THE DEATH GUARD

PHILIP GEORGE CHADWICK

INTRODUCTION BY BRIAN W. ALDISS

A ROC BOOK

ROC

Published by the Penguin Group
Penguin Books Ltd, 27 Wrights Lane, London W8 5TZ, England
Penguin Books USA Inc., 375 Hudson Street, New York, New York 10014, USA
Penguin Books Australia Ltd, Ringwood, Victoria, Australia
Penguin Books Canada Ltd, 10 Alcorn Avenue, Toronto, Ontario, Canada M4V 3B2
Penguin Books (NZ) Ltd, 182–190 Wairau Road, Auckland 10, New Zealand

Penguin Books Ltd, Registered Offices: Harmondsworth, Middlesex, England

First published by Hutchinson & Company 1939
Published in Penguin 1992
10 9 8 7 6 5 4 3 2

 Roc is a trademark of Penguin Books Ltd

Typeset by DatIX International Limited, Bungay, Suffolk
Printed in England by Clays Ltd, St Ives plc

Introduction

The Death Guard is about a naked display of brute force: war. It culminates in 'that strangest of all battles when Flesh and metal met on the plain of Kent and automatically hunted and destroyed each other'.

The novel is a nightmare, a prodromic nightmare of things to come. Yet the nightmare is less about war itself than the Flesh that makes war possible. Here are marching feet, and helmeted brigades, and the irresistible force of armies – all the trappings of previous wars waged on land. But the feet, the helmets, the irresistible force, belong to an 'improvement' on mankind: the Death Guard, the Flesh.

The character who fires the engine of the action is Goble, a man without friends, an ex-soldier casually given a lift by the narrator's grandfather. Goble's mind is clogged with thoughts of the war into which he was dragged. He was forced to kill. 'I didn't ask to have my mind twisted and debased.' (And we see that he was indeed debased: it is indeed an effect of war.)

Goble is referring to the First World War, 1914–1918. He is possessed by an evil vision of the opposing forces. 'Out there, I used to think how each army was like a sprawling, living creature, a powerful but rudimentary creature . . . bursting and dying incessantly . . . Two vast, stagnant armies, oozing and jellying backwards and forwards like immense protozoa trying to feed off each other!'

This appalling metaphor dominates Chadwick's book, blossoming into an imagined future war. His novel, published in the ill year of 1939, sometimes approaches futurism (which is mentioned) while sharing something of the symbolism of Rex Warner's once-famous novel, The Aerodrome, published two years later in 1941.

v

Little is known of Chadwick's life. However, since he was born in 1893, he would have been twenty-one when war was declared in August 1914. The carnage of the Western Front would, inevitably, have affected deeply his perception of humanity's capacity for technologically enhanced murderous excess.

The 'improvement' on ordinary soldiers – who can think, run away, bleed and die – is biologically achieved. An 'artificial life cell', unlike 'us ill-adapted, cringing, little bipeds', is developed into a kind of machine of flesh, mindless, conscienceless, with no purpose except – when unleashed – for war.

Chadwick's slow build – leisurely indeed for the modern reader – prepares us for the legend which lies behind his story as behind so many SF stories: the legend of the dragon's teeth – those teeth which, once sown, spring up armed. Perhaps this is the legend behind all wars: every conflict gives birth to fresh problems. We know for sure – and knowing doesn't help us – that the Flesh will get out of control once they are released. Their masters will be unable to master them.

The second half of the book is horrifying, even in contemporary terms, as the insatiable tide of the Death Guard spreads over England – fighting, eating, marching, killing everything in its path – and Continental powers invade this country. It's August again, the cruellest month. August, breeding hate out of the dead land. The nation is dying. But the Flesh does not die – even when chopped to bits. The dragon's teeth are immortal.

Two-thirds through the book, Chadwick springs his new terror. Like human dead returning from the battlefield, 'their wounds and mutilations with them', the neoblasts rise up, deformed and blind and beyond control. Certainly they are alien, and yet – 'the most natural of phenomena' . . .

This masterly stroke of linking what is most frightening with what is inescapably part of humanity stiffens the narrative with a morality which owes something to Chadwick's master, H. G. Wells. The Island of Dr Moreau is referred to in the text. Wells was the tree under which Chadwick and his generation – and later generations – laboured. But the closest resemblances are less to Moreau than to the war novels like Mr Britling Sees it Through and the most famous future-war of all, The War of the Worlds. As Wells's parasitic Martians were little more than a specialized evolved humanity, so Chadwick's loathesomely mindless killers are symbols of an 'improved' way of mass-killing. The horror is not there for its own sake, but for ours.

There is irony in the fact that The Death Guard was itself overtaken by the war its author feared. The original Hutchinson cloth edition is a scarce book. The publisher's stock probably went up in flames during the first hours of the Blitz, when London burned, and, with it, Paternoster Row, home to many publishers including Hutchinson. Curiously, the author–publisher contract for the novel has survived the years and bombs – not to mention company take-overs. It was tracked down by Nick Austin, the publishing authority on science fiction.

Now this almost unknown novel again sees the light of day. It wakes from its sleep to find that over half a century has passed. SF readers are experts in the art of reading and can manoeuvre their way past what is dated to what remains vital.

No one can foresee the future, not even Nostradamus. Building a picture of the day after tomorrow, we inevitably look into a mirror and reflect our own hopes and fears from the past. So Chadwick gets some details of his predictive fantasy curiously wrong. Here's a prime minister still clad in a frock coat and sporting a buttonhole. Here are the working class, talking in funny accents. And here – the most damaging aspect of the novel to a 1990s reader – is unthinking racism, with blacks referred to as 'nigs', introduced as a kind of slave species. The racism was Chadwick's; it was also part of the cultural climate of the 1930s, an unpalatable historical fact.

Events move at a slower pace than today. A politician addresses a mob. 'They listened to his speech for an hour and then they shot him.' Nowadays, he'd be lucky to get through five minutes.

The plot, too, as I have intimated, is slow to unfold. Some of the props of that plot were familiar even in the thirties. England had been invaded many a time previously. There's a pretty girl with whom the narrator falls in love, who later must travel alone through dangerous territory. That's a useful stand-by to any plot.

London was often laid flat long before Chadwick wrote. Kill the capital, you kill national life and culture: the chicken has no head.

We also encounter a ruined house where menace lurks (good

scenes, these). The mansions in which much nineteenth-century fiction was staged, from *Castle Rackrent* in 1800 to Sherlock Holmes's rooms in Baker Street at the other end of the century, were frequently to undergo ruination at the hands of the new breed of science fiction writers who, once air warfare was an established fact, saw there was no hiding place at home.

A morbid and guilty pleasure is still to be had from reading of one's country being destroyed. We lust for change, however dire. Drama itself changed with the century, or near enough. Once, adultery was a subject scandalous enough to turn the wheels of an entire plot. The Education Acts of the last century, and the removal of taxes on paper, meant a new class of writers grew up to address a new class of readers. Many of them, both readers and writers, struggled against the repressions of the time, inequitable laws, censorship, the patronage of the established church, disastrous housing, and so forth.

They saw in science and education a way clear of inherited muddle, of being free of the past. Often they became – dread word – socialists, dedicated to overturning the world of privilege and the misery that accompanied it. H. G. Wells stands as representative of this kind of man. The destruction of a house, a country, held more excitement – because more meaning – than the destruction of a marriage.

Science fiction is sometimes blamed for concerning itself too greatly with disaster (though others, on the contrary, call it escapist). Both views are wrong. Disaster is the common lot of most of the world's peoples; illiteracy and starvation afflict a majority. Life is a struggle. Catastrophe is no more than realism. SF is one of the mirrors we hold up to nature.

Perhaps Chadwick came to regard that most degrading of all wars, 'The Great War', as its participants called it, as a culmination of an age of privilege, when kings decided the destiny of their peoples and Kaiser Bill could plunge a continent into bloodshed. After the war, Chadwick became active as a Fabian (a movement to which both Wells and George Bernard Shaw had belonged), and later as an Independent of Leftist tendencies. He was an able speaker at political meetings. Although he wrote many short stories, *The Death Guard* is his only published novel.

He was evidently an active man. Nevertheless, he follows literary tradition in giving us a not very heroic hero. Gregory Beldite spends several chapters of the book injured and a mere onlooker.

Although, for reasons stated, accuracy is impossible in any portrait of the future, Chadwick scores some interesting bull's-eyes. The date of his future war is left vague. All the same, 'In '39 it seemed that the end of civilization was at hand'. And indeed so it was: not least for the many Jewish communities of Europe.

The advent of the Flesh war is marked by a non-combatant period, during which foreign aircraft drop leaflets on cities. This corresponds with what was known in 1940 as 'the Phoney War'. The aircraft 'guided by radio beams' are clearly operating early radar systems. Instead of the Willey's Jeeps of World War II renown, our characters drive about in 'dopeys', which serve the same purpose. More broadly, Chadwick has grasped something that English and French generals, imagining themselves safe behind the Maginot Line, failed to understand: that the next war would have no more trenches.

There's also the question of nuclear power. Chadwick calls it 'humanite'. It seems to have about as much effect on a tank as a well-aimed Stilton cheese. But the author's interest inclines more to biology than physics. We must assume he is no relation to the James Chadwick who worked with Lord Rutherford. Still, the mysterious power is there.

These may be small amusements. They remain as guarantees that the author is thinking hard and, in the main, clearly, on his theme. Wells was not the sole author in the thirties warning against the terrors of another world war.

All the warnings in the world did not stop the war. Hitler was not to be deterred by romances. Novels are not designed for such work, apocalyptic though they may be. They cannot bring us to Utopia or our senses. They do, however, exercise us. They exercise our sense of outrage or compassion. If they are black, they comfort the suffering, like black coffee. Occasionally, they may change a mind here and there. Perhaps, too, they help keep the author sane – a not inconsiderable benefit. The dreadful scenes Chadwick describes surely reflect the carnage on the Somme and at Passchendaele, of which he must have been aware.

At present, the threat of even greater carnage to be inflicted on the world has evaporated, with the ending of the Cold War and the 'For Sale' signs going up at nuclear missile sites.

That by no means renders this venerable novel obsolete. All Goble does is to recreate in living flesh those terrible emotions he found in the minds of the men he knew around him. That is what he lets loose on England in surreal form: everyday misery, evil thoughts, the lust for power.

This we understand and have to accept. We see it still alive in our cities today.

Brian W. Aldiss
Oxford, 1991

Author's Preface

———————

THIS STORY OF the not very distant future was written during that unwholesome period, now happily ending, when the imminent doom of our modern world seemed almost as inevitable as next year's football season. It was written in an optimistic mood, in a belief that our suicidal tendencies were not as yet quite sufficiently developed to destroy wilfully the rare chance of civilization which scientific thinking and discovery are at last presenting to us.

That optimism prevails. I find myself and my compatriots still able to look across the dreary waste of the European war which is now opening to the peace beyond, realizing that it is entirely within the power of ordinary men such as myself and those who, I hope, will read this book to decide whether that peace shall be enduring, a gracious peace of heart and mind, or whether it shall be merely a further and even more poverty-stricken pause in the barren struggle of outworn creeds and nations which is our present life.

There are some, no doubt, who will think my conception of the Death Guard a wild phantasy. I hope that phantasy will at least assist in distracting their minds from present fear and sorrow to the imaginary terrors of future days. Maybe it is not so fantastic as it seems. Already, since writing this book, the first peaceful ancestor of the 'bomb-pluggers', the 'sharks of the air', has risen from the back of her mothercraft and flown the Atlantic. The 'bloodless air-raids' are in the news. The attentive reader will notice other forecasts in gradual process of fulfilment, the great evacuations, the depth-penetrating bombs ... Whether or not the Death Guard ever comes to earth – and who can put a limit to the indomitable ingenuity of men in their quest for power? – the call for the human flesh units is once more sounding. Brave men are debasing themselves, stifling their lives and hopes to fight for a peace which war alone can never bring. That fight must go forward into the aftermath of war.

In this book man gains the power to destroy himself, and refuses. If we so will, that choice can be ours and not our children's. It is in the hope that my story will help a little towards the making of that choice that I welcome its publication at so grim a moment.

Philip George Chadwick, 1939

Contents

Foreword

———————————

It is now some three years since it was suggested to me that it was my particular duty to collate and record the full facts in regard to the first creation of artificial life. It was pointed out that no one was better equipped for the task than I; that not only had I ready access to all matters relative to the Dax-Beldite estates, but I also had firsthand experience of the Flesh Factories and of the Guard, both in and out of action; that I had something of an Expert's knowledge of these things.

The proposal attracted me and so it is that the compilation of this projected history has occupied me for some considerable time. Certain of its chapters are fully written and the broad outline of the whole is sufficiently sketched for me to hope that when complete the work will be accepted as an official chronicle, not only of its specific subject, but of the climacteric times with which it deals.

Nevertheless its very comprehensiveness carries within it failure to fulfil what to my mind should be its chief purpose, that of keeping alive in the common world the meaning it holds. The majority, especially in these new days of swift, sweeping reconstruction, has little time for detailed history and, even were this not so, the historical method with its need of careful documentation, its analytical demands, its painstaking, ambient progression, does not lend itself to that dramatization, that personal presentation which drives deep into the human heart to leave its mark.

One reads and studies history, but drama is felt.

From the larger work a shorter, more compact one has thrust itself into my view not only as a possibility but as a need, and as something already existing within the major history waiting to be drawn out and written. This detachable theme has grown to

1

monopolize my thoughts, an increasing reaction to the colder exigencies of my task. I have discovered myself at times to be no longer thinking but staring blankly, idle pen in hand, at one or other of the terrific memories which surge in me.

Some months ago I laid aside my history, and this story of the Death Guard is the outcome. It is intended for popular reading, and at times I have taken a novelist's prerogative in dealing with my subject. If in parts it lacks verisimilitude, this is because I have had to compress it into so small a space. I am depicting a whole world from one tragic angle and that the most difficult of approach. I can only hope to convey in outline its wider background and the many lights which converged upon it.

Nor must the leader expect to find any 'hero' as is the way with romances: at best I and my intimates can only be little figures struggling in the web of great events. This is the story of the Death Guard, and the Death Guard is its only hero.

But if I can to some small degree make my readers live with me through a time when all past conceptions of man were stamped out, and the most fantastic thought in life was of the quiet days before, then I shall have succeeded in my purpose. If they, too, through my writings can feel the horror of the Beast Battalions, then they will join with me and others of my generation, in resolving that there can be no going back to those dead, chaotic years, that whatever may come, whatever passions may flare and fears arise, the Flesh Factories must nevermore be opened nor the Guard march forth to its bloody teaching.

Gregory Beldite
View,
Darnley, W. Yorks.,
October 1971

BOOK I

CHAPTER ONE

Through the Eyes of Aunt Fertile

———————

GOBLE

MY GRANDFATHER, Edom Beldite, discovered Goble purely by chance.

He was motoring through Ripon one early morning in January 1919, returning, I believe, from a snatched visit to his northern factories, and on an outlying road, a little distance from one of the huge military camps which stood there at that time, he noticed a dirty-looking, unshaven soldier sitting on a gate, his eyes fixed dully on the ground beneath him, his hunched body shivering visibly in the bitter dawn wind. Thin snow lay in a hard crust over the countryside. Heavy grey clouds, scarcely as yet distinguishable from the passing night, betokened an early and heavier fall. But the man seemed oblivious of his surroundings, intent only on his gloomy thoughts.

My grandfather did not know what impelled him to stop and to offer the man a lift. It was during the first chaotic period of demobilization after the World War and, Ripon being one of the centres of that hurried traffic, there were numerous soldiers about even at that early hour, awaiting a chance to reach their homes. But this one was different from his fellows. His tall, muscular figure would have been noticeable in any company, and the massive contours of his brow, exaggerated no doubt in that first passing glimpse by the downward inclination of his head, stamped him as an anomaly even in the multifarious army of those days. As the limousine passed, running at moderate speed because of the slippery roads, he glanced up so that his eyes met my grandfather's through the window. Deep-set, heavy eyes they were, cold and confident and, as my grandfather expressed it, 'quietly damning the whole scheme of things'.

My grandfather felt suddenly and irrationally ashamed to see this man in the coarse, vulgar uniform of a private, ashamed of a world which had found no better use for him than to stamp him into the common mould of a soldier. He gave an order to his chauffeur and the car stopped and reversed.

'Want a lift anywhere?' he called. 'Demobbed, I suppose?'

Goble lowered himself from the gate stiffly, then leant back against it, easing his muscles. On closer inspection my grandfather discerned a quality of ironic but kindly humour in the hard eyes which pleased him.

'Why me?' said Goble. 'There're thousands of us here. Like flies in a fly-trap. One line up, choked with trains, and no way of getting out again. Just more flies – coming in.' He glanced back at the endless lines of drab huts lying like a vast herd of dingy, sleeping beasts under the pale, wakening sky. Then he yawned suddenly. 'Been here days, some of them. I've been up all night. The huts are too filthy to go into; stinking of men and swarming with fleas. Blankets stiff with dirt.' Thrusting his blue hands into his pockets he yawned again as one accustomed to such minor evils.

My grandfather renewed his offer of a lift, extending it to include possible friends who might have homes in the direction in which he was travelling which was by way of Harrogate and Leeds to Darnley. But Goble had no friends. 'Some of the others . . . I don't know where they are. Been prowling round by myself all night, trying to keep warm. Hell of a time getting through. Someone stole my greatcoat.' He suddenly bethought himself to thank my grandfather. 'But I haven't anywhere to go. Haven't thought about it. Guess the only home I have is a lot of old books going musty in store.' He stared into the interior of the limousine appreciatively. 'To tell the truth, I feel a bit like a pea out of its pod. But it was a bloody sort of pod. It's good to be out.'

It was curiosity more than sympathy which prompted my grandfather to invite him to accompany him home. So he always insisted. He might have taken him as far as Leeds and dropped him there but, instead, he suggested taking him the whole way to Darnley with a fat meal at the end of the journey and a good bed to follow. Behind that great brow there seemed only the most banal of thoughts, but Goble interested him with his unusual physique and his suggestion of a half-academic background; moreover, he glimpsed possibilities of first-hand information on the war and military life such as was difficult to acquire from the average, uncommunicative soldier. That tinge of humour in his eyes — it was not directed at the ugly world around him; it was commenting on some deeper reality beyond. My grandfather pressed his invitation against the other's uncertain reluctance with the result that Goble, lugging a clumsily packed kitbag and wearing his new friend's motoring coat, came to my Aunt Fertile's home on the outskirts of Darnley. Invited for an indeterminate 'day or two', he stayed there, as I shall tell, for the better part of twelve years, according to my aunt, the least troublesome man she had ever known yet one who was destined to bring to the world a danger such as no other age had dreamed to be possible.

II

My grandfather, at that time, was a man in his early fifties, one of those 'hard-headed businessmen' who flourished so blindly in the latter days, and who had devoted his whole life and an abundant supply of energy to increasing a one-mill woollen business into one of the largest textile factories in the north. He had leading interests in cotton and steel and coal-mining, with a link in most of the greater industrial towns, but was in semi-retirement after a long illness when he met Goble, a man lost for some occupation with which to employ his still active brain.

Unlike many of his type, he did not hanker merely to return to his early life's work. That work had been planned for his two sons, the elder of whom had been killed in the later fighting, and the younger, my father, gassed and crippled and destined to live but a short while. To Edom Beldite it had lost all vitality, its possibilities of interest were exhausted; and sickness, with its prolonged opportunities for thought, had opened his mind to wider possibilities than mere commerce presented, possibilities which must still have been vague to him and largely unattainable to a man of his industrial associations. He had been reading widely. In the mood of one searching for something new and more meaningful than his accustomed life he met this unusual personality, Goble, a man in age and character far from his own, but in the similar circumstances of requiring a fresh start in life. He took him home not in any sense as a trophy, a war-worn hero to show his friends — though that was a fashionable pastime of the day — but more as a book to read, a character to explore, and one which might prove an inlet to fuller experience.

The virtual loss of both his sons had its major part in that: he craved for young companionship, and I, of course, was not yet born.

He would, I suppose, still be showing signs of his illness, a certain lack of vigour in his sturdy form, the square-cut buoyancy of his firm face a little relaxed and weary, and according to custom he would be dressed in quiet mourning, perhaps just a black crêpe band round the arm, that lingering Victorian expression of manly sorrow. Celia Fertile, his only daughter, a 'war widow', as the saying went, of thirty-odd — my uncle, John Fertile, had been the first casualty in the family — would favour a more thorough acquiescence in the dark tradition of visible grief, colouring it, however, out of all sombre association by her sparkling personality. They must have been a lonely couple, too essentially home-loving for wealth and influence to distract them, and with the roots of their lives swept away suddenly and, so I see it, almost unbelievably.

My aunt welcomed Goble's coming as a distraction for her father and that same night, after he had a much-needed sleep, they pampered him into conversation. At first he seemed almost sullenly weary, taking lavish hospitality in the same fatalistic spirit in which, no doubt, he had faced danger and hardship, but over a roaring fire in the evening, sipping a third glass of wine, he thawed sufficiently for direct questions to be asked, and the shivering soldier of the early morning, so heroically pathetic, began to recede as the essential man in him, the science worker and visionary, revived.

I believe my Aunt Fertile had hunted out a civilian suit which nearly fitted him, and that seems to have relaxed his nervous tension considerably.

I imagine him with his feet outstretched to the fire and his tired eyes a little dazed with the wine, not altogether convinced of the comfort he is enjoying. He stares into the flames, rarely glancing up, answering questions inattentively and with only offhand interest; but later he was lured on to the subject of those 'books going musty' which had excited my grandfather's curiosity and, from that, the strange thoughts which had been growing in him through many months of intolerable active service began to find expression as confidence in his hosts grew, and his habitual reserve softened.

They must have hung on his every word hoping he might help to make more real their distant, incredible tragedies. But Goble had little to offer there. He knew nothing of their circumstances nor of their aching interest in the common routines of overseas life, the possible bright spots which might have made his days livable to a soldier abroad. He saw war and military training as a spectacle, as a 'biological extravaganza', to quote his own words, and even his own share in it was of no importance except where it illustrated that spectacle.

Celia Fertile sat almost in shadow at the corner of the big hearth listening to the two men talking, and forming her first preliminary and erroneous impression that Goble was probably the most intellectual man in the country. It was she who told me, many years afterwards, of that wide, pregnant conversation, re-creating in vivid paraphrase the essence of his strange and only half-understood confidences which later explanation and events served to clarify and keep living in her colourful mind. Only once have I known my Aunt Fertile to admit her memory at a loss: she can reiterate dialogue a quarter of a century old in the most vivid detail, 'I said', and, 'He said'. One listens – suspicious – wondering; one listens to a disarmed conviction that here, at least, is the soul of the incident, even though wit and insight have clothed it in a bright new body. And if, on repetition, other lights appear and the past yields a hitherto unsuspected wealth of detail, surely one must recognize that memory at its highest is an interpreter, a selective historian, and no mere meticulous camera.

It was she who told me of following and less charmingly annotated talks and of their singular and lasting effect upon my grandfather.

III

It seems that Goble had already sketched something of his personal life to my grandfather during the journey to Darnley. He had been a research worker in biology before the war, specializing in cytological work under the wing of an elderly and obscure but extremely brilliant individual, who died while Goble was abroad and whose name my aunt can never remember except that it began with an E. It is her only known lapse.

'Cellular growth,' Goble had simplified, trying to avoid technicalities. 'Studying the "Life Force". I suppose that's how a popular "scientific" writer would describe it.'

And there he would have left the matter as one altogether too profound for his host's understanding, but my grandfather, some forty years late, as I have explained, was only just awakening to an interest in things in general and, finding his guest uncommunicative on military life, worked back to this engagingly novel subject at the first opportunity. So we have Goble on that first night struggling in a mood of tired politeness to convey the most abstruse physiological facts and speculations to Edom Beldite's brisk but entirely unprepared intelligence. No doubt he was tantalizingly obscure, but from certain lucid statements which struck home to my aunt's retentive memory, because they were too startling to forget, and from what we know of Goble's fundamental ideas, it is possible to reconstruct the general trend of that talk.

Quite childish misconceptions in my grandfather's mind must have brought Goble to the very roots of his studies in no time, and have started him explaining how even the lowest forms of life, as we know it, are in reality highly evolved, amazingly intricate creatures, chemically if not anatomically; and how the amoeba, most humble and popular of simple organisms, must in fact be the outcome of millions of years of gradual evolution. Life at its earliest is unrecognizable, he would emphasize, even as matter is, a mere momentary result of chance combinations, a flash and extinction. Just that and no more through aeons, evolving finally to tentative essays in permanency, the acquirement of the power to endure, perhaps for a few seconds only at first, and then, ages later, for longer periods.

He used the biggest words he could find, says my aunt, far too lengthy for such a young, good-looking man. Sometimes, she professes to suspect, he strung two or more of these together, so that they sounded just like zip-fasteners being opened in a hurry. With all this erudition he combined a romantically illuminating touch.

And somewhere in that conversation he drove right out of the technical and fundamental into Everyman's land with a suddenness which sent the beliefs of a lifetime all staggering over each other in my grandfather, and lit an ambition in him which he followed for the remainder of his life.

'But!' said my grandfather.

My aunt is perfectly certain he said, 'But!' and avers that in the inarticulate, floundering pause which ensued she could see in his eyes and in the muscles of his face the beginnings of the struggle between hitherto unquestioned tradition and his new intellectual daring, which was evident in him to the end.

'You don't mean – you think it possible – to *make* life from chemicals? To make – just chemicals mixed together – live? Surely!'

My aunt is as certain of that 'Surely!' and of the blended delight and fear with which he exclaimed it, as she is of the 'But!' And she thinks Goble smiled.

'It's as natural a phenomenon as lightning or crystals,' Goble said. 'Before the war in German laboratories they were "making life" as you put it. A *kind* of life. An oily scum which behaved in a pseudo-living manner, moving and growing. And at Cambridge too. They didn't and they still don't recognize it as life, only as an interesting demonstration. They appear to think that nothing short of a whole living cell *can* be life. But that's only their learned blindness.'

'And *you* have made it, you and your friend, *and* recognized it?' My grandfather was patently awed at this confirmation of his first impression that Goble was no ordinary soldier.

'Precipitated it might be a better phrase, released it from the clogging matter surrounding it. There's life, you know, basic, *inorganic* life, in "dead" rock. It's just a simple combination of – elements, shall we say; not material, chemical elements, nothing so advanced. Electrical charges, spatial relationships. That's all too difficult for you, of course, but I'm trying to make you realize that it's no use mixing things together and hoping to make protoplasm: you have to start millions of years earlier than that. You don't "make" life, you discover and develop it.'

In some such words, amused perhaps out of his lethargy by my

11

grandfather's naïve astonishment, but later becoming engrossed in his subject to forgetfulness of his audience, did Goble begin to propound the thesis of life as a primal and ubiquitous element in nature with which his name will always be linked but which, it is certain, originated in the brain of the savant E . . ., whose name my aunt so steadfastly and regrettably cannot remember. For it seems that in this nameless and now untraceable old man, we have to recognize the pioneer whose theories and experiments his pupil was later to carry to such dreadful fulfilment.

'But rock isn't an environment in which it can develop,' said Goble, 'nor is steam, gas, or volcanic eruption. That was Nature's problem – environment. The circumstances which would enable it to persist and reproduce weren't on earth for myriads of years; temperature, moisture, light, these only changed by infinite stages to a degree suited to life's progress. It is our problem, too.'

He dilated on that, transferring his scene from the cosmic to the laboratorial, and latinized this age-long growth environment of his to the homely jargon of a chemist's shop. Then there was a recrudescence from that proliferous dictionary of his, and lots of 'ids and ods and other helpless little monosyllables' were struggling to survive in a flow of strangling wordy tentacles. There emerged a leading, childishly expressed query from my grandfather, Goble answering excitedly.

'It's *all* environment, growth, function, instinct, and intelligence, up to the very highest vertebrates. Once the spatial correlatives can be brought into a relationship suitable for a positive charge to nucleate . . .

'. . . responsive to external stimulae . . .

'. . . the molecules of the ganglionic cells begin to flow . . . spontaneous adaptation . . . why shouldn't we control it? . . . the army . . . artificial, atavistic mutation . . .'

This highly impressionistic version covers a period during which my aunt may have dozed, though she says she was endeavouring to visualize a spatial relationship in process of changing into a kangaroo. Then, it seems without warning to her, the war was somehow back in the conversation, not as a bleak interlude in Goble's life, but as a vital stage in his research, a turning-point. She does not know how.

'I remember how I killed a man once,' he was saying. He was staring with a dark alertness into the flames, his eyes smouldering. 'Of course I've killed,' he flashed: 'like an animal kills – without really thinking about it. That's what I was for. People think of us as heroes but we weren't. We were just killers. They asked for that and they got that. *I* didn't ask for it. I didn't ask to have my mind and talents twisted and debased. I wanted to enjoy life, research, knowledge, and all the bright little things we take by the way. They've changed all that: I've become like some of those immature, cloddish minds I met out there who had a nasty, inquisitive, monkey interest in killing and maiming. Like babies pull flies to pieces, very solemnly and attentively. The rudiments of a faculty which I've matured on to a higher plane. I've started to study death-dealing – as a science.

'I suppose I shouldn't tell you,' he interrupted himself. 'It was that talk of my researches . . .'

'Please do, if it helps,' said my aunt sympathetically, leaning forward, her eyes full of interest no doubt but still, perhaps, hoping for something which she could grip, something to bridge the aching void in her life.

'This man,' resumed Goble. 'I was with the trench-mortars. We'd gone over at dusk to be ready for a big strafe in the morning about fifty yards beyond the front line. The others were dozing and I was on guard, and suddenly a figure popped up on the rim of the shell-hole in which we were hiding. I challenged and the man gave a queer, inarticulate, gurgling answer – like some German word it sounded to me. I wasn't satisfied or I was scared as he. I sprang up and drove at him at the same time. As I did it the moon came out and I saw he wasn't a German at all, but one of our own Tommies who'd been out scouting or something and had lost his way and his nerve as well. I expect he thought he'd stumbled into the enemy lines. That's why he gurgled, his voice went all wrong with fear.

'But by the time I'd realized what he was I had my bayonet in his stomach. I was horrified at what I'd done, no, wild, mad, not just horrified. I jumped up on the edge of the hole and with that poor devil glaring up at me and frothing at the mouth, I dragged out the bayonet and drove it in again. Because I was afraid if I let him live I should be shot. Something like that was in my mind and – a kind of ghastly satisfaction as if I *had* to complete the job. Then machine-guns started to spit about me; I supposed I showed up in the moonlight. I jerked him away and slid back into the shell-hole, and told the corporal who'd wakened at the row that I thought I'd heard something and had gone over to make sure. He cursed me for taking the risk. I cleaned my bayonet after the firing had stopped, and the boys were asleep again.'

Goble rose to his feet and stood brooding over the dancing flames, his large but oddly nervous hands moving with suppressed emotion.

'I hope I haven't distressed you,' he said tonelessly. 'I – wished to illustrate a point.'

'*That's* all right,' answered my grandfather heartily but with a quiver in his voice. 'I expect – something similar has happened more than once. We folk over here don't understand and we *ought* to understand. Even the women,' with a sharp glance at his daughter to see how she was taking it. 'But this study of life,' he side-tracked; 'you were telling us?'

IV

Goble, his face now placid and inscrutable, did not answer.

Above him, gloomy, unyielding, portraits of quaint-visaged ancestors watched the little fireside group, foreign-minded faces with no conception of the tragic future they had helped to fashion, and no manner of interest in it but only in their past which they had deemed eternal. I know the room well and the self-righteous countenances with which my aunt had lined it, laughing no doubt behind her solemn mien; its grand establishment of dark, immovable furniture, its stern but full-hearted comfort which even the vast, moulded ceiling could not chill. It was in that atmosphere of aged gilt and mahogany and forgotten permanence that Goble first voiced his grim vision of the coming Death Guard.

My grandfather sat fascinated as he resumed. My aunt began to form her second erroneous impression in a silent debate as to the exact dividing line between genius and lunacy.

'*I* didn't kill that man,' said Goble. 'I don't suppose any man of my stamp ever killed another – intentionally, consciously. My body killed him, some instinctive response to danger, a reflex action. And he was so easily *killed*: just a stab and all his training, all the effort to turn him into an efficient fighting animal was meaningless, a good, working, thinking thing turned to a base, unnatural use, and as much good at it as a jellyfish in a jungle. But *I* was a good instrument, much better than when I'd been shivering in a trench, my real self.

'The pitiful humour of it!' he murmured, more to himself than to his listeners. 'Millions of us who'd spent our whole lives inventing and making, and when war came there was no one amongst all the nations who could make anything to do the fighting for him. With all our tanks and guns and aeroplanes we had to take our own puny, soft bodies to the firing-line to defend what we'd made; allow ourselves to be turned into the very machines we could not make otherwise. Like trying to smelt putty!

'There was that great war machine eating up everything it could find, brains, money, devotion, and all of it finally dependent on us ill-adapted, cringing little bipeds, things intended essentially for life, trying to be insensate particles in the death machine! Every art, every science applied and squandered except the most essential of sciences, biology. No one was thinking about that, not even I. There was I with my whole mind concentrated on life, at its very roots, and all around me the world was studying and making death. I didn't see the relationship! I should have been combining the two, creating a living thing which wanted to kill, which revelled in killing, and which wouldn't die at the first little thrust.'

He sighed, but his eyes were laughing. Seemingly he found an ironic humour in others' inefficiency and his own civilized blindness to a ruthless world.

'Making soldiers! *Making soldiers!*' he jeered. 'Bladders! Trying to adapt an over-specialized, decadent species suddenly to gross, new conditions, fundamentally antipathetic conditions. Without even knowing what they were really trying to do. Trying to turn us into mute, obedient slogging automata – me – with just this bit of individual life left in us, that when the order came we'd go out to kill the other bladders as though the whole of our bottled lives were suddenly released.

'I became a specimen in that crazy biological extravaganza, I who should have been conducting the experiment. That man, that British Tommy on the shell-hole, was my high watermark of efficiency!'

'You mean,' said my grandfather, with singular insightedness 'that if biological knowledge had been applied ...' That a kind of different race ... Perhaps negroes ...' He became lost in his half-lit understanding.

'I played with that idea. It's elementary, infantile. It would mean the reversal of everything which constitutes Man. Man is evolved for peace, for progress and creation, a sensitive, vulnerable creature by the very demands of his destiny. The lowest man is dependent on brain to survive.'

With his hands thrust deep into his pockets and his broad shoulders slightly hunched, Goble stood staring up at the passive, visionless faces of the past, embalmed and forever satisfied in their burial oils.

'Supposing that instead of turning ourselves into fighting animals we could breed things or make things which would always act as I acted that night. Starting with a different life cell altogether, perhaps, from that which forms the natural creation; an artificial life cell. A sort of beast with nothing but the fighting instincts in it, something which would be useless except in battle, which we should never make until we needed it for battle.'

'You are looking into the far future,' suggested my grandfather half audibly, but Goble continued without heeding him.

'It would be a living fighting machine, a thing entirely without fear or sentiment or blood-weariness; a thing which could not feel pain, which could be shot or cut to pieces before it died. Impervious even to gas, perhaps, as some vegetation is. Life devoted to death, solely to death.

'In the trenches I used to imagine such things, trying to piece together the possibilities of the knowledge of life we already have, planning how some faculties might be enhanced and others suppressed.' For a space he became highly technical then was back again to his fantastic play. 'If only we had the pliable flesh to work on! Environment, prepared environment would create the rest. I can almost visualize the thing which would be made, which some

16

day, long after me, *will* be made. Its great muscles, its soulless, watching face ... A cell, an immutably adapted cell, in a living machine! I have imagined fine, beautiful countries, growing in knowledge and wisdom and, when war came, sending out their beast battalions to guard them. An end to the degradation of man.'

His subdued, thrilling voice became calmer.

'But all this must seem a lot of nonsense to you, nasty nonsense. I suppose it is. Perhaps if I went back to my work I should realize what moonshine it all is. A million years off.'

'It – it is a very startling thought,' my grandfather conceded, uncertain what answer to give, and my aunt settled her second erroneous impression quite finally for that night. 'Making artificial beasts! You don't mean – you don't really think it possible? You *are* exaggerating a little, aren't you, Mr Goble?'

'Perhaps I am. And yet it is what they would have had us to be. If we *must* fight, if science *must* be degraded to war – that is the logical outcome, the biologically perfect killing mechanism.

'It's strange I should be able to talk to you two about these things. We only met this morning. But it is months since I talked. Such ideas – they take hold of one over there.' He yawned, and with quite normal, laughing determination insisted that he must go to bed.

'I hope he's not dangerous – for the servants' sake,' said my Aunt Fertile, expressing her deepest comprehension of that first conversation.

LIFE DUST

They did not return to that subject until some days later. My grandfather was, perhaps, a little nervous, and Goble, after his first outburst, no doubt grew diffident, realizing how far removed were his thoughts from those of his newly-made friends. Yet it must have been implicit in much of their conversation, and I take it that it revived again by degrees out of the long, rambling talks which ensued between them. My grandfather would grow accustomed to Goble's characteristic viewpoint, his mind would widen immensely under its stimulating influence; he would probe more deeply into the other's ideas.

But in all this I am in some difficulty in telling what transpired, for I have to depend entirely on what my Aunt Fertile heard during her comparatively infrequent presence.

I imagine that during those early conversations both of them were doing little more than satisfying a pent-up desire to unburden their souls. The war and its stifling influence was still on them, and in their efforts to reach back to normal they must have experimented over a wide and extravagant field, touching subjects my grandfather had never dwelt on since youth, if then, discussing loosely, romantically, gravidly ... They took long walks across the dingy fields or round the sombre, old-fashioned outskirts of Darnley, and they spent many hours in the library, an oddly assorted couple with little apparently to bind them together.

Echoes of their discussions came to my aunt's ears at mealtimes. The inevitability of future world conflicts figured largely in their talk, my grandfather's thoughts running on how a second such disaster could be avoided. They flung the projected League of Nations up and down the breakfast-table 'like buns at Whitsuntide', my grandfather hoping, Goble scoffing; and for lunch there would be cells and ganglia and quaint biological versions of the army. 'Out there,' said Goble, 'I used to think how each army was like a sprawling, living creature, a powerful but rudimentary creature made of silly little bubbles, bursting and dying incessantly. Us fellows. Two vast, stagnant armies, oozing and jellying backwards and forwards like immense protozoa trying to feed off each other!'

Dinner was reserved for visitors, and no animalcula nor dissection, neither political nor anatomical, was allowed.

Goble dwelt constantly on the probabilities of mechanization, and such talk appealed strongly to my grandfather. 'I'd like to see Britain so armed that no one would ever dare to fight us,' he aspired, and 'You'll never get that,' contradicted Goble. 'Nations will suspect each other of doing the very thing you're suggesting, and will go out to smash each other purely as a precaution,' quoting, I think, from Ponsonby or Mundaine, or some other of the pacifists who were so to the fore about then. Somewhere in those talks, extending perhaps over a couple of weeks, one or other of them returned to the subject which, to Goble, was the one reality of life.

My aunt had warnings that something new and active was toward some while before her father, a little apologetically, broached the subject of the laboratory. She had an inkling at times that she was being kept out of the way.

Entering the library one night she found them sitting very close together. Goble's tousled black hair close to my grandfather's greying head, and so intent that neither heard her enter.

'We shall need a microscope, of course,' Goble was saying, 'the highest possible power. Then there will be a whole list of irritants and counter-irritants, and re-urgents, and some rare mud cultures – fungoid. That may be difficult. The heat apparatus –' He leaned forward and in doing so caught sight of my aunt in the doorway. She went forward, laughing.

'I was listening,' she admitted. 'Whatever are you talking about *now*? *Rare Mud*?' And my grandfather said, 'Chemistry', very curtly, and seemed a trifle upset.

But that half-hearted insight into the trend of their thoughts gave her the clue to later developments in the home. When her father announced that Goble was to stay on indefinitely and was having one of the stables converted into an experimental room, my aunt, professing the expected feminine ignorance and lack of curiosity in mere male affairs, had a very shrewd idea as to what it was all about. Two lonely men, one young but disillusioned and bitter, the other older and bereaved, had found an interest in common, a new and rather astounding hobby. Out in the stable, bizarrely furnished with a continuously growing equipment of deal tables, retorts, trays, electrical instruments, bottles of all colours and sizes, and with the cows lowing in the neighbouring fields and the fresh wind from the west blowing across the mill-strewn valleys of the West Riding, these two would find new life, pottering at their impossible experiments, dreaming of extravagant success, new worlds of invention, goodness knew that!

And because Celia Fertile also had been cut off ruthlessly from the better meaning of things, from marriage and children and the romance of just living happily together with someone else, she too decided that she would be interested in the new game, and made them tell her what it was all about.

For many weeks she fussed in and out of the growing laboratory, intent on making it comfortable until finally it dawned on her that comfort had nothing to do with it. But, because of her, Edom Beldite had his lounge chair to rest in, and, with her own hands, she always took their morning coffee over, and sometimes lunch and tea, and would stand over Goble, interrupting the greatest experiments of all time ruthlessly, until he had eaten.

'It's as hard for me to put sustenance into you as it is for you to put life into those nasty messes you concoct,' she said.

And she had no idea that anything but contented and sometimes puzzlingly excited plodding would ever materialize from their efforts.

II

In such homely circumstances did the work of ultimate disaster commence. For a while my grandfather dabbled in simple chemistry, and the place, at least so far as he was concerned, became an orthodox 'stink-shop' where they pottered about together with no other design than to amuse themselves. Tadpoles and caterpillars and other larvae were introduced for his education, and formed a very pleasant change from the League of Nations at the breakfast table.

There came a day, however when there was great excitement over the microscope. My aunt was invited to look through it, and was expected to show enthusiasm over the cloud of minute specks which she could scarcely see. And Goble was very pale and distraught.

'They weren't there yesterday,' he insisted.

'Dust,' suggested my grandfather.

'Yes, life dust,' murmured Goble. When they looked again the cloud was thinning. It dissipated beneath their gaze, vanished back into its constituent elements, leaving what my aunt described as 'nothing but a movement in the waters'. But the next morning, after Goble's treatment, there were more specks and for some days my grandfather was very worried indeed.

Thereafter there was a new seriousness in their work, though it bore, I think, little relation to those early extravagances from which the laboratory had sprung. It was years later, as I shall tell, that Goble referred to them again, years of innumerable, painstaking experiments which, stage by stage, proved his theory that life is in reality a simple, omnipresent phenomenon needing only the correct circumstances for it to blossom into endless, astounding forms, as it did in the distant days of earth's creation, as easily subject to control and manipulation as is matter, perhaps altogether insepar- able from matter. Material, differently manifested. I seem to remem- ber that he actually used those words. Month by month, point by point, he proved the truth of his astonishing hypothesis to my common-sense, doubting grandfather, until he too was in the grip of its fascination, a believer, a disciple. Thereafter nothing dis- tracted him from the experiments, not even his second son's ex- pected death. Perhaps they saved him on that occasion.

My Aunt Fertile was in it from the beginning, her young, motherly finger in the very matrix. And I, also, was in it, very shortly, for my mother succeeded my father only long enough to give me birth. Tragic little grandson, though I must have been, I was yet too much of an uncertain beginning in life, a tiny baby asleep somewhere in the background to take the place of my grandfather's own boys or rival the fascinating prospects opening to him. Whilst I slept in my perambulator in the sun on the front lawn or gurgled pleasantly to myself and to the very comfortable world into which I had been born, he and my Uncle Gobey, as I was to call him later, were poring over the microscopic particles of another and stranger birth less than fifty yards from me. Later, when I began to toddle, I too put my little eyes to the microscope and watched the queer, lumpy tadpoles of Goble's creation hunting their daily bread in a chemical sea.

'Wigglies!' I said rapturously.

'Not wigglies. Certainly not wigglies. Perhaps – homo juvenis – artificiosus,' laughed my Uncle Gobey. 'Who knows!'

"Omo wigglies!' I chuckled, making the one outstanding joke of my infancy.

VIEW

The house to which my grandfather took Goble that January morn- ing was his in law and his daughter's in all else. Celia Fertile had rescued it from its eighty years of heavy, motionless tradition the day her mother was buried.

Youthful, straight-backed, decisive, a mere twenty-odd in septuagenarian black, she reinspected her birthplace with new eyes, gazed out over the perished fields to the smudgy outlines of Darnley beyond, and into the souls of each, and settled finally and insolubly on her future home. 'I still like it,' she said to John Fertile, who, for me, is only a photograph of a pleasant-looking young man who bestowed a quaint name on my nearest relative and then died, rather heroically, in France, but who to her was everything. 'Father could come to us in Madeira, but I prefer to be here.' And I expect she laughed at him in that rather marvellous way she still retains but with a youth and vivacity which I have never seen.

This large, double-fronted Georgian house, with its decently ugly exterior and great though rather sunless internal possibilities, was her considered choice as being the best possible home for one of her carefully understood temperament. A discriminating traveller with the choice of all earth's beauty spots for home, she elected for the better part of each year to remain within sight of that scarred scrap of Yorkshire, Darnley, where nothing was beautiful and nothing romantic, but where, according to Celia Fertile, everything was to be seen.

View. It symbolized her own kaleidoscopic range of vision. It grew with the years to represent the wealthy mind of an old, world-worn lady who knew life to be a bottomless sea and death the one conceivable haven of rest and understanding. 'Of course, I may be wrong. Heaven wasn't made to sit in. But I do feel we shall understand *something*, even if it is only for a few seconds before we crank up again. Meanwhile, this spot helps me to see just a *little* bit in advance.'

Frontally, View was massive and squat, a fearless and interested observer of the growth and change of its dingy environs. It stood on a broad terrace edged with solid, square-cut box, beneath which the smooth lawns sloped gently to spare, tangled hedges and undulating fields. The garden did not really end: it merged itself with the surrounding country: except where the broad drive was cut athwart by slow-moving gates and round-headed stone pillars with giant's shoulders, and a tiny lodge more fitted to a dwarf than a gardener. There it had the decisiveness though none of the broad-mindedness of its mistress. Beyond, the drive continued less evenly, less comfortingly, as befitted a path leading from long-established security to the dissipated world without, and there were cottages and hens and children I never played with, but to whom my aunt gave sweets and sometimes bulging baskets into which I was not allowed to peep.

To the rear View jutted and spread and eased itself into big, useless spaces and corridors, as a relief from the massive gravity of its front rooms and hall: by walking across ten uneven flags outside the kitchen door one could be amongst the stables with their pent-housed hay-lofts and stamping horses. After that, after an extra, rather meaningless yard to which neighbours' poultry migrated at intervals and in which there were funny little lean-to sheds, the garden recommenced, but without any pretence of being a garden. It was more like a part of the countryside which had achieved some slight degree of education through contact with the big house. The sweep of the fields was abruptly curtailed in that direction by a sudden horizon, and the chimneys and smoke were packed into a small valley and had none of the grandeur of their brothers on the front skyline.

II

My very earliest recollections of Aunt Fertile are of someone superlatively more definite both in thought and action than any other of the grown-ups in my infantile world. What she said was so, and what she did was done before anyone else could do otherwise. From this I deduce that, even then, she was mentally complete, an entirety having the beginnings and the distant end of her life already neatly bound together like a book, a book linked to some unseen, grander volume which was, at once, the prelude and the sequel to her own finite story. Into her home as into her memory she had gathered the crowded third of a century, and was holding its relics holy and mocked around her.

Her rambling, diversified house had been stamped and moulded into an unmistakable whole long before Goble came or I made my appearance on earth. It was not a unity but a totality as the world

23

is a totality, the frame of events in constant progress. Its commodious rooms gave space for commodious thought, and commodious thought there was; its heavily decorated ceilings held a fine suggestion of heavenly surety, and that same immutable certainty formed the foundation of its mistress's being. Even in early youth, so she has told me, she held firmly to the religion of her forefathers, refuting all fundamental attacks with the sole argument that she knew what it really meant better than any other professing Christian. And so felt entitled to joke about the Vicar's 'toy sermons', as she called them, at dogma in all its tottering details, at a tribal morality now comparatively obscene. 'Free love isn't coming. It's here. Been here this few thousand years. But it's not for me, nor ever was. I had one man and he had one woman. John and I were not so far in our minds from the days of Calvin when, if you did not see Hell clearly enough you went there.'

Night and morning and Sunday noon she prayed, requiring such observances of no one else. 'You may play football on Sunday, if you want, Gregory, but I shall not.' She worshipped her own abounding deity, and could quote the Devil's inmost plans.

'What does a vicar know of God!' she scoffed, leaving church one morning. 'Moreover, what does God know of the Vicar.'

The Vicar called her 'that dear, generous atheist', knowing the largest coin in the plate to be hers.

But in all matters except those she deemed eternal verities, hard, bright rocks of belief, as far away from everyday life as is the earth's core and, to her, just as vital, she was the apologist and advocate of change.

The entire world radiated from View, the essence of its polychromatic thought was concentrated within the old bricks, a sense of distant lands, thronging, intimate, essential permeated it pleasantly, peeping at you subtly from a host of unobtrusive souvenirs. Celia Fertile had travelled and collected and understood. Returned to Darnley, gazing at the sooty mist or at the sudden revelation of unexpected colour in the dense smoke drifting insultingly across the setting sun, she would sigh as if the centre of the universe had been achieved at last.

'You know, I always feel as if I'd put on my spectacles when I come back to View,' she would say, and walk into the kitchen, an ultra-modern kitchen which almost ran itself to give home-warming orders to her many superfluous maids, China, the States, the Soviet put in their places. Well, she was used to maids just as she was used to foreign parts. Why dispense with good, familiar things even though they had become redundant? If the old clock on the stairs did not go one could remember the time when it did.

Magnificent, huge, immovable, the suites of View were more monuments than furniture, 'Like Egypt but less approachable.' The electric cleaners which flitted over and about them could not change their nature. 'I always fly if possible, but if we ever remove it will be by horse-van.'

Mahogany, gilt, oil-paintings rubbed corners with aluminium and futurisms, and that subdued disposition of souvenirs. Didn't fit? Neither did the world. That was the world's one certainty. Medley.

III

I feel that no other home than Aunt Fertile's View could have absorbed successfully into itself such foreign human elements as Goble and myself. I arrived some three years later than he, a double-sided orphan in long clothes, a scrap of squalling barbarism intent to reorientate the household which had adopted me. Nurses followed in my wake, and their stiff demands and my more human ones, plus Goble and all that Goble was then introducing, must have compelled most unusual adjustments not only of routine but of ideas.

My aunt's breadth of mind requires no greater emphasis than the fact that she could accept the making of artificial life as a fit subject, not merely for serious experiment but also as a suitable light pastime for her own father, for that must have been how she regarded his interest for quite a long while. Many women would have considered it to be nothing short of blasphemy, but Aunt Fertile's god was much thicker-skinned than most. 'A good father likes his children to surpass him even in his most cherished achievements.' I remember her saying that.

My first memories of the laboratory are inextricably confused with what she has often told me, so that I really do not know where my own observation begins and where I am only repeating her recollections. I probably witnessed the most astounding experiments without knowing it even now, for I used to trot in and out as I wished, having a natural reverence for Goble's appliances which precluded my ever touching them. And there was a period extending over some weeks during which my grandfather was ill and absent from the laboratory, and throughout that time Goble utilized me as a foil. Faced with some difficulty he would prowl up and down the floor of the old hay-loft, his powerful hands thrust deep in his trouser pockets, his shoulders hunched and pugnacious. Then he would explain to me, a tubby, wide-eyed little boy of five or six, the most intimate details of what he was essaying. It was a necessity for him to voice his problems to however dumb an auditor. Afterwards he would scribble furiously in one or other of a chaotic pile of notebooks which I revered like so many new and tiny Bibles. Once, probably in answer to some of leading question of mine, he became too jestingly explicit even for a tiny child.

'Men,' he answered; 'big men like you and I. Soldiers.'

It took my attention and I pored over one of his flat, oily troughs, puzzled but intent to believe, trying my generous best to see little soldiers in it who might be expected to grow bigger when given more room; for I was always intrigued by Uncle Gobey's partiality for little vessels. The pigs and horses had much more impressive ones. At length I shook my head, loath indeed to doubt my hero's word but unable to believe. 'There's only teeny little specks,' I told him, trying to conceal my incredulity.

'You were a little speck once, a teenier little speck than any of those. But you've grown and grown into a real big fellow,' he answered.

'I'm not big enough to be a soldier,' I regretted, slightly comforted.

'You won't need to be,' he said. 'When you're grown up you'll have my big men to fight for you, hulky brutes who won't mind if they're knocked about or killed.'

'Were you killed in the war?' I asked gravely.

I remember he laughed and then muttered something about not being sure. After which he became altogether certain, and told me he had never been killed and that he would not let me be killed either. It appeared that killing was worse than smacks or even being runned over by motors, and I had to go back to the trays to look for the big fellows who would not mind this quite impressive disaster, only to come away disappointed again.

I watched him for a long while maturing a great thought, a masterly argument. I knew he was concealing something.

'When was I just a little speck?' I asked.

'Oh, long ago,' said Goble. 'Before you were born.'

Born meant little or nothing to me, but I found a meaning in that moment and it fitted my tentative revelation.

'I'spose little specks have to have mummies before they gwow,' I ventured, laying bare his secret, and for two days or more I kept a wary eye on Aunt Fertile and the maids, watching whenever I saw them near the stables. And, one day, after my aunt had spent an hour or more inside the laboratory, my imagination almost fully convinced me that she had been acting in the capacity of mummy to the teeny specks, and I went in vividly expecting to meet a lot of new little boys like myself, though probably dressed in khaki and carrying swords. But there were still only the little specks, slightly larger and darker, and my aunt was clearing away the dishes which it had taken her all that time to persuade Goble to empty.

Innocent childhood could not let the matter rest there. Though more than doubtful of my knowledge, I was immensely proud of it and, one day in the kitchen whilst I sat watching Bessie the old maid mixing a pudding, I began to boast of it. Probably the dark, treacly appearance of the mixture, reminding me of some of Uncle Gobey's brews, brought it to mind.

'Uncle Gobey's making little men,' I announced.

Bessie continued stirring without paying attention to me, so I proffered my startling announcement again adding, as a further attraction: 'They'll gwow. Bigger and fatter than 'oo, Bessie.' The personal reference drew her and she looked up, her round, simple eyes contracting. I perceived I had made a hit and followed it up.

'He makes them in the lavatry,' I amplified, using my own version of the most difficult world I had up to then encountered.

'Master *Gregory*!' she exclaimed, emphasizing my name in a truly Papal manner. She was shocked, but whether at my version of laboratory which I knew to be the subject of surreptitious laughter, or at my front-page announcement, I was not certain. I made more than certain.

'Sometime they'll all come marchin' out, sojers wiv guns. An' dey won't kill 'oo an' me. Dey'll kill all the uvvers. Pop, pop!' I added, with gory relish.

'What's the child talking about!' whispered Bessie and, 'They didn't ought to say such things to a child. Taste this pudden, Master Gregory, an' don't you go repeatin' an' thinkin' all you 'ears. Most things you 'ears is lies. Makin' men, indeed! Wot next! It's 'igh time these kemmical folk was put a stop to, makin' of all sorts of *things* an' not 'esitatin' to tell wee bairns!'

But apparently I had placed Bessie in a similar position of knowledgeable pride to my own. Where and when she passed it on can never be known but, like a boomerang – or should I say a dozen boomerangs? – it flung back upon View, first via the chimney-sweep, then through one of our gardeners, who had garnered it from a favourite public-house, and, at length, from more influential sources.

It was the Vicar who, one Sunday morning, hurried round from the vestry so that he might catch dear Mrs Fertile before anyone else did.

'And what is this I hear about your Mr Goble?' he asked, after he had remarked briefly and introductively on the splendour of the day. He was one of those vicars who believed himself possessed of some divine prerogative to ask all questions and to receive dutiful answers. He had what Aunt Fertile called, 'a noozy smile', and he had apple cheeks, a large but interested nose, and tin-tack eyes. I reproduce her description of him. And he always spoke of 'your Mr Goble', as though there were other Mr Gobles, respectable ones who came regularly to church and did nothing of importance; certainly nothing smelly and secretive in someone else's stables.

'I hear the most extraordinary stories.' He smirked, encouragingly.

'We all do,' said Aunt Fertile comfortingly. 'Especially if we are vicars.'

The Vicar's smile veiled itself. His cheeks grew riper – it was a hot day – and he puffed slightly as though to cool the situation a little.

'But what I hear is blasphemous. Indeed, highly blasphemous. They say . . .' He had a fat hand with two fat gold rings, and when he said 'They say,' he waved it with separated fingers, sensitive fingers like aerials receiving the unanimous opinion of the diocese. 'They say he is experimenting with *life* itself. That he has a black art – you know how these poor villagers talk! – and that he is deluding the little children – *my* little children,' encompassing the parish with his fatherly fingers, 'into believing that he is . . . Really, dear Mrs Fertile, I scarce like to repeat the ideas, the ridiculous, blasphemous ideas he is putting into their wee minds.'

Celia Fertile smiled politely in a manner which indicated complete boredom with the subject.

'The chimney-sweep told my maid that Mr Goble was making *men*,' she said. 'I do hope it isn't true, though of course they might be better church-goers than the ordinary kind. They'd feel so inferior and in need of a little grace, wouldn't they? Just made out of old chemicals and things instead of coming along in the proper way.

'But really, Mr Chubling, I shouldn't believe it. You, a minister of religion, listening to old wives' talk!' She bent towards his ruddy shocked countenance. 'What he's really making is – is –'

'But, Mrs Fertile.'

'That's it. Fertilizer. You know. Chemical manure to make the cabbages have twins and grow fifty potatoes to the square foot. He's going to sell it. That's why the chimney-sweep is cross. He thinks no one will want to buy his soot any more!'

The Vicar's tin-tack eyes had discovered amazed white rims. He was far from being convinced.

'I fear greatly that you are concealing something, Mrs Fertile. These scientists with their unbounded intellectual conceit – some of them trespass into the very provinces of the Almighty Himself. I am most loath to appear inquisitive, but I have to remember that *I* am the Vicar and, as such, am responsible for the welfare of my parish, both temporal *and* spiritual.'

Aunt Fertile acquiesced, gravely and silently.

'I'll speak to Mr Goble about it,' she promised; 'and then perhaps he'll refrain from adding to the parish.'

In after years, after many trials and humiliations, this Mr

Chubling lived to realize that Celia Fertile was a greater power in the district than he, but at the time he was new to the parish and she was young and vivacious, and with no more respect for dignity and self-assumed authority than a kitten, and there was an arctic coolness between View and the Vicarage for many long months.

IV

From that day the powers of science were on their guard against me; I was no longer allowed in the laboratory, and when discussions on its mysteries were in progress I was securely shepherded out of hearing.

Though some days, at Aunt Fertile's instigation, my Uncle Gobey explained to me that he had only meant toy soldiers and, sure enough, one afternoon he came out of his home of forbidden mysteries with his arms loaded with brightly coloured objects and, strolling to where I and another little boy were trundling each other over the lawn, playing at garden rollers, presented me with the finest selection of wooden warriors that ever a nipper feasted his eyes on. All suspicions were dissipated and I was over thirty before I learnt that it had taken them a fortnight to unearth a man competent to undertake the construction of these super-toys. Twelve inches high they were, and impressive enough in colour and design to account for the long hours of work in the lab.

After that I wallowed in playthings, for under my watchfully expectant eye its new reputation had to be kept going.

The hush-hush campaign did not stop at me. For the benefit of a gossiping locality it was considered advisable for Aunt Fertile's fertilizer brainwave to be substantiated in fact, and Goble devoted much valuable time to the invention and preparation of an original brand of chemical manure which was judiciously presented to the more troublesome critics. It was a very remarkable product based on entirely new principles, and was soon in such great demand that its commercial possibilities become unmistakable, and a couple of spare sheds at my grandfather's Darnley mills were set aside for its production.

Fertilizer, however, could not account for everything and gossip persisted. There was a particularly pokey-nosed railway van-driver who, having delivered some new and interesting crate at View, would wonder audibly at doorways and other convenient points along his route what there could be in it. 'It was this long if it was a hinch!' Arms extended to match his eyes. 'What they wants with all them bottles passes me!'

So it was that each new enlargement of the laboratory or its equipment was accompanied by a hidden barrage of comment and suspicion, and the laboratory, after a time, began to enlarge with extreme rapidity. The little trays were no longer adapted to the expanding possibilities of Goble's progress; structural alterations became necessary. A huge sun-window was let into the top storey, the whole bottom floor was devoted to a chemical bath; there was complicated heating apparatus, a plant for artificial sunlight and, later, living specimens for observation. A trained assistant, Betts, was placed in charge of these, a man whose sole pride was in keeping secrets. The 'homo wigglies' which had made my name as a humorist had long been surpassed. By what my aunt did not know.

'It's fish this morning,' one can hear the van-driver announcing, well aware that his hearer needed no explanation as to where and how it was fish. '*And* cephalpods, the d'liv'ry note said. Last week it was seaweed an' 'lectrical things, coils an' such. Come Monday they'll happen to be having a helephant or an 'ipperpotermus. I gets frightened to take the old 'orse through them gates fear they'll nab 'er. That I do.'

It must have been during that period that Goble's mind harked back to those fantastic 'beast battalions' with which his imagination had once played. My aunt is of the opinion that the fascination of humbler but concrete results had driven such ideas far away in the interim. But perhaps she is quite wrong in this supposition. Perhaps the visionary in him was always working in consort with the scientist.

'You remember those talks we used to have?' said Goble suddenly to my grandfather one night as they were chatting idly. 'Did I really believe what I used to say? I mean that sentient creatures capable of control, capable of controlling themselves, could be made. Did you believe it?'

'I think we were only romancing – then,' answered my grandfather.

31

'You mean you're beginning to think it possible?'

'There's that thing in the laboratory,' guardedly. 'If *that* can be done!'

Goble rose and went to his room, returning after a long search with a yellowed piece of paper, on which were some pencilled sketches.

'I thought I had destroyed it,' he said. 'I drew these – probably a couple of weeks after we met.' He handed it to them, and for a while the three pored over those first crude drawings of the Flesh units as Goble had conceived them. Then my grandfather began to pace up and down the room in high nervous excitement, and my aunt fell to wondering whether she had been right in encouraging them. Goble, she says, was staring intently at his sketches, as if his mind were working back to something almost forgotten. Or was he only concealing his satisfaction at the long patient conquest of his patron?

'*Must* we – devote all you have done to war? The greatest of all discoveries?' My grandfather ceased his pacing.

'If we don't – others will,' murmured Goble. 'Perhaps in a more enlightened age we could have concentrated on – well, some kind of robot worker, a synthetic human being. Or woolly puppy-things, "pooms" as that chap Damstruther called them, for the kiddies to play with.' He stared at his sketch. 'It seems the world is in need of such a beast as this,' he said.

'Yes,' my grandfather whispered; 'yes,' and 'If you can make *that* . . .' throwing out the suggestion of infinite possibility.

At a question from my aunt he turned on her sharply.

'It's not suitable for a woman,' he said. 'You'd dream about it.'

What 'it' actually was no one but he and Goble would ever have known had it not been for the failure of the incubator one cold January night some weeks later.

THE STRANGE BABY IN THE KITCHEN

They say it was one of the coldest nights they had ever known. A steady north-easterly wind was sweeping across the hills, whining and ferreting round the house; torn black clouds hurried across

Goble's original sketches of the Flesh units

the bleak, crowding stars like witches racing to some unknown tryst, a scurry of trailing cloaks and whispy brooms. Out in the back passages cold draughts had found their way inside. Bessie, in her old-fashioned way, said the wind-folk were getting tired and cold and were creeping into the house for warmth.

Aunt Fertile had shut out all this, elements, witches, frost, and imagination, and before a roaring fire, in company with the gilt-edged ancestors, was reading a prosaic book on ruins. In between the ruins she was thinking of going to bed. But beyond the yard, her father, Goble, and Betts, the assistant, were still busily at work, and she always liked to see the two former safe indoors and the latter fortified with supper and a hot drink prior to his homeward journey before she settled for the night. Otherwise they tended to work till dawn.

The first warning of anything wrong was the sound of the assistant's heavy boots ringing on the frozen flags. Then the back door slammed and there were voices. Bessie appeared with her hands in her apron, a sure sign of a troubled mind.

'The Master wants us to build a huge fire in the kitchen,' she announced. 'Mr Betts says so. Now.' Having delivered her message she added her personal postscript. 'This time of night! I hope, Mum, they're not bringing their hexperiments into my kitchen. There's no room as it is what with all the maids.' Bessie never hid the fact that she considered she could have run the house better by herself without help from vacuum cleaners, electric ovens, or extra servants.

The back door slammed again and my grandfather came into the room. With a brief, repeated order to Bessie to stoke up the kitchen fire, he closed the door after her and stood staring at his daughter enigmatically.

'I'm sorry, Celia,' he said, 'we shall have to bring it in. The incubator has gone wrong. We can't get the current to flow, and it'll be stone cold in a few minutes. We'll have to bring it in.'

'It?' said Aunt Fertile.

'Perhaps you'd better get to bed,' said my grandfather.

'I'll see to the fire,' answered my Aunt Fertile, laying down her book on ruins and beginning to prepare her mind for something entirely unexampled and appalling. 'Bessie will go to bed. All the others have gone. We've plenty of wood in the house.'

My grandfather stared at her speculatively for a moment.

'And blankets,' he said, surrendering. 'Lots of blankets and hot bottles. And a big basket, a clothes-basket. I'll go tell Goble. He's frightfully upset.'

'We mustn't let it die,' agreed Aunt Fertile without the slightest idea of what she was speaking. But she had known for a considerable time that there was something in the incubator, and things in incubators died if they were exposed to the cold. 'Hurry,' she said, and experienced a chill, tingly sensation in her spine.

There was a struggle before Bessie consented to leave her domain to the unknown mercies of science; she, too, like her mistress, had set her mind on seeing whatever there was to see, even though she incontinently died from shock, which she was quite prepared to do. She had always known that there was *something* out there in the laboratory. It had not been her business, nor was it her business now, but it took Aunt Fertile over five minutes to convince her that she could attend to the fire by herself, that there was no need to peel the potatoes at that time of night, in fact, that Bessie was tired out and *must* get some rest.

'Very well, Mum,' Bessie surrendered. 'But don't forget, Mum, that Mr Betts likes his tea real hot an' the cold 'am's in the cupboard. He doesn't take no mustard with it. Sure you've got enough *coal*, Mum?' She cast a curious eye down the passage to where my grandfather was fretting impatiently in the cold then with a resigned shake of her grey locks, began to mount the stairs with extreme slowness. She had rheumatism that night.

Immediately she was gone there was a rush for blankets and other warm things. Rugs were hurried to the kitchen floor; Mr Betts darted backwards and forwards across the yard, returning with, amongst other articles, a thermometer, a small chest of bottles, and a number of flat cases with holes in them which he carried with great care.

'Spawn,' said my grandfather.

Then Goble entered, his head and most of his body hidden behind a bundle of rugs. 'Has that woman gone?' sounded his muffled voice. 'Thank God!' His face, perspiring even in the intense cold, appeared round his burden for a second, seeking direction. Then he snapped out orders for all draughts to be excluded and doors closed and, with gingerly care, deposited his bundle in the clothes-basket which my aunt had placed before the blazing fire. Betts, the assistant, had gone back to the laboratory to renew his struggles with the wiring. The three of them were alone.

'Now, Celia,' said my grandfather, 'I don't want you to be startled. I know you've never really taken our investigations seriously, and perhaps it may be a shock to – to see how far we've progressed. Some people, of course, would – well, they would disapprove of what we have been doing, but I credit you with sufficient common sense, Celia, to understand that the cause of Science allows of no prejudice . . .' And whilst he was talking, quite unnecessarily, Goble was removing the blankets.

Aunt Fertile says her mind was prepared for anything. If a small devil, complete with tail and horns, had been revealed, she says she would not have been surprised. But it was something much more real, much more believable than a devil. For a fleeting second she says she thought it was a baby: there was a glimpse of dull, pinkish skin and a round smoothness as if of baby muscles. Then she knew quite well that it was not a baby, that it was not anything which she had seen before, either in reality or in pictures, or that anyone else had seen before except the two men with her and, probably, Betts.

Goble, having completed his unpacking, stood back from it, folding a thick, woolly blanket into four exactly like a mother, and Celia Fertile had a complete view of the creature.

It was fat, amazingly fat. That was the first impression she had, and so strong was it that momentarily she imagined that that was all it was, just a lump, living, but not in any way impressive. Then the thing itself dissipated that misconception by raising what was indubitably a head from the fatty rolls of its tub-like body and pushing it forward, tortoise-like, towards the welcome heat of the fire. There followed two pudgy appendages, one growing from each shoulder, which lifted and flopped back, lifted and flopped. Arms! My aunt peered downwards into the basket, fascinated. There, sure enough, all curled round and useless-looking, but quite unmistakable, were its legs, fine, promising legs with lumpish, toeless feet on the ends. My aunt tells me that she did not even feel sick, she was so stupefied. Both the men were watching her intently, anxious to witness the effect of their masterpiece on her.

'We might have called it Adam,' said my grandfather, 'but we chose Alpha as being more suited to these times.' He was smiling in a thoroughly benign fashion, if a little uncertainly, and Goble was chuckling audibly in an altogether homely, unscientific way. My aunt realized that this quaint monstrosity was, after all, a commonplace to them, that it had grown upon them gradually and according to law, an inevitable result not a nasty miracle.

'Little Alfy,' she said weakly, trying to live up to the occasion. And there was general laughter, to which the creature in the basket paid not the slightest attention. Then Goble began to wrap its body in blankets and to distribute hot-water bottles about the basket. My aunt had time to look more closely at its head; up to then the fact that it actually had a head had prevented her from examining its features.

Strictly it had no features apart from a loose-edged hole in the lower part of the face which was obviously a kind of mouth. There were certainly no ears nor suggestion of ears, but above the mouth-gap the skin was of a different texture, as though some subtle change were in process. This difference – she always found it impossible to give any adequate description of it – was more marked where the eyes should have been. The skin looked more sensitive and was darker with a ruddier tinge than the body parts. There was a hint of embryonic shape about the mask, not dissimilar but much less defined than that of an early foetus. Otherwise, there was nothing whatever pre-natal about the thing: it was alive in its own separate existence, responding visibly to the heat, moving its flapper-like arms up and down in a remote suggestion of play.

'It's horrible and wonderful, but I can't believe it,' said Aunt Fertile. 'I feel it ought to make me ill, but it doesn't. It – it makes me sympathetic. It looks so helpless, so baby-like. But it seems happy,' she pondered. 'Is it really alive?'

'In a way,' answered Goble. 'Life is relative like everything else. It's more alive than most plants, though it's not so highly organized. But you mustn't imagine it has feelings. It likes the heat, but that's only our way of putting it. What we really mean is that its surface cells react to heat, as material a fact as that our cells respond to gravitation. That pellicular appearance of the upper part of the face: the cuticle is becoming sensitized to light. Already, in the broadest sense of the word, it can see.'

'Do you mean it will have eyes?'

'Not exactly eyes. At least, I don't think so. Parts of the face which will be able to distinguish light from dark, movement from quiescence. And perhaps not this particular specimen. I've already seen signs that his power of adaptation is failing. All life, when it achieves the faintest degree of safety, survival value, tends to congeal into a set form. But that remains to be seen in his case. I haven't abandoned hope in him. Danger or strain, if we can find something suitable, may restore him.' He spoke of 'him' and 'his' . . .

There came a sudden sound from behind, a creaking and the shuffle of soft substance pushed aside. My grandfather had padded under the kitchen door with an old coat. Then Bessie's face appeared, round-eyed beneath brown-paper curlers. Afterwards, she explained that she couldn't abear the thought of Mum getting the coal, but in that moment she had no words.

'Hex,' she said – it was probably the beginning of 'excuse' – and then she emitted a strangulated gurgle as her eyes fell on the bladder-like head of Little Alfy. Against all her training and instincts she came straight forward into the kitchen, her gaze never veering from the clothes-basket and its inexplicable contents. It was a matter of swift seconds, during which Goble alone made a belated effort to throw a blanket over that shimmering pink pate. Then Bessie's gurgle recommenced and became incorporated in the unconscious groaning of one about to faint. She sagged, and slumped down on to the floor.

II

It was a climax for which none had made the slightest preparation. The men would probably have tried to brave out whatever results occurred, to repel gossip and animosity by downright rudeness, barricades, patrols, anything; assuming, of course, that Bessie spread her story, which no one seems to have hoped to avoid. It was the twentieth century, the Great War had come and gone and had changed everything; anyone was entitled to continue that change, to vindicate the existence of another century in the waste of time, in his own way and in his own backyard. But Aunt Fertile knew her Bessie and her locality better than they. She was the only one who did anything practical.

Before nine the following morning Bessie, in excellent, almost violent health (rheumatism miraculously removed by shock), was on her way to a distant friend of Aunt Fertile, who ran a secluded establishment for non-homicidal eccentrics. By half-past ten my aunt was paying strategic, disarming calls on the Vicar (the first in years), and other locally celebrated busybodies, collecting for an orphanage remembered at ten. By one, tired but determined, she was settling the future of Goble, Little Alfy, and whatever else might eventuate from their association.

She knew her Bessie's tongue.

'Anywhere,' she said; 'the farther the better. You can't expect to carry on indefinitely in the West Riding. These Alphas and things you're making! By the time you reach Delta they'll be running about the garden, bothering the chickens and playing with the cottage children. There's Gregory to consider. Go abroad. You need heat for your experiments. Go to Africa, the Sudan, Arabia . . .'

She had taken every precaution to safeguard Bessie from all human association until she should be in an environment where delusions might be expected and would pass unnoticed, but in that she had failed. Probably she had expected to fail. Bessie had three minutes – separate minutes – with one of the maids. In the early afternoon heads were seen bobbing about beyond the hedge at the far end of the lawn, and there was a growing crowd from the cottages outside the big gates. A rough man who was inclined to be socialistic in an illogical, eruptive fashion, came right to the front door and rang the bell. Aunt Fertile answered it.

'The people's saying that somethink's up here,' he opened. 'I ain't got no wish to intrude, but they arst me to come see.'

'What are they saying?' asked Aunt Fertile coldly.

'Well, some's saying that there's unholy doings – not that I personally holds with *holy* doings – and others sez whatever it is it ought to be stopped. And there's some thinks that Mr Goble, wot lives here, has made a baby, and that he's keeping it in the kitchen.' He paused, peering beyond her into the hall, and resumed confidentially. 'I knows, Ma'am, that these folks has no objective reasoning. They just hears and imbibes and never thinks. I've tried learning some of them Marx, but they just giggles as though it was the pictures. But they're frightened, Ma'am, and some of them's getting nasty, and you won't have no peace until you settles them.'

Beyond his head, down the broad drive near the little lodge, which was more suited to a dwarf than a gardener, there appeared the short, busy figure of Mr Chubling, the Vicar. Drawn into his wake, as it were, by his determined passage an uncertain retinue bobbed and wavered in his train.

Aunt Fertile stiffened herself. Behind her in the hall appeared Goble, hands in pockets, shoulders hunched menacingly in the way which even I remember. All obstacles, human or abstract, caused him to adopt that characteristic attitude.

'Tell them it's no business of theirs,' he said harshly, coming forward. 'Tell them to clear off; that they shouldn't listen to what fools tell them.' But Aunt Fertile was cleverer than that.

Over the afternoon tea to which she invited the Vicar, the rough socialist man, and two or three carefully selected neighbours, she discoursed charmingly for three-quarters of an hour on everything under the sun but scientific research. Goble had to sit through it, nursing a fragile cup and saucer, and with subtle tact and a few apt scowls, was lured into confessing an interest in a most astonishing series of everyday subjects ranging from rugby football to textiles and poultry and poetry. Francis Thompson was his particular anathema, it emerged, and the Vicar fell for that bait and its Catholic content, and they reciprocated their antagonism most agreeably.

Then they inspected the laboratory – Mr Goble had always wanted to show them round, hadn't he? but he was such a busy man – and were invited to examine closely, under the pretext of its great interest, everything which did not matter in the least. Everything which did matter had been carefully removed under Aunt Fertile's urgent instructions. Whilst the Vicar tried to air his archaic science and the others sought for incriminating clues in vain, Little Alfy was squatting only a few feet away from them in his incubator which had been neatly covered with sackcloth and excited no curiosity whatever. Betts had completed the wiring in the early hours, whilst Bessie was still uncertain whether to continue fainting or not.

'Not at all the kind of man I imagined,' the Vicar opinionated to the rough socialist in a voice which no one was intended to hear, but all did. 'Though he has a strange look.'

'You must all come again,' invited Aunt Fertile, 'when Mr Goble is actually experimenting and there is something to show you.'

I dimly recollect that I tried to take part in that friendly leave-taking, but was lured away with an unexpected offer of a visit to town if I would go to get washed *then*. No one knew how much I remembered or had forgotten.

From that day the house entered on a new period, the general impression of which is still in my mind. There was much private conference, a frequent going and coming, a sense of hurry and unease in the home. No doubt I noticed it the more because of Bessie's absence.

'What are you going to do with us now?' asked my grandfather of Aunt Fertile that evening, when the visitors had gone. 'You seem to be more practical than us men. What next?' It was patent to all that the extravaganza of View must end forthwith. Aunt Fertile, departing from her first suggestions, would have settled it out of hand with a country cottage on the moors, Haworth way or, better, on the Sussex downs; but Goble, while he was nursing his cup of tea and criticizing Francis Thompson, had really been visualizing a whole series of desirable possibilities let loose by those larger proposals.

'Why not central Africa?' he asked with a signal disregard of my grandfather's finances. 'Sunlight, tropical heat is of paramount importance to us. Lack of it has been our main drawback,' and he launched into a dissertation on infra-reds and ultraviolets.

III

It was then that Professor Dax came on the scene at Goble's urgent call, abandoning a boring chair and narrow research facilities for illimitable opportunity. They had once worked together, but Dax's dynamic personality had carried him to early and now much-regretted academic distinction, and had severed the partnership. He brought with him a large, recent inheritance, an established reputation extending far beyond his 'varsity associations, and a quite unscholarly push and business ability, all of which Goble visualized as being vital to future progress. He looked too bald to be young and too pinkly fresh to be old, but he went about so quickly and talked so rapidly that it was impossible for a small boy to gauge his age. My aunt said he was full of vitamins.

View overflowed with him. He was like an electric current flowing from Darnley to Africa.

Within the month he and Goble sailed. We said 'goodbye' to them under the front porch, and I became sole heir to the now vacant stables, a wonderland of odd relics and lingering scents.

They fed my imagination for many weeks afterwards.

To Africa, also, some six months later, my grandfather followed.

My Aunt Fertile says he never settled after Goble's departure; his heart was in Goble's work as though it were his own. 'I wonder how he is getting on,' he would say. 'I wonder if his hopes are being fulfilled.' For Goble was a sparse letter-writer.

He would stand at the window staring outwards and southwards dreamily. Sometimes he visited the stables.

Once again he became active at his factories, working hard and late, but it transpired that he was only arranging matters so that he, too, could leave.

I remember his going quite distinctly; there were tears in his eyes at the thought of leaving his only daughter behind. But there was another quality, something beyond description, a youthfulness, an excitement. Only a week before he had received one of Goble's rare letters.

HOW THE COMPOUND GREW

I have chosen this way of writing my story, admitting the reader to a prelude which was undreamed of by myself and most others until many years later, because what I am writing is in the nature of a history and only, incidentally, a record of my own experiences. I have been at some pains to describe the events of that early period.

Nevertheless, I do not intend to continue these beginnings. I wish to depict the coming of artificial life to the earth as I and the millions who shared my ignorance actually witnessed it, and I must ask the reader to be patient in rediscovering through my eyes what is now a commonplace to him; that shortly after the World War men were making living things which Nature had no hand in designing, and that from the commencement they had in mind, romantically at first perhaps, but later with a growing certitude, the creation of a fighting animal which would assist and eventually supersede the use of men in battle. Of the years between I propose to give only such particulars as will make unnecessary any repetition of the endless speculations and questionings in which we outsiders, presented suddenly with the accomplished fact of life-making, spent many brain-racking hours. The growth of the little Congo experimental station into the famous Compound and training centre, the exploitation of Goble's subsidiary inventions – for the fertilizing agent was only one of many by-products of his main research – and the secret linking of these into the great Dax-Beldite Combine, these are matters on which I can only touch most briefly.

For a number of years my aunt was kept fairly well in touch with events in Africa. After only a few weeks Professor Dax, prospecting by air, discovered the perfect situation for Goble's further research work, a lonely tract of territory in the Congo, half savannah, half jungle, some eight or nine hundred miles inland from Boma and far away from all administration, railroads and highways. A handsome payment no doubt disposed of all official curiosity, and within two days from their signing the lease Goble was settled again in a makeshift shanty with a sun-scorched clearing in front on which he could spread his tanks of spawn and a special nursery for Little Alfy, who had survived the sea voyage most phlegmatically. There, in a while, further Little Alfies began to make their appearance, and the sheds spread and enlarged until they formed a definite settlement.

The intense heat produced results beyond all expectation. 'The latest specimens have entirely lost the cloddishness of their forerunners,' writes my grandfather shortly after arrival. 'They respond instantaneously to heat and light and any movement close to them causes a noticeable excitation.' And, later, on the same subject, 'Food dominates them. Fear and even the most rudimentary sense of fellowship are altogether absent. When fed the little beasts are

torpid, but as soon as hunger recurs they attack each other mercilessly, and us too, in what I suppose is the urge to feed themselves.
How they scrap! But they are so soft they cannot injure themselves
or each other. Goble says he has discovered a method of toughening
them without bad effects. That will be most interesting. But we
shall have to watch out. D 16, our latest, weighs over six stone.'

Through innumerable sidelights such as these one can trace
something of the steady conquest of obstacle after obstacle, the
overcoming of the natural flabbiness of a loose cellular structure,
the evolution of a primitive form of musculation. Bones, it seems,
and the reinforcements of nerve and sinew eluded Goble's genius,
but he was at no loss for effective substitutes. And growth presented no problem whatever.

In truth, the very opposite! Goble's main difficulty was a propen-
sity in the specimens to grow surplus arms and legs, to effloresce
into useless bulges and, at a later stage, into quaint, unfinished
imitations of themselves. 'Neoblast', he called it, new germination.
This 'misguided effort at reproduction' was, he contended, inevitable; for in its essence life is growth and procreation merely a
separable growth.

The specimens, however, aspired to no such cellular specializa-
tion as is evident in the more complex life-forms, and sprouted and
budded and proliferated like tropical plants, and he had no alternative but to carry on incessant combat against this 'neoblast' of
theirs.

There was never any hope that it would supersede the process
of separate creation: the 'offspring' were altogether too protean. Sometimes they inherited one thing and sometimes another and sometimes nothing in particular but a capacity for inordinate, gelatinous
growth. The tendency increased with each advance in his products,
and was only curbed by special treatment and injection.

'I wish they wouldn't,' writes my grandfather, with the note of a
pathetic parent complaining of his wilful children.

Within three years the palisaded compound, later to become
world-famous, was in existence in miniature, and there was a
steadily growing need of extra assistance. The first helpers were
mostly laboratory-trained men, but these were difficult to come by,
and reluctant to exile themselves in Central Africa in conditions of

secrecy amounting almost to incarceration, and so resort had to be made to the coastal towns from which was gradually recruited the strangest assortment of men, tempted by high wages and privileged circumstances, and trained and disciplined through the months into skilled, trustworthy assistants.

Professor Dax had it in his ambitious mind from the beginning that they were founding something much bigger than a mere experimental station, and concentrated on developing a high sense of *esprit de corps*, encouraging these early experts in artificial life-making to create their own isolated world, planning for their peculiar needs, salvaging the riff-raff souls he had collected with sound, if ruthless, psychology. It was he who introduced native labour from faraway districts and invented a new kind of idolatry based on Goble and my grandfather specially for their benefit. 'Foresight', Dax defended his action when the latter protested against the 'Glory Service' he had instituted and wanted them to be Christianized in the usual way; 'we'll need all the superstition we can soak into them later to prevent their spreading what's going to happen here.' Goble laughed at the squabble, saying he did not mind so long as they did not make images of him. But that was too good an idea for Dax to neglect and images were forthwith made.

II

The Compound from its earliest was of roughly circular shape surrounded by electrified palisades close inside which were built the laboratories, flesh houses, and living quarters. The remainder was an expanse of hard, beaten earth set apart for exercising and 'educating' the specimens and, later, for the Experts' 'games'.

Education covered a wide experimental field, cattle playing the major part in it. They would be let loose with selected specimens for scientific observation of the latter's behaviour to be made. Often enough in the early stages the specimens paid no attention to their companions nor the cattle to them, but sometimes the animals would take fright and stampede and bellow. And then these overgrown Little Alfies, great bloated lumps of flesh, would wake as if from eternal torpor and blunder a few yards after the fleeing cows. Any which excelled their fellows became the objects of closest analysis. All lethargy being eventually overcome, exercise became a dangerous business, and it was then that the Experts began fully to realize the sporting possibilities of their charges and introduced bigger game.

My grandfather's communications, however, at a time when the most startling progress was being made, became more and more reticent. He speaks of anything but the specimens. 'The Experts are difficult,' he writes. 'They are amazingly staunch, but resent any kind of control of their way of living and they are such harsh, wild men, a class to themselves. We have given them a new world and they have made it their own. Their "games" are a monstrous institution! I cannot understand how Dax ever countenanced them, and now they have become a tradition and cannot possibly be eradicated. And yet, perhaps, Goble is right. How else could the specimens be trained and their powers developed but by pitting them one against another?' (Creatures altogether different from the early specimens are suggested in this, but he offers no description of them.) 'They call it the "Red Try-out", a name dreadfully suggestive of what must come later. It is preferable to their "cow-runnings" in which real, live animals are introduced and sometimes killed. That is horrible!' He refers once again to the idolatry of the negroes. 'This worshipping business! This "White Man's Glory", as Dax irreverently calls it! He contends that it is the only way to keep them blindly loyal and I have to admit that loyalty is imperative. He argues that all patriotism is a kind of idolatry, and that there is no real difference between praying to Goble and Beldite and shouting for King and Country. But I hate being treated like a demigod even by savages. I verily believe some of them think *we* made them! They call the specimens "the Brothers", as if they are kin.'

Nothing in detail. Exclamations. Doubts. My Aunt Fertile concluded that he had bound himself to secrecy in certain matters and implied the most astounding successes, imagining as best she could creatures which ate and ran and slept, but were like nothing else on earth, artificial beasts which fought each other ... During that period he fills his letters with descriptions of Goble's minor inventions, telling of remarkable results achieved with different varieties of fertilizer, of how Goble grew artificial flowers and immunized the Compound against fever, and for some years appears to have given his main attention to lightweight cellular rubber ('Imitation muscle'), for the construction of aeros, which brought him the bitter rivalry of the German synthetic rubber manufacturers. This development took him away from the Compound to the new factories which were being purchased in England. He gives no hint of a parallel but entirely secret expansion which was proceeding in those same factories; nor does he mention the visits paid to the Compound by Sir Godfrey Human, the inventor of humanite the super-explosive, and other influential friends of Professor Dax: Rufus, the financier, Erasmus Pollen, the Home Secretary who abolished capital punishment, and General Tankerley who, having had no wars to run since he rose to eminence, took to playing with fire in his retirement.

On all these matters my grandfather is silent. He makes no mention of the Belgian Government's increasing curiosity as to their activities, nor of the great negro uprising which culminated in the establishment of a black mandate over that area and stifled all uncomfortable probing. The Compound was henceforth left free from interference, one suspects as payment for secret services rendered, and no objection was raised to a second compound some miles away where Experts and blacks could be trained in larger numbers. By then much greater interests were at stake than the mere guarding of a scientific marvel.

III

And that, apart from one or two vivid insights given to me in after years by Haggard, the Process Expert, is all the light I can throw on the evolution of the Flesh from ultra-microscopic ephemerons in the little vats at View to its final emergence in the growing pans and mills of Darnley. Through the years the Compound expanded farther and farther until eventually the palisades were over half a mile apart and outside were acres of artificial vegetation and other subsidiary aspects of the business, employing in all some several thousand persons. The whole formed a little isolated world of its own, an island of fantastic civilization growing in the jungle waste hundreds of miles from the nearest town, its only communication being by air. Rumours of it probably leaked down to the coast, but their very truth and apparent connection with native ju-ju courted disbelief. Professor Dax's sparkling ingenuity, his White Man's Glory Service, with its cleverly planned idolatry, the fervour of highly paid, widely privileged Experts, guarded their secrets. Simple, credulous fellows (or downright liars!) – no one with intelligence would believe them. Africa is overflowing with tales of magic, and both Goble and Dax preferred the reputation of being white witch-doctors who could make animals by waving their hands and incanting to anything more approximating to the facts. Highly influential assistance was theirs whenever required.

Those were the great days of the peace movements when both governments and peoples, shocked into action by the futile and inconclusive slaughterings of the thirties and early forties and the economic impossibility of forever increasing their defences, sought temporary relief in a tangle of international pacts and armament controls. The great standing armies of the Continent declined, giving place to cheap militia and other safeguards against insurrection on the home fronts; navies were reduced to a plausible minimum and aerial bombardment placed on the blacklist together with a galaxy of gases and lethal powders. 'Humanite', the atomic explosive, was discovered, sold to all nations, and its use promptly prohibited.

Nevertheless, its inventor, Godfrey Human, attained his knighthood and continued to amass great wealth. Beneath the political surface militaristic minds, sceptical of all permanent peace in that trade-strangled world, were re-orientating their ancient prejudices, seeking new ways of arming, cheaper and less visible ways. After all, such vast and expensive aggregations of war material as had once been were no longer needed for the highly mechanized warfare the new military were visualizing.

An armament technique suited to the time was sought ... here and again methodical, disinterested intellects were throwing up unprecedented possibilities, acquiescent in the most complicated subterfuge providing their discoveries could be commercialized. Shadow syndicates, invisible trusts ... individual firms suffering the prohibition of their deadly specialities without apparent loss. The Dax-Beldite Combine, hidden, tortuous, ever-growing, was perhaps only one of these.

Within the framework of national planning, which for a while damped down industrial unrest during the recurrent economic crises of that unbalanced civilization, it grew unsuspected, its component firms contributing immensely with their fertilizers and imitation muscle to the periodic prosperity campaigns. Trust in the web of international pacts and understandings and in a disarmament which was little more than the natural evolution of munitions, trust that mere fear and hatred of war must preserve and consolidate peace, these were the veils behind which it grew. The Compound was like a distant gland, feeding, controlling . . .

One can see my grandfather, ageing and vacillating in all his later letters, complaining without explanation that Professor Dax overrode him in everything, deploring Goble's entire unconcern with the exploitation of his genius. 'He sticks his hands in his pockets and hunches his shoulders and glares. Not at me; at his thoughts. Then he seems to remember me and laughs and is his old self. Sometimes he says terrible things. He lives for his work and I can scarcely persuade him to leave the laboratories. "Let them have their toys," he laughs as though it were young Gregory again. No, I don't suppose he will ever return to England.'

Only once does he break his silence under some unusual stress. The Hon. Rupert Vessant, then an under-secretary, was brought into their confidence and visited the Compound.

Vessant was the man they had been awaiting.

As a mere chrysalis of a politician he had established a reputation on the theme that old-time strategy and weapons were ludicrously outworn and that future war would be a quite fantastical occurrence, a fight between laboratories rather than physical beings. He rose to cabinet rank on his masterly exposition of how Britain could be wiped off the map within weeks by any powerful and intelligent enemy. In his famous phrase she was 'as vulnerable as a naked man fastened to the ground with falcons assailing him.' As Secretary for War he continued to urge these views throughout a period when merely to mention the possibility of war was to be considered unpatriotic and bellicose. He had no faith in peace and said so. The pacifists used his warnings as an argument for peace at any price.

My grandfather describes him in one letter. 'A pug-nosed fellow with a quality of – how can I put it? Logical imagination seems to describe it. He should be the means of completing our plans of which, Celia, I must not tell you, but I am rather afraid of what he may do.

'He is so typical of this age, one of those thrusting men who goes by instinct from power to power, who cannot resist using a new power when he gains it. He sees power in Goble's work. Whenever he looks at it there is a cold appreciation in his eyes which in any other man I should call excitement. He seems to hanker after it if you know what I mean.'

Indeed it was Vessant's nature to use ruthlessly whatever came to his forceful hand. Another scientific miracle had been brought to earth, a new gift to his military genius, hitherto denied expression. He would have utilized a descent of heavenly angels – or an eruption of black ones – in the same impartial, logical spirit. An aged, deeply rooted Prime Minister was presented with reports and affidavits, gazed blankly at the films they showed to him. 'If these creatures exist then they exist,' he said wearily. 'But what can *we* do with them? There isn't going to be any war. And the Army! What would the Army say!'

A long-hoped-for change in the premiership took place . . .

IV

But I can do no justice to that political dissension nor its counterpart amongst the directors of Dax-Beldite, the feud between patriotism and the basest commercialism, between idealist pacifism and cynical war preparation. These personal quarrels, hidden intrigues, the cumulative needs of secrecy to avoid disturbing the trustful social surface, all are dramas deserving separate treatment. Across that trust, war rumours, prophecies of imminent world collapse, swept at intervals and passed. The mass peace feeling was too strong, the time not ripe. Heat flared up between one nation and another, between classes within nations; poverty spread as freedom declined. Sudden winds of disillusion whirled up the seemingly dead leaves of revolution – and were gone. So the cooling earth must have frothed and spat and threatened millions of years before in the aeons when life was but a scum on the hot pools. Human society reproduced in itself that early dawn – and brought forth a new scum; a bestial rival to itself.

All of these can be no more than threads in the story, backgrounds to the vivid pattern they wove.

Into these backgrounds Goble and Edom Beldite and Professor Dax must recede with the years, and it is only the chance of his senior position and a public name which later brings my grandfather back into the limelight to brand him as the arch-purveyor of living munitions.

And Goble, that very human but inaccessible figure. I hope I have succeeded in dispelling the illusion, so common in these latter days, that he was a superhuman ghoul, a maniac scientist whose mind had become unhinged during the World War.

He was not. Perhaps his was a deeper sanity than ours, a humble sanity merciless in its demands. For some twelve years he lived rationally and contentedly with my grandfather and aunt, homely people though with minds more vividly alive than most. He was my Uncle Gobey and as good an uncle as ever a small boy had. I have romped with him on my nursery floor and admired his surpassing imitation of grizzly bears. We have shared surreptitious apples together . . .

CHAPTER TWO

Time and the Beldite Factories

THE MILLS AT DARNLEY

IN THE YEARS immediately preceding the destruction of Darnley, the Beldite mills, always of imposing size, had grown to be the most outstanding feature for many miles round. The three unsightly hulks of the old factories were dominated to the south by massive new offices, many-windowed and sunny except on the mill-yard side where a vast blank wall pierced by one small door frowned down on the steamy activity below; far too many offices it seemed, of which the upper floors remained neglected and empty. Those vacant rooms in their turn were shadowed to the east by a towering storehouse, the end one of a quarter ring of identical buildings circling round the factory on adjacent plots like huge blocks of solid concrete, grim, eyeless structures in the then modern anti-air-raid style, their ugliness relieved only by the soft curve of their carapace roofs. A fortress, a bastille: seen pygmy-like from below, or from the hills, a featureless cluster in the smoky distance, one could not avoid the comparison. That? *That* tremendous place? Only Beldite's, the fertilizer works. Used to be a woollen mill, but they've transferred that part of the business to smaller premises. Yes, they think big. Surprising how these new industries grow.

Beldite's did not end with the surface. During the first rearmament scares when, following the example of the thirties, efforts were being made to make the whole population gas-conscious, Beldite's led in the construction of raid shelters. In the interim the problems of deep and inexpensive excavation had been solved by soil converters and humanite blasting apparatus, and many large businesses and hotels and most municipalities had sunk deep undergrounds. It seemed merely commensurate with the large thinking of Beldite's that ours should be on a super-scale, extending beneath the whole of the works. But they were not distinctive for their size only nor for their air-renewal plant, gas-absorbers, heating arrangements; their design excited comment, consisting of a large central hall entered through a sloping runway and with interconnecting galleries running from it to lesser halls, all equipped with heavy doors. They had an oddly stable-like appearance.

I took my place in the Darnley mills when I was eighteen, after six months' struggle to join my all-but-forgotten Uncle Gobey in Africa. This ambition was painstakingly discouraged, I was told that our holding there was an uninviting swamp of fevers and dead monotony (!), though prolific in fertilizing elements, and the uncertain native situation was used heavily against me. I had perforce to find interest in the more prosaic industry of cloth manufacture and accept the sternly kind yeoman tradition of my family that boys should begin at the bottom. A promise made by my grandfather on one of his infrequent visits home that I would later go to the new cellular rubber works shortly to be opened outside London finally settled me, though it never came to anything, and being a hefty youngster and destined to inherit the Darnley mills some day I soon overcame my disappointment. Gliders and certain youthful inventive ambitions in which the engaging products of Rubber Treatments played a big part were already occupying me. Both cloth and fertilizer with their perfected processes bored me, but Darnley, provincial and dull and dirty as it was, was as good a place as any other for a slogging young investigator with no taste for giddying round, and I settled to it easily. A dash over to the Continent now and again or a tour of some new rubber factory was all the change I needed.

What did I know of it all? I knew that the fertilizer ingredients came partly from the Congo and partly from certain laboratories in Herts; I knew the complex formulae for the treatment, and that if anything went wrong, and at times large quantities would go bad and smell abominably, we had to send samples back to Africa forthwith. Some of the simpler varieties went directly into the market while others, which had to mature before they could be of use, were either sold to a large firm of factors in Manchester (whom I never in the least suspected of being a part of ourselves), or deposited in the dim, heated interiors of our own great store-houses. It was just an uninteresting affair of seedy-looking jellies, and much of the work on it was, I feel, solely designed to puzzle the inquisitive, of which I was not one.

After we took over the old sewage works in the fields below View our range of products widened. Open-air tanks were laid down to receive the pulverized produce of a number of mushroom batteries (we nicknamed the noxious stuff 'ketchup'), and this we were told was for use as cattle-cake and as a basis for synthetic foods which the Chinese found most palatable. An oily extract from it became soap.

No ordinary mushrooms those. Much more flaccid, inclined to bulge and blob shapelessly and vigorous beyond measure in dissemination. The neighbouring fields were under constant survey for outcrops. But who would be suspicious of mushrooms!

Cloth receded and fertilizer and soap spread. Beldite's grew and I grew with it, accepting the strange order as natural. Our adverts, our goods were everywhere. Our massive conception of architecture inspired confidence. What could be more reasonable than that my grandfather should utilize his own lands and factories as soon as Goble's discoveries became marketable propositions? Nor was it to be expected that even the managerial staff should know anything about such valuable trade secrets. My main concern was a secret regret that my Uncle Gobey had degenerated into a clever chemist: cellular rubber had been such an inspiring beginning.

One grew used to the perennial jokes of outsiders. 'Beldite cloth? Mind there ain't mushrooms in the pockets'; and, 'They're going to hide all Darnley under Beldite's when the next war comes!'

For some years the national schemes for intensive agriculture and the steady conversion of pasture into arable land accounted adequately for our prosperity (though these seemed to cancel out the demand for cattle-cake); and there was no shortage of Chinese who might, for all we knew, be coming cleaner and buying our soap as well. But during the last eighteen months queer rumours rose that Beldite's was not all it appeared, strange officials inspected our works, there was a murmur that in some inexplicable way we were concerned in those secret preparations for war which popular gossip persisted were afoot in all lands.

I had no patience with such yap.

My grandfather a warmonger!

Returned to England some years previously, he moved in and out of my life spasmodically, a thick-set, slightly bowed, but well-preserved figure who, more and more, seemed to sink into himself. He was over eighty then, a very lonely old man, wealthy but without friends, who at times impressed me as struggling with something terrific and, perhaps, unmanageable. I did not follow up the clue. Spending most of his time in London or at the rubber factories he had little time for me nor I for him, and such hours as we did spend together were mostly in younger company introduced by myself. The immense, unknown hinterland of his life meant little to me, as little as did the historical background of my time.

I was a pretty big sort of chap, long-limbed, with what always struck me as rather a chunk of a face. I have heard it called 'pleasing', though it never pleased me particularly, and 'dynamic', and once a soppy girl described it as 'dreamily pugilistic', whatever that meant. Anyhow, my face be what it might, I had all the assurance which normally goes with healthy size and slightly unhealthy security, and my lack of interest in things greater and more complex than my own little busy round was probably due to a rather stupid instinct for playing a lone hand. I did a solid day's routine work, slogged away to the small hours nightly at research into the weight-carrying capacity of gliders (far outstripped on the Continent long before, though I had no means of knowing that), and took my relaxation either in the air or the boxing ring. Knocking someone's face about or having my own beaten up had an equally exhilarating effect. I never poked my nose into other folk's ambitions and I pushed theirs back from mine feeling confident I could make a go of anything I essayed.

Sometimes, it is true, I felt like breaking out and going adventuring, but there were no new poles to find and no lost worlds. If anyone pointed to the adventure of politics or commerce, well, I'd only to look at Beldite's.

Beldite's romantic! Those rumours . . .

Yap!

*

55

II

But to hear Manders on me, on Beldite's, and on politics.

'Hell! It's all damn spoof! The whole universe doesn't need so much fertilizer!'

Manders was my under-manager, and not a very thorough one: dreams of internationalism and a communistic world evermore distracted him. His grandmother had been a militant suffragette of the man-mauling order and I suppose he had inherited a likeness of spirit, much refined and diluted in transmission, and now fretting tentatively behind a scrupulous toilet and over-brilliant shirts. He read and quoted endless illegal pamphlets and would have carted them around for others' improvement, but they bulged his pockets badly. A nice boy suspended in his intentions by mixed ideals.

One aspect of him expressed itself in pomade and a shy liking for girls: the other in the assiduous collection of facts and rumours relating to rearmament, exciting guesses not excluded. He seemed to think I wanted to hear all about these, always wanted to hear about them. There was a *sotto voce* quality about his mind. No one took him very seriously.

'Perhaps I shouldn't say it about my own firm. But, hell!' (Quite a mild little hell it was.) 'In the End of War Movement we hear things.' He dabbled in movements. 'It has its eye on Beldite's and it's not all sentimental peacemongers. There's Mundaine. And Hogbin. I'd like you to hear them, Betty.'

Not very encouraging but quite charming sound from Betty Corrall, my typist. In between pamphlets, as it were, he was in love with Betty.

See him perched any morning on my office table, on a canteen table, or some other table, or even the banisters, fixing me with his black eyes. Quietly fervid. 'You make me sick, you do. War isn't ended; the whole world's driving to war. We're preparing for war, here in these very brick walls. And look at you!' His naturally pleasant voice would become monotonous and then it was time to joke before he became deadly serious.

'Please look at me, Betty, I hate looking at myself. And they're

not brick, Manders; they're ferro-concrete with matt faience fac-
ings.' Poking fun at him amused Betty but never deterred him.

'You, strong, young, with a brain of your own! We need men like
you in the EOWM, and you spend your time flipping about in the
sky. You pretend politics doesn't affect you and you can't even
have an engine over about ten horse because of the disarmament
laws.'

'That should please you. Besides, we up-to-date birds don't need
engines. My latest model –'

'But it's all damn camouflage. What about –'

'What about a small spot of work?'

'*Work!*' With Armageddon on the doorstep again and the millennium down the street! 'All you think about!' Manders would gaze at his
daintily creased trousers, pat that day's pretty tie, and retreat to his
own office, postponed but not defeated. And Betty Corrall would toss
her fair mop, smile, and look very charming indeed in her baby-like
way before resuming work diligently. Sometimes I feared rather than
flattered myself that she accepted his genuine but politically tinted
courtship as a not inevitable second-best and might also, at any
moment, begin to sit on tables near to me. What affairs I'd had I'd
crashed into unawares and it wasn't in my nature to streak at a girl
like some do, even when the girl was like a jolly little toy, fluffy and
irresponsible as Betty was; smiling distance, especially with my own
typist, was quite near enough.

'Wasted! Six foot odd, time, and money. You don't gad around
like most. We *need moral* men who can discipline themselves for
the struggle that's coming. You prefer to put up with all the irksome
restrictions they've invented to prevent progress: vote qualifica-
tions, the corporate form of election, "legislative continuity", sitting
like dead hens' – ('On addled eggs!') – 'on even the mildest reforms.
You prefer to be one of the crowd waiting to be massacred!' ('I've
been waiting to be massacred so many years!') 'And you actually
remember Shanghai and Guernica and the Slav bombardments!'

And, indeed, Mars seemed nearly down and out to my preoccupied mind. Our civilization might be 'a decrepit old hag kept young
by dope and artifice' (one of Manders' gems), but surely we had
outrun organized murder! It was good to me and I felt I could give
well in return. You can imagine me and a score million others I

scarce thought about, blasé to scare headlines and surreptitious pamphlets, skipping the new rearmament revelations ... The humanite scandal, the accusations and repercussions of the Chemical Warfare Commission, the persistently recurring story abroad that Britain's mild face hid the most dire of all weapons, then ... what was it? France contravening the bomb-carrying capacity agreements. Official denial, facts and figures, legal imbroglio over the exact definition of a bomb, France as anxious to solve as anyone. Manders – perfervid – 'hell'-ing excitedly (was there no one left on earth to convert but me?), quoting over a century from Marx and Nietzsche to Lenin, Lloyd George, and Eden, and on to Vessant and Mundaine and himself ... 'Of course France is making super-aeros, but we shan't find them. We're all making something. In the EOW we get to know things.

'Candidly, I'd be rather glad if war broke,' confidentially, with an eye on Betty. 'Rather damn glad. It'd give the Movement a chance to show what it can do. The TUs would be out, general stoppage; the Government would be clapping us into gaol right and left and then the wardens and police would strike. They're with us at heart. Hogbin has a little book on it, Ye Who Keep the Peace. Betty's read it, haven't you, Betty?' Remote but presumably satisfactory sound from Betty blended with the click of keys. 'The B double-O A, Brotherhood out of Arms – that's another peace body – has a million people pledged to defend each other – passively – and prevent others joining the forces. Of course, there'd be scrapping.' His eyes brightened, became apologetic. 'The B double-O A has plans to mass its forces. The Army of Peace en route. It'll take some arresting.'

'This is all very illegal; I think you're a bit of a fool for talking like this, Manders,' I commented and, growing facetious, 'When I become a Massed Brother or an Ellamennapeekue Comrade –'

'I'd like to know what we're making here, anyway,' interjected Betty and, 'That's the spirit!' applauded Manders, mistaking feminine curiosity for political awakening. 'I know one thing,' tightening his gaily striped tie; 'when war does break the first thing I do is to hand in my resignation here. I'm not working in a munition factory.'

More in Manders than met the slightly dazzled eye. Had I taken his accusations seriously I might have recommended a change in my under-managership, but I never could translate our jammy products into gas or explosives or even poison. Still yap, at least as concerned Beldite's.

The rumours passed from the front to the inner pages, dwindled into conversations and assurances, international lawyers, chiselling formulae lucratively.

The Congo massacre burst upon a reassured world with the effect of a gunshot heard after the echo.

THE CONGO MASSACRE

The evening before the first news of the Congo massacre came through stands out in my memory in the brightest of detail. I have had reason to revive it time and again, for it was the night my guardian fates in their inscrutable foresight decreed that some months later I should still be a living man instead of a useless corpse. And much more than that.

At that time I was living by myself in a small flat in the town convenient both to the mills and my private workshop. Aunt Fertile, elderly as she was, had been travelling in the Near East and on her return had sent me a message asking me to run out to View. 'I found a very original souvenir in Cairo,' she wrote (she was still the most incorrigible of collectors); ' I want your opinion of it.'

I found her on the broad terrace, knitting. Three kittens were frolicking round her feet and tea stood on a table at her side. A warm breeze blew from the west bearing the somnolent lowing of cattle in the fields below and the mellowed clanking of a distant, old-fashioned steam train shunting. Perhaps the most settled and peaceful house on earth, View. Seen from its calm altitude all events seemed minimized and irrelevant like the tiny, far-off figures moving along the roads and labouring in the quiet fields and the dwarfed industry of the town fringe straggling along the skyline. Or was it my Aunt Fertile who made it so?

'And what do you think of this new war talk, Gregory?' she asked after she had kissed me and informed me that I was bigger and more stubborn looking than ever. Placing her knitting on her lap she extended her lean hand to remove a kitten from her skirt. 'Pretty puss. Go find the little mother. It's time we had a war to kill off all these kittens.

'Do you know, Gregory – I know you don't because you never have time to think of such things – I must be growing old fashioned. And I used to be so up to date. I've been listening to war scares these thirty years – long before Mr Baldwin discovered there was no defence against aircraft – and I still believe in them. Look at all these peacemonger people – are you a Brother or a Friend or a Comrade or anything very fraternal and determined and secretly illegal, Gregory?'

Before I could answer, 'Of course, you're not. You've too much work and money. Though I'm told peacemongering is a wonderful racket and pays better dividends than making armaments. Not that they're all on the make. There's that man, Mundaine, with the beard. He's the Irish kind of pacifist, the man who threw General Tankerley down the stairs because he considered it an insult for anyone to visit him in regimentals.' Aunt Fertile nodded approvingly at the far landscape. '"You can come naked if you wish." That's what he told him. "You can come naked if you wish and if you're indecent it's because you've allowed your body to grow old and ugly. I shan't care. But that dress you have on is as unholy as skulls and blood-paint. You're like a hangman sick-visiting with his rope. That's why you're going down those steps." Those were his very words; it was in the papers. And down went the General. A great man, this Mundaine, even if it were only publicity as some say.' She wiped appreciative tears from her eyes and, replacing her glasses, looked round as a movement sounded behind us. I found myself facing Aunt Fertile's 'Cairo souvenir'.

I might have guessed. Subtle in all else, she had a crude way of thrusting charming girls into my presence. 'Well, if I don't practically throw them at you you never see them. And it's in our family to marry before we're sixty.'

'Ah, here you are! Miss Paddy Hassall. My nephew, Gregory. Now did you ever see anything like that come out of Egypt before? There she was in Shepherd's lounge when I dropped in, as though she were waiting for me. She was secretary to someone very rich and elderly who had just died – nicely before I came. Providence always knows when to strike. Leaving poor Paddy alone in the desert.'

'With nothing to drink but cocktails,' laughed the girl.

'And in a positive sandstorm of admirers. Isn't she sweet? Don't blush, Paddy. There's red in her hair if you rub it the wrong way, though it looks blue-black in this light. She's travelled so much she scarcely knows England and she only likes big, sensible, plain men. I brought her all the way to see you. Little men are permissible if they're very sensible and quite definitely ugly.'

This Paddy Hassall, of the wide experience and exact tastes, laughed up at me with candid, dark blue eyes, and established a friendship on sight. There was no mistaking the firm grip of her small hand nor the candour of her straight gaze. Nothing artificial, nothing soppy nor sleekly inviting about this clear-cut young personality; as definite and natural and balanced as her slimly built body. There was a soft tan on her cheeks and the cleanness of the open in her eyes. I guessed her age a year too much at twenty-five.

'And that's all there is to know about me,' she laughed. She seemed to study me for a moment with deep interest. 'I'm glad you're Greg'ry,' she said. 'You see, I've known all about you ages ago from a loving aunt – first tooth to splendid manhood.'

'And I come up to expectations?' I smiled.

'Well, you're not exactly a fond auntie's darling.'

'These subtle compliments leave me tongue-tied,' I laughed. 'I suppose I ought to return them, but –'

'But you couldn't. Listen. What was it? "He's the sort of man who thrills at the sight of a cog-wheel. If he looks at you twice – be flattered." Of course, I'm not, but then I don't believe half the things Mrs Fertile says about you.'

My aunt rustled in her chair. 'Am I still here or are my old eyes deceiving me!' she murmured with mock pathos.

'Oh, I'm so sorry,' said Paddy Hassall, turning quickly. 'You know how I adore big, silent men,' and she glanced up at me wickedly.

I could remember a great deal of that conversation were it of any importance now. The blue expressiveness of this Paddy Hassall's eyes and a charming, cheeky surety of manner and word made me at home with her from the first and I did not feel it necessary to pretend to be anything but myself. Whenever she spoke to me she looked me straight in the eyes and that's a way I like. Then she would say, 'But listen –' and give her final opinion on the subject firmly and brooking no contradiction. If she had no opinion she would be silent, intent to understand, and not full of silly exclamations like so many girls. Her abounding interest in everything and a way she had of living into the talk have stamped any number of slight matters into my memory. We became Paddy and Gregory – 'Greg'ry', she called me, with the half suggestion of a lisp on the first r – because it seemed quite natural that way.

I was amused and, odd though it was to me, interested by her. She was more like a pal than a girl.

At the risk of being boring I told them something of my recent research ('Stodgy, isn't he?' said Aunt Fertile, and 'How can I tell till I know what he's really talking about?' said Paddy. 'Go on.'). We sat on into the cooling evening discussing the strange customs of distant lands, flourishing air routes, and declining seaways, touching at times on the familiar home things Aunt Fertile and I had in common, but which were strange to our little Anglo-foreign companion, and returning as dusk began to shade the east to the war rumours which still brooded over it all. I recollect that far away in the fields near the old sewage works the Home Reserve was drilling.

'They say they're out every night nowadays,' said Aunt Fertile. 'Drilling and forming threes and shouting and trying on gas-helmets like Paddy tries on hats. (She's terrible on hats!) Poor little ninepins! What possible use could they be!'

'I don't see that,' asserted Paddy. 'Everyone abroad seems to think Britain tremendously powerful, though I suppose it should not be, now we're disarmed.'

'Disarmed!' said my Aunt Fertile glancing up. 'And they're saying that.' Turning to me she changed the subject. 'Gregory, does your grandfather ever talk to you about the business, I mean the – other sides of the business?'

'You mean rubber and so on? No. I scarcely ever see him. He doesn't seem to have very much use for me.' I laughed.

'Use for you,' she repeated and, as if to herself. 'What use can we have for anyone or anything with this dirty thing out of the past leering at us all the time like an obscene old man! Use! There's no health in man as the Prayer Book says; not enough sunlight. Like Little Alfy,' she murmured.

'Little Alfy?'

'A sort of Adam. Eve wouldn't have looked at him. But you don't know *what* I'm chattering about, do you, children?

'And now, Gregory, what do you think of my Egyptian souvenir? I believe you've broken your record and looked at her at least three times in between all my wise words, so you must have formed an opinion.'

Paddy Hassall turned on me in mock anxiety and I joked away a slight embarrassment by pointing out that such a valuable curio was useless as someone was bound to steal it soon, and Paddy replied that that would be most unwise as she carried with her a curse equal to that of ten ancient mummies.

I stayed to supper and there were a number of young folk there invited for Paddy's entertainment and dancing and games under the high, heavenly ceilings. Paddy did not sheer off from me like most girls for someone bright and with more airs and graces but steered my rather clumsy steps sympathetically and made me feel I ought to go in for more of this sort of thing. For a few minutes at parting we stood under the porch watching the disappearing lights of a friend's baby-plane and admiring the night; then we walked round to where my road-car was garaged in the stables, the same in which Goble had conducted his early experiments.

'Funny old buildings,' commented Paddy. 'That great big window with the moon shining on it! They look – they look as if something wonderful happened in them long ago.'

'Probably the magic aura of my childhood,' I laughed, without knowing how close my joke was to the truth. '*Now* what is it? You're looking at me again.'

'I always look at people when I think about them,' she answered. 'I was wondering – if there were a war would you join something or other? I mean would you fight?'

'You do get down to things, don't you?' I smiled. 'Candidly, I don't think the question will arise.'

'No-o: it doesn't seem possible – here,' she answered, looking up at the peaceful darkness of the sky and its sprinkling of faint summer stars. She looked a very solemn little person standing there, wondering.

'Don't we laugh again?' I asked.

'I don't want to laugh,' she answered, very seriously.

Something had brought that funny little sentence back to my mind the following evening just as I was leaving the canteen to resume work and saw Manders approaching me carrying an evening sheet.

II

I was irritable that night. Extra work had come in when I was in no mood for extra work, and the sight of Manders and his eternal news-sheets exasperated me.

'Have you seen this?' he asked.

'One of your pet politicians in gaol?' I responded sarcastically, looking beyond him at the pale blue of the sky between the glooming storehouses and thinking how much better another evening up at View would have suited me than sticking down there in the dreary factory.

Manders paid no attention to my sneer. Doubling his paper he trust it under my nose aggressively. 'Just this,' he exclaimed, and reread it with me, staring over my arm, one of his soft, almost girlish hands fumbling with the edge of the sheet. It was featured on the main news page, a breath of fantastic romance such as many papers specialized in.

'WHITE NEGROES SACK A VILLAGE,' I read, and ran my eye down a whole pyramid of sub-headings.

'EUROPEANS DIE FIGHTING'

'HUNDREDS OF PEOPLE MURDERED'

'ASTOUNDING STORY FROM THE CONGO'

'WHAT THE PLANTERS SAW FROM THE GLIDER'

The story was slim enough in essentials though well padded by astute copywriting.

The young planters had been gliding down to Matadi in the early morning using, apparently, one of the new catapult gliders then becoming popular. They must have been skimming the jungle at quite a low altitude when they came in sight of the sleeping village of Opo. The sudden, frenzied bellowing of oxen and barking of dogs attracted their attention and in a moment they saw natives rushing out of the huts to protect their animals against what they no doubt thought was an attack by wild beasts. The planters rose sharply, perhaps alarmed, or more probably curious and seeking a wider view. And so it is from above, with everything foreshortened and indefinite, that we had this first glimpse of massacre and horror tucked away in the primeval wild.

Their description is necessarily insufficient and probably modified to suit the incredulity of their listeners. From a jungle road there issued what the planters called 'white blacks', huge men wearing helmets and carrying spears, who 'made a noise like shod horses' as they closed in on the village. Those who had left the huts started to race back again, terror-stricken, their screams sounding clearly to the circling watchers. The cattle, which must have been hidden from sight, had ceased their clamour.

The advance seems to have been rapid and the actual attack mostly concealed by heavy dust from the marching feet. Only two scraps of the killing were visible. A missionary who had accompanied the first outrush to save the cattle remained behind, standing, they agree, with one hand raised and his eyes to the sky. The 'white blacks' quickened their pace. Then his hand fell and for a brief moment it seemed he appealed to them, facing the unthought-of monsters heroically, with gesticulating arms. His tiny voice, exhorting them in the name of God, rose distantly to his helpless audience.

He fell with a dozen or more great spears driving into him, after which the horde hurried on villagewards. One remained behind prodding at the body.

And then, in a sudden subsidence of dust, two men, apparently white, were seen momentarily fighting with their rifle-butts. Shots had previously been heard.

The last thing the witnesses saw was the attacking force disappearing into the jungle in rough marching order.

Many minutes later the planters descended close to the village, but did not land as it would have been impossible to relaunch their glider. To the north lay the scattered carcases of some fifty oxen and the whole village and its environs were strewn with bodies, none of which moved. Even the hut dogs were dead. They rose again and, returning to their plantation, telephoned the Commissioner.

Such was the unbelievable yet absorbing tale the newspapers printed that June evening. It shot round the world like all such stories, a thrill for the millions, and by morning confirmation had followed. The village of Opo had been visited by Belgian officials and had been found to contain no living creature. A parrot had been killed in its cage the bars of which had been burst inwards. A week-old black baby had been speared through the mouth. When it was moved it was found that the spear had been driven a foot into the earthen floor beneath. A broad shuffle of indecipherable tracks witnessed the approach and retreat of the ravagers, but these ceased at the bank of a small river with swampland beyond. It was as if they had risen from the water and, after the deadly work, had returned there.

That night, however, we had no confirmation.

'Hell, it'll cause a whoop whatever the truth is,' said Manders. He began rummaging the paper about and prophesying the most extraordinary international complications. I had not noticed his extreme pallor nor the way his hands were shaking. Mentally, I was cursing his politics. If you had asked him why a cow looked over a wall he would have found a political explanation of it.

'It happened in the Belgian Congo,' I said irritably. 'It says so. It doesn't concern us. Why the deuce do you want to worry me with scare headlines tonight! I'm busy!'

But he had found what he wanted and silently pointed to a short paragraph in the stop-press. 'It says here that this Opo place is close to the border dividing the Belgian Congo from the native mandated territory, and that the whole of the land for miles along that border is owned by a British firm. 'Rubber – Treatments – Limited,' he read slowly, as if nervous of the result on me of this bombshell announcement. 'Isn't that associated with us in any way? With Beldite's?' He faced me with what I now realized to be an almost sickly intentness, waiting for the item to sink it.

I reread that stop-press note, read it over and over. It made no sense except a sense I hated to believe. Could it really be that this devilishness, mass murder, wild canard, whatever it might be, had to do with *me*, with my grandfather? I had little patience with those who scented sensational mystery in Beldite's most gratifying if abnormal expansion but, if this tale were true, then here was the mystery in the very heart of my personal life, grimacing at me from the gloom like that ugly old man of Aunt Fertile's imagination.

'In the EOW we hear things,' began Manders.

'Oh shut *up*!' I said rudely, but he knew that at last he had captured my attention whether I liked it or not. In his fervour he had even forgotten the set of his tie which looked as excited as he.

'Those storehouses! Full of what? Not fertilizer. Not anything we know. We've never behaved like a normal firm. Making soap! Soft soap for the sloppies! If we're hiding something here – and who but you doubts it? – why shouldn't we be hiding something else out there?'

'You've said all that a hundred times,' I snapped. 'What are we hiding? Invisible Zulus?'

'You can't tell,' he answered grotesquely. 'We're living in a time when the most red-tapish military men are ready to believe in impossibilities. That fellow, Churchman or something, had a hell of a job to persuade the War Office to take up tanks in the last war, but now they've got science stuck in their minds: they'd sooner follow Wells than Wellington. Perhaps it's nothing to do with war. There's more than rivalry between Rubber Treatments and Reibenberfatic, the German firm. It may be that.

'Has it ever occurred to you that we might have a private army of our own? Such things existed not long ago. Hitler and his Brown-shirts and General Shanks in the States. And there was a fascist crowd here financed by the big assurance companies. These cartelists have one idea, and that's to keep selling. They'd sell flames to the devil.'

'That's bunk. Of course, it *is* possible we're part of a cartel,' I allowed, mentally fingering this odd suggestion of his and trying to fit in my grandfather with it. 'Most probably it is just some of our niggers run amok and the rest news-sheet tripe. Anything these days for a shout.'

So we speculated. Six struck from the factory clock and Manders left me for Betty as a more appreciative audience. My mind was filled with unease. When I finished work it was too late to see Aunt Fertile and secure her views, so I ran over to Leeds for a midnight show. I was too restless to sleep. On my return to the tube I recall staring up at the flashing lights of City Square. One, a great sky-sign, on the lofty roof of the Light-Absorbent Brick Corporation building had always given me a slight glow of pride.

'BELDITE FERTILIZER FLOODS YOUR GARDENS WITH FLOWERS', it flashed, cheaply but majestically. Just one spot of truth on heaven knew what secret workings!

In the morning was the confirmation of the slaughter and details of three European slain. And by night the Empire Press evening sheet was out with the truth of the connection between Rubber Treatments and Beldite's.

The name 'Beldite' was on everyone's lips.

The massacre was due to Beldite's.

There were rumours that the Belgian Government was about to demand drastic investigation.

III

'Beldite's!' shouted the news-vans in the streets, 'Beldite's!' flared the placards on the walls.

It was the beginning of the end of the great Dax-Beldite camouflage. Where everything had been hidden everything was to be seen. The Press opened a long-nosed investigation into Rubber Treatments, and the Darnley factories were forthwith implicated as the parent body. Fertilizer production, mushroom growing, questionable soap, and reputable cloth manufacture were displayed indiscriminately and invitingly for the public mistrust. Our Manchester factors and their maturing warehouses were unearthed and linked to us together with further enigmatical firms in Leeds, Barnsley, Burnley, Liverpool, throughout the whole northern counties. There were extensive tanneries, chemical works, laboratories. All mysterious, all one perhaps ... All Dax-Beldite's? One wondered why these things had not been noticed before. One wondered whether someone had given an order that information long withheld could now be released.

A three days' furore followed the inexplicable but incriminating discovery that our northern steel factories had long been producing steel helmets of an entirely novel pattern and much too large for the average human skull, queer hoof-shaped metal boots, blades, poles, and mechanism to which no one could give a name.

My grandfather became the 'Mysterious Myriadaire', and 'the Man who Murdered Hundreds', though there was a strange lack of speculation as to how he had murdered them; the financial manipulations of Professor Dax and Rufus were unravelled (judiciously), and made lurid in a light which left all other financiers in respectable gloom. Goble, less accessible, a name let loose for public execration, underwent specialized treatment on the journalistic dissecting table (they had not even a photo), and was impressionized as a cross between Alva Edison, Dracula and the Invisible Man, and the four of them were banded in an imaginary gangster-like plot to rule the entire world. No one suggested how. For a considerable while Sir Godfrey Human pulled effective wires and kept his name unsmirched.

The less cautious socialist papers openly accused us of being a secret munition trust with the Government behind us – or us of being the hidden power behind the Government; and one all-too-progressive journal dispatched a special representative to the Congo to acquire first-hand information. He sent a couple of brilliant descriptions of the hut-lines, offices, and vegetation-beds surrounding the Compound, of grinning negroes, evil-looking white men, and high palisades enclosing strange, enigmatic noises, all journalistically embellished with red flamingos trailing across gorgeous sunsets, mysterious jungles, and oozy swamps. On mention of the Rt Hon. Rupert Vessant's name in conjunction with Beldite's the articles ceased suddenly.

All of this, of course, took time to work up. It was the home facet of an international tangle. Some, if not all, of the complex web which was Dax-Beldite's was allowed to be ferreted out, these revelations forming the pivot of our diplomacy; the onus of the Opo massacre could be thrown on an irresponsible combine. Britain promised Belgium a full investigation and ample recompense. Belgium accepted but indicated that its own nationals demanded a separate Belgian inquiry also. With British encouragement the native mandated territory rebuffed this projected infringement of its rights.

As soon as it became evident that diplomacy had secured the maximum delay the whitewash brush came out and Dax-Beldite's was metaphorically enveloped in flags as the outstanding example of spontaneous loyalty of all time. Edom Beldite, 'the power-mad myriadaire', 'the arch-fiend of armament', become Edom Beldite, 'the man who sacrificed his millions that Britain might not be disarmed when the crisis came.'

IV

Feeling against us was reflected from the first day in the knots of people which gathered outside our gates staring and gossiping and sometimes booing. There was an effort to hold factory-gate meetings to reach our employees, but these were prohibited. Manders gave me a lecture on the subject at wrathful length.

'The people must be told of the rivalry between the great financial interests. They'll welcome war. It means markets, markets, *markets*! The whole world's starving for markets and unless the people are told they'll welcome war for the work it makes. Hell! All you've ever done is to let yourself be trained as a potential pilot for the slaughter.

'Girls are worse,' he flung at Betty's curls across the office as her voice rose in my defence. 'If a fellow tries to tell them they don't listen.'

'Your voice lulls me to sleep,' shot Betty laughing, inspecting her pretty face in a diminutive mirror. 'I do hope there won't be a shortage of face creams. There's always a market for them. Poor Mandy,' she chuckled as he withdrew in offended dignity.

'Why don't you treat him better?' I rebuked. 'He's fond of you, deuced fond. And he's worried to death, you know. All this ranting's just his steam valve. He sees things differently from us.'

Betty eyed me speculatively. The calm, feminine understanding in her eyes was unmistakable.

'He'd willingly die for me – on the soap-box,' she shrugged. 'The idea doesn't tickle me frightfully.'

Far apart from the criss-cross of our bewildered reactions, unknown to us, to Manders' revolutionary friends, and to the unawakened millions, a nerve-racked cabinet was struggling within itself like a bomb trying not to burst, arguing and counter-arguing whether Dax-Beldite's and all its works should be finally repudiated and damned or whether certain long-standing agreements should be honoured and cryptic instructions, in print these many years, be issued.

Said Vessant, 'Give me the little I ask and you can throw the world at me!'

And Erasmus Pollen, mild and conciliatory, 'But you are speaking of war! That is the whole point. When our power is seen no one will dare to attack.'

The Dax-Beldite directors, facing the alternatives of possible war and certain sales, or peace and commercial suicide, were only too glad to accept the somewhat contradictory assurances of Vessant and Pollen. The larger the sales, the smaller the war. For the safety of the realm their agreements must be honoured immediately.

V

The events of those first restive days ran athwart my personal life with the oddest effect as of sudden shadows flung over sunlight; it was as though I were a piece on a chessboard trying to keep only to the white squares and constantly and maddeningly finding black ones where the white should have been. The inescapable thought of my quiet, worried old grandfather as a myriadaire, a mystery man of veiled, pernicious power had me beat. It was ludicrous – and unavoidable. I wrote him two long, almost bullying letters, receiving no answer. Probably they were not forwarded.

That first day I dashed out to View convinced that Aunt Fertile would dispose of Manders' disagreeable theories, but found she had left hurriedly for London some hours before. It seemed to confirm the worst. If her father were in trouble she would be there. With new respect for Manders' sources of information, and feeling a little like one of Kipling's 'muddied oafs and flannelled fools', brought up to date in air gear, I accompanied him to an open-air political meeting, letting him talk his full.

But I was known. 'That's Beldite,' I heard them whisper. Wot's 'e doing 'ere? Spying?' They were mostly rough men, some from our own mills. They knew Manders, but he seemed nervous in their presence and inclined to fiddle with his tie. Why couldn't he leave it off and look less genteel if it made him uncomfortable! My sympathies were more with these workers: they were real, rather too bitterly real. His romantic proletarianism irritated me (these were not heroes but solid stuff); a mild possessiveness in his manner towards me as to one now converted and anxious to learn made me wish to kick his beliefs and revelations to limbo. As we left someone started to hiss.

I had never realized before that I am something of a bully. I bullied Mr Thoms, our manager, unmercifully. Mr Thoms was a methodical little gentleman in a nineteenth-century white waistcoat who found a tepid romance in the carrying-out of prescribed duties year upon year and a silent but torturing exasperation in any undigested innovation. He was visibly suffering tortures now. 'I am no more in their confidence than you are,' he sighed. 'These stories are most disturbing, most disturbing.' I told him bluntly I did not believe him. His mute acceptance of the role of puppet manager had lost him my respect and sympathy and I continued to pester him with news items. I was still in the first conceit of imagining that I had a personal responsibility to know everything. He continued to hedge or lie outright, and avoided me.

Close upon that mood followed its opposite. If I were still to be kept in the dark, as apparently I had been for years, then damned if it were my responsibility!

CHAPTER THREE

The Eve of New Days

PLEASURE SOUTH

ON THE FIFTH day of mounting revelation Mr Thoms called me to his office to announce the coming of change to the Darnley factories. He welcomed me in his usual brisk manner, stroked his little beard, cleared his throat with gentle decision, both sure portents of some important announcement to come, and launched himself pedantically.

'Mr Beldite. I wish you to understand that what I am about to say has nothing whatever to do with the foolish rumours we hear from time to time. In uninformed quarters there is some slight antagonism to our firm. Baseless suspicions. But owing to this I wish you to be most discreet in passing on my information.'

'That goes without saying; all of it,' I said sarcastically.

Mr Thoms glanced out of the window at the vista of mills and roof-tops which his office commanded, apparently found no inspiration there, sighed suddenly and profoundly from the very depths of his gentlemanly principles, and launched himself again.

'Hitherto, Mr Beldite, as perhaps you are aware, we have dealt only with, shall we say, primary aspects of the commodities we manufacture.' I had not been aware. 'But now it is the directors' wish that we undertake the final process also, what is technically known as the Fourteenth Process. The *Fourteenth* Process. This will necessitate an added staff of manuals who will be special experts trained – elsewhere.'

'And where are Fourteenth Process experts trained?' I asked quietly.

He stroked his little beard knowing that this item at least he could not conceal.

'In the Congo, Mr Beldite,' he answered.

'In the Congo, Mr Thoms,' I repeated, indifferently.

When I left half an hour later I was little wiser than when I went in.

'Something's moving,' I answered Manders' inquiry. 'New instructions – from somewhere. Only a few of us have to know.' I gave him the gist of what I had been told. 'Some of these new hands will be white, but most'll be black. You know what black's like, don't you? Don't spread it about.'

I sat down broodily at my table and, 'Damn niggers!' exclaimed Manders, flung out of his political depth.

'Now whatever can we need with blackmen in Darnley!' said Betty Corrall.

'You've heard the explanation,' I snapped. 'These men are merely workers and experts – in this Fourteenth Process. That's why we need them.'

The following morning further instructions were to hand. Mr Thoms had handed them to Betty before my arrival. I do not think he liked the way I looked at him the previous day. I found her with the typewritten paper in one hand and a vast news-sheet in the other, determined to gain as much excitement as possible out of both.

'More about this funny Fourteenth,' she greeted me; 'and it's thrilling, all this war talk. France has half a million air boats, at least someone guesses so, and there's a new ray discovered. Russia is "watching events". Can't you imagine it! They tarred and feathered a peacemonger in Portsmouth last night. Have a read. And here it says we've to prepare a dozen "clamping sheds", whatever they are, and it advises the coming of all sorts of queer things. A thousand drums of A stroke, five stroke, fourteen, and thousands of other drums with other references, and five thousand quad – riff – aynes. Yes, "aynes". What are quad-riff-aynes? And oh; Mr Thoms says these experts will be here tomorrow. They're coming by air direct from Africa. I do hope they'll be nice.'

But I saw neither the arrival of the first drums nor the preparation of the 'clamping sheds'. I had a message from Aunt Fertile that evening to say she was with my grandfather who was seriously ill in Brighton where he frequently stayed. She asked me to join her. That decided me. Probably this new process would illuminate part of my problem (maybe by blowing us all skyhigh); and I had decided to get some of the truth out of these Congo workers if I had to wring a few necks to do it. But now all that could wait. Ill or not, my grandfather would have to answer all I wanted. I was busy arranging my departure when the Experts arrived the next morning.

I am afraid I paid little attention to them, though I was cordial enough. They seemed a surprisingly scrubby lot, all deeply tanned, wearing topees, and still dressed in the dirty drill which had no doubt passed muster in the Congo. They looked well capable of having had something to do with the Opo massacre ... There was an extremely bright-eyed, sunken-looking young fellow who smiled at me charmingly and cursed confidentially at the pleasure of meeting a younger Beldite; and there was Hutterding – I caught his name – gaunt, tragic and silent, who appeared to be their overseer. I was informed that some other individual, Godman, seemingly in still higher authority, was following later with the 'pattern', whatever that was. My general impression was of men jerked suddenly away from long, arduous toil without even having had time to wash. But they were singularly unlike most workers. They were loudly cheerful in divers languages, and confident with a swagger all their own.

One spat in his hands on being introduced as though about to hit me. But it was merely a makeshift cleansing preparatory to a hefty shake. 'Mucky oily 'ole!' said one, alluding to Darnley.

I had no time to look at the blacks who were pouring into the yard from a fleet of lorries. Betty Corrall passed on snatches about them in between my parting instructions. (As if *my* orders mattered any more!) Hundreds, she said, all white and ebony smiles. Like a revue. She was not going to be afraid of them one tiny bit. 'You can have them all to yourself,' I smiled; '*and* the new process.'

'Mandy thinks it may be gas,' she whispered in a hushed voice.

The Experts had a rowdy meal at the canteen and then boarded the lorries for the old sewerage works. Mr Thoms was fussing around. 'Splendid fellows!' he said to me; 'splendid fellows!' looking a little white about the gills. Hutterding's gaunt frame, towering at his side, was like a threat to all things decent and respectable.

I caught the earliest aero south, and after I had settled from the rush of leaving and we were skimming across the drab, sunlit towns of southern Yorkshire the dark atmosphere of ominous and incalculable change around me gripped my mind. Perhaps my grandfather could tell me nothing; perhaps he too was a cipher like old Thoms.

And I began to realize the oddness of those Experts.

They were like the first distorted view from a world beginning to turn itself upside down.

II

When I reached the air stage at Brighton, sunlit and thronging, all this darkness passed. War clouds, angry workers, that brief vision of strange Africans in the familiar Darnley mills, all seemed parts of a heavy, unhealthy dream, the inevitable shadows of life. Perhaps deeper shadows than usual. Who cared! By three o'clock in the afternoon I was sitting in a first-floor balcony room at the Carfax Hotel watching the easygoing crowds strolling along Brighton's gaily floriated sea-front and listening to my aunt and grandfather exchanging unimportant items of news. Paddy Hassall was there and dashed out to meet me like the oldest of friends. I think she just stopped short of kissing me in her enthusiasm. I remember she was wearing a loose white suede jacket and a short motor skirt with pockets in which she thrust her hands like a boy; eyes, skirt, and blouse seemed of one blue.

'Now this is important,' she said. 'Listen, Greg'ry. I hope you're not working every minute of the time you're here because I've hundreds of things to talk about to somebody or other and I don't know anyone but you.' *This* was reality, the china on the little table, the refined service of a perfect hotel, the idly swelling ocean beneath the soft afternoon sun, pretty frocks, leisured voices. My grandfather was laughing quite like his old self of years before; I think Paddy had a lot to do with that. And though my main reason for coming was to talk to him, well, I was not altogether sorry when I was told to keep off all serious subjects for a few days. The mere sight of him soothed my apprehensions: it was impossible to associate him with the uproar in the north. This kindly faced old gentleman, propped up on his pillow, discussing everything on earth but national affairs, the great Man of Mystery, the arch-fiend of armament! I felt that Manders and his ilk, together with the news-sheets and some millions of my fellow-countrymen, were still in that dark dream of mine, that if only we three relatives – and Paddy Hassall made a good fourth – sat talking in this pleasant hotel long enough they would forget all about us and would awaken back into their normal lives like I had done.

'I'm afraid I'll have to be that somebody or other,' I teased Paddy; 'there doesn't seem anything else to do,' and perhaps because I knew at heart that all brightness was soon to pass from my world I allowed her eager little personality and the intimate, irrelevant south to capture me. I looked at Paddy and I looked at the sun and they seemed to fit. 'Orders, please,' I laughed, feeling exactly like a kid starting on his summer hols.

III

Brighton was, I suspect, knowingly planned to make one forget not only its own more sordid aspects but the rest of the world. For the wealthy it was a delightful place, a haven of luxury and seclusion. One could imagine an invading army marching to within sight of it and then suddenly drawing to a shame-faced halt. Take war to Brighton! No! And the army retreats on tiptoe, nervous that it should be suspected even of having hinted at such a crudity.

I suppose, as the Americans say, I had my rosy eyes in. My recollections centre round the splendid white-façaded hotels which had reared themselves before the wide ocean scape, and the Flying Stage arching gracefully over the one-time famous Aquarium and adjoining pier. The soft, unobtrusive music of these places persists in my mind altogether to the exclusion of the blatant speakers of the town thoroughfares.

These things, the lights, the music, the luxuriance, were the setting of Paddy and myself, and had I been of a romantic disposition or of such easily disposed morals as most of my kind, and she not so level-headed, we might have imagined ourselves in love. Everyone else did, I think. We must have tried every decent pleasure in the city and the best were only atmosphere to our jolly companionship. Only once and again did Fact creep in, questioning, pointing ... But if one did not read the news-sheets nor listen to the shrill calling of the radio-vans and kiosks along the busier traffic ways one scarcely noticed that overshadowing pressure of events. It was the time when Belgium and Britain were still reciprocating polite notes, when rumours of Continental statesmen conferring were being circulated and denied, when the mass of the people were content to incriminate Beldite's without realizing that, slow and preparatory as it was, the last great movement to disaster had commenced.

We attended dances in the Flying Stage dance-hall and on the windswept top deck, gorgeous, hilarious affairs; and the more stately balls at the Carfax as well as the crowded shilling hop-floors also saw us. Paddy said I could nearly dance after five days of it. We idled on the water, tore frantically over the water, and had our roaring thrills beneath the water; the catapult gliders flung us heavenwards daily. We visited all the better sterio houses and spent one evening immensely amused at the old, flat-screened talkie show.

I ceased to ask questions or to bother about anything, but Paddy was a running commentary of flitting inquiry, and for two days I became 'Psyche', which had nothing to do with Cupid but was short for Cyclopaedia. How the catapults worked, what *was* the basis of the ingenious experiments in localized weather control proceeding out on the downs, what was I really trying to do in my researches, why did English people never look at anything but just mooched respectably on? I had to answer them all. On the sixth day she announced that I was exhausted. She contradicted me in the middle of a sentence, no unusual event, and I found her regarding me with that calm, determined note of correction in her eyes which always made me want to spank her.

'Greg'ry. You're not trying. I think you're the most disappointing man I ever met. You know all about those big, interesting things a girl doesn't and each time I mention them now – off you go, making jokes, *amusing* me.'

'Most girls prefer that. You don't exactly glue yourself to a subject.'

'You won't let me. And I'm not most girls. And you don't know much about any sort of girl, anyway. This isn't all of me, laughing and playing. Abroad, in those *dead* hotels, the only idea anyone had was never to betray an idea, but here, everywhere, there are ideas bubbling up and being pricked and bubbling up again –'

'Sounds quite champagnified to me.'

'Don't interrupt. – people doing big things, preparing – terrible things. It fascinates. Like the work crowds in Darnley. They all mean something. I try to puzzle it out and so I have to think very deeply, politics, war, all this about Beldite's. How can I make anything out of it without your help? I shall have to get another Psyche,' she decided.

'And I'll retire between my moth-eaten covers and take to knitting.'

'No, you won't. You'll dig yourself into all kinds of enthralling things, far too deep for any *girl* to understand, and work like three devils and tell no one anything. This will be your last light hour. Some day, I suppose, you'll marry in a spare moment and organize a wife and children like you've organized everything else. You'll be a horribly *good* husband just because you've no time to be anything else. You'll enjoy a mechanically perfect marriage.'

'Brilliant!' I applauded. 'Do I now open the page headed MAR for Marriage?'

She cheeked me with her eyes. 'I never knew the big man knew such sentimental words. Race you to that lamp near the Carfax?'

'Serious ladies don't race in public. Paddy!' But she was gone and I had to show I could beat her.

She clung to my arm, breathless and laughing. 'Don't – really – want another Psyche,' she gasped. Still breathless, as if from our brief round of gaiety, we ran up to my grandfather's suite to say good night.

THE POWER BEHIND DAX-BELDITE

That night there was a change in my grandfather.

Hitherto he had been a most obedient patient but that evening he was wide awake when we returned, fretful, overtired, and determined to stay awake, his bed littered with the day's papers. They were the editions announcing Belgium's final intention of undertaking her own inquiry into the Congo massacre.

'Gregory,' he said, calling me to him; 'I must talk to you.'

It was the moment I had been waiting for, but I knew he was still unfit for serious discussion, and the sight of the newspapers, forbidden fare, had forewarned me. 'Tomorrow, Grandad,' I began and, 'Tonight,' he insisted, gripping my hand. 'To the devil with doctors, they don't understand. It's more important I should talk than live. To the devil with 'em!' I had never heard him swear, even mildly. I glanced at Aunt Fertile.

'Perhaps you'd better,' she said.

'Fancy a millionaire – twenty times a millionaire! – in bed – not allowed to talk! Bossed!

'Millionaire!' he repeated; 'I never felt or acted like a millionaire. It came too late in life when I'd no interest in wealth and grand show and suchlike. No-o . . .' I sat down on the bed and he gripped my hand tightly.

'You never imagined I'd all that money, boy, did you? I didn't want all the fuss and fame and I was afraid it might turn your head. But I was wrong, almighty wrong. If ever God gave power to a man to use he gave it to me. Unasked. Aye, unasked. I've been thinking, lying here all these days. I ought to have made a grand show, got myself knighted, owned newspapers, made other folk kow-tow to me, and all I did was to stick around the laboratories until it was too late, letting the power dribble out of my hands – dribble out of my hands.' Weak tears came to his dim eyes, then, suddenly, he smiled up at me feebly.

'Somehow, I've never been able to get it out of my silly old noddle that you were just a boy, Gregory, a young boy. Old folks are like that, they can't see young folks are better and stronger. And I'd the idea I was doing something no one else could do, certainly not a youngster like you. It's only since I've been lying here that I've really seen I wasn't doing anything. I've been clinging on, boy, defeated, without knowing it, an old sick fool with his life's work in the hands of blunderers and knaves, just an ageing, dwindling old dodderer growing less determined, less capable, every year. As if *I* could fight all those politicians and folk. And there were you, a grown man, six foot, stronger than I ever was, and I couldn't see! You seemed so wrapped up in your work and flying; and perhaps I was jealous, too. Who knows! I was wrapped up in my sport as well.'

For a few moments he rested, his eyes closed, and I glanced an inquiry at Aunt Fertile. 'Let him talk,' her lips shaped.

'I want to tell you about everything, boy,' he resumed, his eyes still closed; 'but it's all so difficult. You've got to know soon because I'll be dead and gone; though I don't see what you can do. It'll be yours – you've known that a long while, haven't you?

Financial resources you can't imagine, and political power if you care to use it, and all manner of industries. You'll have the biggest holding, my holding.' His eyes opened, staring at me dimly. 'Boy, you won't believe it, but I might have been the most powerful man on earth. I am, on paper. I could have given the world peace and happiness, that's the power I had, but I'd never the wit or ruthlessness to use it. I put almost every penny back into the combine for development, for others to make use of. Idiot, I was. Fool!' His fragile hand moved to a firmer grip, his eyes, now feverishly alight, were unwavering. 'I could have stopped this war.'

'There isn't going to be a war, Grandad,' I said, speaking for the first time.

'There'll be war, boy. The countries are frightened. They'll attack when they see our power. I could have worked it differently, but I can't *see*. I seem all blind and withered inside. Yes, one man. I'm not joking.'

II

Propped up on his pillows, his steel-grey hair seeming almost coloured against their whiteness, he stared beyond me passing, it seemed, so silent did he become, into his memories, surely the strangest memories man ever had. Paddy's hand sought mine. 'What does he mean?'

'Gregory's waiting, Father, dear,' Aunt Fertile said. 'You know, you want to tell him about all the power which will be his.' She spoke as if to a child, but her eyes were strained, waiting for him to continue. 'You must try to understand and believe,' she whispered to me.

The murmur of late traffic, the distant hum of hotel life, these and a faint wheezing in his breath were the only sounds in the room. How old and feeble he looked. Yet it *was* such tired old men as he who held nations and history in their hands. A small thing in himself, a kindly, disappointed thing, he epitomized the vast, concentrated forces of the age; like five letters open a strongroom or a tiny lever releases a bomb, just as small, just as portentous. That was what he was telling us: that he was Edom Beldite, the great myriadaire, who held the lives of millions in his hands, who had it in his power to save or to slaughter. Propped up on his pillows uselessly, an old, *dead* man whilst others prepared disaster in his name.

'Listen, Gregory.' His eyes were on mine again. 'The papers are telling the truth, a bit of the truth. All the factories they tell about are ours, a hundred or more of them. And the tanneries and great steel works. We're the biggest munition trust this side of the Atlantic, hidden all these years. They're bringing it out now to play for time while the factories get ready. That was the scheme, prepared long ago, a huge stunt to hide the facts and blame us. I had to agree. And all those poor people in the Congo – we killed them. Yes, we killed them. Dax-Beldite's. It's going to be hard for you to understand. I don't feel I can make you understand. The Guard has to be seen to be believed.'

'What do you mean by "the Guard"?' I asked, leaving a dozen other questions untouched. All this talk of millions and power! Meaningless, wild stuff it seemed. But this killing, this making of munitions, that was something I must understand. Was I to be heir to a foul massacre as well?

His voice had fallen to a whisper when he answered.

'The Death Guard. Goble called it that. It – it's a – fighting contrivance invented by him. You remember Goble, don't you? Uncle Gobey? Of course, you do. I'm old and I forget what's known and what's secret. It's alive, this Guard. No, not men, not men differently armed. Living things but very different from men. They're grown in the laboratories, grown and blended and treated . . . Seven and eight feet high they stand. You don't believe me? Of course not, my boy. I saw you glance at your aunt to see if I'm raving. I'm not; I'm just telling the simple truth. Living fighting machines, that's what they are, and the Darnley mills and all the other mills are ready to turn them out. Turn them out in millions; there's no limit. Did I say "ready"? They've begun, Gregory, they've begun. They can't hide it from me. They've brought the Experts over, haven't they, and the negroes, and the patterns? Haven't they, boy, haven't they?' He was not listening to my answer; he had forgotten he was explaining to me, his heir. His voice rose excitedly, passionately – sobered again until it was no more than a husky whisper.

'We had an agreement to supply certain quantities of the Guard when needed, and we got valuable trade privileges in exchange. The Government daren't manufacture and they daren't pay us money; the peace movements were too strong. That was the new technique: it's done all over Europe. And now there's a chance of sales, cash sales, they've met behind my back and given orders for production to start. The Government'll hold them to it. They're planning to put the Guard on the road, now at the worst of all possible times with every nation afraid and suspicious, and our own people against us. Vessant must have his glory. He's lived for this day. I always knew it, I always knew it. Damn them! Oh, if only I could really damn them for ever and ever!'

'Darling, you must not get so excited,' said Aunt Fertile, leaning over him. 'Try to control yourself, dear. You're telling Gregory. He doesn't know anything about this.'

'No, of course. I'm sorry. You see, Gregory, we planned it all for peace. England all-powerful. We had it all arranged to win public support and then reveal it to other countries so that they'd never dare make war again, never any war again. But it's war now; we can't hope any more. These military men and politicians, they altered all that. Afraid for their votes, afraid of common honesty. They didn't really want the fear of war abolished because it paid to arm in secret, it paid to pretend we were disarmed. The whole power of Dax-Beldite is in its ability to manufacture the Guard. The fools! Armaments will out; you can't hide them for ever.'

'And – it is alive?' I said stupidly in his pause, uncertain whether I were trying to humour him or was beginning to believe.

'I have some photos at View,' interjected Aunt Fertile. 'Your grandfather sent them to me a long while ago.'

'He doesn't need photos. He'll see them living.' He sighed wearily. 'I can't talk any more. Go back to the mills, Gregory, and see for yourself, see that it isn't just an old man's wanderings. Any day now you may inherit my share in Dax-Beldite and Rubber Treatments and the rest, responsibilities and secrets and inventions you know nothing about.'

'But this massacre!' I said, suddenly exasperated that he could tell me no more. 'If all this power is yours, can't I act for you, see someone –'

'They'd laugh at you, boy, they'd twist you round their little fingers. The Experts have the real power, and they'd jeer at you; they're like a race to themselves, serving the Guard, living for the

Guard. It's a different world, Gregory; you can't just walk in and order things about because you've money. The very nigs would laugh at you, poor souls, though they worship *me*.' The grip of his mind seemed to loosen again. 'I don't know what you can do; *I* don't know what you can do. You're young and strong and there's a power about you . . .

'In three, four weeks' time they'll be marching out of the mill gates, officered by soldiers who don't know a thing about them, hated by the very folks they're going to defend. I've seen it coming, but I couldn't decide what to do, I was too old, too weak.' Suddenly he snatched my hand again. 'It mustn't be too late, boy, it mustn't.'

'I'll do everything I can,' I said, bending over him. His head shook wearily and he breathed something I could not hear.

'Don't talk any more,' whispered Aunt Fertile. 'I'll tell you all I can in the morning. He'll feel as if *he*'s come out of an incubator when he sees it all, won't he?' she added aloud.

My grandfather's expression softened, becoming almost childish, and his eyes lit to a mirthful appreciation.

'What a night that was, Celia,' he chuckled feebly. 'What a night!'

III

'Would you like to go out?' asked Paddy in the corridor.

'Out? That's an idea. Yes.' She was back with me in a moment in a light wrap. 'My eyes feel staring out of my head,' she said.

'You're only the first of millions; or rather the second,' I laughed grimly.

We chose quiet streets and walked without speaking, Paddy's arm through mine and her soft little hand tucked into my coat pocket. 'I'm letting you think – deeply,' she said once. 'But I'm not,' I answered; 'I'm just staring blankly.'

We wandered about for an hour or more while I pondered on my grandfather's words. It is not my nature to be excited, but there was a tremor in my mind which could have been nothing else. Another part of me, that comfortable, jog-along streak which is in all of us, was telling me not to believe what he had told me, for it did not want to believe and so have to uproot itself and deal with it. It wanted neither responsibility nor millions.

For a while this meagre spirit was uppermost in me, childishly resenting the world events drawing darkly together, massing to explosion, and compelling my reluctant mind to submit to them. But my grandfather's helplessness was urging me on, even Paddy, I knew, was fascinated by that monstrous grouping.

Darkness and quiet streets are great sedatives. In time all this rankling was gone and I was facing up to myself coldly.

We had supper at a late restaurant, and I encouraged Paddy to talk on Egypt and the Far East. I did not want to talk. She had a bright faculty of peeping beneath the surface of countries and drawing out quaint, illuminating threads from their hidden souls. It was all very simple and artless, just the passing impressions of a mind which instinctively saw through life and was puzzling over the depths beneath. I sat watching her and listening with few words, getting it clear with myself what I intended to do and missing the obvious point that the one thing keeping me back was unwillingness to leave her. Had someone told me that I should have laughed; I had never allowed any girl to hold me back against my will and I could not recognize the new, subtle emotion working in me. I suppose mine is a chunky sort of mind with a one-way method of thinking.

I remember helping her into her wrap and how her dusky hair curled beneath my lips, darkness over hidden fire. I had never kissed her, not even her hair. I don't kiss easily. Her face was tilted up and backwards to mine, quarter profile, laughing. Making laughter. The faint tan on her cheek seemed deeper, spreading from within. I remember thinking she was the dearest little woman on earth; but already I had erected a barrier between us. My mind was hard and set.

'Conclave of Continental Cabinets,' a news-speaker was calling, muted to the late hour. '*I* have the latest story of Continental Cabinets in Conclave.' We walked on until we came to the Flying Stage and, mounting to the promenade deck where it was dim and quiet, we stood watching the billows being broken and dissipated on the steel reefs surrounding it.

'I'm going back to the mills tomorrow,' I said. 'I've thought it all out. I've got to get to the bottom of this thing before I can do anything. Dig myself in and get a hold. I sha'n't do anything else or move out of those mills until I've got the grip I want. I didn't know I'd such a damnable sense of duty.'

'You haven't,' she answered. 'Listen, Greg'ry.' She was leaning on the rail, chin on hand, her eyes looking outwards. I had never known her talk to me without looking straight into my face. There was a difference in her voice, a toneless, halting quality. 'You don't know yourself one bit, Greg'ry. This is everything you've been waiting for, something big, something – adventurous. You'll know when you get back. This is your *real* work, getting that grip. The other wasn't important any more than running about with me – or any other pretty girl – is important.'

That seemed an odd thing to say. I placed my hands on her shoulders and bent to look into her face. Her eyes were glistening. She turned further away, and I could feel her body quivering under my touch.

'Look at me, Paddy,' I said.

'No. I know I'm crying. I'm just upset – about your grandfather.' She wriggled out of my hold and glanced at me. Her lips were stubbornly compressed, her eyes almost sullen. I had never seen her look that way before. 'Now you've decided, let's go home. Thank goodness, it's one o'clock and dark. I feel *ugly*, all screwed up like a monkey. All these horrible ideas . . . They're fascinating you now, not me.

'I'm bothering you,' she said, taking my arm. 'You haven't time to worry about me. Have I helped – just a little?'

'It's funny but I think you've helped me a lot. Just by being there.'

She whispered something, it sounded like, 'I'll always be there,' but my thoughts had gone back to the mills, and I did not quite catch it. 'What was that?' I asked.

'Hush, never mind me,' she answered.

LAST BROADCAST

In the morning my grandfather was feverish, and the nurse admonished us severely and unjustly. I had two disjointed and unsatisfactory talks with Aunt Fertile. She was constantly breaking off to visit the sick-chamber, and I fear I held up her efforts at explanation with technical questions she could not answer. That Goble was making living things and that these were responsible for the massacre at Opo became distantly true to me because I could not doubt her reiterated assurances. I no more visualized what it meant than I should have visualized a statement that we had all died the previous night and were now somewhere else in time and space. I was left with a sense that there was some comparatively commonplace explanation, and twisted Aunt Fertile's artless, matter-of-fact comments into an additional cause of doubt. She was not sufficiently scientific in mind to see its impossibility; clever as she was, she had still the woman's quality of passive acceptance. Goble was making some kind of living thing, cross-breeding, perhaps, or grafting and vivisection. I recollected H. G. Wells' Dr Moreau . . .

I postponed my return to the last minute hoping for another talk with my grandfather. War fever was in the air, the papers had been splashing wildly; people were discussing the imminent prospect of teaching little Belgium a lesson for doubting our good intentions. If larger nations were behind her, then they could have a lesson too. 'Why should not Beldite's make munitions?' asked one sheet. About noon a spattering of flags appeared, poking loosely and uninspiringly from upper windows. The motley variety of these slackly dangling symbols indicated an ingenuous anticipation of a similar grouping to 1914–1918 (Belgium excepted). There must have been a hurried withdrawal later. A breeze sprang up and the flags waved. More flags came out. There was cheering from somewhere. The boundless political ignorance of a holiday resort was epidemic.

Paddy had little to say; she kept watching me in an oddly calculating fashion. There was no sparkle in her. 'I wish you weren't going,' she said once. 'I don't feel this power he talks about means anything. Once, perhaps; but think of all the huge organization, the authority which must have grown up round this – this Guard. You can't fight that.'

'I'm not fighting anything, I'm going to school,' I laughed; 'going to learn my own business.'

My grandfather was too weak to be troubled, and I decided to take the last aero north that night, but at eight o'clock we learned that the air service was temporarily curtailed and there was no late 'plane. There was a rumour that all heavy aircraft were being withdrawn for conversion into bombers.

So I 'phoned the railway. A train in fifteen minutes had a good connection in town. There was just time. My grandfather was white and silent, giving me the feeblest of handshakes; Aunt Fertile distressingly worried. Rushed, unsatisfactory partings both of them. Paddy went with me to the station, and we had to race for the train, which we missed by seconds.

We did not return to the hotel. Instead, we wandered out into the brilliant streets to find ourselves shortly in front of the Radio-scope Hall, where the music and speeches of the whole earth could be heard throughout the day and night. 'Let's go in,' said Paddy, and so it was that we heard Mundaine's great plea for the future in his world broadcast, the last non-official broadcast which was to be heard for many months.

II

Mundaine's broadcast has its definitive place in this story, not so much because it carries the narrative forward as because it halts and breaks it. To the world at large, as in my own life, it marks a period. Thirty years of unease and dark prophecy with life struggling and pleasuring regardlessly and then, peremptorily, this commanding voice calling the last hour, the zero hour. All must attend.

Mundaine was the unelected but acknowledged leader of all the heterogeneous peace movements, a unifying personality for a score of different views, a man whose eloquence and character had carried him through difficulties which thwarted others into the antagonistic atmosphere of that most carefully balanced of institutions, the 'National' Parliament, and into the columns of every newspaper professing even a shred of impartiality. Mundaine, MP, author and publicist, was allowed his broadcast where lesser lights were referred to regulations with which they could not possibly comply if they were to speak at all. He had access where others were gagged.

But not all even of his speech came beyond the studio walls that night. Already the mesh was on him. Censorship, for some years comparatively dormant, was awakening and, ever and again, at the behest of an unseen hand, his great, bearded figure would be left mouthing and gesticulating silently on the sterio plates, his words cut away from the ears for which they were intended though still conveying, in the living likeness which was left to us, something of his message. Then again, in mid-sentence perhaps, the rich voice would boom out.

'These are the days when you can press a stud and light a whole city; press another and blow it to smithereens. These are the days when you can pull a lever and an automatic factory will grind out aircraft parts like a sausage-machine sausage; a second and a third lever and the aeros will be assembled, tested . . .'

We made our way to the nearest seats in the almost packed amphitheatre.

'. . . and will propel themselves alone into the sky, guided by some distant man who has never seen them.'

His huge figure and powerful head brooded over the audience as though he were there in reality, alive except for his magnified proportions. In a thousand such halls, in a million smaller stations, in countless homes, the people who feared war were listening to him, awaiting the advice of the great peace leader.

'That is what we have been doing during our days of disarmament: making the studs and the levers and the factories, pretending they were for other and peaceful uses, perfecting them ready for the time when they would be revealed.

'That time is now. Make no mistake, it is *now*. The factories are already at work.'

I have an old news-sheet giving the gist of that speech and many verbatim paragraphs. With its aid and my visual memory I am still able to picture that night very vividly.

'As far back as 1920, people were prophesying what I am telling you now; in the 1930s war returned, war upon war, until in '39 it seemed that the end of civilization was at hand. Peace returned, a dark and evil peace, and, as the years passed, those who resisted the illusion of disarmament, who saw the mockery of that peace, wondered that its feeble threads still held. But hold they did. Like gamblers who have staked their all, the nations continued to draw cards from the ever-rising pack of deathly inventions, hoping that the next would be the ace of aces. Like gamblers, they discarded their useless cards, the effete, overgrown battleships, the crawling foot armies.

'And now, at the end of these years of waiting, it is Britain which has drawn that card and . . .'

Silence fell and we had nothing to do but watch his broad hands moving in slow, almost rhythmic gesticulations, his long form swaying on huge, immovable boots as though they were a part of the platform. Minute after minute we waited and it seemed to me, watching his lips, that time and again they were shaping the same words. B, quite distinctly, the mouth wide with some following syllable; then the lips withdrawn, as though D were being pronounced, and then, perhaps, T.

'He's talking about Beldite's,' I whispered to Paddy. 'I'm sure he is.' She gripped my hand quiveringly.

It seems he had no knowledge of that interruption; he continued evenly until, suddenly, his rich Irish voice was swelling once more across the hall.

'. . . and all that our peace movements have done is to drive armaments underground. The power is in the machines and in the chemicals, and one paid dupe with those in his hands is worth a thousand heroes. Face it. Face it, you people who thought that your resolutions and your pacts and promises had won. They're not depending on us to fight their war; they'll need a few only, and that few they've got.' His upheld hand clenched expressively. 'For the rest they'll use machines, and machines to make the machines, and in the machine-shops, to be safe, they'll have blacks – yes, blacks – and scalliwags from overseas. And if ye're thinking of taking the power from them, remember it's the machines ye have to beat.'

He proceeded to outline the known resources of a fully equipped army, the feed-guns which were replacing the older varieties of machine-gun, which by means of diminutive soil-conversion plants made and rifled their own bullets and cartridge-cases and could carry a sufficiency of humanite percussion-caps to fire hundreds of thousands of these without replenishment from the rear. They could be used accurately by any novice within an hour. The greater guns, with their ever-extending range and powers of destruction; aeros from the old-fashioned bombing-planes to autostats and gyrostats and stratoplanes and the automatic 'sowing-machines', gliders dropped from above, their bomb-dropping controlled by the air-currents caused by the irregular contours of built-up areas.

'They can turn them all out like screws! Like screws!'

Gases and powders, water-poisons and vegetation-contaminators. Aerial gas-sprayers, thermite-bombs, acid-firing rifles, which would penetrate the thickest rubber suiting in preparation for the vesicant projectors which would follow. He listed them for us, calmly, ticking them off on his fingers. Perhaps the nations would at first hesitate to use the more devastating of these weapons, 'the indiscriminating killing agents'.

'But, after a while, when we've heard the bombs exploding and after a few of our friends have been blown to pieces, we may not be so particular. And when our stomachs begin to get thin there'll be plenty ready to use the foulest of contrivances and more rushing into the chemical and munition works, if so be they're needed. It isn't everyone who can sit fast on his principles when the very floor is blown away beneath him. If we wait for that time we peacemongers'll be a gnat's buzz in a barrage.

'We've got to decide what we're going to do *now*.'

III

He came to a decisive pause as though finally separating one aspect from another. His right hand moved to a dial, his eyes narrowed as if staring into something.

'He's looking at the audiences,' whispered Paddy. 'Going from hall to hall. I can't get used to that, it's so wonderful. London, Manchester, Brighton . . . He may be looking at *us, now*.'

'I don't think ye'll stop it.' His voice was low and soft-toned, and scarcely louder as he repeated those words. 'I don't think ye'll stop it. When the avalanche has begun it isn't much use trying to stop it. And this avalanche, this war, has already started. Make no mistake: it comes as surely as the Day of Judgment. It *is* the Day of Judgment on most earthly things. Way back in the twenties and thirties it might have been prevented. But the hates have grown, and the poverty of the world has grown, and the suspicions and the fears, fears of the powers which were falling into men's hands, powers all too great and terrible for blind, jealous little men to wield. All these years the world has been in labour; all these years the devils of death and mutilation have been preparing for the day of birth, the birth of war such as god and man have never seen. Refuse to fight if ye must. But they don't want ye to fight. Start your insurrections, your strikes and your boycotts. I'm with ye. But let's know what we're fighting. Let's understand from the beginning that we needn't smash anything, that we can't smash anything. Ye've got to face it, people, and it's not just a government and a system, not an army with hearts and feelings like your own and a handful of scared autocrats ye've got to face. It's the machines and the chaos they're bringing. Ye've got to keep going while the power breaks itself to pieces and breaks everything ye love and cherish in the process.

'A month or two and we'll be living the life of rats, in and out of holes. Ye won't train in neat little camps with weekend leave and then be cheered off to the front by enthusiastic thousands. Ye'll be requisitioned to clear the dead from your own home streets or do it just because ye can't stand the smell.

'War? It won't be a war. It'll last a little while and, during that while, it won't matter much, except to your individual consciences, whether ye fight or not, nor who ye fight, the enemy or each other. From the beginnings of this war there's something more terrible coming, something which will fight all sides, all people, without meaning. Pestilence, perhaps spread by mad patriots, some new indiscriminate death-dealer. Let loose. And then chaos, chaos in which there is no Britain to fight for, and no Germany, and no France, in which there's no one to recruit ye and perhaps nothing except your starving fellow-men, ruin, disease, to fight against. It will come swiftly, collapse, disintegration, a strewing of death, a disruption of all communication, all organization, everything which gives sense to our present standpoints. The imprisoned war-resister if, indeed, they trouble to imprison us, will find himself free because the warders are dead or the prison walls blown to the ground. The patriot in his colours will find himself a prisoner in a starving camp surrounded by armed civilians who fear and hate him as a trained and powerful man wanting food. Yes, wanting food. Starvation will be one of the enemies we shall all meet. There will be no war after that, for war means organized life. I tell ye that the world around us will shatter, and all our prides and progress and ideals will decay until men will kill women in the streets for the food they have on them, when fathers will murder their children to have less mouths to feed or to forestall a slower and worse death.

'If war comes –' His voice suddenly roared out, a rebuke to the earth man had made; 'and it comes as surely as death out of the blunderings and madness of our days – then there is only one hope, one hope for the future.'

His voice modulated again, his hands fell to his sides. His body leaned forward until it seemed that he was going to fall. Someone tittered inanely.

'All ye have to understand clearly is that these are the last days of our civilization, that men are declaring war not on their fellow men but on themselves, and that what ye have to do is to band yourselves together to keep some little order in the chaos which will be here before the year ends. Turn yourselves into salvagers, planning to save whatever can be saved from the wreckage. It may be only hopes, ideals. They'll need saving. Say to yourselves from now on, "Tomorrow everything will be changed." There'll be no trains, no road-cars, no proper food, only ruins and shell-fire and gas-clouds and thousands dying. Prepare in your little districts to deal with *that*.

'Preserve one spot of order in chaos.

'Do not add to the chaos.

'Keep cool, keep together.

'Remember that *you* are to be the makers of the new world, if a new world is to be made.

'The world will be full of beasts, human beasts. Kill them. Such words as pacifism, pity, revolution, loyalty, these will mean nothing except for the few who are with ye. They are dead now. Peace is nothing but the smile on the face of a skull. Dead. And soon the skull itself, the skull of militarism itself, will be dust.

'Bah!' he exclaimed. 'I'm talking as if I'm still trying to win votes, orating, gesticulating with plain words! Get this. If we can say, Here is the first spark of the new order, lighted even before the destruction has begun, then perhaps we can drag the remnants together. It will be the proof that we peacemongers *haven't* failed.

We've told the truth, and when folks *see* the truth we've told – in the sky and in the streets and in their own terror-stricken hearts . . .' His hand swung outwards.

'And that's all. It's little enough. I want ye to understand that that's *all* that can be said, all the hope there is. Don't waste time spitting into a volcano. Wait till it's blown itself out. There aren't any heroics for this occasion, no grand defiance: just a resolve to keep the spark alight. To tell ye anything else would be lies, damnable lies.'

'We shall have to go,' I whispered. Paddy's hand gripped mine, for Mundaine was speaking again.

'And the greatest of these lies is that Dax-Beldite . . .'

The end of his sentence never came through to the outer air. Other voices cut into it, then misty figures, out of focus and blotchy, appeared behind him. He turned, expostulating, his voice, echoing strangely, called something fiercely but unintelligibly. With the effect of a light turned off silently, his voice was gone and the image of his gesticulating figure faded as if into the blurred faces behind. We were not to hear any more.

A quiet, cultured voice filled the auditorium, announcing that broadcast would be resumed in ten minutes. 'A commentary upon sterio film stars in their own luxurious homes.' Refreshments were on sale. Listeners were invited to patronize the amusement wings. We rose to forestall the crowd.

At the exit there was a crush of excited men. 'He should lead, he should damn well lead, not tell us we've damn well failed!' one was shouting.

'In a month you'll find him on the recruiting platform bellowing for cannon-fodder. If the workers rise –'

Once more we had to hurry for the train. We neither of us spoke until I was in the carriage. 'As soon as I get the hang of things I'll drop over for a day,' I said.

'I may come to see *you*,' she answered. The whistle blew and she held up her mouth to be kissed. I felt a sudden, cutting reluctance at leaving her, a reluctance I had never felt over any other soul.

That restrained little kiss, her lonely figure standing out from the crowd on the glaring platform, mingled with the grim echoes of Mundaine's speech far up into the Midlands, where the smooth flow of the train lulled me to sleep.

BOOK II

CHAPTER FOUR

Experts of the Fourteenth Process

———————

THE WASHING OF THE PUGS

DARNLEY, COLD, DRAB and depressing, returned to me with a shock of shameful discovery in the unsympathetic light of early morning as I ran into it on the train from Leeds. I felt I had never really seen it before. It spread itself out, the mill-crowded valley, the stodgy, residential hills with their weakling trees, nakedly, presumptuously, like a muscular, ugly little man proud to show himself.

From early sunlight and a flash-by of high, whitened quarries, green-topped with scanty grass, we drove into the shadow of massive flat-blocks. Grey, lumpish buildings, infirmaries, schools, churches, circled out of the crushed confusion of masonry, the central Beldite works hurried to us, dominated us, passed ... A sharp turn in the lines, the whole hill-gripped town swaying to new and dirtier aspects, an endless multiplication of one nasty street, Beldite's commanding again in the distance, sudden resounding dimness and the station. It came to my mind as darkly fitting that such squalid, low-browed towns should be the hidden centres of rearmament, half-cured blemishes still festering dirtily. Elsewhere flags could fly, the gay pretensions of war flourish, but here was the truth, the works of it, the cogs and the grease.

And the grit in the wheels ...

In my absence the walls had been plastered with vivid posters calling for munition workers, their appeal to loyalty mingling cynically with the offer of abnormally high wages. On pavements and walls nearby, crudely chalked inscriptions bade the passer-by not to be misled by these alluring invitations. 'Don't help to murder your own sons!' 'Filling shells is filling graves!' Some of Manders' friends had been busy. There was a lowering atmosphere, a gloom of bitter unwillingness in the colourless streets and the early workers I passed.

As I left the rail-station three lorries moved slowly out of the Goods Depot, lorries laden with huge drums of a kind I had never seen, each conspicuously labelled 'Beldite's'. They went ahead of me in the same direction and, before I had gone far, a second fleet rumbled by.

A silent group of workmen lounging at a corner turned to stare after them. One of them spoke.

'Blasted things!' he growled, speaking overloud as if for my ears. Probably he knew me by sight. 'Blasted murdering bombs and stink gas in Darnley! Yah. Beldite's!' he snarled, and began shouting after me. 'We doon't wanter kill no damn Belgiums an' they doon't wanter kill us.' Others joined in. A girl, hearing shouts, came to a cottage doorway. 'Rotten *scab*!' she said.

That was it. I was to be a blackleg besides a cursed munition worker, a man apparently selling his soul for money while others, needing the money, refused. Well, I had chosen it. Hurrying on to the factory gates I came face to face with Manders staring through the wicket grid at the early traffic. He was the last person I had expected to see there. His place was up in the office and then not till two hours later.

'Yes, it's me. Why not?' he answered my exclamation. The kind of remark usually accompanied by a smile, but there was not a vestige of a smile about him. 'A chap can't starve,' he mumbled, suspicious that I might be thinking him a renegade from his principles. His acute consciousness of his position was pitiful, though no doubt his ideals were still strong within him. I gave him a sympathetic word of understanding and passed through the door he had unlocked for me.

'I suppose you know about it?' He was staring at me queerly and, forthwith, my thoughts passed from his humiliation to what lay ahead. Disconnected sentences from my grandfather's words came back to me. 'They've given orders for the factories to start production.' 'Living things . . . different from men.'

'I don't know *what* I know,' I answered briefly.

Through the gatehouse window I could see great piles of drums, red drums in the early sunlight, receding far across the yard to the high, blank wall of the offices. Two black men, woolly headed, hastening, passed across my view. I became conscious of unusual silence in the factory: the machines were no longer running. But in that comparative silence there was a new hum of rushed activity, voices, hurried movement. A strange, pungent odour permeated the place. Not bombs and gas at all. Living things? A fighting contrivance?

'You'll find things changed,' said Manders, still staring at me. He turned aside to shut and lock the outer door carefully.

II

'We're like this. Mostly,' said Manders, and drew my attention to his appearance. He was wearing a crumpled, dirty collar, his clothes were greased and torn, and he was grimy and unshaven and dog-tired. He straightened his scarf with a filthy hand, almost blushing at his un-Manders-like state of neglect. There was a shortage of overalls, he explained.

'The wash-ups are always full of pugs getting scrubbed,' he amplified; 'and who wants to wash there afterwards, the rotten, mucking swine! We're not supposed to go into the office lavs.'

'Pugs?'

'We call 'em that. They're like pugs. Hutterding, the Boss, calls 'em "Piglets", but it's too damn endearing. Pugs! Blast their slimy skins!'

'You'd better go up to see Thoms,' he continued, without explanation of this outburst. 'You'll find things *changed*. We're all on the way to being blasted Experts now.' He yawned suddenly and prodigiously. 'Thoms won't be here yet,' he recollected. 'I'll show you round. You'd better get ready for shocks.

'God, I'm sick,' he muttered; 'I'm deadbeat this morning, and the whole thing's on my brain.' He did not heed my questions. He was so tired I doubt that he heard them. 'I guess the work's got me down; we're short-handed, It wasn't many who could be relied on or were willing to work in here. I'm still one of the Movement, of course, but I hold rather a different view. I'm here from choice. I'm willing.' He stared vacantly ahead as we left the gatehouse, visibly not one of anything, just a lonely, doubtful soul playing up to something, trying to adapt his ideals to new urgencies.

'You look devilish willing,' I scoffed.

'We have to do what we can. That's why I'm on the gate. Nothing much to do in the offices. Look at it all!' He indicated the piled drums through an avenue of which we were passing, and gave me some explanation I could not follow about their contents and its uses. 'But it isn't all work. We play cards and sing sometimes and tell rotten stories most others. And we make the pugs race, little blasted fools that they are.'

There had been some confusion in my mind about the pugs being another word for the negroes. This became patently wrong. I jumped to the only other conclusion, feeling that my grandfather should have prepared me better.

'They're the things we're making here?'

'Not exactly here. They come during the night from the Growing Pans, packed almost to pulp, and with plugs in their mouths to prevent them squealing. Quadrifanes and ketchup and chemicals by day and pugs all night. That's the round. Come and see 'em,' and he drew me towards what had once been the factory washing-rooms, a series of sheds near the outer wall.

They were still the familiar 'wash-ups' in appearance. The rows of basins and showers were there as before, a credit to the care Beldite's gave to its employees' comfort, and for the first look it appeared that they were being used for their normal purpose, except that black men were washing themselves instead of white. There was a haze of steam through which it was difficult to see but, as it cleared in the draught, I perceived the truth of what was happening. It was a blend of joke and nightmare.

A half-nude negro, grinning cheerfully at us, passed with some-thing fat and of a pale yellowish colour squirming in his heavily muscled arms and, incontinently, I discerned that nearly all of them had such burdens. How can I describe them? To those who have never seen a pug in its raw state and, I hope, never will, it is impossible to convey the peculiarly comical abomination of them. The words sound contradictory. They are not. It was instinctive to laugh at the lumpish, shapeless bodies, fat in great rolls and bulges and, or so it seemed to me at the time, faceless if not headless, being washed by those great grinning negroes. That was what they were doing, washing them in masses of white lather, whilst others stood by to whisk them away and still others to replace them with further wriggling bodies. It was an amazingly quick process, executed in nigh scalding water which left them rose-red for a few seconds, the vivid colour then fading rapidly to a drab yellow. The negroes, I noticed, wore some kind of long gauntlets. One would hand a squirming pug to another who, dipping it in the steaming water, would rub it ferociously for some twenty seconds with the bubbling lather, then jerk it backwards over his shoulder into a waiting padded trough with a soft thud and a gasping expulsion of air, and a third would yank it out and bear it away.

'Our splendid supply of hot water wasn't altogether for us,' said Manders, over my shoulder. 'It's funny, isn't it, the first time? But it grows nauseating. Look at this one.'

A negro held it up for me, smiling all over his glistening ebony face as though it were his only child and he were paternally anxious for my admiration, and as I examined it my amusement changed to sudden disgust.

Up to that moment I know that deep in me I had refused, wilfully and blindly refused, to believe what I had been told by my most trusted relatives. I would not face it; and Manders, with his 'pugs' and 'piglets', had confirmed me in that reluctance. And even on seeing them, though obviously these creatures were neither, my mind in some obscure way had momentarily accepted them as something of the sort – to enjoy the joke of the ludicrous scene as it were, and in defence of the doubts to which I was still clinging. But, gazing into the blank, uplifted, bladder-like face, I knew that it had nothing in common with the wholesome if grubby little grunters of the farmyard nor with any living creature on earth. It was not an animal at all, not a young thing, the grotesque offspring of some uncouth, unknown mammal, but a half-made thing, a separated lump of life still in the hands of the moulder.

I say 'face', for on the fleshy surface of what I rightly took to be its cranium were blotchy markings as of sketchy, embryonic eyes and, below, a bubbling slit which might have been intended for a mouth. But it was merely the part-formed suggestion of a face, noseless and earless. I only received a general impression of it, of pallid repulsiveness and masses of fatty tissue, for my mind was not thinking clearly. It was starkly and blindly fascinated.

I suppose it and its fellows were not dissimilar from Little Alfy, but my aunt's description which I had then only half-heard is of a much more primitive and less suggestive creature than these latter-day descendants. Descendants. No, specimens. There was no hered-ity in their production: each one was to itself, a thing apart. Apart, yet an exact replica of all its fellows. Careless, experimental Nature would never have produced that photographic similarity.

'They're just blubber,' said Manders and, obviously nerving him-self to show off, pushed his hand into the belly of the thing. It went in and the fat bubbled up round it like a jellyfish engaging a choice morsel.

'Makee pug brothers jolly clean,' grinned the negro, a privileged overseer it seemed. 'Much careful or squash, squash, pug brothers makee jelly.'

Manders withdrew his hand and wiped his brow.

'They're quite clean, scalded,' he said. 'It just makes the skin cold – and a bit clammy.'

We turned away – I had seen enough for the while – and passed into the sunlit yard.

'These things,' I began, muddling for words and fully formed thoughts. 'Are they grown – or *made*? I know they're not natural life, they're –' I lost the word and Manders supplied it.

'Synthetic. Synthetic life.* I know it's hard to believe, but it's there. We've got to believe it. Most of that fertilizer we turned out was synthetic life-stuff, minute seeds in jelly which preserved them indefinitely. Oviplasm it's called. You remember Metchnikoff and that Dr Willard who froze monkeys and brought them to life again? And the younger Huxleys. I suppose we ought to have been prepared for something like this. It was coming – if we'd had eyes to see.

---

* In speaking of 'synthetic life' Manders expressed what has since become the general viewpoint, but it is only partially or relatively true if at all. Goble held that life was inherent in all matter and the truth may be that he grew and moulded visible creatures from a previously existent ultra-microscopic life. On the other hand, the complex chemical and physical treatment to which the first flabby pro-ducts were subjected altogether warrants the use of the term 'artificial', if not 'synthetic'. Whatever was natural in the completed specimen was a mere basis of 'pliable flesh'. – G. B.

'They do something to the stuff, treat it with other kinds of "fertilizer" – God knows what they do! – and the life in it which has lain dormant for months or years begins to ferment and grow. I don't know the exact way of it. It starts out at the old sewerage works, in the Growing Pans, and they come to us like this, budded off from the mother-stuff, I expect. Or perhaps they grow separately. I can't say. They're untouchably greasy, and the grease clogs their pores so they scald 'em and wash 'em in some different variety of that damned fertilizer. They use gallons of it. Otherwise they wouldn't grow.'

'They grow?' I said, knowing they did.

'It's an amazingly quick process. They say that from start to finish, to turning out the finished product, is less than a month. They treat the oviplasm here, then they run it out to the Pans. There it ferments twenty-four hours and the germs or cells, or whatever they are, are forced electrically under terrific heat. They come back here just as you've seen them, and we harden 'em. That's the Fourteenth Process, stiffening them up, making them solid and usable. Feel? No, they don't *feel* anything, not even that scalding. I suppose they feel in a way when they're grown, otherwise they wouldn't be much use. Probably in a plant-like fashion. A plant doesn't feel pain but it has sensation.'

'Use?' I repeated limply. I had been forgetting that aspect. Of course, it was obvious that Beldite's would not have turned itself to such grotesque manufacture without a sufficient purpose. Perhaps I was dull-witted, but I was shocked and mentally stumbling, and I could not link up those helpless monstrosities in the wash-ups with my grandfather's 'fighting contrivance'. These must be some other branch of the same discovery.

'Food?' I asked, shuddering, with some illuminating idea of prospective blockade and starvation. Manders' sceptical stare wiped out my disbelief. 'You don't mean – those flobby things . . . For fighting?'

'I was telling you. They're hardened,' said Manders. 'I thought you understood. That's what the quadrifanes are for. Those,' he added, and pointed.

Three negroes in overalls came out of a shed. Each was carrying a dull steel bar some six feet long and three inches in diameter. At

103

one end was a queerly shaped knob and at the other two broad
spearheads set through each other at right angles, so that their
points were one. These crossed blades sloped sharply back from
the point to a breadth of six or seven inches, where they terminated,
backed by a thick, round steel plate.

I give an exact description from later inspection, but at the time
my only impression was of vast, unusual spears, more like parts of
a strange machine than weapons. The negroes moved slowly as
under heavy weights.

'Quadrifanes,' said Manders again. 'That's what they use.

'You'd better see Thoms,' he said, avoiding my eye.

III

After half an hour with Mr Thoms my first impression of something
dream-like and infernal risen to earth began to disappear. If
common-sense Mr Thoms could believe the incredible, then so
could I.

He talked to me confidentially as one thunderstruck individual
to another, untwining his previous untruths without a blush in his
relief at being able to speak openly. 'It gave me a very great shock
indeed,' he kept repeating, alluding to some years before, when he
had first learned the truth. There was a suggestion of some half-
forgotten religious doubts and both shock and scruples had visibly
been revived during the past week.

'I accepted it purely in a scientific sense,' he explained, expecting
me to understand this peculiar moral subterfuge. 'I never for a
moment credited its full significance. These creatures, the fully-
grown ones, are beyond my powers of description.' And then,
apparently more shocked than flattered at the privilege: 'I was
allowed to see the adult pattern they brought from the Congo. No
one else but I. Unless it is entirely necessary, I do not wish to see it
again.'

He was a badly shaken man, whitely drawn and worried to
sickness.

The whole factory had been turned to new purposes and nine-
tenths of the staff dismissed. Only special volunteers remained,
and these had committed themselves to temporary confinement

within rigid bounds and had been sworn to secrecy before knowing anything. The mystery of our many superfluous offices was thereat explained: they had been turned into dormitories. But all this would change shortly when the nature of our product was made public. 'And popularized,' said Mr Thoms, as though he were speaking of some new textile. 'Though that in no way concerns us,' with evident relief.

He made me a kind of speech, standing with his back to me and his nervous eyes on the sky. I imagine he had made it to others. The national danger – shortage of labour long foreseen – black workers trained in readiness. Regrettable but unavoidable. 'All volunteers are expected to take a fair share of even the most disagreeable and menial tasks.' No, this did not apply to pug-washing. That was skilled work performed only by the negroes, and all matters concerning the growing creatures were for the white Experts alone. 'The Government has ordered seven thousand "units" as a support to the regular troops in the event of war. This may be quite a passing phase of our activity.'

During the conversation I pressed him at intervals to assure me I was understanding rightly. When he reiterated that indeed the pugs grew and strengthened until they were capable of fighting, I asked how they fought. 'Do they use rifles and machine-guns? Can they control aeros?'

'Nothing so fantastic,' he answered, as though the reality were not fantastic enough. 'They have their own method.'

'Quadrifanes,' I recollected.

'Yes, quadrifanes,' he confirmed, and avoided my further curiosity on this aspect by hurrying on to the 'rough but high intelligence' of the Experts. Wanderers, adventurers, civilization's waste, criminals, perhaps, picked up as difficult conditions allowed, they were nevertheless the most suitable class for the purposes of a secret undertaking and, being the only men who understood the concluding, vital stages of our manufacture, we (he included himself humbly) had to accept their authority on many matters. Then there were the black workers who did the rough and seemingly very filthy duties of the process. Understanding was required. They were not the usual kind of negro. He hung on that so long that the most startling ideas came to me.

'You don't mean – they're like the pugs in some way?'

'No, no, no,' to my relief. 'But some of them – well, they don't seem sure.' ('Good God!' I exclaimed.) 'They're only poor, simple savages, Mr Beldite; they treat the units as – as a kind of inferior brother. Very pitiful, but I fear they have not been encouraged to see the difference. But please do not imagine there is no effort to teach them anything: they have their service every night, Glory Service they call it, in their simple way. Something adapted to their peculiar primitive needs, I am given to understand, and naturally we are not allowed to attend. Mr Hutterding takes it. He never discusses it.' Remembering Hutterding, I could believe that.

'We have to realize,' said Mr Thoms, 'that this life-making is not a new thing. It has its traditions, its customs. It is one of those scientific discoveries of which the layman rarely hears until they become of some practical use. Why, actually, it is older than you, Mr Beldite,' he smiled. There was no depth in his smile.

IV

It is unnecessary to recapitulate all the events of that day and how in close contact with others already steeped in the new order I began to accept as rational that which in the early morning had seemed impossibly bizarre. Was it really more astounding that man should learn how to make life than that he should discover how to see through solid flesh and walls or transmit invisible messages over thousands of miles? There must have been many would-be Frankensteins and Rossums.

Obviously, henceforth, all things were bound to revolve round this new and startling manufacture, and I could be prepared for the most extraordinary innovations.

As I entered the canteen for breakfast Betty Corrall rushed at me, almost crying with pleasure. She was one of the few office hands allowed in the yards.

'Why, it's Gregory!' she cried, as though I had been away months, and clutched my hands. 'I suppose you know all about it *now*? As we do. It's amazing, and horrible, and terrific, isn't it? All this making life and things to fight for us? Fancy us, all the time, and we didn't know! Making these funny little pugs or rather what they're made of, I mean! Thinking it was soap and cattle-cake!' Other familiar faces came to greet me. 'I'm the only bright spot left,' laughed Betty. 'Everyone else is caked up to the eyes.'

By evening I was accustomed to the sight of black faces, cheerful and smiling, low-browed and savage, and had added considerably to my knowledge of the pugs. I had toured the clamping sheds where the units would later be harnessed, the shoeing forge, and a second forge for branding; I had learned that our famous mushroom 'ketchup' (artificial mushrooms!) was being returned to us in immense quantities as food for the maturing pugs, and how all but one or two of the skeleton office staff still retained were not allowed in the works nor the works staff in the offices. The huge blank office wall, with its one tiny door, assumed new significance.

I had examined and tried to use a quadrifane, but could scarcely lift it. In the bomb-proof shelters below, I was told, the growing units were housed together with the adult 'pattern', and these were as taboo to all but Experts and nigs, as was the yard to the clerks. There was to be no leakage of information before the appointed time.

Through that investigatory day the Experts, our new, unofficial lords, came and went, cursing in a dozen different languages, including their own Compound jargon, shouting, laughing and bossing the show. One spoke to me. 'Hey, mugger,' he called. That was what I was: a mugger, one who mugged about for others. Well, I had told Paddy – Paddy who, only some fifteen hours distant, already seemed so far away! – that I was going to school. It was my first experience in life of being an errand-boy, and I was enjoying it; the Fourteenth Process, with its startling glamour, was beginning to grip me, these flesh-makers, and their competence with unknown miracles, fascinated.

In the early afternoon I was sworn in by Thoms and Hutterding. Hutterding made trouble because I had been allowed in the yard unsworn to secrecy. 'He's Mr Beldite's only grandson,' explained Mr Thoms. 'It makes no odds if he's Mr Beldite's only sacred grandmother,' said Hutterding. 'This isn't a peep-show, it's a death factory. He'll have to sign as a mugger. There's no privilege here.'

'*I* don't want privilege; I want to go through it all,' I said.

'You won't when you *know* all,' answered Hutterding sourly.

Absolute secrecy, never to leave the factory without permission, to send no letters, only printed 'greeting cards', to serve my country as a munition worker and auxiliary road-hand until 'my services are no longer required'. So ran the oath.

I hesitated over the last clause. Signing up for the duration of a war which might last years had not been in my plans. And there would be no visit from Paddy nor to her; not even correspondence. That incident was to be closed, indefinitely. Well, it was better so. A man starting on man's work is best without a woman, for both their sakes. This was no time for me to be falling in love or growing sentimental.

'You shouldn't have come in,' said Hutterding, gruffly sympathetic. 'Perhaps your grandad'll bail you out.'

'I'll bail myself out when the time comes,' I answered and, swallowing the clause, the dirt and the grind, scrawled my signature.

IN THE FLESH FACTORY

Within a couple of days I was as unkempt and dirty as Manders. I, who had come 'to get a grip on things', was made more conscious hourly that it was the Experts who had their grip on me. I was a pawn in the Fourteenth Process.

The Experts, as I have already suggested, were of the type one would find in an army of mercenaries, hard, untamed men, to whom civilization was a soft thing, to be despised except in so far as it offered scope for carousing. Perhaps Hutterding, the Boss, was a cut above the rest. He was a tall, grimly silent man, with a kindly look hidden in his eye and an accent betraying a somewhat obliterated education. He was both hero and villain of the Opo outrage. There was Coe Gardy, five feet four of smiling silence, whose peculiarly round eyes seemed always to be searching for something; long-legged Tim Lafferty, 'Sump' Bjorraman, the Scandinavian, and a man from Harvard, who rarely forgot it. And, of course, Haggard. And a little man with a clerical cast, the only one who publicly admitted having been in prison. Those were the pick. The remainder, there were forty in all, were less approachable, less individual. They were not interested in bridging the gap between their own strange world and the homeland.

They had been virtual though voluntary prisoners in the wide spaces of the Compound and its environs, and it was part of their agreement that they should remain practically the same in the factory for some weeks. They took an hour or two's leave, two at a time, never more, and as this was granted in rotation and was dependent on our very elastic work hours, the town saw little of them. In truth, it would not have been safe to allow many out together: public antagonism combined with the temptations of a modern town might have created a riot. They amused themselves in the too brief rest intervals gambling blasphemously and in novel ways, drinking and telling yarns and, perforce, we muggers from the regular staff had to make ourselves sociable (when they deigned that we should do so), and had to accept the restrictions to which our superiors were subject. The injustice, otherwise, would have caused trouble for they were the Process Experts, our new bosses in fact if not in name, and we were merely wet clerks and mill-hands. Haggard, sub-overseer, and next in authority to Hutterding, told me so quite frankly, without any suggestion of offence. It was just a fact.

'Thoms is only a clean face for show purposes. It's Hutterding's mug you have to watch.'

Their sense of values was a Flesh standard, faintly tinctured with Harvard survivals and other individual and discordant relics of half-forgotten pasts, and all other standards were 'sick-livered', to put the politest construction I can on their characteristic phrase. Knowing nothing of the Process, its problems, triumphs and adventures, brought up to the tepid excitements of cricket and football as against their own bloody 'Games', we homelanders were as novices at the feet of the mighty. Perhaps we disapproved; we did not say so. Yet, cosmopolitan race to themselves as they were, some long-established, unwritten code of Beldite ethics kept a check on their behaviour before strangers.

I grew to like them and to respect them even more though I was glad enough, once and again, to escape into the open streets for a brief spell and experience my separate existence again. I was too disreputable for public places and took the air in quiet back streets; nor was it advisable for a munitioner to be seen abroad with feeling running so high.

Because the Experts dressed merely to cover their nakedness and were not too particular about that, we also allowed our clothes to grow shabby and our bodies unclean. To have tried to keep smart would have been to court constant derision and to have lived a life of uncomfortable ridicule. Even Thoms modified his spruceness and abandoned his white waistcoat in deference to the spirit of toil. In any case, with the wash-ups given over to the pugs, the offices barred to us, and no convenience for laundering or keeping spare clothing in our dormitories, it would have been well-nigh impossible to keep sanitary during the hundred and one 'muggering' jobs which fell to us.

II

We worked anything from fourteen to sixteen hours a day. Hutterding, silent and ubiquitous, indicating and hastening with a thick, scarred finger, kept us to it, himself labouring harder than any. Each night there was a long break about ten, and the nigs would jabber down into the raid-shelters followed by Hutterding and one or more other Experts for their 'Glory Service', whilst we betook ourselves to the canteen there to listen to yarning about past 'cow-runnings', 'gulletings', and other of the Experts' Games, including the 'Red Try-out' in which, as I believe I have mentioned, adult units were pitted against each other in deadly combat. Our only adult, the 'pattern', who went by the name of 'Bloody Omega' (being of the Zed variety), was never on view, but we got to know him quite well through descriptions and records of his feats in the Games.

We also sang, sometimes to accordion accompaniment, at others with our own unsweetened voices brawling with the heated, smoke-thick air into the cool outer world and, no doubt, impinging on sensitive Darnleyite ears with an effect of riotous drunkenness which was never allowed to become the fact. We sang of Joey Cutts – a mythological Expert, I gathered – who lost his guts and didn't know where to find 'em, and we chanted through never-ending verses of 'Old Man Brother', a paean of rhythmic slaughter sung preferably with a pseudo-negro enunciation.

I remember a verse.

'Old Man Brother, he
Didn't have a momma, he
Didn't have a poppa, see;
Hadn't gotten no one.
All along de ribber de
Niggers are a shibberee,
Waitin' for de Brother to come . . .
Come . . .
Come – come – come.
Slish!
Slosh!
See – that – splosh!
Now dere ain't no nigger for to shibber in de sun.'

At the 'Splosh!' a cup might smash across the room or a table castanet suddenly under heavy descending hands, and once one Expert delivered his emphasis, humorously, on another Expert's nose. But fighting was never permitted. Experts were too valuable to be incapacitated even for an hour.

'Old Man Brother, he
Met a little Portugee.
Chuckled in his gullet, see;
Wriggled like a dance-girl.'

Ad infinitum.

In thought-provoking contrast to our lusty bawling was the singing which ascended from the shelters, wholehearted, melodious, harmonizing, as though Heaven had got a word into Babel. The words I could never hear, but the music was mostly of the simpler variety of hymn. We in the canteen had our response. 'Glory, gory Bally-hoo-yah,' sung to the air of the latter part of 'John Brown's Body', a sufficient commentary on what the lordly White Man thought of the dope service.

'That Glory Service make you feel damnfool,' said Haggard, 'but it's great dope for the nigs. Keeps 'em rev'rent. Don't forget they're mostly just joss-worshipping heathen an' they don't get no kick out of the more classy breeds o' religion. Though I guess there ain't that much diff'rence. It ain't many's so Lord Almighty in theirselves that they don't need a joss of some sort, an' I guess it's what yu think about him matters not the sort o' joss.'

Certainly, when the negroes returned they would be humming brightly and chattering about 'the Brothers', or the 'Pug Brothers', in the case of the little ones. It was their whole life. Apart from their overseers we were not allowed to converse with them, nor had I any wish to do, for they were a primitive, bloodthirsty-looking mob even though they did sing like angels.

I grew accustomed to them and to other things gradually and knowledge of our manufacture, of which I will speak more fully in a later section, came to me incidentally arising from the different jobs I was given. Those first two days I spent in and about the factory, mostly in a mill-yard office, totting up pugs and items of harness instead of gallons of fertilizer, with Betty Corrall enlightening me at intervals with an air of vast superiority and, at others, speculating with me ingenuously. 'I was supposed not to know *anything*, but I shouldn't have been a girl if I hadn't found out,' she confided. 'I dig things up. Just can't resist it.' It appeared she had promoted herself into being Thoms' confidential clerk by 'digging things up'. I suspect that neither loyalty nor extra pay had persuaded her to cut herself off temporarily from home and friends by becoming a munitioner: it was solely the undying wish to know.

'Eve all over again,' I laughed.

'It's an entirely different sort of knowledge,' she corrected me sternly. 'It's everybody's duty to *know* these days. For instance, I know there isn't going to be a war; we're far too sensible nowadays. All this is just a big selling boom. They won't let it go too far,' with doubtful shrewdness.

'Manders doesn't think that.'

'Oh, well, he's so solemn. He's growing more solemn. Or should it be solemner? Why can't he get the spirit of the thing and be jolly like the Experts?'

'I shouldn't encourage the Experts too much,' I advised. 'You're the only pretty girl here – the other two typists don't count and they're scared to death of them anyhow – and if two of them happened to become jealous over you, well, they're capable of slitting each other's throat.'

'That'd be thrilling,' she said, gleefully; 'so long as I didn't actually see it.'

A step sounded outside. Manders, always ridiculously suspicious when Betty and I were together, entered gloomily. His grimy, perspiration-streaked face gave him no added attraction as a lover. 'You're wanted over in the clamping sheds, Greg,' he announced, with ill-concealed relish. 'Hutterding reckons you're acclimatized by now.'

I left them and thenceforward settled down to the finger-straining intricacies of fitting belts and shoulder-straps together. It was there I re-met Haggard, that bright-eyed, sunken individual I had noticed when the Experts first arrived. Our positions were now singularly reversed.

He came to fix his glowing eyes on me, smiling sympathetically as he watched my clumsy hands struggling with the stiff hide.

'Yuv got fingers like wet dafferdils!' he said. 'See here,' and, taking the belt from me, taught me the knack of fitting on the massive front buckle.

III

I liked Haggard from our first meeting. Though younger than I, in some definable way he looked older, a young man experienced in harsh, unmannerly ways. Slight in figure, the bones of his face standing out, there was fire in his eyes and, despite his frail appearance, he was as tough as a mule. Fever had taken all the juice out of him, he said. 'Ought tuv bin sent home years ago, but there wasn't any sending home. Afraid we might split. They used us an' buried us – with no sort of ill-feeling. Just, "Now yuv come that's the way of it. Here's a bloody good bonus for the old relatives." I didn't bury easy as some.' He was the son of a trader who, before dying, had secured him a place in the then new Rubber Treatments, Limited. 'Thought he was starting me off on the grand career! All spawn!'

So his whole adolescence and manhood up to the day when, with only six hours' warning, they had been flown over to England, had been spent in and around the Compound. The Death Guard was his life, his education, his ideal. 'All spawn! All bloody spawn!'

he said of Darnley, and I suppose he was not far out. But he had access to my grandfather's library, and lying about in his mind were undigested glimpses of art and poetry and history, which made him more accessible to me than were the other Experts.

'All droppings!' he would say of the gems of the nation's genius, 'but there's a sort of itch in 'em,' and seemingly I aggravated this itch, for once we overcame first barriers he sought my company regularly, and would listen to my talk with strained attention as though seeking clues to the solution of a mystery. He had an urge to beauty, but everything had to be passed through the sieve of his narrow, intense experience. 'I don't see where it all goes,' he would mutter. 'It's like wanting something yu can't have an' ain't worth having.' And one day I showed him a photograph of Paddy Hassall.

I do not know what made me do that. It had come with the first of two short letters, and I was not in the habit of looking at it. 'I know you have little time for either reading or answering letters,' she wrote. 'But I *would* like to keep in touch.' There had been a second brief note in response to my official 'greeting card'. Nothing much in them, certainly nothing of the real Paddy.

Wiping his greasy hands Haggard held the card gingerly, staring at it for a full minute.

'Josh!' he muttered. 'I didn't know gurls like that *was*!' He brooded on the picture again. 'Yurs?' he asked.

'The photo? Yes.'

'No, the gurl.'

'Just a friend,' I answered.

'Guess yuv bin a bit of a spawny fool to leave it at that,' he commented. 'Muckin' round in a flesh fact'ry with *hur* waiting.'

'I take a different view,' I said. 'It isn't fair to a girl to let her grow fond of you at a time like this.'

'Time like what? Oh, yu mean can't settle an' just mop around an' watch the babies grow. This war. Feeling more like a "rendez-vous with death" than with the gurlfriend. P'raps yur right.' He thought deeply for a while, then smiled at me in a friendly, twisted way. 'I guess such gurls like their men sick-livered,' he said. Then, at least ten minutes later, 'But luv ain't all hoots, is it?'

It was Haggard who took me in hand to raise me from the level of a mere mugger. We conversed as we worked or over our hasty meals, and he had me moved to the Growing Pans so that we could be together. Gorey, he called me, an abbreviation of Gregory, and sometimes, Young Gorey; and Manders, who was with us a great deal, was Manny Boy. 'Talks too much that Manny Boy. He's let it loose to me that he's neck in with these Soashlist crowds, an' he's full of fat ideas about the People an' how they'll kick the guts out o' monop'ly an' governments an' take over the fac'tries. An' then they're going to turn out heaven like you sweaters have been turning out fertilizer – in bucketsful. Slop!' He despised Manders. 'Thinks he luvs that office gurl, Corrall. See it in his wet eyes. How can a man who wears a spotted tie *luv* a gurl! It's just a sort of snivelling itch.'

He believed in hitting for the sake of it, in seeing blood flow. Artistically, he believed in these, in a spartan, quite non-brutal manner. 'When yuv seen a Brother split his twin in two yu'll know what life is.' And he dispelled my not over-strong illusion that the factory was only undergoing a temporary break in its normal routine. 'Seven thousand!' he scoffed, when I quoted Mr Thoms' words. 'He forgot a bit! Vessant's orders is seven thou a week. Get that stuck in yu, Gorey. D'yu suppose they've aeroed all us Experts an' nigs an' patterns over here for a little show-out? Spawn! Yu didn't know it, but there's dozens of fac'tries like this an' thousands of us fellows. We're England now until no god knows when. Before we're though, Cow-running an' the Red Try-out'll be yur national pastimes.'

IV

Throughout those early days my mind was adjusting itself so rapidly that they will always have a slightly unreal quality to me. But, day by day, it was as gross and definite as booze or the heavy women the Experts seemed to admire, as the bricks and mortar in which it all took place.

All the while we had gorgeous sun beating into the oily mill-yards and a delightful sense of early summer in the breeze and the hot blue of the sky; and despite growing fatigue we were all extremely vigorous, hurrying, and shouting, and singing our ridiculous chanties as we hastened about our work. There is nothing dreamlike about vulgar, toiling men and hard work, even though the men are differently coloured, or from the scrap heaps of the earth, and the work is centred round the incredible. The incredible made the most mundane demands on us, it kept us going day long, and later when I rose to be an Auxiliary Expert ('One o' the Oxy-Exy Boys', as the song had it), and took my place with the growing Guard below, was there groaning and pushing and slobbering about wherever one looked. I merely knew it to be incredible.

Whenever the life became too impossible I would seek one of the higher windows and gaze out at Darnley's homely ugliness. People on their daily round, police, traffic, street-corner loungers, a procession of unemployed, these told me I was still in the same old world. On a distant, barren field-path lovers could be seen, midget lovers, imagining themselves unseen, or not caring, oblivious of the gaunt piles of the Beldite masonry and their toiling secrecy.

But the details of those weeks have oozed together; one day was the previous day and the following day, hard striving in a fog of impressions. Here and there incidents stand out like things jagged and frowning in a misty sea.

During my sojourn in the Flesh Factory I suppose I went through all the stages of the Fourteenth Process itself and in equipping the Guard for 'Marching Condition', as it was termed. I learned how to test 'ketchup' for the units to feed on, to see that it was fresh and that refrigeration had not devitalized it, and to re-can it ready for the road; I assisted for a couple of days out at the Growing Pans (night journeys each way), and watched the miracle of a scummy-looking liquid poured out of tanks into shallow vats, bubbling and frothing under chemical treatment into globular, living organisms, jostling and struggling insensately and eating each other up, for ever eating each other up, until at a certain stage of growth the winners in this digestive contest were run down a kind of sink and separated, each into its individual incubator. There they commenced to take form, thrusting out rudimentary limbs to the warmth like spineless cacti, fattening and bulging, and turning into pugs before our eyes. Less than a week it took, life, freed from all the innumerable restrictions of nature, without any great refinement of bone and tissue and organ such as exists in all but the most lowly natural organisms, bursting with uncontrolled growth-energy. Like bladders taking shape as they are filled.

I never loaded them into the lorries: the grease on their hides nauseated me. But I watched Haggard, and Coe Gardy, and others, pack them, thrusting a rubber cork into each gaping mouth, not to prevent their squealing, as Manders had said, for the Guard had no vocal organs, but to stifle the raucous breathing of the little brutes. Word of them was all over the town, but there was no object in arousing deeper curiosity than hearsay and rumbling of lorries by night engendered. Nor was I encouraged to handle them, for the pugs at that early stage were easily injured.

They continued their abnormal growth at the factory down in the raid-shelters, subjected to constant washings, squashings and pump-feeding, and complex injections, about which I was never enlightened, though I know that some were to counteract neoblastic tendencies, and others to toughen their blubbery flesh. By this means, also, certain portions of the skin were sensitized, later to become the retina and other perceptive surfaces in which can be included the outer sides of the calves which were the only parts made susceptible to pain. The nerve ganglia there had a life all its own.

At three weeks old, when they stood close upon six feet high, they were harnessed and shod. At that growth point they were still comparatively harmless, unless one got crushed in between them or had one's feet trodden on, but they were as tough as hemp and had already developed that uncanny knack of sensing a foreign presence, which was one of their chief guides in battle. Constant vigilance was necessary. Their entire skin, from which their optical and auditory organs were artificially refined, was in some rudimentary way sensitive to light and scent, and to the less clearly recognized emanations of organic matter, and I was told that it was the rule rather than the exception for them to continue fighting with a quite accurate location of their enemy after they had been blinded or even with their heads apparently mortally injured. They did not depend on a centralized brain like real animals. Units, they were called, units of a living fighting-machine, but each was a fighting-machine in itself composed of other units. Their nerve-centres were distributed throughout their bodies, the head being of purely relative importance, though, without it, they became blundering and useless.

In appearance they were like hairless, pig-coloured gorillas, but with shorter, heavier arms and thicker legs. Their hands were prehensile, a thick pad with an opposed thumb, their feet mere lumps. From tremendous shoulders and a single-muscled chest a foot and a half thick, the head, all but neckless, projected forward, the occiput sloping and negligible, the brow prodigiously but meaninglessly massive during the first fortnight, after which this surplus matter sank to form the mask, leaving the forehead broad but receding. The 'eyes', pinkish, shallow convexities, looked more like circular scalds than anything else, having neither lids nor eyeballs, and the centre of the mask sloped outwards, noseless and without nostrils, to an oval, gaplike mouth eternally gaping over a loose chin, which was as much a part of the neck as of the jaw. They shuffled, rather than walked, with hands crooked oddly in front of their chests and, until they had finished with the injections, they were lethargic and slow-moving.

Such were the units at three weeks old, huge, naked lumps, impressive in their bulk, horrible in appearance but still awaiting the final maturing of their deadly instincts and that last toning up which would make them fit for the road and battle.

They were harnessed with belt, shoulder-straps, helmet, leg-strappings, and hooves before they were fully grown. This uniform was an inch or so too big for them in each item and had temporary fastenings attached which were afterwards taken away, and thereafter their rubbery flesh grew into these trappings so that they could not possibly be dislodged. The leg-prongs, sharp spikes below the outer side of the knees, and the quadrifanes were fitted only just before they were ready to march.

Entirely boneless, the solidity of their flesh supported them as firmly. They had no blood as we understand it, but were more akin to a plant which will bruise and exude moisture but cannot be said to bleed. I was never able to convince myself that this was the fact until I actually saw them in action. They looked so human in a grotesque way. Haggard offered to show me by cutting lumps out of one of them with a knife, assuring me that the creature would feel no more than an apple would, but I refused the offer. Branding had been sufficient, for each Brother had his number like a real Tommy, stamped with hot irons on the only part, as one humorist expressed it, where a brave soldier is safe. 'If he keeps his face to the enemy it can't be blown off, and he won't wear it away because he never sits down.'

V

About noon one day during the early part of my third week news of the second Congo massacre came through on the air.

A small group of Experts was gathered round the speaker, listening eagerly, as I entered the canteen.

'Ssh!' said one, his eyes alight. 'Home news!'

'As previously announced,' the newsman was saying, 'the Belgian Government had decided to institute its own inquiry into the affairs of Rubber Treatments, Limited.' More Experts hurried in, shouting questions, and fell to attentive silence. 'This inquiry took the form of an armed force of some thousand infantry, native troops officered by white men,' proceeded the newsman, blandly, 'a sign of the seriousness with which the Government is regarding this matter,' and, as if reading from script, continued with carefully spaced sentences.

'Accompanied by a small body of mobile artillery, they entered the outlying parts of the Rubber Treatments' reserve some twenty-four hours ago. Their departure inland had been kept strictly secret, as was their presence in the reserve. No correspondents were allowed to accompany them, nor were even supposed to know of their intentions.

'But we are now able to reveal – able to reveal – able to reveal – that our special radiographer, in constant danger of arrest, has kept closely in touch with them from the start.

'Risking discovery, he has now transmitted his first message, a brief résumé of recent events.

'I am now about to broadcast the first message of our special radiographer, who is accompanying the Belgian armed inquiry into Rubber Treatments, Limited in the Native Mandated Territory in the Congo.'

A slight pause.

'He tells us that he would very much like to describe the journey up-country through the jungle and how he has avoided discovery, but that he has more immediate material to send. He will, on return, write a book on his full experiences, announcements of which will be broadcast in due course. He proceeds to say that the Inquiry Force having revealed itself, there has been a period of parleying between its commander and the company. Apparently extending over some hours. The Inquiry Force peremptorily demanded the immediate handing over of all books and papers, and the right of unopposed entry to all buildings.

'My own comment, Listeners, is that this is quite unexpected, far exceeding what the Belgian Government stated to be their intention. Radiographer's report continues:

'These demands being rejected, they advanced to within sight of the company's premises, after which further protracted negotiations followed. These negotiations also failing, five shells were then fired into the "Compound", a large central space used, it is believed, for experimental purposes.'

'Glory!' ejaculated one of the Experts.

The newsman's delivery quickened.

'The company, using radio, then responded, saying that if further shells were fired or any other force used, they would have no alternative but to retaliate. On condition that the surrounding force withdrew they offered to commence evacuating their premises immediately. The answer was a further volley of shells, one of which destroyed a bungalow. Machine-guns and mortars were trained on all exits. Infantry began to deploy and encircle the buildings. White people and natives who, up to then had been visible outside their houses and offices, retired hurriedly to what little shelter there was. A number tried to escape towards the jungle, but those who did not turn back were taken prisoner. Another round was fired into the Compound.'

One Expert glanced at another, and I saw Haggard's bright eyes positively glaring with excitement. 'The carrion!' he muttered; 'the rotten carrion!'

'There's only a handful of us left there,' said one. 'Ev'ry qualiguy worth his gulleter's over here by now. Nigs too.'

'Goble's there. He'll deal with the bleeders! What's *he* to fear?'

'Where's Dax these days?'

No one knew where Professor Dax was. There was a mention of women. Many had womenfolk out there and some even legal wives and children. Anxious faces pressed round. One swarthy countenance close to me was making an angry, spitting noise through gleaming teeth.

'If thu touch mah Loo!' he kept mouthing thickly.

'That is the whole of the very brief first message from our special radiographer, relayed by Central Broadcasting. It was received twenty minutes ago.'

'God, it's happening now!' said Coe Gardy. 'I thought –'

'It was withheld pending a further instalment, but as no more news is to hand . . .' His voice droaned on.

'Think of it! Shells bursting in the Compound. Killing us! Goble, perhaps. I wish I was there. I'd give 'em guns!'

'This means war. Our Government can't keep squatto after this. Killing Britishers!'

The radio hummed softly, as though far-away, indecipherable voices were busily gossiping the news. Then a sharp crack and the automatic 'Announcer' was chattering its stock call for attention.

'Onthespot news! Onthespot news! O.N. T.H.E. S.P.O.T. news! NEWS! Onthespot news! Onthespot news!'

The mechanical voice was cut out and the newsman resumed.

'A further message sent direct from the news-point by our special radiographer. Our "on-the-spot service" is the latest and most up-to-date news disseminator in the world. Our radiographer has just told us that the surrounding infantry is advancing in open order and that regular machine-gun fire is being directed at any unlucky person who shows himself. Two bodies are lying near one of the hutments. One is still moving, trying to crawl away. The offices of Rubber Treatments are burning at one end.

'Ah, again. He continues to say that great gates are opening in the company's palisades surrounding the Compound. The machine-guns are now directing their fire through the gates and the elevation of the mobile heavy artillery is being lowered. I'm sorry, Listeners. The gunfire is audible on the air, and it is difficult to hear the message. I wish I could put my listeners direct through to the scene of fighting, for this is the first time a battle has been wirelessed from the spot. History in the making. Our "on-the-spot service" marks a new triumph. Ah! Troops are now issuing from the Compound. No effort has been made to return the attackers' fire, and there is no reason to suppose that the company possesses firearms of any size. But our radiographer says that troops are marching out, though there is a difficulty in seeing them for smoke-bombs in great quantity are being thrown to cover their advance. Now the infantry are closing in and motor machine-guns are dashing up to advanced positions. Shell-fire has been resumed. The microphone dislikes the explosions. It buzzes like a great fly on a paper.

'I am repeating his news exactly as he transmits it. Listeners, you are in at a great moment. Not a minute elapses between an incident happening and your hearing of it.

'The smoke is clearing away and the two forces are at grips. Our radiographer regrets that he is in a somewhat difficult position for witnessing this fight. He says he is now about to use his field-glasses, and will resume transmission in a few moments.' There was a brief pause. 'He sounds as if he is saying something to himself or perhaps to his driver. Exclaiming. Yes, that was perfectly clear. He is very startled. He said – I hope my listeners will excuse me – "Good God in Heaven!" And what was that? It sounded like, "Bill, they're *not* men! They're beasts! They're animals!" Now he is shouting to his driver. "Get the mike, Bill. Tell 'em we daren't stay any longer." Now the driver's voice saying that our special radiographer instructs him to say that they cannot stay any longer. I can now hear the motor starting. Some distance away there is screaming, but no rifle-fire. Radiographer calling us again in person. Says, "Belgian troops in flight. Others in pursuit." Something . . . Sounded like, "not human". "Massacre. Leaving nothing alive."'

His next words were drowned in a sudden scream of cheering from the Experts.

'Silence,' roared Hutterding's voice.

'That – seems to be all. No doubt our radiographer is moving to a safer position. The next part of his exciting narrative will be broadcast as soon as it is . . .

'He's on again. Says, "Cannot escape. Engine running badly. Troops advancing from a new quarter down the jungle road. In-

human monsters." Someone is screaming violently in terror, probably the driver, Bill. Radiographer again. Speaking. Says, "It's all
up. Give my love to the wife and kiddies, someone." Says, "Goodbye, Central Broadcasting. Goodbye, Listeners."' There was a
breathless catch in the newsman's voice but it went on stolidly. 'I
have heard a crash as though something had struck the car. The
transmitter is still working. There is a strange medley of sounds –
a strangulated noise, half scream, half cursing. Now I can hear – a
kind of thunder as though heavy animals were charging past. And
raucous breathing. Hurr-h, it goes, hurr-h.

'The transmission – seems to have ceased.' A long pause. 'Yes,
the transmission has now ceased. That completes – our news –
from the Congo for this morning. Our "on-the-spot service" is the
latest and most up-to-date news disseminator in the world.' There
followed an odd sound like someone drawing in his breath deeply
and wearily, a rustle as of papers turned, a sigh. Then, 'The
controversy on the survival of county cricket has reached a new
phase,' the voice resumed tonelessly. Hutterding stepped forward
and switched it off with a curse.

By two o'clock the news-vans were shouting in the streets
beyond the factory walls. 'Massacre! Massacre! No survivors in the
big Congo massacre! Belgian Inquiry Force wiped out!' And by
evening great placards, 'Belgium accuses Britain. British Government denies all responsibility. Is it to be War?'

The effect on us was such that not even Hutterding could keep us
down to our routine. An angry restlessness gripped the Experts,
infecting us homelanders, spreading to the nigs. 'Now, boys,' he
would admonish, grimmer than ever. 'This gets me even more'n it
gets you. I feel sort of responsible. But I'm not slacking. It sure
makes it more necessary to turn out the stuff.'

Back to work, concentrating against smothered excitement.

'They won't settle any more this damn side of the war,' I overheard
Hutterding say to Haggard. 'Something's to be done.'

It was as though, in deference to a civilization they did not
understand but had been taught to respect, they had been trying
to forget about their normal lives, and now everything had flushed
back thirstily, unquenchably. They ceased to be cheery, boisterous

imitations of buccaneers having a land holiday and became dour and savage in their manner. Something had been released in them, an opening made for disturbing influences which had for days been fretting at them. The Congo Compound had been a world to itself, their home world, but here they were prisoners in an alien, barren land. With the steady influx of new mugger labour in response to the advertisements had come tales of bright life in the cities, and crowds of grumbling muggers, who growled unceasingly from the moment they fully realized the nature of the work they had undertaken in the dark, lured by high wages and perfervid appeals, and this had its repercussions. The Experts began to complain openly. They were not attracted by the 'bright life', it was mostly spawn, but if they couldn't have that, then they wanted something of their own life back again.

'Cooped in all this bloody smallness!' said Haggard. 'Thu can't just sweat an' sleep. Thur'r missing thur women an' thur games.'

And the thought of coming war was in them. What was the good of high wages if, before they could be spent, bombs splashed them all out of existence? Even the nigs were muttering; they, too, had revived memories. The half-curbed savagery of them began to show more clearly; they worked less willingly as with a grudge against someone unmentioned. Groups would assemble, staring up at the blue sky. It was the way they had come; in their minds it was linked with their homes, a pale imitation of their flaming sky. But the sky did not attract and disquiet them for one reason only: they, too, had heard of the bombs, of gas. They would cease their chattering as we approached, glancing round and showing the whites of their eyes like suspicious dogs. They shared the general feeling of the Experts that imminent danger overhung the Compound, that even now it might be a waste of smoking ruins.

In this vibrant atmosphere subjects came to the surface which previously had always been shielded from conversation, old grievances, bitter criticisms of those in authority above them. Vessant's name was mentioned and forthwith the whole miserable explanation of the Opo massacre was being cursed out before me and the rest.

Vessant's thoroughness in detail had laid it down that all specimens sent to the Inland Compound for training the Experts there should be marched across country instead of being sent in a half-grown state. 'Liked to see full dress rehearsals when he dropped over so that he could swell out his belly and feel big. Proud as a pink pug he was.' This had been done through months until one day a tropical storm delayed them unduly, so that the dope which was always given to them before marching wore off. The oppressive heat toned them up and the scared, half-mad cattle near Opo put the finishing touch. 'Their jolly little instincts jacked up and they broke quad' (a reference to the method by which they were fastened together), 'and had a Red Try-out all on their sweet own.'

Hutterding was the hero of the occasion, having herded them into order again besides to some extent covering their tracks. But he had to accept the blame for the tropical storm also.

'Hasn't been the same since,' said someone. 'Sort o' bittered.'

'So'd yu,' said Haggard, 'if you struck blame for a crowd o' women an' kids bin killed, even if they were nigs. He don't give one damn now. Guess the real blame's to the Right Hon. Pot-Belly Rupert, if anyone.'

'He's the Gov'ment sort of, ain't he?'

'He's a whole chunk of it. But it isn't their mush. All scratch-yu-backs, most of these politicians, but Vessant's got a liver and doesn't sick himself at seeing other folks killed. They'll follow *his* nose when he snorts, not their own.'

I noticed Hutterding with greater interest after that. His grimness, his curt, streaky kindliness, had found an explanation. Not very particular whether he lived or died; getting on with the job, drinking heavily. Fine waste, growing steadily worse. His sympathies were all with his 'boys'; he wanted them to live while they had the chance, and for a couple of days he was noticeably at loggerheads with Mr Thoms, demanded privileges, pointing to the Experts' increasing unrest. Then, suddenly, their whole mien changed and a new spate of strange jargon cascaded over their talk. Haggard solved the little riddle for me in characteristic phrase.

'Yu better get yur kidneys stiffened up for tomorrow,' he announced; 'there's going to be fun at last. The men're spitty with this spawny existence; they want a bit of ripe hell in life, if it's only a sniff an' if they don't have some soon they'll bust the gates an' play Old Man Brother in Darnley, an' the nigs'll spill over after them. Hutterding knows it so he's goin' to give 'em a Cow-running and a Try-out to follow. He wants it himself like hell he does. It means squeezing out some valuable flesh from the first contingent, but the boys'll make it up.' He was animated with mysterious expectations.

'It'll be something of an event, too. Out on the hot line the units were armed with trifanes, three blades, yu know, an' this will be the first time quadrifanes have been used. "Blooding", the nigs call it, the bloodthirsty savages. Rule or no rule, Hutterding's bringing Omega out to do a part. Hasn't had a go since the Opo mush. He's a spiller in the games, a real split-yu-through fighter. Yu'll see. Hell, what yu *will* see!'

And we set to work on our preparations for this 'blooding', careless of the Belgian demand that all Dax-Beldite works should be suppressed, that Britain should help her in demolishing the Congo Compound. Trix cartooned it in the *Empire Press*, representing Belgium as a flea shaking its puny fist at a whimsically surprised British Lion. Mooney answered with an almost identical cartoon, but into it he had introduced a great black cloud in the background, a clever network of cross-hatching, in which could be discerned the shadowy outlines of all those heraldic eagles and other creatures, which have long been the conventional representation of the powers of Europe. Its significance was patent: behind the cheeky little fist of Belgium was the threat of a whole continent.

We glanced at these things in the papers and talked about Bloody Omega and his deeds. Europe was drawing together reluctantly, nervously. Between many of the powers there was no other common interest than this newly arisen fear of a hidden power greater than any of them, greater, perhaps, than all of them, and Britain had many friends abroad. But the secret of Dax-Beldite was known in every foreign office; incredulous ministers and officials questioned and requestioned their informants and, convinced against all their manifold doubts, faced up to the prospect of an unconquerable land power. Weaker maybe in the air for the nonce, when that defect was remedied – and what but immediate war could prevent that revival? – she would dominate for good or ill the entire world, the Grand Imperial Dictatorship to which so many had fruitlessly aspired and which was now to be accomplished. Peace or war at her command, all colonies, all trade at her mercy, the endless humiliation of her inevitable interference in others' domestic affairs. Who dare listen to the plea that her strength would be used to bring peace and prosperity to the earth? Better freedom than slavery to the overlord however beneficent. That ancient military-cum-pacifist ambition, a land so powerful that none dare attack her, was being revealed in all its immense falsehood, twisted to a new, ironic corollary: a land so powerful that none dare fail to attack her before she became all-powerful. The dream of Napoleon and later of the Kaiser Wilhelm, a Europe united against Britain, was being fulfilled.

The web of pacts and understandings strained and broke and began to reshape itself. To the end there were some who played with the policy of retaining Britain's friendship; yet to be her successful ally was to become her tool, her jackal, even more than if one were her defeated rival. And what chance had she against a whole continent!

Lurid publicists deepened the immemorial red of Britain to vampire hue, discovering unbelievable ambitions to add the western shores of Europe to her colonies! Stories of dastardly slavery in the Compound, honest workmen forced into the Flesh Factories at the point of the bayonet, atrocities on pacificists, all had their vogue. Another school of writers called the British worker to revolution, to rise and crush the military cartelists above him. Bearing within it a hundred dissensions, France moved towards the grand European bloc which was forming.

I questioned Manders, my only accessible authority, on these international affairs and the probability or otherwise of insurrection at home, but he had grown very uncommunicative on such subjects. He did not know; it was impossible to say. He seemed to be suffering from some great and suppressed strain for which mere overwork could not account. He turned the conversation to Betty Corrall, a subject he had never broached with me before.

'What d'you think she feels about me?' he asked. He was lonely and I his only friend though, in a very negative sense, his rival. I could not dash his hopes, nor was it my business to anticipate

Betty's responses. 'She's the only thing I have to hope for,' he said lugubriously. The comfort of ideals had, apparently, collapsed.

He chose the night before the 'Games' to ask her to marry him. Where he asked her or when he proposed marrying her I do not know. I had a coffee with Betty in the canteen, and she told me in one uninterested sentence. 'Mandy's proposed.'

'Oh.' I looked inquiringly.

'How can I know what I feel when he's so dirty, when you're all so dirty? I can't think about such things – *here*. What's all this fuss about, this excitement?'

I had to pass that off. None of the office staff were to know about the Games.

THE BLOODING OF THE QUADRIFANE

Cow-running was the logical development by bored and lonely men of those early experiments of Goble's when the specimens and cattle took exercise together in the Compound. As soon as the former began to take active notice of their four-legged companions the sporting possibilities must have become obvious. Whilst my grandfather was in evidence it was, I gather, a comparatively humane sport with the cows or other herbivora – hartebeest and wildebeest were favourite victims – heavily padded so that they suffered little worse than shock and fear. After his departure, however, necessary experiment paving the way, protection was dispensed with, and it grew somewhat along the lines of bull-fighting though, after a number of violent deaths, matadors ceased to be allowed. Experts with the necessary courage were too rare to be thrown away. There never was a toreador; the specimens in their fighting glory offered no scope for one. Quite as dreadful to watch as bullfighting, it was in fact less cruel. There was no lingering torture of animals. They had their few moments of fear or defiance, according to their nature, and then that particular 'round' was over. More 'cows' would follow.

Cow-running was a sport in itself, but it was also used in a modified form as a preliminary to the 'Try-out', a curtain-raiser without which it was impossible to persuade the specimens to fight one another, for they were constructed so as to have no natural animosity to their brothers, and needed steady preparatory inflaming if they were to perform to the satisfaction of a critical audience.

Bloody Omega, I learned, had earned his name in the Games – he had once killed a rhinoceros – and had crowned it with his part in the Opo massacre. One Expert could be heard arguing with another as to whether through disuse new germination, that bane of the Expert, might have started in his inside. No heavyweight champion could have been discussed in greater detail. They knew his every measurement, his method of attack, his outstanding qualities. Of his prospective opponents less could be said; they were immature and doomed, a foil for his prowess. Keen betting, running to quite surprising figures, had commenced as soon as it was known that the combined Running and Try-out was to take place. They betted, apparently, on the number of seconds the star performer would take to finish each round, but there were other more complex forms of betting which I could not follow.

No one ever backed a cow.

We began to gather in the mill-yard about two o'clock. This was our first afternoon off and, though it was understood that the valuable time would have to be made up later, no one allowed this thought to spoil the holiday.

The social divisions of the factory were strongly emphasized by our grouping. The negroes had rearranged the piles of drums into tier formation, like so many tiny grandstands circling round the yard with the 'arena' in the middle. They sat together on the larger piles, serried rows of white teeth and flashing eyes. The Experts and Oxy-Exys like myself chose a point as far away from them as possible, and the muggers were left to shift for themselves. Some occupied the remaining drums and odd packing-cases, whilst others stood about uneasily. A specially high pile of drums was surmounted by chairs for Mr Thoms and the sub-managers still remaining. The expressions on the assembled faces varied from the keen interest of a boxing fan to sheer funk. My feelings were very mixed, curiosity being upmost, but Manders was much less at ease. Haggard took obvious joy in his nerviness.

Hutterding appeared and, taking up a position in the centre of the yard, held up his hand.

'This cow-running won't be quite what you're used to, men,' he shouted. 'In this old land there's no jungle where we can trap all the creatures of creation. I've had a hell of a job to get cows an' I had to pay heavy, but you boys have clubbed together well. One *is* a cow, just an ordinary, two-horned milk-giver. No. 2's a horse, an old nag. The running mayn't be long enough to stir up Omega, so you'd better be ready for the Try-out to be a flop. An' if they just lope round rubbing noses like pet poodles, don't blame me. I've done my best in this gosh-darn town.' There was an encouraging cheer at that and some friendly booing.

'An' now you people who haven't seen a cow-running before. There's just that bit of danger to the spectators that isn't in any other sport, so if you feel scared take care there's a quick getaway behind you. An' *make* it quick if there's need. Or go now if you feel that way.' He grinned. This was a new Hutterding, a Hutterding at the height of enjoyment. No one moved. It came to me with an uncomfortable shock how all of us were trying to live up to the standard set by the Experts.

'We're not over-particular what the cow is, but we don't like them two-legged. If you sit quite still neither Bloody Omega nor the other units will ever see you. They're not interested in still-life. And as soon as the show's over, there'll be a good dish of ketchup for whichever's living to stick his gullet into, and he'll gorge himself half-asleep. If by any chance our performers charge the spectators we've matadors ready to take the quad first whilst you vamose.'

His grimness had evaporated; he laughed aloud as a number of the muggers began to seek safer vantage points. When three or four started to clamber up on to the roof of the canteen a roar of laughter ran round the yard.

'That's the one creature on earth who doesn't give a hoot for the Guard,' cried Hutterding as the laughter subsided. 'The monkey.' He turned as Mr Thoms, appearing from the office block, approached. The old man's face was yellow-white. We saw Hutterding bend towards him and shake his head sympathetically. His hand swung round the yard as though indicating the eager audience. Then, taking Thoms by the arm, he led him gently towards the side. Half-way he paused.

'Remember, men, that this is a man's sport. It's a bit too like strong meat for the folk round here. So – and this is important – don't *talk* about it, not even to the office staff. They know nix. They'll see nix. They're upstairs working like lambs while we enjoy ourselves. Not a word. *You* understand, you *muggers*?' His voice rose ferociously.

Coe Gardy appeared, leading a somewhat thin, somnolent-looking cow, and grinning broadly. Hutterding went to meet him, leaving Thoms alone. A murmur of comment rose. The Experts near me fell to discussing the animal's points. 'She'll shake 'er legs okay w'en she sees wot's coming' to 'er,' said one.

Manders, who was next to me, nudged my arm.

'This is a foul, bloodthirsty business,' he whispered. 'I wish we could be out of it. Old Thoms is nearly sick.'

'It's their life,' I answered; 'I suppose we've got to think of ourselves as soft and over-civilized. There's something about these chaps you know, something I like.' Manders muttered, which was his way when he disapproved of me. His opinions were no doubt shared by a majority of the regular staff and muggers but intense curiosity was in them as in me and bored, fatigued men will stand a great deal to have their interest aroused. Pride, false pride maybe, had its part too.

Released from its rope the cow lumbered forward, a frightened animal, glaring round uncertainly at the human concourse. A titter arose as, for a moment, Thoms and the cow had the centre of the stage together. He walked to the side and was assisted up to his chair; he knew more about what was coming than any of us and the expression on his face was anything but reassuring. Old age, perhaps. His high sense of duty could have been his only reason for being present. 'They shouldn't! They shouldn't!' he was muttering to himself.

Another second and we saw that Haggard had opened the door of one of the harnessing sheds. The chatter of the crowd ceased; the turning of heads towards that opening, black in comparison with the sun-glare in the yard, was the only movement amongst us. In the open flagged space the cow was still swinging its head right and left doubtfully. The heavy murmur of afternoon town life came to us from the roads outside; motors hooted; a news-van was calling the sporting news. Someone was laughing near the main gateway, rough girls' voices. The pungent odour of ketchup was strong in the air, blending with oil and chemicals. All of us were silently expectant.

It was, perhaps, four minutes, four minutes of intense waiting, before Bloody Omega came out. I understand that in Africa affairs were arranged more efficiently, that a whole technique of managing these cow-runnings so as to extract the utmost excitement from them had been developed. But here we had to await Omega's pleasure; the light would draw him but he seemed to respond to it only slowly. His appearance as a dim, pale shadow inside the opening was the signal for a sudden running exclamation amongst the negroes. 'The brudder! The brudder!' they chattered in their various dialects. 'The brudder comes!'

The 'matadors' moved forward a pace into the arena, lithe, watch-ful figures.

II

Like a creature emerging from the nether regions, Bloody Omega shambled out into the factory yard.

I had heard more than one description of the brute from Haggard and others, but only then did I realize how inadequate these were.

Omega's head was only an inch or so from the top of the door, his shoulders seemed almost to touch the jambs as he came through. Just outside he stood, feeling the heat on his retinae, as if posing for a photograph, and it was possible to examine him in detail.

He was in his full war harness, the dull leather showing almost black against his piglike skin in which it was deeply inset as were the dulled steel helmet and hooves. They seemed part of him. His quadrifane, gripped immovably in massive hands on a level with his waist, swung ever so faintly, the chains which linked it to his wristlets clanking in a soft ghostly music. His head was sunk deeply on to his tremendous chest, his knees bent slightly with his weight. Three hundred and fifty pounds he weighed, three hundred and fifty pounds of rubber-like muscle, muscle no natural creature could acquire, muscle chemically hardened by constant injection until its slightest movement exerted the power of an average man's blow.

One could see the crinkling of the sensitive skin beneath the fleshy ridge supporting the helmet as it responded to the light and heat; his mouth gap widened exuding a pale scummy saliva, and the deep breath intake sounded like a low growl. Hurr-h, he breathed, hurr-h. The shapeless projection of the centre of the mask quivered faintly as the mixed odours of the mill-yard acted on his rudimentary olfactory nerves. Then he moved forward, following the sole instincts which dwelt in his vast body, to drive blindly at whatever moved before his sight, irritating, exciting: to seek food.

The quadrifane vibrated to his breathing, working backwards and forwards expectantly.

'The brudder!' a negro voice hissed ecstatically, the only voice in deathly silence. 'The brudder,' whispered a tiny echo from the great wall of the office block. There was no slightest movement in the intently watching crowd. Thirty yards away the cow stood with lowered head gazing at this strange monster. Its tail flicked ever so faintly.

In another moment it must have moved, probably to amble slowly away as nervous beasts do when a man approaches, turning soft, uncertain eyes upon him, retreating gradually as though hoping not to be noticed. That would have been sufficient to arouse the instinct in Omega, an instinct no doubt dulled to some extent by weeks of disuse. But in those seconds as we waited, horrified at what we were going to see but, withal, excited to the depths of our beings, the door which led from the yard to the office staircase opened and Betty Corrall came out. Her pretty face was flushed with interest, her blonde hair was flying wild.

'Whatever's happening?' she cried. 'Where's everybody?'

Her brightly excited eyes ran round the strangely still faces now all turned towards her and she stepped forward into the yard in puzzled amazement. What had led her to break the most stringent rule of the office staff none of us knew. She had discerned that something untoward was afoot and, as always in her case, she had to find out what it was. She knew so much; she had seen so little. Perhaps the temptation had suddenly grown irresistible.

As her eyes fell on Omega she became suddenly rigid. Her hands, which were raised, stayed in mid-air, the smile on her face set into a frozen grimace. Haggard's harsh voice broke the silence.

'Keep quite still, Miss Corrall,' he called. 'He's quite harmless if you *keep still. Don't move!*'

I do not think she heard him. 'Ah-h,' she said. *'Ah-h! AH-H-H!'* the first whisper rising to a scream. Her hands jerked into the air, waving frantically, her head tossed. She stepped forward as though hypnotized by what she saw.

I remember hearing a quick clank of metal on stone as Bloody Omega turned in her direction. I half saw the sudden clenching of the lax muscles, the way in which the head dropped further on to the great chest muscle. Then he had gone forward.

It was not a run, it was a shuffle, with his steel-shod feet striking sparks as he moved, but it was so swift that not a sound rose from any one of us before he had reached Betty Corrall where she stood with her hands now clasped over her eyes, emitting scream after scream. I saw the fourfold point of the quadrifane touch her breast and then the transverse blades passed through her and only the steel shaft driving deeper and deeper was visible. Thoms fell from his seat with a half uttered whimper in a dead faint. I heard Manders — like some animal squealing in a trap. Haggard was racing across the yard. There was a horrified screeching from the negroes and people were running hither and thither. Then Hutterding's voice bawling: 'Stand still, you bloody fools, stand still!'

Bloody Omega had withdrawn the quadrifane and was standing like a thing at bay, his head swinging right and left, maddened, distracted by the sudden, violent movements around him. I could not look at what lay at his feet. Then the head sank and in a fraction of time his dripping weapon was driving into Hutterding who had flung himself in front to attract attention from us others. He doubled up at the impact and was flung aside in the great onrush. His body thudded on the yard floor and he lay spread-eagled, his chest and abdomen gashed open into four as though a crucifix had been driven into him.

Haggard was leading the matadors at a run. Omega drove forward and as smartly as their namesakes they danced aside so that he went straight into the steel mesh of a net which others behind were holding. Another moment and he was wrapped in it, as helpless as an animal in a cage. His breathing was like the muffled bellowing of a bull.

I suppose I am as naturally sensitive to suffering or bloodshed as any normal man, but that first sight of violent and useless death had the odd effect of making me suddenly cold, almost callous. I stiffened as though the same death were coming upon me the next moment. Then Thoms' white, unconscious face caught my eye and, recovering reason, I bent to attend to him.

Haggard joined me as he was coming round. He was smiling, or grimacing, in a queer, lopsided way, like a man about to be executed might smile, and puffing at the fag-end of a cigarette. His face looked emaciated, his eyes sunken. But they were shining like bright steel.

'They've gas-gulleted him and lugged him back to the shelters, Gorey,' he said unnecessarily.

I stared at him, unanswering, and in that stare I know I admitted responsibility with him and the rest.

'We're murderers,' I said, foolishly.

He answered with that lopsided smile and a shake of the head. 'That door should ha' been locked. Yu don't understand the men an' yu don't understand me. If anyone'd yapped an' stopped the running Hutterding'd have drilled him. Our life hasn't bin all chaw an' sleep an' the boys were ripe for hell's trouble.' I experienced a vague impression that he wanted something from me if only my company, that he wished to defend himself and his life and have me with him.

'Great joss, Hutterding,' he muttered. 'Yu didn't known him. Yu never will now.' He was staring across the yard to where negroes were busy with something hidden. 'Chucked his life away to save you muggers, an' us. Guess he didn't care much after Opo; no guts for just anyhow bloodspilling.'

'You and your hellish games,' I began, but he cut me short. 'We're trained to be hellish. We *make* hell an' we amuse ourselves with it an' we don't pretend we do it for God or honour either. I'm sorry – about *her*. It's a bloody way to die but it's no worse than being slushed up by a bomb which she'd like as not have got in a week or two. An' she'd no job to be there.' His strained, glittering eyes fixed me. 'It's just one o' those bloody happenings, Gorey, see?' He hesitated, balancing something in himself. 'I'm Overseer here now, Gorey. D'yu get it? Don't make it tougher. I'll see yu again.'

He hurried away, visibly uncertain in his mind, to take charge of that crushed day, bitterly determined at least that neither sentiment nor weakness should hinder him. He was sorry – about *her*! Well, that was his way of expressing the inexpressible. Tardily I realized that he wanted my support, that in some subtle manner I was nearer to him than his fellow Experts and that he knew it.

There was an effort amongst the men to get back to work. It was voluntary. A few groups hung about, talking. Everyone gave the impression of watching everyone else. No one went near the office wall where nigs were busy cleaning, muttering among themselves. For a while I tried to find Manders, but he had hidden himself somewhere. No one seemed to be expressing any opinion on what had happened and no one was asking for any. Uppermost in my mind, a defence against my own feelings, was the memory of a child who had been torn to pieces beneath a road-bus. Almost commonplace, that. I had not seen it, only the crowd. At least we did not stand gaping, revelling in morbidity. Orders coming through from Haggard to resume work, in a short while it was as though life were normal again except that there was no singing and we worked mostly in silence.

I fell into conversation with Haggard again about tea-time. He had recovered much of his sang-froid. He had a grip.

'How about – outside, when they get to know?' I asked him.

'They won't know,' he snapped. 'Think I'm doped? I'm Overseer, I'm Boss, an' this biz'll be smothered. The parents'll know only; an' just what I tell 'um. An' be told like hell not to yarn it about. Oh, thur'll be a Death Certificate . . .

'Thur's going to be new rules. No one'll leave those gates till I say. Oh, I know yu privileged devils have been creeping out more'n yur share, but that's done now. Even for Thoms. He can doss in here with the rest or he'll go preachin' a sermon on it or yappin' in his bloody faints.' His eyes glanced round; they looked bloodshot at the corners. 'It's in here I'm thinking about. Those muggers – thu just sick-livered now an' emptying thu bellies. But when thu through with that . . .'

His arrogant tone modified to a friendlier and less confident note.

'An' the nigs have gone silent. Thu'v never seen a white boss killed that way. It'll itch 'em in thu religious beliefs. Bound to itch 'em. Thu *may* think – If the Brothers can do that, so can they.' I must have expressed my question very obviously on my face, for he suddenly turned on me growling: 'Part of the dope,' he snarled. 'D'yu suppose those nigs do all this hell's work an' sing with it – from fear? Thu think thu'r born to it. Many of 'em were, at the Compound. Thu'v bin coddled in thu bellies an' doped in thu minds from burth, an' Goble's the big, holy joss to 'um, an' Beldite's the littler joss. Some of 'um's not sure that before thu made the Flesh thu didn't make *them*. Why not? Who're they to know? Dax dished 'um up a worship that's part thur old fetishism an' part Christianity – case thu'd heard missions – an' most just original bunk an' 'tween it all thu don't know where thu are. Black flesh to slave for the God-whites an' pug flesh to guard 'um.

'See, young Gorey,' he impressed; 'thu've seen life made, seen how the White Man brings it out from nothing an' makes it grow into the bloodiest thing on earth. Why shouldn't thu wonder if thu were made the same way? Not all niggers, just thur sort. When a nigger went amok an' had to be sent up country somewheres he couldn't blabber – well, it just got put about that he'd been pitched back into the pulping pans as bad flesh.' He pondered this extraordinarily unjust arrangement and went on. 'Having kids makes 'um wonder, but thu take it that's just the way the Whites have ordered things an' yu can take it straight that thu'v no Mammy an' Daddy songs out thur: thu sing Flesh an' thu think Flesh. Thu'v seen, Gorey, with thur own eyes, an' it's drug into 'um at ev'ry chance. That's what the Glory Service is for. Keep 'um rev'runt an' won'dring.'

His eyes were challenging.

'While thu've life thu must give ev'ry minute to the White Man. P'raps he gave 'em life, thu don't know; an' it's sure he can take it away if he wants. That's thur religion. 'Tain't any worse than living an' dying for yur country or any other joss. 'Sides, thu could have ruined everything in thur heathen ignorance without some dope.'

Suddenly he moved away and shouted in some African dialect at a couple of negroes who were loitering some distance away. They slouched towards the wash-ups, glancing back.

'Yu see what this war's brought to yur old country, Gorey. Savages. An' I'm one of 'um, so get it. Our job's to prepare to kill, an' thur ain't no damn ideal an' slobber an' droppings goin' to stop us. Thur's a couple of thousand Flesh down in the shelters that's got to be put on the road in marching condition an' thur's more thousands to follow. That's what us Experts have been trained for, an' that's what we do if we've to drill ev'ry mugger an' nig in the damned mill. Those nigs, if thu got loose, if thu lost faith, would just slit us up an' set the Flesh free. What happens to yur Darnley then?'

Again his tone moderated.

'Gorey,' he said. 'D'yu know what thu'r saying since the Congo news come over? Thu'r saying Goble's dead. Thu'r god. That Dax is dead, an' yur gran'dad. An' now thu'v seen Hutterding, thur boss, split in four. *An'* a white gurl. Thu'r saying we can't protect our womenfolk, 'hat we're spawn, that thu'r workin' for spawn.' He glared. 'Some of those muggers have put the idea into thu black skulls that thu'r as good as we are. That Manny Boy, the young blaster, perhaps. I wish . . .' He left that, an unspoken threat, and cursed violently.

'It's my job to do the Glory Service tonight,' he resumed more softly. 'I'll have to show 'um what glory means just to settle 'um. Thu'r just raw savages below an' thu'd kill for pie. P'raps I'll plug a few first.' ('You can't do that,' I said, and he grinned.) 'Well, it ain't just hymns an' tales tonight. Dax's little parribles an' other junk won't be enough. An' I'll have the lot of yu in, muggers an' all before anything gets going. Yu'll sit with me, Gorey, just to show this Glory dope keeps in the fam'ly. The nigs think big bones of yu an' p'raps thu wonder why yu don't come along. Yu don't look godly to me, Gorey, but there's no understandin' tastes.'

He stood looking round the half-empty yard, facing his responsibility primitively according to his training, conscious of being the pivot on which life and death for many might hang. An exotic, outlandish figure even in his familiar overalls and rubber boots. But, as I watched him, I realized that *he* was the reality, he and his fantastic Glory Service, his murderous heathen, and all the groaning, terrible power of the Flesh below for which they stood, and that it was the drab, old-fashioned buildings around us, the meagre commonplaces of Darnley and its helpless, packed, ignorant masses which were bizarre. Science and civilization were still blind to themselves, like sorcerers telling the entrails of the dead they were calling on the primeval, on bloodlust and ruthlessness, to protect them. In all that wilderness of civilization without, there was no one on whom he could call to do his job. Little strutting police, not knowing the first needs of the times; soldiers who might shoot our nigs but could never replace them and their skill. This was an Expert's job, as the war was to be an Experts' war, and the world an Experts' world. They had to decide and they had to carry out.

'All spawn!' spat Haggard, as though he had been following my thoughts. 'I'll show 'um Glory!'

WHITE MAN'S GLORY SERVICE

By ten o'clock the entire works staff of the factory was assembled down in the bomb-proof shelters. The place was suffocatingly hot, for it was here that the pugs grew to maturity, and powerful electric heating had been installed. The floor was almost as dirty as the mill-yard, straw-strewn and muddy with here and there trickles of slimy water. It reminded me of a half-forgotten description of the Augean stables which Hercules cleaned but, instead of the three thousand oxen, we could hear the muffled breathing of a more than equivalent number of the Guard shackled in the further shelters. Their heavy respiration and the dull thudding of their restless movements formed an unbroken accompaniment to our 'service', a thematic undercurrent like the viols of an orchestra supply. Ever and again the whinnying of No. 2 'cow' broke in shrilly.

The shelters were low-roofed, echoing, and brilliantly lit. There were no seats. The blacks squatted on their hams down the centre of the main hall which we occupied, and the whites stood round the walls. In this order, after a great shuffling and a command for silence, we settled down to worship. Deep below the old woollen factory, in the heart of the stolid West Riding, we gave ourselves up to what I can only compare to a form of devil-worship, though there was no reference to any satanic power. It was Man we worshipped, White Man, the beneficent and supreme. Solemnly, for there was no heart in us to find fun in the absurd ritual, we settled down to the worship of ourselves.

During the latter part of the evening I had been with Haggard in the gatehouse which served as the Overseer's office.

'You're snickier with a pen than I am,' he said, and so I had the job of writing a report of the afternoon's tragedies to an address in London of which I had not heard, apparently the headquarters of the Experts. Godman was the name of the man I wrote to, and we 'awaited his instructions by return', my commercial phrasing of Haggard's 'an' tell him to be damn quick in telling me which way I've to jump.'

After that I wrote to the C/O, Pontefract Barracks. 'Thu said we could have Tommies if we wanted 'um an' guess they're due,' said Haggard.

A hush fell on the gathering as Haggard and I entered. His customary, easy-going manner had fallen from him; he was fiercely keyed-up and, I felt, self-conscious. In one hand he carried a book. Any old book would do, it seemed, so long as it was in print which no chance, inquisitive negro could read, and this was a Greek copy of Aristophanes' plays which Hutterding had always used. In the other he held an empty revolver; he opened it for me to see. These were important symbols. Taking up his stand at one end of the hall he raised his empty hand. This was the signal for the blacks to rise from their crouching positions with a great shuffling of boots. Tired and heavy-eyed most of them looked but expectant, one might almost say excited. Others appeared sullen, critical, and rose less willingly, these being the more intelligent. The muggers were whispering to each other, their eyes fixed on Haggard and me. What the hell was all this about? One could see the sneering inquiry on their lips. One could feel the undercurrent of antagonism. The meanest type of worker, a blackleg type but, for all we knew, leavened with socialist troublemakers intentionally planted in the factory.

From a side doorway a little procession emerged. Big 'Sump' Bjorraman led it, carrying, of all things on earth, a ketchup tin, as though it were the most fragile, valuable vase in existence. I suppose it was a holy ketchup tin with some especial significance. I never asked. A hum went up at sight of it.

At any other time I should have laughed but, had there been nothing else to control me, the appearance of Bjorraman's face would have done so. Big, rough fellow that he was, he had a heart hidden in him. His face showed drawn and muddy white as if the tan had been brushed away; his eyes were staring blankly ahead, still witnessing the horror of the afternoon. He held the brightly painted, idiotically symbolic can in his huge hands and gazed over the top of it in suppressed misery.

Behind him a bunch of four others came dragging the heavily doped carcase of one of the half-grown units, naked and harnessless. It could scarcely walk, its head hung forward, its legs dragged. They hustled it in front of us and let it sag to the floor where it sat, with the can at its side, throughout the proceedings. Then a scared negro came shuffling from the mass of his fellows and crouched down by the swaying beast to complete the tableau, a third symbol of the White Man's gifts to the earth. Little images in clay were produced, I recognized conventional resemblances to Goble and to my grandfather, and there were others unknown, and were distributed around the squatting figures.

'To the Power of Man, to the Word of Man!' The negroes had begun to chant. 'Maker of Life; Maker of us poor black bodies and of the Brothers who will guard us in time of war. To the Power and the Word of Man! The Black Flesh bows to the Power and the Word of Man!' I reproduce the chant in correct English though, in fact, there was a variety of queer accents and some used their native tongues. They shuffled into a squatting position again, some thudding wearily on the miry floor, and began to listen with rapt attention while Haggard pretended to read 'the Word of Man'. He had a well-thumbed typed slip in between the leaves, and was reading one of some dozen 'lessons' written specially for use at these services.

Before it was ended I had grasped most of the crude but effective symbolism employed and the psychology behind it. 'The Word' was understood to include the secret of making life, the history of life, and other impressive dogma. The Power of Man was unmistakably symbolized by the revolver, a revolver so symbolically sacred that it never needed to be loaded. The two symbols together effected a nice blend of religious awe and human fear, and inspired the needful reverence in the intent congregation.

This particular lesson dealt briefly with what at first puzzled me, but soon became evident as the making of the Flesh. It was in pseudo-Biblical language.

'And the ꞁ crawled on their black bellies into the Lab of Goble, and there they beheld the seeds of the Brothers floating in the waters. And after many days they crawled yet again and lo, the seeds were grown into living creatures, greater than any, and the Brothers *were*.' One black head nodded to another. They had seen. Some who had been glaring at us suspiciously began to hang their heads. They, too, had seen.

'But the Brothers spake not, having no need of tongue, neither did they sow, nor delve, nor tend the machines. But when the day came they marched forth in their might and slew all that stood before them, man, woman and child, the dogs of the kraal, and the cattle of the field. Not one life did they leave breathing. And they returned, silent in their strength, to rest in sleep unbroken. And all praised the Brothers, saying, Without you should we be dead and over. Without the White Man who made you should we be in the grave. And their fears slept with the Brothers and their living bodies worked joyously.'

Haggard's harsh voice ceased and the round, black heads nodded again one to another in reverence and confirmation. This was truth to them. They had seen. Why should they doubt. White eyes were turned towards the muggers, accusingly: they had been lied to. *This* that they heard was the truth.

The muggers were staring, round-eyed, uncertain. Manders' white face came to me out of their darker ones, staring at the floor as if not listening.

Some of those muggers were already beginning to follow out the quite far-reaching implications of this mumbo-jumbo service and why Haggard had ordered them to attend it. The authority above them might represent itself through restituted criminals and uneducated backwoodsmen who besported themselves in bloodthirsty ways and had little regard for human life, but it had powers of which they had no comprehension. Sure it could make life and, probably, take it as easily: that revolver suggested the guns and gas behind it. They were here to be told that *they* were the scum who had to keep quiet and just work – like niggers. That was it: they were being told there were more sorts of Black Flesh than one.

We sang a hymn. I seem to remember it as 'O God, Our Help in Ages Past', words and music intact, each left to construe God in his own way, after which Haggard gave a short address, a queer blend of sermon, with the infinite superiority of the White Man as its theme, and instructions upon the work for the next shift inter-larded with comments on the previous one. A pug had been roughly handled and spoilt and 'though it cried not yet the little Brother was suffering'. 'Handle the created work of the White Man with great care,' admonished Haggard. And there was praise for good work as well.

He came to a long pause. The negroes began to shuffle uncomfort-ably. A murmur of whispering arose. From beyond the black shadows of the corridors leading to the inner halls sounded the deadened groaning of the sleeping Brothers.

II

Haggard's book rose for silence. Hitherto he had been reading or repeating well-known phrases, but now he had to speak on his own. His voice was halting, harsher than usual.

'This day the Brother, hero of a hundred Games – did – too well. He saw enemies where there were no enemies and he slew. He slew – our white sister and the White Man who was placed over us as the Greater Man so that now *I* am the Greater Man. He slew too well. We must grieve for our dead. But who shall blame the Brother? Was he not made to slay! Who shall blame the White Man that he made so good an instrument! Bow yu heads, yu black bodies an' yu White Men. Bow to the dead.'

There was a slow, uncertain movement amongst the blacks, many of the muggers came forward from the walls. No one bowed; that was not their mood. Then one massive negro with a shaven head and a slash-scar on his cheek rose to his feet, his heavy hands wiping their palms on his dirty overalls. He advanced to stand next to the symbolic, seated negro. After a few silent seconds others rose in support until half of our black congregation was standing.

'The woman – is nothing,' said their spokesman, speaking in rich, almost perfect English. 'She came unwanted. Whoever owned her should have kept her safe. She did not please the Brother. He who fights bulls, who drove his trifane into the heart of the rhinoceros! Why should we bow for one of whom the White Man thinks so little that he leaves her open to death? And why should we bow for the dead White Man who is no greater than that he dies to save us Black Flesh; and for muggers who know not the way of life-making and shuffle before the sacred emblems? Is it, then, that the White Man knew these to be of more value than he?' His face was grim in suspicion of his tottering faith.

'The White Man knows when an' how to die an' it is not for the Black Flesh to question,' countered Haggard smartly. 'Though he be greater than a thousand black bodies, to die is a little thing, for death is not dust and decay to the White Man as to yu.'

The black was puzzled. 'Then could it be that the Boss Hutterding wished to die? That if one of us black bodies had turned mad as the Brothers grow neoblastic and tried to kill the Boss Hutterding . . .'

'Ask 'im w'y you should slave for 'im,' a voice shouted from the rear of the hall. 'Ask 'im w'y 'e's better'n you, w'y you can't be Experts an' boss them abaht.'

'This is all very damnfoolish talk,' said Haggard quietly. Raising his revolver he swung open the empty chambers for the negro to see. Then, leisurely, he drew out a handful of cartridges from his pocket and began to load.

'Rush 'im,' called a voice, and, 'Ain't they murdered enough!' There were angry shouts, but no one gave a lead.

'Take,' said Haggard, snapping the revolver and leaning forward to place it in the negro's hand. 'Answer yur own question. See if I can die. Raise it – so. Pull the trigger.' He mimicked the action with finger and thumb raised. 'And shoot down the grandson of Beldite who stands with me. Look how he laughs at yu, yu black bodies, yu brothers of spawn, yu mugging, swinish black flesh.

'Smile, yu fool, smile,' he hissed over his shoulder to me.

And, thank heaven, I smiled.

The big negro fumbled vacantly with the revolver. He had never held one before. He glanced up at us foolishly then behind at his intent, spellbound supporters. Even the muggers, rough men who could admire pluck when they saw it, were silent. Not a foot stirred.

Haggard held out his hand and the black returned the revolver sheepishly. He toyed with it momentarily. Then, as everyone thought he was about to replace it in his pocket, he cocked it up with an idle gesture and fired point-blank from the level of his hip. The round eyes of the standing negro widened, his huge white teeth flashed in a sudden, vast grimace, and he sank down to the oozy floor. His limbs jerked outwards and he lay crumpled and half spreadeagled at our feet. For the second I thought that he was dead, and then I saw that he was gibbering and cringing, that the other nig had joined him, grovelling in the dirt, and that in the body of the crouched Brother were six hotly-red round holes which seemed to be quivering and enlarging as I gazed at them.

'Just *flesh*!' shouted Haggard; 'pug flesh! Is the black flesh any more than the pug flesh?' He had reloaded the revolver. The muzzle rose, pointing down at one of the fawning negroes.

'No,' screamed the congregation, and bowed down in reverence, impressed perhaps as much by this unprecedented use of their holy symbol as by its threat. 'Just flesh! Just flesh!' They were not just flesh to me, and Haggard's blazing eye brought me forward in my chair ready to spring if he went too far. He caught my movement, and the smile which flickered across his face told me I was a fool, that he knew how to handle his problem and was in full control of himself.

'The pug Brother does not die,' came his quiet voice. 'See, it struggles to rise. But a black body full of lead is useless carrion and, dirt as it is, it is needed to work through the long days in the service of the Guard.' There was a click and he was replacing the cartridges in his pocket. 'Bow yur heads to the White Man and the White Woman who are dead. Glory to the White Man who created the great Brother Omega.' He closed his eyes and stood silently.

Beneath my lowered brows I saw the set faces of the muggers

staring blankly like so many wax-works round the walls. One by one they bowed. From the centre of the hall not a face showed, only the bobbing, cringing heads, some shaven and glistening, others black with woolly hair. Coe Gardy's round eyes became visible, grinning cheerfully at me. Bjorraman came forward, relief written in his face, and began to haul up the apparently uninjured pug.

'To the Power of Man, to the Word of Man. Maker of Life. Maker of us poor black bodies . . .' The chant rose from the bowed faces. It continued even as Haggard began to speak once more.

'Let all learn from the wisdom of the Black Flesh, even those whose skin is white yet have black flesh in their hearts. Not only the Black Flesh must slave an' sweat but all, *all*. Let no man raise his voice against the spirit of the Glory Service lest the Power of the White Man fall on him.' Linking his arm in mine, he led me down the hall to the chanting of five hundred negro voices.

> 'We are the Black Flesh
> Who work with joy in our hearts
> That the Brothers may live to guard us
> As the White Man has willed.
>
> All others be our enemies.
>
> But there shall be war
> That our enemies be slain.
> There shall be *war*
> That our Brothers may slay,
> To the Glory of the White Man
> And the truth of his Word.
> Wherefore with joyous hearts we work,
> We, the Black Flesh.'

At the doorway of the runway leading to the surface he button-holed Manders.

'Tell yur mugger friends that the next time there's need of shootin' it won't be only pugs,' he said. 'This fact'ry's for work an' no blabbering. Today's *done*. Yu get it?' Manders stared at him with unblinking, expressionless eyes. He did not move as Haggard's hand fell on his shoulder. 'See yu here, Manny Boy; I ain't no hand at expressing feelings, but I want yu to understand I know what yu felt about – hur. There ain't one o' the boys who wouldn't have taken the quad to save hur. I'd go to hell to get today back an' do it diff'rent.' He hesitated, his rough sympathy holding him, then walked on with me.

'Yu thought of droppin' me one, didn't yu? Out on the hot line one o' those nigs'd be a gonner now, but it doesn't seem to fit in with this spitty-mouthed land. An' guess there's bin enough killin' for today. That gurl! Tell yu what, Gorey, I've never seen a dead gurl before.'

He whistled two bars of 'O God, Our Help in Ages Past', absent-mindedly, then seemed suddenly to remember that there was work to be done. 'Night shift,' he bawled at the outflowing congregation, black against the vivid light of the bomb-shelters beneath. 'Rest – get yur sleep an' no talking.'

A group of negroes separated themselves and passed us, humming and chattering excitedly. I walked back to find Manders, then recollected I was on shift. I did not run across him until later that night, when I discovered him close to the side factory wall, deep in shadow. I had an impression that he had just thrown something over. I waited for him to join me.

'Getting rid of some rubbish,' he mumbled. 'It piles up so in here. Makes me sick to see it.' Collarless, begrimed and dispirited, he was a mere shadow of his once vivid self. I began to say something about Betty, and stopped at the strained, tearless state of his eyes. He hurried away into the darkness, wordless and half running.

III

That was only some four days before our first contingent was to be ready for the road. Haggard kept us so hard at it that there was time to think of little else. The nigs worked like devils and the muggers sank back into themselves, awed by the undefined power under which they laboured. Within a day the tragedy of the Games was a thing of the past.

I was one of many who went to pay my last respects to the dead where they lay in the gatehouse. The horror on Betty's face had softened away into peace, a baby's face beneath her bush of curling blonde hair. Hutterding, too, looked oddly childish. The grimness had relaxed; he had the appearance of tired disappointment.

The hard eyes of the Experts showed little as they bent over them. 'Sore luck,' they said and, 'Bloody shame,' inexpressive comments which conveyed more than they intended. Coe Gardy was smiling as always, his face was set that way, his eyes rounder and more glistening than usual. 'Maybe it's better for them than being burnt out with gas, Gorey,' he said. 'They're just leading the way. That's how I look at it. Like a funny little doll, ain't she?'

By noon, Godman, one of the chief overseers, was in the factory, putting the finishing touches to the discipline started by Haggard. He brought with him a breath of aloof authority, but for which, like all Experts, he had little respect.

'Good work,' he told Haggard. 'Vessant asked me to convey his congratulations on the way you handled it all.'

'*I* don't want the Pot-Belly's 'gratulations,' slung Haggard.

'But you get 'em. Just a slice of that other glory service they've been running for centuries, the land of hope and glory service. Made a speech on you, he did, to some of the bug-mugs. Called this Miss Corrall of yours a "fruitful source of trouble suspected of spying", whilst his heart bled for her and her relatives. His heart bleeds very quickly when he's making a speech. Knows better what you did than you know yourself. "The White Man can be killed but the White Man has no objection to being killed. The grandson of Beldite has no objection to being killed. What a thought for black, superstitious minds to play with!"'

'Who's his yapper in here who tells him all this?'

Godman grinned. 'He knows all.' Godman had a long face with a twisted nose, a permanent cigar and a sense of humour. Walking or sitting, his long legs seemed always slightly in the way. I don't know whether he could read thoughts, but he knew all about a man on sight. He sent for me and said, 'What are you doing here?' as though he knew all about it. 'You ought to have a swagger job somewhere. Your grandfather's popular just now.' That and the look of the man conveyed so much that I had no inclination to lie.

'He's not popular with himself,' I answered. 'Doesn't like the way things are going.'

'Who does? But they are going. Him and you and us won't stop 'em. We're not politicians, we do a job. I'd stick around, Mr Beldite, until things have moved a bit further. I get your idea, but you don't know what to do about it yet, do you? Who does? We'll have a talk sometime. Maybe you'll be my boss some day. Think it out well; we're rotten cusses to boss.' He arranged his legs for rising, and yawned without moving his cigar.

'The time's come, boys,' said Godman to a crowd of us, 'for us to be adopted openly. They're giving us a chunk of glory all to ourselves. They're going to make us national heroes. Perhaps Pollen, the Home Secretary, is hoping to deal with his own white rebels as you did with your black ones.

'We're going to be the very latest in White Men for the nation to come honeying round,' he told us. 'When you take the road they're going to doll you up romantic to attract the ladies, so you'd all better start learning to wash. But don't imagine that means more freedom: idols just sit on pedestals and do what they're told. No more cow-runnings for you, boys.'

'We'll have cow-runnings if we like,' said Coe Gardy. 'They won't stop us.'

'Course you will. Course they won't. But you just won't like, Coe, will you now? Maybe they'll print picture postcards of us and we'll be so busy wallowing in our fan-mails we shan't have time for other amusements.'

Despite Godman's cynical views on authority in the works he was the supreme speeder-up. His job, like Haggard's, was producing the Guard and he did it; his opinions did not interfere with that.

During the evening sentries were posted round the walls and there were machine-guns in the gatehouse. The appearance of the soldiers was greeted with hooting and booing and after nightfall crowds began to gather outside the walls at a little distance.

We were told nothing of events outside, part of the policy of preserving us from disruptive influences. Newspapers were stopped to us and the radio cut off. We were like prisoners in a penal settlement except that we worked harder, toiling like galley-slaves. If any sequel followed the killing of Betty Corrall we did not hear of it: the entire affair became the concern of higher authorities.

ties. We concentrated on the final equipment of the first contingent and scarcely noticed our increased isolation.

But, ever and anon, from the higher windows of the factory one could see the crowds in the streets demonstrating against the introduction of the military. There was shouting and singing and, once, a wild scuffle and the crashing of broken glass. It passed out of sight and hearing towards the town. A posse of mounted police went galloping by. Our inquiries as to whether this outburst arose from the funeral of Betty Corrall were answered by denials. Foreign aeros, said to be Russian, had been over the town the previous night showering revolutionary literature into the streets. This was the response.

Next day gyros appeared droning in the sky and we heard the peculiarly muffled clangour of tanks and armoured cars passing beyond the walls. Darnley, it was said, was seething with unrest, a town of dour, frightened people ready to break into fury at any moment. The presence of the military now openly on the side of Beldite's increased the rancour but prevented active trouble.

What a different picture came to me in Paddy's infrequent letters! I was more than glad to receive them. It was good to know oneself remembered when one had almost forgotten oneself!

In the comparative calm of the south, minds were healthier and tempers better. There were no munition blacklegs, no negroes to arouse resentment, no angry, incontinently displaced workers deprived of their livelihood.

The undercurrent of fear which must have existed did not show in her writing: Brighton seemed to be crowded with gay, brave young officers – I could have been jealous had I not long pushed all that out of my mind – and there was a brave affectation that this war was to be the greatest of all joyrides, a long hoped for opportunity for heroes, a splash of vivid colour at the zenith of existence. There was much doubt about there being a war. People who had been trained to believe that war would open with the cataclysmic destruction of London and the major cities were unprepared for this deliberate, prolonged preparation. The cynical asserted that the re-armament ramp needed a good war scare to get going.

The news-sheets were now featuring semi-documented assurances of Britain's preparedness and unexampled defences. Faced with the grave war danger the Government had seen no alternative but to accept the oft-repeated offers from certain far-seeing but hitherto neglected firms who, in the course of purely commercial enterprise, had happened on discoveries of supreme military importance, discoveries they had hoped never to reveal! In such fashion was the last shred of camouflage on our secret armaments removed to the satisfaction of millions of loyal but peace-loving people.

My grandfather forthwith became the subject of widespread Press publicity. He became the super-patriot who, year after year, unrecognized, scorned, vilified, had poured his millions into preparing for the war which he, almost alone, knew must come. His view that a peaceful but all-powerful Britain, the sole aim of Dax-Beldite, was the best possible guarantee of peace, was flaunted before the public, a final argument against the advocates of disarmament. For was not war on our very doorstep! Its immediate origin in the Congo was allowed to die from the columns and attention concentrated on the primary causes of financial and industrial rivalry and that jealousy which is the ill-fortune of any great empire. From these highly complicated arguments the average man must have taken refuge in blind patriotism as his only way to an intelligent understanding.

I do not remember that the truth about the Death Guard was ever publicly stated. Starting from an unknown source it passed from mouth to mouth, a spread of distortion, half-truth, and ridiculous exaggeration. The truth fell more palatably for this clever garbling.

My grandfather, wrote Paddy, was much more vigorous, newsmen keeping him busy and hopeful, and he was able to leave his bed and move about the room. Then it came to him that his views were being perverted to a war propagandist purpose. He relapsed and was ordered back to rest. 'I do wish it were possible for you to visit him, but of course you cannot,' she said.

Regulations apart, there was no chance of that. Every minute of our time was in demand during those last days of increasing strain. It was as though we were living over a hidden mine which might explode at any moment. We were racing that moment. The Guard contingents must be ready.

The day of the first marching dawned cold and dull. We rose an hour earlier than usual, eating our meals at work.

'This is where we start,' said Haggard. 'Keep those gates greased. This is goin' to be sheer non-stop an' no variety: just solid flesh in blocks of a thousand. We'll spew 'em out like tadpoles!'

CHAPTER FIVE

The Marching of the Guard

THE FACTORIES DISGORGE

AT HALF-PAST ten that night the word went round for hot coffee and rum to be served. It was the signal that the first contingent was ready to leave the factory. The deep, discordant hum of activity took a higher note, a note of excitement, of jubilation. This was the crowning hour of our labours. In a little while we should assemble at the gates, weary but triumphant, to witness that strangest of all marches. What matter that our lot was but to turn once more to our incessant labour, that no man knew the end of this drama we were beginning? In half an hour the whistle would blow and the gates swing wide!

In the gloom weary men began to make their way towards the canteen, shouting and laughing to each other. Outside the wash-ups, just clear of the whitely steaming doorway, the negroes clustered, chattering ecstatically, and snatching at the steaming mugs handed round to them. Haggard emerged from the clamping sheds whistling. The light of the canteen flushed on, spattering the wet yard with shimmering reflections, sending the shadows sliding and humping away behind the ramparts of the piled drums. Some-one began singing.

I remember standing for a while brooding on the scene, wearily impervious to the exciting infection of the night. Something of my original horrified repugnance assailed me. I was jaded, mentally and physically, and I cursed having to enter that canteen for my rum and coffee. Why could I not have my coffee brought out to me here where it was cool and where I could be alone! This inconse-quent irritation absorbed me for some minutes like a sharp new pin-prick distracting from a deeper, permanent pain.

In the quad-shackling sheds the first thousand of the Guard crushed and grumbled like cattle. The low mutter of their breathing sounded over the yard and ever and again the boardwork of the sheds would shake as some vast bulk heaved against it ... as though the sea were pressing on our thin walls, an eternal, ever-rising sea, approaching its destined time of flood. Someone drew down one of the canteen blinds and a shadow started out suddenly from the black immensity of the further yards and rushed like a wave to my very feet. I jerked, nervily.

Why should men, clear-eyed, clear-thoughted, beautiful men spend their days in this welter, turning out this filthy imitation of themselves, this bastardized version of nature's supreme gift? Above, there was the peaceful, star-flecked sky brightening to a hazy radiance where the moon was rising from beyond the dark line of the distant quarries, and here was this steamy yard, soaked in water, reeking with obnoxious smells! Only the god in man which made it so immeasurably loathsome could account for man suffering it at all. Animals, good, healthy, godless animals would, I felt, have fled nauseated as they would from putrid food.

What was it we were doing? Preparing to defend our homeland, to protect those we loved, the country we loved. Or were we just maniacs, blindly turning our hopes into decay and dust, fascinated by our own self-destruction? Already two people I had known were uselessly dead ... God knew what might be happening in the other factories scattered throughout the north.

Why was I there, munitioning, blacklegging, slaving as though my bread depended on it? Was I still trying to get that grip, hoping, perhaps, to become a leader in this mad effort so that I could stem it, control it, turn it to peaceful purposes? Or, bored with my sedentary life, did I actually enjoy the heavy manual labour, the rough company, did it serve as an excuse for shelving the problem I had set myself? Peaceful purposes! when we sang of war, glorified killing ... What would my grandfather say if he knew? And Paddy, who imagined ... But I did not know what she imagined. Nor care. She was distant and meaningless. A glimpse, a broken idea; what had she to do with me!

A biting shiver took me. I had been working heavily, riveting thick steel wristlets on the units, and the late air was cold. The thought of hot coffee, stinging rum, steaming food, and a shouting company of lusty men incontinently drew me, driving all thought but that of mere creature comfort out of my mind. I hastened to the canteen, glad now of its stuffy heat.

A brief ten minutes and we were out once more. During that short interval floodlighting had been switched on turning the yard to daylight, whitening the towering blocks above us. Beyond their effulgence the night formed a vast cap of blackness over our insect-like activities. It split suddenly as the beam of a searchlight from the quarries jetted across it. The night broke into defeated fragments as further beams flashed zenithwards, coldly triumphant. We were no longer insects: we were gods.

This was the end of secrecy. That day of lies and pretence was over for ever. The people had growled and threatened and suspected; now let them see what Dax-Beldite's and their thoughtful Government had done for them, the impregnable defence which was to be theirs. Already the news-sheets had been preparing the way, thrilling in anticipatory headlines; in future all the arts of publicity would be used to popularize the Guard, the Royal Death Guard. Such was the official title.

The grand secret was floodlit; the flinging light beams called the town to its uncovering. Some might think it an air-raid: they would rush into the streets terrified to seek the public shelters – to find that it was Safety, Impregnability on the march!

At eleven o'clock, when the traffic had settled for the night and the roads were clear, our mill siren broken into a vast, commanding roar, summoning the townsfolk from their suppers and beds, their night-clubs and sterio shows, and the gates swung wide for that great outgoing.

II

At that time there was a man called Hitchin who kept one of those very small, out-of-date shops which still lingered on selling, mainly, newspapers and the gaudy periodicals of the day, but also tobaccos, confectionery, and a pitiful uneconomic medley of similar small goods. It was close to our main entrance.

He took a quaint, old-fashioned pride in his tiny business, one of the very few left in Darnley. And, because he and his dismal shop stood for a past tradition, he felt it a duty to defend most other past traditions. At least, that is how his distinctively narrow mind presented itself to me. Some similar, lingering instinct in me drew me frequently to patronize his little store, and we knew each other and the clash of our ideas very well.

I mention him now because the marching of the Death Guard which he witnessed must have meant to him the crashing of an entire world as, indeed, it actually symbolized, and because he was one of the very few from whom I gained a first-hand impression.

There must have been a dozen or more altogether different effects created in the little crowd which first gathered. Rumours had leaked, distorted rumours, but sufficient to prepare some imaginative minds for the reality; and these rumours had varied results. There were those who understood clearly enough, having read their newspapers intelligently, that what they saw was designed to be their saviour against foreign aggression, and some of these essayed a sporadic cheer or so. Others, equally enlightened, were terrified out of all rational sensations. There were many who stared dumbly, incomprehensibly, and there was one young girl who, when more than half the contingent had passed into the road, screamed, madly and uncontrollably, and still screaming tore down a side street, her hands tearing wildly at her flying hair. One of her shoes fell off and she hesitated, brought momentarily to her senses by this tiny mishap, and glancing backwards. Then she screamed again, pitifully, like a stricken animal, and was gone. I saw her through the crowd and Hitchin, the newsagent, also witnessed her flight.

Hitchin had been reading in his back parlour and, hearing the sudden belching of the siren, strolled out to the shop door. He thought it might be a fire. Not an air-raid for he did not believe in anything so fantastic. A fire. No other explanation of the uproar occurred to him, though he had heard as many rumours as anyone. His standing joke was that he always ate salt for breakfast to shake on his newspapers. Town talk he soaked in like a sponge, squeezing it out again as readily, but anything beyond the confines of what he considered normal was not only unbelievable but anathema to him.

'I heard 'em,' he said to me afterwards; 'I read abaht 'em. But did I believe! Not until wi' these own eyes I see. Myers used to be on me day arter day. The man what rented me back room. "It's true," he'd say, slobberin' a bit wi' excitement as he always did. "They're makin' things, *living* things, to fight for uz. A sort o' soldier it is, but not *born* as you might say. Made. Turned out by machines. Robots."

'There *might* be something in it,' the newsagent pretended to agree, eyes glimmering humorously behind his glasses. 'If sausages *could* be made to fight, I guess they'd have a good few old grudges to pay off. But I don't think we'll see 'em on their hind legs yet awhile. Robots, heck!'

That was how he treated everything he heard; and though he never mentioned it to anyone, he believed that the Beldite mills were making a new explosive, and only his reluctance to abandon the archaic business of which he was so proud prevented his moving to some safer spot.

So, expecting to see flames and smoke at the worst, he strolled to his shop door and stared at the mill gates. The brilliantly lit yard confirmed his thoughts. Nothing happened. Then he noticed that some dozen or more people who had collected there and were obviously awaiting something were behaving differently from the usual fire crowd. They were lining up not clammering to see inside. Many others were running to join them. When the gates began to open he settled himself against the door jamb and commenced to fill his pipe and to enjoy whatever transpired.

It was only then that he realized that if Beldite's *were* making explosives he might be blown to Kingdom Come the very next minute.

That idea had no time to develop; it died as it rose.

And he never lit his pipe. In telling me, he laid great stress on that little point.

'I never lit me pipe,' he said. 'I stood with the match burning me fingers, and I don't think I knew. And when it was all over, there was me pipe on the ground, freshly filled, and in three pieces. I'd never lit it.'

The gates moved open in jerks and a sergeant became visible, looking behind him and waving an arm. He re-entered out of sight and, after a moment, a platoon of soldiers with bayonets at the slope and bombs slung round their waists marched out. Close upon their heels followed the Guard accompanied by the Road Experts.

'I thought as 'ow they were big fellows for a moment,' said Hitchin. 'I saw their helmets sort of shining a bit muddily in the glare, an' towering above the little chaps who'd come first. "What woppers!" I thought. I took those spike things they carry for bayonets, huge big bayonets at the trail, an' their skin – well, I expect I thought it was a light-coloured khaki though, of course, it ain't like khaki at all. But I remember I was just struck by their size. "Good God! What men!" I said.

'An' then I sees they wasn't men.

'I tell you, I didn't believe. I didn't believe anything. I never *lit* me pipe! I stood – like sommat struck dead, but still seeing. The sodjers passed me, whippersnappers of boys with white, scared faces, looking as though they were getting ready to be corpses. Then the others went by. Within three feet of me they was, just across the causeway, their metal shoes hittin' sparks off the road as they shuffled by, their beastly bodies gleaming wi' sweat, an' their breath comin' – how does it go? Hoo-uh, hoo-uh. Hoo-uh, hooh-uh. The ghastliest sound God ever allowed. Beasts, they was, but worse than any beasts as ever lived. Seven foot high! Rigged out in bits of dull armour with bulging fat between their pig faces sunk down on their thick necks an' their eyes – if you call 'em eyes – glazed an' dead-lookin'.'

'They were doped,' I told him. 'When they're not – when the life flows in them – then their heads come up and their flesh stiffens and they're altogether a different creature.'

'There couldn't be a creature more different,' said Hitchin. 'They was like a dead army of horrors! If ever they comes to life, God preserve me from seein' 'em! I watched 'em out of sight, though it seemed as 'ow they'd never stop until hell was emptied, right up the hill towards the station. All alike they was, all dead an' sweatin'. They didn't look right nor left, not at me nor no one. It may have been just that I were dazed, but the air seemed to grow hot as they passed, and there was a cloud of steam over them as they disappeared, a sort of whiteness in the night. Then I went in an' woke Myers, who'd gone to bed, and told him. He cursed at me like a man what's been robbed an' grabbed at his boots. He didn't put 'em on. He just raced after that hell's crowd in his pyjamas, carrying his boots in one hand. *I* didn't laugh. I went an' sat me dahn in the parlour an' tried to shut me eyes to get me senses back, but each time I shut 'em I could see those sweaty brutes going by, thud, thud, hoo-uh, hoo-uh.

'Myers found me that way when he come back, an' he sat himself down on the chair opposite without a word. Then he got up an' went into the kitchen, shivering' an' gulpin', an' in a minute I heard him being sick in the sink. I didn't see him again that night. He'd had his bellyful.'

III

That was the impression made on Hitchin, the old-fashioned news-agent, and his over-enthusiastic lodger, Myers. There must have been many such. From fifty factories that night, scattered over the North and Midlands, the beast battalions issued, the last, and the strangest, and the foulest of all earth's armies. A thousand a day, that was each factory's quota, and Darnley, at least, fulfilled it until the day I left, the day I talked to Hitchin, which was well over a week later. Each night at eleven, heralded by that ululating roar, watched by larger and larger crowds, cheering, booing, scream-ing, and fighting crowds, the mill gates opened and the day's product marched out and tramped southwards to the immense depots which had been prepared in the old, disused coal-fields of south Yorkshire.

That first night, as I stood near the gates watching, they came to me anew as things rediscovered, those cloddish lives to which my life was being dedicated. For units during the growth period were only units, injected, drugged, aimless; except for their animal appearance and size of little more import to an unknowing observer than the mushrooms on which they fed. Even in full harness they were grotesquely pitiful in their helpless somnolence. But the Guard on the march was a creature in itself; though still doped and blind it was a beast awakening, achieving purpose and deathly power with every mile it marched.

Close to me stood a little group in deep shadow, a shortish, heavily built man in a big fur coat, a tall, military figure, and others. Word went round that it was the Rt Hon. Rupert Vessant and General Tankerley. It was symptomatic of my mood that I did not make myself known to them, that I had no form of ideas to put before them. I felt raw, a novice, a human unit. Perhaps Godman, with his shrewdness, was expecting me to do something. What was there to do?

Every detail still lives with me, the scared Tommies at attention, others at every door with bayonets on guard, a huge pile of smoke-bombs in a corner and another of tear-gas grenades. Experts were openly jeering at these precautions. As if *they* did not know their jobs! Bayonets! Spawn! Owl-eyed nigs, released from their last-minute tasks, went to stare at the soldiers silently. I heard one ask another what they were for. Officers were bossing needlessly, probably to cover their nervousness; Experts scowlingly obeyed their instructions. There seemed to be running trouble between the officers and Godman. Inside the sheds the thud of heavy bodies grew louder. Everything was in black and white, silhouettes mounted one behind another, rising to the sky, with brilliant walls beyond; in the foreground little figures hastening on a black and white stage.

The Guard came out in double file, blundering clumsily against each other, recoiling as their projecting leg-prongs tore into the sensitized parts of each other's legs, leaving dull, reddish-brown abrasions as on a bruised apple. A little while and the automatic process of marching would become ingrained in their nerve-centres; they were a herd by the planned results of their manufacture, a herd with the instinct to keep close and to go straight ahead.

They carried their quadrifanes at the trail and, by an ingenious coupling device, the rear knob of each was attached to the front of the one behind at a point just below the cutting-head, so that each file was linked slackly but inseparably together until the couplings were struck apart. Every tenth pair were cross-linked to prevent their straying apart. The ooze of the yard squelching beneath their shuffling hooves, a hazy suggestion of steam beginning to rise from their permanently perspiring bodies, they went forward like a living chain. At spaced intervals came the wheeled barrels carrying their dope-food. Three officers and the head Road Expert ended the procession, the former visibly ill at ease with their companion and trying to look oblivious of the grotesque company of which they were in command. A couple of lorries bearing spare equipment and other gear rumbled behind.

Nine hundred and ninety-nine left the gates; the thousandth, a brute somewhere about the middle of the column, was neoblastic, so Haggard said. Its instincts were insufficiently matured or already degenerating, and part way across the yard it made strenuous efforts to lumber out to the side. Its sight-ganglia were enlarged weirdly in the floodlighting.

A whistle piped, a roadman dashed forward. Two deft strokes of his uncoupler disconnected its quad and detached it from the column. Another roadman inserted a substitute quad. The unit came blundering into the open and in a fraction the net was over him. It took ten nigs to drag it back to its shed, an awesome struggle. Insufficiently doped perhaps, or tougher than standard.

'Why didn't you have it shot straight away?' one of the officers was asking. 'What are our fellows for?'

Godman was standing near him. 'Young man,' he said; 'you don't know these big boys. They *don't* shoot. Pumping lead into them sure wakes them up.'

We turned to watch the last files disappear, and for ten days I witnessed the same procession at eleven each night. But the net was not in demand again and in the third contingent were one thousand and one units. The factory quota had to be fulfilled exactly.

THE CALL TO REVOLUTION

There can be little doubt but that during those ten days, even as the Guard was beginning to pour out from the Flesh Factories in its hundreds of thousands, the Continental powers were still vacillating in their attitude towards Britain. An all-European demand that she should cease Flesh manufacture forthwith and surrender its secrets to an international convention had been made and rejected, with the tiny loophole left that the suggestion would be considered if all other nations would reveal their own secrets first;

a pious pact of mutual defence (for who honestly believed that Britain would attack her Atlantic neighbours?) was spreading erratically, but not all favoured that early aggression which was patently the only logical method of dealing with an embryonic All-Powerful. Even the most inimical to us favoured delay, for though this also favoured Britain, it was vital to them: to re-arm adequately, to gain allies, to win home approval. So it was that, to cover these preparations, they fell in with elements which were striving frantically for peace, promoting useless parleys, assisting in the 'propaganda bombardment' and 'bloodless air-raids', which were the Soviet's preliminary contribution.

All armament agreements and prohibitions had been swept aside and, with a great show of extemporaneous revival which deluded very few, each had set its munition centres to work; Britain's crop of unsuspected inventors was paralleled abroad in much greater measure, inventors who, for the past decade, had been living lavishly on undeveloped patents and, with no encouragement whatever, had developed their marvels to the highest lethal pitch. Some of these were pooled, notably the famous 'mother-machines' and their 'bomb-pluggers', but other novel innovations were kept jealously within national bounds. Concurrent with the lightning adaptation to military purposes of every available air-liner, new air machines were rising from impromptu factories as though they were self-generated. Weapons which a child could use with deadly accuracy were being manufactured, as Mundaine had prophesied, 'like screws', and there was at least one disastrous humanite explosion a week before its production had been generally agreed. The new Latin Communist republics came out best from that ironic phrase: they had never professed to any major degree of disarmament being still in fear of counter-revolutionary intercession.

The bloodless air-raids in which foreign craft scattered leaflets over all our main cities, penetrating as far west as Liverpool and Bristol, and, once, Belfast, calling upon the populace to demand the immediate cessation of Flesh manufacture, formed the opening chapter of Continental policy and underlined our obvious accessibility. Darnley was the aim of this propaganda more than once. Our night shift was startled to see the sky suddenly raining paper and spent a jolly quarter of an hour waking us others to make us read.

Light, dummy bombs, inscribed with quaintly worded warnings, were deposited in Trafalgar Square and in Princes Street, Edinburgh, apparently from very low altitudes; London woke one night to a terrific roar and the winding Thames was lit for a distance of two miles by brilliant chemical flares; flame-writing was seen in the high sky, a fugue of friendly appeal repeated over a rough circle visible to the larger part of Yorkshire and Lancashire.

These efforts to assist public fervour against the Guard were followed by the destruction from the air of a half-mile section of road on the wolds north of Ripon, an old bridge crossing the Tay, and a short section of disused railway in South Wales, each spot being undoubtedly chosen for its solitude so that life should not be endangered. This aerial publicity left no doubt as to the silence of modern aeros nor the high degree of accuracy developed by foreign pilots.

But because delay was essential to Vessant's plans it was a part of his early policy to reveal Britain as a country disrupted from within, to magnify all elements antagonistic to war preparation: this would encourage the enemy both to underestimate our solidarity and to hesitate to attack so pacific a population, even perhaps to hope that Britain would solve their problem for them and abolish its own warlords. He extracted every ounce of publicity value from the anti-Beldite campaign; he worked for the retention of Erasmus Pollen at the Home Office, though many clamoured for his removal as being too weak for the looming insurrectionary situation. Pollen's old-fashioned democratic leaning towards free public expression was given play to an extent far beyond what latter-day law sanctioned, not for friendship's sake, but because Vessant considered that a little insurrection would do no harm. Censorship was relaxed, though not on broadcasting which reached too wide a field. Mundaine being feared, Mundaine was imprisoned together with a few hundred others; the foreigner must not think Pollen too flaccid. But Hogbin and Stamper, more violent, less universally respected, were left free. The more peace propaganda, the bigger the protest meetings; the more acrid the demonstrations the better. Vessant, via Pollen, played astutely on these chords to encourage peace feeling abroad to hinder Europe's militarization. No irreparable harm would be done. The aces were all in his hand.

Vessant had gauged the situation to a nicety. At the inception of war the prime need is for enthusiasm on the home front, speedy but not too sickeningly murderous victories. The first throes of war madness are still only a veneer; heroism, righteousness, the spirit of the crusade must be encouraged. Dour, unfeeling death-dealing comes only with time and there is a nice game of luring the enemy into foul deeds as a palatable excuse for reprisals. Britain was largely exempt from these considerations, but not so Europe with its dependence on man-power. The Continental generals would make a big show of attacking the Guard and the munitions centres, of killing as few civilians as possible. Neither the means nor the will to sheer massacre is present in war's opening phases; when holocaust came later Britain would then be ready. It was all fore-seen by Vessant's foresighted genius.

II

Of those ten days I remember very little. To us in the factories it was a timeless, intolerable strain under which even the negroes flagged and became dispirited. More than one of the whites col-lapsed entirely. But how, during that time, I degenerated into what Jack London used to call a 'work-beast', and how the tedious grind bit into my soul until I felt I could not carry on a day longer are of no particular moment in this narrative. The long hours, monotonous food, and dirty, makeshift living quarters began to undermine my health, but, above all, was the sense of taking part in the running of a madhouse, a feeling that one was dedicating one's whole self to the creation of a nightmare.

Outside our high, barbed walls, the world, mad but healthy and virulent, was preparing vigorously for suicide; nevertheless, out there, real human companionship was to be found, not hymn-sing-ing negroes, sullen muggers, and foul-mouthed, bloody-minded Ex-perts. And there was the open, and free, unpolluted air, danger and adventure; and, to a mind like mine, history in the making, the climax of a civilization. I say a mind like mine though, indeed, interest in such matters dated back less than a month; but it seemed to me that that month had laid bare my true mind to me, which so long had frittered itself away in sport and amusement.

Each day a thousand of the Guard had to be fed to marching condition and made ready for the road, whilst another thousand, to follow them, was being harnessed and equipped, and still a further thousand was undergoing the last tests of fitness. Then, at night, the searchlights would splash their bright flowers above us like a mocking crown, the siren bay out its message and, through the dark hours, the contingent having passed out, the lorries would begin rolling in, bearing the pugs which, three weeks later, would be matured and ready for battle.

Food and sleeping accommodation degenerated, there being no time to attend to it; we workers degenerated. Nightly some of our numbers passed out on to the road, freed men, and others came to take their place or we ex-muggers were promoted.

On the ninth day Haggard came to see me. His eyes were sunken and bright with a slight attack of fever, his cheek-bones showed prominently.

'I'm clearing tomorrow,' he said. 'I'm marching with the eleventh contingent. Like to come?' He regarded me frowningly as though questioning my eager agreement. 'No, you're too bloody worn. Tell yu what. We'll be hitching up with the main drove tomorrow night in Leeds an' then it'll be all slog an' slush until we get them to the coast. Yu slack off for a day. I'll work it. Rest, booze, what yu want. Get some hell into yuself. An' take that Manny Boy with yu.'

'Why?' He had never shown interest in Manders before.

'There's trouble banking up. May be tonight, tomorrow, any day. Coe Gardy – he's takin' charge from me – wants rid of him. Seems his riots an' busting in the fact'ries is comin' right from what I hear. There's bin a sort of scared, creepy look in his eyes an' I've a wind that he knows. I'm guessing things about him. Maybe just his gurl's worrying him; he blubs when he's alone, some o' the boys tell me. But I may be guessing right. He's soap, wet soap, an' I don't want the job o' putting his bullet in him. Gardy don't either. We'd sooner he hiked out an' got himself killed in his revolution before we know for certs. Take him with yu an' if he does a getaway, *spawn* to him! I don't want him on the road with us.' Haggard made a spitting sound with his lips. 'He was always too bloody clean for me. Washed his hands for fodder if he could find water. As though the fodder wasn't as full o' muck as his finger-nails! He's muggered in okay, but he's spitty.'

In that way, with less than twenty-four hours' warning, I left the Flesh Factory. I harboured a delusion that away from its restrictions my mind would come straight. Experts, however powerful, were only workmen with the minds of workmen; with the assistance of my grandfather I would release myself from military service or, better, wangle myself some influential post, and from there I would get amongst the politicians with all the experience of the factory to weight my efforts. I failed woefully to visualize the extent to which the Death Guard was already monopolizing the limelight, turning all but the veriest few into lookers-on – or rebels if it took them that way – or toiling pawns such as myself, and how slight and tortuous an influence the once powerful Edom Beldite could exert on this new and paramount phase of existence. His popularization was a mere stunt. I did not realize my value as an Oxy-Exy. The nickname, 'Vessant's Saviours' (I do not know what brilliant mind conceived it), had sprung into use, and the country was being lured by every means into regarding the Flesh in this way. We fellows were one of the means. As Auxiliary Experts we were of great value and we were living publicity for our charges as well; if the girls liked the looks of us then some part of our haloes would reflect over the sludging beasts we tended. 'You'll not get out,' smiled Godman who, perhaps foolishly, I confided in. 'You're too big and sweet-looking. It's your sort they're wanting for the pantomime.' I wondered how straight Godman was, and how clever. His interest was in his pay.

'See yu on the march, p'raps,' was Haggard's parting. 'Don't be later than midnight at the Road Depot.' And feeling very much as Adam and Eve would have done had they been allowed back into the Garden of Eden, Manders and I went out into the early dawn, a couple of grimed, scarecrow figures with a look of expectant freedom in our eyes and cash to burn in our greasy pockets.

III

Manders was about the last person I would have chosen for companion that day, and I guess he must have felt the same about me. I was tired, drab, and preoccupied, and he was like a rag from which all colour and pattern have been washed away. We had scarcely spoken for a month; the factory had cut right across our business friendship, revealing how little we really had in common. We could have parted outside the gates and gone our separate ways, but I think his listlessness aroused my sympathy. I invited him along to my flat to enjoy the amazing luxuries of a hot bath and a clean change, hoping, perhaps, to put some life into him. He picked up some clothes from his lodgings on the way, and I was pleased when he began to doll himself up. In half an hour, apart from his stained, calloused hands which nothing short of a thorough course of manicuring could have remedied, he was his spruce, spotless self again, complete with a new, almost ecstatic scarf.

It was only habit. He scarcely spoke. What talking there was I did, and he seemed reluctant to leave the flat. Minute after minute he stood before the mirror adjusting that scarf while I noted how the reflection brought out the weariness of his face, lined in the shock of sorrow lurking in his eyes. It should have helped me to understand, but his inability to get going and what appeared to me as a quite unwarrantable suspicion of myself (I could see it in his every look and word), maddened me. I am glad I did not show it. As he revealed later, he too had his plans for release, but he had no strength of purpose. He was afraid to go forward. Those plans were only a continuation of the horror of which the mills had been the opening phase to him. Of all things he needed talk to drag him out of his repression, but I could not get him going. He was too suspicious.

It was something I said as we repassed the Flesh Mills on our way to the tube which first stirred him out of his silence. I expect I cursed them fluently, expressing something of his own feelings. And then we ran into old Hitchin, returning from the station with his morning papers and, because he was the first outsider I had seen for many days, I stopped to chat and accepted his invitation to share breakfast in his dingy little back parlour.

Everything about Hitchin must have helped Manders to recover himself in the quickest and best way open to him: anger. There was a surreptitious look in the old man's eyes, and he spoke and moved stealthily, glancing up at any unusual sound. He seemed very poor, but scraped together a passable meal over which he gave us his version of the first marching of the Guard which I have already told. He pressed us almost pitifully to stay and join him in dinner; Myers had left and he was lonely and afraid. His hatred of the Guard equalled Manders', but his traditional unimaginative mind could not rise to any hope of ever being free of it again. Beliefs were dead in him, too dead to give rise to new beliefs.

It was as Hitchin was clearing the table that Manders broke out. 'I'm not going back to it,' he said, his sudden voice high with anger. 'The hellish swine!' He was glaring at me across the dirty pots, a cup of tea half-way to his mouth. 'I'm not going to the depot tonight whatever you're doing. I'm going back to the comrades. D'you understand?' He paused to see the effect of this.

'I don't know that I blame you,' I answered, more to encourage him than because I had formed any real opinion. I had scarcely considered Haggard's view that he might bolt; I had certainly not expected the latter to be so outright about it. Manders, however, had reached that point when further suppression was impossible. He had to defy somebody. He had to shout, to make a brave show. He had to *tell* – all that was in him. If he could have cried it might have acted as well, but he was too taut to cry.

'You think we've been doing nothing, don't you? Well, I'll tell you. I've been getting news in there. I've been *giving* news. You thought I was in there for the money, didn't you?' Hitchin, some cups and saucers in his hand, stood to listen, his mouth slightly open. Manders made a jarring noise in his throat which might have been a pretence of laughter. 'I'll tell you,' he repeated. 'Tonight they're holding mass meetings all over Leeds, protest meetings, and then they're going to march on the Hunslet Flesh Factories. The police won't interfere, Pollen won't interfere; they're afraid, though the law's damn against us. We mustn't hold big meetings? We're *doing* it. All over the country it's happening. The people are rising and they're going through with it.'

Hitchin's head shook doubtfully.

'Through with it. Anything may happen. Anything. *You* don't care. You're thick in with those disgusting Experts.'

'I'm not,' I objected. 'My position's different, that's all.' He glared at me. He was no longer interested in my opinions, nor in changing them, nor even in how I might have changed them. But he took my words as an admission of partial support. Circumstances were so overwhelming to him that he could see only two sides, his hated Experts and revolution. If I were not wholly with the former then I was with him. Or perhaps he didn't care. He had found a way out of himself. Though I had him arrested forthwith he had to get away from the chaotic suppressions in his mind.

'What is there to do but fight and fight now while there's still hope?' How he talked! He was in the mood to stride up and down the room gesticulating, but he did not do that. He sat at the table with his hands clenched on the cloth and his eyes roving round. 'A month ago I thought if war came we'd just to win the forces over to our side and walk into power, but this life-making's altered everything. Everything goes to hell. Those devils! They're Flesh themselves; they almost eat it. Soon, *we're* going to live Death Guard; they'll be top-dog, a handful of blackguards with all the power of science in their hands. Unless we act now they'll be top for ever, machines piling up against us, the Flesh marching against us.'

He had set a limit for the fulfilment of his political faith after which democracy, socialism, communism, would be dead for ever. 'Just the few – overlords, sending their beasts and machines against humanity, a few hundred men ruling the entire world and the rest – Black Flesh.' He predicted compulsory sterilization of the proletariat because they would no longer be needed, and used Hitchin as an example of what he termed 'mental sterilization' – with Hitchin and his cups and saucers standing gazing at him openmouthed; he tore the famous Russian revolution to shreds. 'A silly little struggle between barbarians! Scarcely a struggle. A failure to govern, a pushing aside; fighting afterwards as a desperate afterthought.' This was the real machine age, the age of living machines. 'Just a crazy Tsar and a lot of medieval hangers-on. You can't do *that* again.' He wiped out the Latin revolutions as well. Ten years had changed everything. He had the quality of blaming someone or something bitterly for a fatal lack of foresight: the Marxist theory, Sovietism, his associates, himself? His gods were gone. At the same time he was clinging to their crumbling feet in a last frightened grovel of hope. Without that hope he felt he would have gone mad. He said as much. 'I'm not the sort of chap to be alone,

Gregory. In *there* I nearly went crazy. It made me feel I'd thrown my ideals into a pig-sty in mistake for the millennium.' He made that jarring noise again. It was obvious that he was afraid to face either his past or his future. He was sublimating his grief over Betty and his hate of those he held responsible for it, hiding in the belief that retribution was at hand.

'I did my job,' he said wearily, and leaving me to guess at the meaning of that rose to examine himself in Hitchin's shaving mirror. His fingers considered the back of his neck distastefully.

'Hell! I'm going to have a haircut,' he said inconsequently. 'I suppose it's daft bothering about appearances, but I want to feel clean and decent. Morale. And God knows what may happen to-night. Not that I care. I *want* to fight. I want to forget everything.'

He did not want to fight. He could not forget.

Watching him and Hitchin I had my first insight into the fate which was beginning to overtake people. Both, in their different ways, were cracking. They were haunted, haunted by the new, terrible powers soon to be loosed upon humanity. Their eyes held the same secretive, furtive quality. Any moment insupportable terror might come.

I thought of Haggard, coarse, uncreative, fearless, the fundamental creature for which the hour called, helping to blast out a future of which he had no conception. I was nearer to him. How near to him I seemed watching those two, drinking more tea Hitchin had brewed, and struggling to control their wavering, complicated minds.

Old Hitchin came with us to the shop door to watch us go and we turned to wave as we passed round the corner; and then, I suppose, he went back to his semi-basement and his niggardly trade, waiting in dread for the siren call which would herald the eleventh contingent. Manders, glancing nervously from side to side, was beginning to tell me about the self-made nightmare of his life in the Flesh Mills. 'I don't know why I'm telling *you*,' he kept reiterating. 'I just can't keep it to myself any longer.'

IV

Amongst the many histories of the Death Guard which will one day be written I suppose Manders will have his little niche of fame; or ill-fame, according to the angle from which the writer approaches his subject. Whatever ethical view one takes there can be small doubt that it was he who precipitated the revolutionary upsurge which flared that day we left the factories and, in few places successful but nowhere altogether suppressed, contributed so immensely to the chaos which supervened.

Insurrection was 'ripe', as the saying goes, the fear of war, the hatred of the munition cartelists had both reached a pitch where organized effort at a complete overthrow had become, I suspect, inevitable. Nevertheless, had it been delayed a very little longer, it could never have taken hold of the popular imagination in the way it actually did. It preceded the first European onslaught by a matter of hours only, yet those few hours meant the active participation of thousands who, had they experienced the aerial bombardment first, would have united with the Government in fighting a murderous enemy. A span of six hours or less committed them to revolution.

And so, perhaps, by one of those flukes of fate which are no less crucial because they are slightly ludicrous, we can lay on Manders' carefully groomed head (he had his haircut and a shampoo) the responsibility for untold suffering and death in the civil conflict.

I had never thought Manders strong enough to be a spy; his pose of being a renegade, conscience-stricken and with few excuses, fitted him too well. When I got it clear that this was his only reason for staying in the factory he went up in my opinion, and down, in the same illuminated moment. It was a complicated sensation which prevented my reaching any clear judgement of his actions.

He was apparently amazed at himself. He would halt half-way through a sentence as though questioning its truth. Had he done that? There was little in it but the usual trickery and risks inevitable to all espionage, but it was more than that to him. He took me back to the time when we used to argue together and frankly admitted that he had been very small fry in his 'movement'. His principles were always faintly in doubt among his rougher associates. Too idealistic. And his clothes militated against him. 'It wasn't fair to judge a fellow by his ties,' he expostulated. 'They were as bad as you and –' But he avoided mentioning Betty. '– some of the others,' he substituted.

After the Congo massacre, ideals or no ideals, he was made to see bluntly that his part was to stay in the factory and act as contact. They had no one else suitable. And because he valued their opinion or shared it – I am unsure which – he accomplished his spying with the most methodical thoroughness in quaking dread of discovery every minute of the time. He supplied his comrades outside with plans of the factory, described details of manufacture, listed everyone inside as certain opponents or likely supporters and, at the end, passed on the news of Betty Corrall's death the very same night, so providing the final spark for rebellion and the content of the slogans which massed thousands of hesitant workers to its call.

I had seen him do it without suspecting. There was an old rubbish dump beyond the wall where I saw him that night and he used to toss his messages, wrapped in old rags, on to this heap from which a neighbour retrieved them within the hour. Most of the messages were written in bed in the dark. Whether he felt any compunction at using such a personal tragedy as propaganda, or whether he did it blindly in the carrying out of his conception of duty he did not explain. I cannot think how he found the courage to write on paper what he had seen that afternoon. I imagine him as weeping, scarce knowing what he did.

He took no pride in his spying, though he made no excuses for it. Until that evening when he saw the great banner, 'Down with the Murderers of Betty Corrall', I am sure he had no conception of what he had really done, nor knew how his leaders had held back his fatal message to act as a detonator for the great explosion.

He had exhausted his anger and had the air of being acutely conscious of his unsatisfactory little self, a rather footling soul who against all his and others' expectations had carried out a difficult, hateful task to the very end, had debased and racked himself to carry it out. He had the air of having won some concealed argument within himself – and of being nervously doubtful of his victory.

'I don't know why I tell you all this,' he said. Bitterness flared up again momentarily.

I recollect his standing stock-still suddenly, emphasizing some point angrily, and how his hand gesticulated over the drab street, the early, hurrying workers, a slatternly woman who came wiping her hands to a sunken doorway to stare at us, and the high massive coping of Beldite's frowning up above the squat, ugly clutter of cottages and warehouses with the cold wrack of the dawn scattering beyond. Despite his worn face and fierce words he looked almost puppyish in his smart clothes. Hating, vilifying, there was about him a touch of modest apology to the more powerful and brutal things of life that *he* had scored over them.

He glanced at me and coloured slightly at his cheap, soap-box rhetoric. Manny Boy, who kindled the fires of revolution!

V

After a stroll round the city together and a little shopping, Manders left me to look up friends, and I spent the remainder of the morning in an hotel writing to my grandfather and answering Paddy's letters. They did not answer easily. I found myself thinking in a way I don't usually do, wishing all this blasted war business was done with, a pretty useless sort of wish, anyway, and that made me mad with myself. Some fellows when they are soldiering, if they haven't a girl of their own, will pick on any girl and write to her, making a big, sloppy pretence out of it. Perhaps it comforts them, but it is no comfort to me. I dashed off a finish and gave her my address which, on Haggard's instructions, was 'Auxiliary Road Expert (ARE for short), Beldite, 27th Contingent, c/o Road Depot 3, Leeds.' Letters so addressed would be forwarded. Then I had lunch, the choicest lunch I could order, glanced over some papers and felt thoroughly at a dead end. Though I had satisfied myself that no long-distance aeros were flying and the trains were no use whatever I was still playing with the idea of getting to Brighton somehow for the day. Little more than an hour's flight in normal times, it was now quite impossible.

There were plenty of acquaintances I could have visited, but I knew they'd talk Flesh and Death Guard and little else, and this was my one 'day off'. I ended up at the Heavenly, that gorgeous new entertainment hall which was destroyed the same night, and went into one of the sterios. They were successful in taking my mind off myself until the newsreel came on and then I had to listen to a patriotic speech by the Prime Minister, inspect the South Coast Air Fleet, and good God! see the 4th Contingent marching out from our Darnley works through a huge crowd of roaringly enthusiastic spectators. I do not know from what popular demonstration this particular crowd had been lifted, but it was a very clever piece of photographic faking.

'Vessant's Saviours Marching to Save You,' ran one caption, and another, in the cheap rhyme which had such a popular appeal, 'Hear them Cheer! Victory's near!'

It was received by a smatter of hand-clapping followed by groans from some of the cheaper seats, and for a couple of minutes all sense of amusement and relaxation was gone, and the atmosphere of the vast hall was tense. Then Clouding, the American producer, was smiling and bowing on the sterio plates and announcing, 'the most glorious, heart-breaking, love-soaked drama of all time.'

At five Manders and I re-met over tea according to arrangement. There was excitement in the streets; it was known that strikes, uncertain in extent, threatening in attitude, were to commence that night. Manders seemed worried, distressingly alone, and anxious that I should stay with him as long as possible. 'Chuck this idea of deserting,' I urged, not mincing words. 'You know you're dead scared.' 'I know I am,' he answered flatly. 'Can't get myself going. I feel a bit alone; they're nearly all strangers to me here.'

So because he seemed to need someone to look after him, and maybe with a hope of getting him to the depot in the end, I threw in my lot with his for the remainder of the evening without expecting that anything very particular was going to happen. He had always been something of a scaremonger. And if there was to be any excitement, well, that would suit me better than hanging around. In that way, led diffidently by Manders, I came upon the fringe of the revolution and, at neither his wish nor mine, was caught up into it.

In a shabby, first-floor room in a once good-class residential district I was introduced to Ben Howroyd under the unexpected alias of 'Comrade Gregory'. The room was very big and ill-lit and had a bed in it, a smudgy gilt overmantel, and peeling paper, and on the landing, between two broad, carpetless flights of stairs, was a 'kitchenette', as I understood it was called, where a silent, thin woman stirred a pan and produced endless chipped cups of over-brewed coffee for an interminable, heavy-footed stream of callers.

Ben Howroyd was a big-fisted railman, unemployed, as silent as his thin wife, who spent much time listening wordlessly to information brought to him by the visitors and making some unknown use of it upstairs where a typewriter clattered at intervals. Farther above we could hear squeaky voices now and again and once a baby cried and ceased with drastic suddenness. Apparently there were children in the house being kept out of the way.

Most of the evening our room was crowded, and it was obvious from the noise that other rooms were in the same state of conges-tion. Our crowd's individual composition was in constant flux, people coming, drinking their coffee, and leaving, but its general complexion remained the same, harassed and poverty-stricken, grim-faced and brooding. No one smiled apart from a chubby-faced, middle-aged tyke in ill-fitting blue serge, and his permanent grin seemed more a defence against harsh circumstances than a reflec-tion of any real brightness in him. He told me he had been a rat-catcher in Batley in his younger days and had given exhibitions of killing them with his teeth, hands fastened behind his back, but since vermin had been so largely exterminated he had taken to doing odd jobs in carpentering and to selling from a barrow any-thing he could buy cheaply. And there was a young, wizened-looking girl-woman who perched on the end of a painted deal sideboard swinging thin legs in twisted, laddered stockings, and smoking whenever she could borrow a cigarette. In the absence of a cigarette she bit at her nails. She was much respected by the callers and had eczema on her arms due, no doubt, to underfeeding.

Seemingly I won her respect, for she smiled at me whenever our eyes met, an arch but somewhat sidelong smile owing to a gap in her artificial teeth of which she was conscious. These two were with us the whole time.

The room was stuffy with smoke, coffee fumes, and perspiration. I sat until I was cramped on a pile of assorted papers in a corner. Then I stood. The girl-woman moved up to make a space, but I said I was stiff. Manders pointed people out. A bright young girl plied me with coffee. The rat-catcher told me about the increase of illegitimate children in Batley, how cabbages were almost unprocurable, and how he had told all the councillors about a very smelly drain, but couldn't get it altered. No one talked politics.

It was impossible to credit that these folk were in the process of executing a plan to overthrow the Constitution, though I gathered that their part was primarily to set the example in Leeds for other centres to follow. I felt that poverty must have made them foolishly romantic, that they took a bitter glory in their poverty, finding the only pride and strength left to them in flaunting it rebelliously. Possibly beautiful things to them were redolent of selfishness and tyranny. But, as the evening wore on, my opinion began to fluctuate. Not all were poor, not all downtrodden, and many of the men were much more than rough worker types. Nevertheless, they all accepted the leadership of Howroyd. Manders in his finery excited no scorn, nor did they seem to realize how out of place I felt. Though many of them used factory dialect and drank their coffee with a no doubt courteous show of enjoyment, their eyes brooded and their thoughts seemed far away. Except when there was some task to carry out and then they became amazingly alert and competent.

A slim, academic youth, immaturely bearded, slouched in wearing a vivid red scarf, and was pointed out to me as Stamper, the notorious firebrand and poet. A study of industrial conditions had drawn him north during the early war scare, and he had chosen to stay and assist in the organization. A thick-featured, massive-shouldered, almost dwarfish man was Hogbin who had been permanently deprived of his seat in Parliament and, I gathered, should have been in gaol at that moment, but wasn't. He wore a cloth cap after the fashion of the early century, Lenin and Keir Hardie, and I had thought him a typical worker, not one of the intellectuals.

He was an international figure and his entry caused a muttered interest. The wizened girl-woman leaned forward and shouted, 'Hillo, Hoggy. How yer blowin'?' and he answered. 'Fine, Charlotte,' and stretched out a hand like a boat to grip hers.

'Gotter cig?' said Charlotte.

Hogbin's appearance ended the small talk and there was a sudden run of controversy, centring round Mundaine. I perceived that at least in some circles Hogbin was the popular heir to the Irishman's waning star; the width and vision of that final broadcast had been lost on many cruder minds. The rat-catcher sidled his head towards me confidentially. Jerking a thumb as if at a thing that passed, he said, 'Mundaine didn' lead hadn' got th'reet *line* me an' Charlotte was speakin' on t' same platfoorm las' Feb an' 'e woz wobblin' an' 'is speeches theze las' weekertwo! Gum!' Hogbin shook hands with a number of us and was gone in a couple of minutes after spreading a big smile round the room. The atmosphere was immensely encouraged by his brief visit.

Quickly after that Ben Howroyd entered and spoke.

'Zero,' he announced expressively. 'You've orl got yer jobs? Do 'em.' A murmur passed round. Probably no more cryptic order from a commander-in-chief of either legitimate or illegitimate forces had ever been heard. But these rebels, it came to me, had developed through years of underground working a method of conveying information to each other by veiled hints, odd words, gestures which could easily pass unnoticed. Even the very latest comers seemed to know everything necessary, but not a vestige of their plans had been suggested to me. Though, on Manders' guarantee, I was accepted as one of them I felt it would have been an indelicacy to ask and might have aroused suspicion.

Manders sat with me most of the evening with occasional visits upstairs to the typewriter room or to secure coffee, but had little to say. He was introspective, tired, almost less at home amongst his own people than I was.

'When the bells ring just stand yer ground,' said Howroyd. I did not understand that and had no time to ask. He was near the door as I passed out and unexpectedly clapped his thick hand on my shoulder.

'You're in wi' uz, lad,' he said.

I do not know whether he intended it as encouragement or a question, but I smiled reassuringly. Unless I made a dash for it, leaving Manders to face the inevitable accusations, it seemed I was to be in wi' 'em for quite a while yet.

Outside the house we formed a brief cluster stretching across the road. A small group was busy on the pavement and then that crude, red banner which later led the march on Hunslet was unfurled on its twin poles. I saw Manders staring at it, I saw him blench. His hands and head moved vaguely as if he would have stopped this blatant utilization of a pitiful death.

'DOWN WITH THE MURDERERS OF BETTY CORRALL.'

He turned in Howroyd's direction and, I think, tried to say something. Howroyd patted him on the back.

We scattered into twos and threes. The banner was furled and disappeared. I found myself alone with Manders and Charlotte hurrying down an alley-way and Manders was very white and Charlotte archly vivacious. But shrewd.

'You'd like us better if you knew us. We're chummy. You're a bit bourgeois, aren't you?' No apologetics about her!

It was my chance to get away, but Manders' dejection held me. As he practically admitted, he was not really one of these comrades; but then none of them was of each other. This workers' movement was not a whole, it was a fluctuation, coalescing, dissipating, gone – then suddenly roaring and powerful again like a tide from the ocean bottom called into being by magnetic voices. It was not an entity, but a vision jealous of its own eyes, the miasmic birth of something. Little and envious and inchoate, it had existed around me all my life, a life pulse, and, intent on my clearer pursuits, I had never sensed it. Tonight the pulse was high.

I glanced at Manders, wondering what was passing behind his strained eyes.

'Gotter cig?' asked Charlotte, smirking sidelong.

WHEN THE BELLS RANG

War fever, a restless urge to be as near as possible to the sources of information, had filled the central streets of the city early in the evening. Wild rumour was afoot. It was said that Continental aircraft were about to strike, that the peacemongers and socialists were in rebellion, that demonstrations and meetings were to be held in defiance of all authority. The story of Betty Corrall, released simultaneously from a dozen strategic points, passed on from mouth to mouth, was on every lip.

There was tension in the air, a craving to have the strain of blind waiting assuaged by amusement or excitement, however slight, which drove people from their homes to wander aimlessly about the streets from one passing conversation to another, carried them into theatres and out again as the idle foolishness or irrelevant drama palled, drew them, curious and sympathetic, to hear what the Internationalists had to say. Business folk on their way homewards had their attention irresistibly arrested by a sense of impending crisis and, according to their nature, began to plan to leave the city or, more fascinated than afraid, snatched hurried teas in the crowded restaurants and stayed. Workmen, having downed tools for none knew how long, came crowding from the buses and subways to add to the already congested streets.

Long before the first meeting was due to start, City Square was a solid mass of patient watchers except where the police were keeping a narrow, precarious route open for the more important traffic. There was no effort to move this mass, every precaution taken not to annoy it; it extended unbroken along all the main thoroughfares where the news had spread that the speeches in the square were to be relayed from concealed loudspeakers. Incoming traffic sought new and narrower ways along the by-streets.

The vast, pregnant crowd was heralded as the first sign of victory. It was against the law to congregate in large numbers, it was against the law to hold outdoor public meetings, but no effort was being made to enforce these laws. The authorities knew their limitations, the Government was yielding, Erasmus Pollen, the sentimentalist, the weakest Home Secretary in fifty years, was leading the way back to true democracy, to the overthrow of Beldite's and all munition-lords!

Exactly how we three became part of an organized procession I cannot say. One moment we were a separate group in a broad stream of people flowing citywards and the next, as if by prearranged signal, that stream was forming itself into fours, drawing in the ignorant with it, sprouting standards and banners, and swinging into marching step to the stirring cadences of some traditional revolutionary song. Suddenly, music was leading our singing, crude music of accordions, ochorinas and mouth-organs. We passed a side road and there was the head of a second procession led by a ten-foot banner, 'Death to the Death Guard! To Hell with the Flesh Guard Killers!' They roared at us in greeting and we roared back. City Square came to us as a single, crashing note of spontaneous welcome and, as if by magic, they made way for us where, it had seemed, there was no inch of space to spare. We gathered round the pedestal of the Black Prince, and the Black Prince was draped in flaming red, and from his upraised sword fluttered a long scarlet pennant, 'Workers Unite'.

Manders was still at my side. His face was cold white, his eyes shining, but all depression was gone. He glanced towards me proudly.

'Think of it. Every city in the country. Yes, every city. Like this, tonight!' From near Whitehall Road a voice began shouting and the crowd took it up, screaming it violently, passionately. 'Down with the murderers of Betty Corrall! Down with the Flesh Guard Killers!'

'You gave them that,' I whispered.

His face was stiff with understanding. Sorrow or no sorrow, it was irresistible. He smiled nervously, apologetically, and his hand sought his scarf, leaving a black smear on his collar.

A shrill, heroic voice jetted above the turmoil screaming, 'Up with the old flag! Go an' put yer khaki on, yer cowards!' Shouting arose, there was an eddying movement in the crush, cries of trampled people, a frantic yell. Then someone high on the statue was bawling, 'To hell with the Bloody Beldite brutes!' The crowd surged round as to a new command and took up the cry. I saw a young girl of about sixteen, a pretty child with flying auburn hair and tears streaming down her cheeks. 'Bloody Beldite *brutes!*' she was screaming. 'Bloody Beldite *brutes!*'

II

Though it must have been well over an hour later it seemed only a short while before the processions were reforming. There had been much half-heard speech-making from the plinth of the statue, Hogbin, and Charlotte, who was no longer conscious of her teeth, and others I did not know, and intermittent singing. The brilliant lighting of the square symbolized the spirit of that fiery concourse. The flashing signs on the high, glimmering façades of the buildings were as coloured sparks flung upwards from our enthusiasm until, above all, separated by a width of darkness, shining in the sky itself, the eye was caught by the neon writing snaking mockingly across the dimly outlined roof of the Light Absorbent Brick Corporation. 'BELDITE FERTILIZER FLOODS YOUR GARDENS WITH FLOWERS.' It was like the sneer of superior beings safe from our threatening rabble in the high heavens.

For some twenty minutes it dominated our ardour then tiny figures were seen moving on the lofty parapet, there was a distant clatter of glass and the lights were gone. Some intrepid spirits had removed the glaring insult. Shouting followed from that side of the square, there was a moblike rush defeated by the backwash of an unseen struggle. Minutes later more little figures were visible on the roof, police . . . They disappeared and we turned again to the speech-making.

Rain began to fall, a sharp, heavy shower which left the ground wet and glistening. Then a movement of banners near the entrance to Boar Lane proclaimed the end of the demonstration, and a tall, cadaverous man was bawling encouragement to the crowd with exaggerated rhetorical flourishes and quotations from back in the nineteenth century and earlier.

'I suppose you'll be going now,' said Manders. 'Thanks for staying. It's – been a help, somehow.'

'I'm not going, yet,' I answered. 'I never imagined this could happen in England in these days; I'm going to see it through to the end or see it begin, whichever it may be.' Oddly enough, though there was danger in the air, I had been wishing Paddy with me: she would have revelled in the crowd, and I felt sure that the danger would have added spice.

'You're beginning to believe in it?' eagerly. 'You're starting to understand what's kept us people slogging away underneath, the faith of it, the bigness –?' I never heard the end of that question nor tried to answer it. We were being swept forward. I do not think I could have answered it. Belief? In what? In that huge, passionate crowd, its purpose, its courage, its inevitable victory? It fascinated, it seemed unbeatable. Crude and violent, it was but the spuming, thundering wave thrown up by the deep, ever-returning tide of humanity. But belief?

I saw Howroyd a couple of yards away and he had his hand raised as if commanding silence. Above the roar of the multitude a bell began to sound, an unmelodious church bell tolling rapidly.

Dang, dang, dang, dang, it clattered. A second, clearer bell followed, a third, and a fourth, more remote. I looked at Manders inquiringly, saw Howroyd shoving his way through the press, calling as he went. Every face in sight was lifted, listening.

'That's the signal to clear the streets when the contingents are marched out. They have to come through the city. Sirens and maroons if it's an air-raid, bells alone, the contingents. That – it must be for the Eleventh Hunslet.'

'But it's only nine,' I objected. 'Unless . . .'

'They're sending them out two hours earlier,' said a man next to me. 'That's what it is. The swine, oh, the swine! That's why they've left us in peace here. Government giving in be damned! Have our shout and let off steam and then they think we'll scatter at them blasted bells!' He raised a useless, menacing fist as a string of mounted police moved into the crowd. Then a distant voice rose shouting, a voice which quelled the uproar commandingly. 'Never mind yon bells. Hunslet. To Hunslet!' it cried and the banners moved forward like red, bellying sails, passing into the narrow duct of Boar Lane.

'Down with the Beldite murderers! Down with the Flesh Guard Killers!'

'You'd better go,' shouted Manders in my ear. 'There'll be trouble. There's bound to be trouble.' A rush of young strikers with a banner separated us; I was hustled along into the living current of marchers. I might have fought my way to the side, but there was no side: from wall to wall everyone was falling into line and step. Where the road widened the crowd was so dense that procession and followers, if there were any real difference, could only be distinguished by the more rhythmic movement of the marchers. A woman shrilled as she was crushed against a shop front. I saw an old, white-haired waving man crumple and disappear as into a flood and there were shouts of, 'Keep back! Keep back!' A huge, plate-glass window starred and shattered amidst cries.

'Shout, you bugger!' yelled a man, jerking his elbow into my ribs, and laughing in crazy, uncontrolled excitement, and I shouted and sang with the rest.

As we rounded the corner some kind of fight was in progress along Vicar Lane. Mounties were threshing with their truncheons, stones were flying. There was a big navvy in an open space striking right and left with a yard-long sliver of sheet glass gripped in his electric-drill gloves.

We swung past and shouted our greeting to the open sky of the bridge and south Leeds.

'To hell with the Beldite murderers!' I roared, and heard Manders swearing and marvelling close behind me. In a little while we were in the Hunslet Road between blank-eyed, silent shops. Ever and again one would crash as some enthusiast passed. Ever and again the flow would clot into cheering groups. An old, bent flower-seller was standing precariously on the edge of the pavement. Her hand dipped shakingly into her basket and withdrawing a bunch of roses she threw it at me. Her eyes were laughing in sheer joy and her toothless gums mouthing praise of us. I thought I distinguished two words. 'My boys! My boys!' her lips repeated.

Showers soaked us at intervals, leaving behind a chill, inter-mittent wind. From side roads sporadic raids were made on our outskirts by police, but only to be met and mobbed by over-whelming numbers of our supporters. Besides encouragement, warnings were shouted at us from open windows, warnings that the Guard was coming, that the way must be kept open for the Guard to march through. A police official on a low roof har-angued us through a megaphone. All roads must be kept open for the Guard to march through. His raucous voice dwindled behind.

Many such efforts, forcible and appealing, must have been made to turn us from our determined route, but even those who would have obeyed had little chance, hemmed in as we were. There was a rumour of tear-gas in use. A silent, low-flying aero commanded us to dissipate immediately.

To the steady tolling of church bells and the rhythm of our own hoarse singing we marched on through the narrowing road until racing messengers appeared round the a corner and word passed down the lines that the Eleventh Hunslet was close ahead.

III

A quiver seemed to run down our column as, rank after rank, we halted. The crowd on the edges of the road surged ahead, realized that we had stopped and sagged back in front of us. Round the bend a disorderly mob appeared shouting and waving.

Up to that moment I had stayed in the procession for a medley of reasons. Genuine interest and expectation, a dislike of being thought a runaway even by men I had only met half an hour before, unexpected conscience that Manders was heading for trouble and I ought to look after him, mingling with a hope that after he had ended his rebellious fling he would accompany me to the Road Depot. Moreover, after the straining monotony of the factory, this marching and shouting and singing was a fine lark to me: it was like getting drunk in a new way. Haggard had told me to get some hell into me and this was the novel method which had presented itself. In Yorkshire dialect I was as bright and active as a 'scoparil'.

Then we were standing in the cold drizzle, shivering, and the cheering and singing were over. The shouts of those in front came solitary, threatening in the silence; grim faces surrounded me, craning forward awaiting their orders. No one looked back. It came to me, who had known it all along, but had avoided the thought, that this was a life and death game, that the glimpsed fighting had been real, not something seen on the sterios. These men were not going to break and run, they were going through to Hunslet to occupy and wreck the Flesh Factories.

In every city in the country . . .

'Marching eight abreast! Road blocked!' The news spread.

That wasn't the usual formation. It was dangerous. Two abreast was the limit. Someone was heard calling for Manders, and we two found ourselves the centre of a dour group of leaders, authorities on this imbroglio.

'Never more than two.' I settled the question with brief, technical reasons, Manders supporting. 'It's one of two things. Either they're trying to get them through the city as quickly as possible or else it's their counterstroke to stop us.' I said 'us'. 'There's nothing for it but to go back.'

'Back!' barked Howroyd with a look which branded me as 'sick-livered'.

'Or round,' I substituted.

'There's plenty others going *round*,' Howroyd responded. 'Our job's on this road. And there ain't any *back*.' He turned into brief consultation with his fellows.

'It isn't as if it *were* the Eleventh Hunslet,' considered a calm, cultivated voice, sending a new thrill down the ranks. 'We might wait for them to pass. They tell me it's the 27th Road Column starting for the east coast. Thousands of them. They've been herded in the mines. If we stand firm they'll stop them; they'll have to stop them.'

'They'll have to turn 'em down the side streets, eh?'

I heard Manders. 'They can't stop them. It's madness.'

And Howroyd: 'Nah, lad! You've done your bit an' you done it well. This is oor bit. Keep aht of it.'

The little cluster of anxious consultants in the centre of the expectant crowd broke up. Shouts arose. There was a hurried scattering to the rear. Someone bolting past me with white face sent me reeling and, when I recovered my balance, they were already forming themselves into a solid press across the road. One man linked his arm round the next until they extended from wall to wall. Howroyd was shouting encouragement to others at the back. A second row formed, and a third. Within two minutes the thoroughfare was a packed block of humanity extending twenty or thirty yards back, spreading steadily into the gloom.

'Let the quitters get out,' cried Howroyd. 'We don't want no weak links in *this* chain.' People were struggling and fighting close by me for egress to the rear, but that was more than my pride would allow me to do. With my arm round the waist of a shivering-faced boy on one side and a squat, shirt-sleeved factory-hand on the other, I became one of that amazing phalanx. Manders was not with me. He had been with Howroyd and the other leaders when I last saw him.

There came a clatter of hoofs, and troopers engaged in clearing the way galloped into view round the bend, drawing to a halt a couple of yards from our advance line.

'Now, you men, you can't stand there,' called their captain. 'Get right back, right away. Road column of the Guard close behind. No one is allowed on this road until it has passed.'

In the silence which followed Howroyd's voice rang out with hoarse clearness.

'This is our road, mate, not theirs. There's some on uz have dug it up an' put it dahn a hundred times an' it's uz 'as paid for it. Yer can take yer Guard another way. We're staying 'ere.'

The captain's horse pawed at the ground impatiently; others beyond, highly strung and, no doubt, previously excited by sight or scent of the beasts they heralded, began to prance and caracole nervously. The captain was a model of calmness. His voice was strong and commanding, but almost soothing in its intonation. He leaned forward with a suggestion of sympathetic confidence.

'You don't understand, boys. This Guard doesn't halt when it's told; it doesn't about turn or break ranks or do any of the disciplined things we soldiers do. Once it has started it just keeps going, through anything and over anything, like – like an army of sleepwalkers until it begins to get hungry and wakes up. And then it's a big business feeding it and quietening it down again. We can't do that in the middle of Leeds. It's coming along a quarter of a mile behind us eight deep so that we can get it through the city as quickly as possible, and then you boys can go on fighting the police if you want to do. But it won't stop for you nor me nor thousands like us.'

An NCO interrupted loudly.

'The men can't keep their mounts quiet much longer, sir.'

'Right,' over his shoulder, and to Howroyd, 'You may be right or wrong in what you're saying. I'm not judging. My work is to warn people of what is coming, and if you value the lives of the crowd behind you – and your own – you'll move – like blazes. Every man-jack of you.'

'We're not moving.'

'See those horses? Behind. They're going mad. You've got my men pinned in between your folk and the Guard. In another two minutes the horses'll go mad with fear. If *you're* not afraid of the Guard, *they* are. Those men are only doing their duty and you're putting them in a position where they haven't a chance in a million. Yes, and me too.'

From the black shadow of the turning where a lamp had been shattered came the metallic clatter of steel on stone and a deep grumble like giant runners gulping for breath. Something sparked on the rough wall of a house. Fifty yards ahead, dull white in the reflected glare of the nearer lamps, the first rank of the Guard strode into view. Silver seemed to splash from their hoofs as they shuffled through the shallow puddles of rain. The ranks behind were black in the shadow of their leaders.

Perhaps it had been in the captain's mind to do what was no doubt his duty, to order his men to charge into the crowd. There was no need of that command. A great bay stallion, the nearest to the approaching column, reared frantically on its hind legs, whinnying in mad terror. It swung round, throwing its rider into the centre of the road, and with head strained forward tore down upon us.

In cavalry shows there is a favourite exhibition of jumping over the heads of standing men and, maybe, in that horse's distraught mind the memory of such a feat came uppermost. Six feet from the crowd it rose in a splendid jump, clearing the heads of the first eight or nine rows. It came down well to the right of me, its bared teeth and gasping nostrils white with foam, its eyes blind and upturned in fear. Even as it fell, smashing down a dozen screaming people, I saw its rider half rise from the wetly glistening road. He, too, like the advancing Guard and the ground on which he knelt, was patterned jaspé in black shadow and silvery white. His hands lifted and I heard the tiny shrill of his cry pierce the pandemonium around me as the vanguard of the beasts went over him.

I felt the boy I was gripping fall limp in my arm. Two of the other troop horses had followed the bay stallion and were floundering in front of the crowd; another, reared to full height, was battering at the faces of the leaders with its hoofs, and the remainder were wheeling round in the narrowing oblong of road, their riders struggling to spur or back them towards our phalanx. A second, and the Guard was upon us.

Over the heads of the intervening crush I saw their dull, vacant ganglia staring above and beyond the wild turmoil, oblivious of it, all appetite and ferocity asleep in them. Their helmets were on a level with the mounted troopers' shoulders and their breath, condensing in the damp atmosphere, formed a white steam over their heads. Across their chests ran a steel band, fastened in some way I had never seen, so that they came forward as one, joined and inseparable.

'Stand firm. Block up behind.' Howroyd's voice rose above the tumult. He must have been pressed close to the steel and flesh in front of him.

For seconds that row of blank masks faced us unmoving. I could see the helmets of the following ranks pressing upon them, the linked quadrifanes clashed and rang. Then it was as though we were being squeezed between two closing valves. I saw a woman upright in the crowd, crushed to death. I could hear the crack of broken bones. People were jumping through the glass of nearby windows. The narrow causeways at the sides of the contingents were the only exits, but on to these the cavalry had drawn their rearing horses. A raving, clutching figure was projected upwards and came towards me clawing over cringing heads, kicking and striking. An elderly woman who had been watching from an upper window flung open a door so that some might enter. Her grey, tousled hair disappeared and she was trampled underfoot by those who sought safety in her home . . .

As if some barrier had melted before them the ranked helmets moved forward, man and horse, soldier and revolutionary crushed beneath. I tried to drag away the unconscious boy at my feet, realized that I was as doomed as he, and was flung away from him. The road as far as I could see was pushing or being borne backwards. With the Flesh less than a yard from me and only a tumbled heap of writhing humanity between I was thrown head foremost into a tiny snicket congested with fighting people. The heavy body smell of the units, blend of greasy sweat and oozing chemical from their injections, was in my nostrils; the heat of their breath was still on my face.

I recollect shouting to my companions in the alley-way that they were safe and must make way for others, then that I was clambering over a low wall in the company of a filthy, ragged man who gasped and choked, but had alive, over-bright eyes. I tripped over some obstacle and fell sprawling, and in a second his hands were in my pockets robbing me. I struck up and backwards feebly.

He was gone, none the better off, and heavy boots were trampling over me.

From the main road a clattering rumble as of iron-shod traffic blended with the roar of hundreds in flight. Somewhere in that hideous thoroughfare, beneath the pounding hoofs of the Royal Death Guard were Howroyd and the rat-catcher and many another face I had grown to know that day. And Manders, who had dressed for the revolution and died for it.

IV

Some five minutes later I had reached a spot out of hearing of the main road, an open patch of ground with hoardings at one side and littered with the less easily destructible rubbish of the mean neighbourhood around, old iron and bottles, a wire mattress, a broken chimney-pot ... Aching and dazed I sat down on one of the end stays of the hoarding and it was whilst I was sitting there regaining my breath that I heard the first bomb explosion.

The damp air was vaguely murmurous with the multitudinous sounds of a great city, and that remote concussion came to me as though it were a part of that whispering circumfusion, as if faint echoes had aggregated at some deep, distant point. The tiniest mutter of sound. I did not realize that I had heard it until it was repeated thrice in rapid succession. There was a pause and then it came again. Boh! Boh! And a scarcely perceptible shudder vibrated in the atmosphere. There followed a far-away tattoo as of minute drums beaten swiftly or as if someone were dropping pebbles into water. Plop, plop, plop.

I had never heard that sound before, but I knew it. Guns. I rose to my feet, straining my eyes at the lightless sky and, as I did so, again the concussion of the bombs sounded, but nearer, noticeably nearer. Far away on the heavens, ten or fifteen miles away to the south-east – I could not judge – splashes of misty light appeared, hurrying hither and thither.

Suddenly I hated being alone on that dark patch of discarded ground. It was like being dead. I began trotting down the strangely silent road, glad of the bright lamps, the lighted windows and, soon, the groups of nervous citizens gathering in the streets to gaze skywards. I slowed to a quick walk and inquired the shortest way to the city of a man at a doorway. 'I don't want to go near the main road,' I told him without explanation. I hurried on, struggling with his complicated directions and then, incontinently, the street lights were gone and, close at hand, a factory siren burst into raucous warning.

Other and more distant sirens opened their throats until the whole city and its environs were in chorus. Laggardly, a mile or more north, maroons began to add their shattering accompaniment. Lights died from the windows and the streets began to fill with dim figures. I noticed they were mostly women and children. The men of that district were in the march on Hunslet. I passed dark houses with open doors from which anxiously shouting voices and hurrying footsteps sounded. Candles glimmered and were hidden. Then, round a corner, a wide spread of light on the road ahead dazzled me for a moment. It came from a long, low building, a school or church house which was brilliantly lit from end to end. Someone was calling that the lights must be covered. There were no blinds it seemed. I came level with it and had a glimpse of the interior through open double doors. Men in some kind of half-uniform, some ambulance corps, were frantically busy within, running backwards and forwards, folding and packing bags and kits on the floor. Through a window I saw a table piled with gas respirators, of out-of-date pattern I was sure, and a second table of what I took to be decontaminating gear and oxygen revivers. Rubber-clothed figures entered from an inner room like divers in air. Some of the vesicant-proof suits did not fit and the wearers moved uncomfortably and clumsily.

The siren chorus diminished and gasped and sighed into silence and, as the last trailing whistle of its warning died, the air shook with a distant thunder of explosion.

The blackened streets were alive with people. As I rounded a bend, their movements and voices became a mere fractional part of a steady roar and once again I came in sight of the Hunslet Road. It was broader at this point than farther out. I had a glimpse only of a thrusting, howling mob lining the pavements whilst between towered the helmeted Guard, then I was hurrying down a back street having realized my location. Very shortly I was at the entrance to the subway beneath the Aire. I joined the steady stream of frightened but on the whole controlled citizens who were seeking refuge in the raid shelters below the river.

It was not my intention to remain with them: my one thought

was to reach the Road Depot as speedily as possible. There, irrationally enough, I felt I should be safe. The Experts, uncivilized but competent, would give me new confidence. Haggard would be there – I thought of him as the only friend I had left – cursing and spawning and taking death and destruction like he took his raw whisky, staring at it distastefully, gulping it down, and then forgetting it. My whole mind was rebounding. The people of that city had become sordid and pitiful to me, crowding, revolutionary creatures clinging in their domesticated fashion to mild, unachievable ideals, ready to die herd-like because they had not the strong, selfish will to live. I wanted the rude health of forgetfulness, of callousness, to revive me. I came up at the far side of the water struggling against a crowd which stared at me amazed that I should be making for the open and elbowed my way into the black cavern which was Boar Lane, detesting their mean lust for safety, despising it, as though I, in my flight to a life I had hated twenty hours ago, were not a greater slave to self-preservation than they.

Between the shadowy roofs high above, the narrow sky was white with wheeling searchlights. I became wedged in the crush unable to do more than free myself from the spate of safety-seekers. There I stood, pressed painfully against a wall, my face towards the junction of four roads across which the Guard was passing.

It marched through an avenue of perhaps the most violent hatred the world has ever seen. The packed multitude was in frenzy with loathing and wild, mirthless laughter, careless of the death which swept upon them from the skies in mad desire to express their passion. From open windows above the shops dusky shapes leaned far out pelting Vessant's Saviours with every missile they could find. From one window, endangering the entire city, a spotlight shone throwing a little circle of light through which the heads of the Guard came and passed. The masks of the beasts were smeared and bespattered with mud and refuse. One was streaked yellow where an egg had smashed on it. Many were slashed and bruised, some almost unrecognizable, and their bloodless flesh revealed these scars vividly as if they had been painted on them. And there was one with a broken bottle embedded deep in its mask like a glistening snout. It thudded by, oblivious of its grotesque adornment. Others had great splinters of glass in them.

A brick hurtled past my head and thudded on the cheek of one brute. It recoiled and marched on heedlessly.

'Flesh Guard!' they screamed. 'Royal *Flesh* Guard!'

'*They* can't feel. Smash the bloody Experts! Smash the bloody Experts!' The cry was taken up, a slogan of transferred hate. It died. There were no Experts. Clattering above all other sound, a small, toad-like tank between two contingents hurried by. Every missile was concentrated on it and a ribald shout went up. There was a chain of such tanks. 'Vessant keeps his skunks safe,' jeered someone.

Heavy gunfire resounded from the south. Like fingers pointing the searchlights swung together to an apex. The gunfire increased and there was a strange, spitting rattle of some unknown death-dealing weapon. The bitter, chatterbox sound of machine-guns rattled far up in the air, then, as though the invading airplanes had at last discovered their objective, bomb after bomb crashed terrify-ingly beyond the river.

A pause and then, a mile or more nearer, a succession of heavy roars, another pause and, again, as if the city split asunder. A gash of vivid flame lit up the nearer sky, windows rattled and came sparkling down in the illumination of the spotlight. Fear came alive in the crowd and, like a single living thing, it surged helplessly in its narrow prison. The light flashed out and, dominating all other sounds, a leading voice in the dwindling *motif* of the rumbling echoes, the metallic roar of a low-flying machine rushed upon us.

It passed, twenty yards over the heads of the marching Guard, lower than the tops of the buildings and flying in line with the road, a mere narrow streak of grey travelling at hundreds of miles an hour, deafening in its passage, the first bomb-plugger that ever descended to its carnage. As it passed, a black shape dropped from it at the very junction of the roads cutting one of the marchers to the ground. It lay, a second, two seconds, with the Guard marching unseeingly over it whilst thousands of terrified human beings fought with each other insanely. Then with a crash, deadening in its power, a sheet of flame starred outwards, scorching and blinding, and tossing brutes and humans like scraps of paper, tearing them to pieces in mid-air. A mass of bleeding flesh struck me on the side of my face. A second and a third explosion up Briggate seemed part of the first.

It was gone. Pinned between a tumble of fallen masonry and an uprooted lamp-standard, a woman's clothes were burning on her living body and by the fitful light of this screaming human torch we could see the following ranks of the beast battalions blundering over the ravaged road surface oblivious of the scorched, ripped forms of their fallen fellows, senseless of the death and wreckage around. Ahead of them, the high, once graceful pile of the Heavenly was glimmering into view as fire broke out in its ruined towers. Northwards, the bomb-plugger was still spreading destruction along the line of route. The whole city was trembling to the vibration of ceaseless gunfire.

I reached the Road Depot near one o'clock. The raid was over and it was brightly lit and jolly, a haven after the riot and tumult of the outer world. Here there was a grip on events, a sense of meaning and design.

I produced my papers and was checked in and dished out with road kit and told I could rest for an hour. A bright canteen crowded with laughing men, soldiers and Experts mingling, invited me for a moment, but instead I went into the rest room and threw myself on an empty bed, one of fifty or more night-weary sleepers.

With the first glint of dawn we were awakened and tumbled out into the bleak, windy night of the roadway. Haggard found me there. He was deadbeat and soaked through but brimming with life.

'Thur'r fighting Hunslet way,' he informed me. 'Machine-guns an' tear-gas out. Those bums of Manders' fight like devils. It's the furst bit of red blood I've seen in this spawny isle!'

CHAPTER SIX

The Battle of the East Riding

VESSANT'S SAVIOURS

THAT FIRST BOMBING of the civilian population split the country in twain. The last phase of warning, designed to emphasize that the Guard was the enemy against which all should make war, it turned millions of vacillating citizens into shocked, ardent patriots, circumscribing the rising spirit of rebellion to Leeds and other industrial districts.

How the papers of the following midday screamed!

'Helpless Civilians Destroyed!' 'Pacifists Murdered as they Cried for Peace!' And across the afternoon sky in the black smoke lettering of the Empire Press, 'Damn their Bombs! All together for King, Country and Vessant's Saviours!'

That was what they dubbed them, our oozing, repulsive charges; and those who had not seen or saw blindly what they were told to see instead of what was actually there believed them. Sentiment was smeared all over them. I can picture old ladies, after reading some of the gush which was emitted, shedding tears over the poor brave things which had been created to fight for us, dying pitifully in the blood-sodden streets of Leeds, while feeling, perhaps, that the foolish, interfering pacifists got all they deserved. Some, I know, regurgitated the slush back into the correspondence columns. Was it not feasible, asked one, to convey them under cover, in armoured trains or tanks?

Godman's 'chunk of glory' came our way too. In that chill, drizzly dawn I was dished out with road uniform which consisted of a heavily belted leather jerkin, corded breeches, and specially sprung marching boots, zip-fastened up to the knee, which gave the wearer a jaunty, cocksure step guaranteed to fascinate. Artistic bronze medallions at the top of the zip were matched by similar badges on the sides of our arms, and senior Experts wore brightly coloured splashes on their breasts to denote that they were real 'Congos'. Divers impressive gadgets, quadrifane uncouplers, ketchup-tin openers, gas-gulleters, hung from our rich leather belts, clanking commandingly, and our romantic ensemble was crowned by casques – they were called casques to differentiate them from the unit's helmets – which, shadowing even the plainest face to a manly charm, fell sharply over the ears inside our jerkin collars. Gas-masks could be clipped on to them in one second and they had the added, though unadvertised, advantage of providing protection for head and neck against stray onions and brickbats.

We had lightweight, cream-coloured stetsons also for hot weather wear and chemically treated undergarments to keep us at body temperature in any weather. As Haggard said, they could not have done us better had we been already corpses. And though there were no picture postcards the papers were full of our photos and heroism.

The Road Experts!

After we had passed beyond the ambit of the strike and were beginning to taste the freshness of the country air crowds assembled in the villages to cheer, and there were flags flying and patriotic songs by school children on unexpected half-holiday, their childish alto sometimes shivering into sobs and screams as we came well in view with our sweating column of beasts. A military camp we approached in the dawn became suddenly flooded with khaki mixed with underpants and a few gay pairs of pyjamas, all converging in our direction and sputtering with anticipatory cheers. The first dozen who reached the road into full view of us went blankly dumb, and only when a half-clothed non-com arrived and, visibly clinging to his instructions with a sickening heart, led the cheering was their shocked obmutescence overcome.

Placards and newspapers were everywhere to tell us we were coming. The units trudged and groaned, our little tanks, long ketchup drums, and big equipment cars clanked and thundered, and we with our casques and elastic tread flanked the whole in human splendour. Hell in its Sunday clothes, said someone. Hell or not we marched to the cheers of a simple people rapidly turning to us as their main safeguard.

Billeted in the Town Hall at Market Weighton that night we listened to Vessant's broadcast answer to the outcry for air reprisals. 'They have made our inalienable right to defend ourselves an excuse for murdering those who were actually demonstrating against war and harboured in their hearts only love for the foreigner. The free, vigorous flower of our race shattered in the streets because we in the Government who have a duty to fulfil will not leave them unprotected.' He gave figures. Over five hundred dead, twice as many injured. Humanite had been used. If only the raid instructions had been followed and all taken shelter in the undergrounds there would have been few casualties. The possibilities of depth-bombs with a ground penetrative power designed to carry them down to raid-shelter level had not then been revealed. 'Britain has no need of such savagery,' he said.

There was a televisor attached and his picture was thrown flatly on an improvised screen. He was a stout but clean-figured man with a pugnacious nose and he radiated confidence and encouragement, chiding the strikers paternally on their misguided opposition to the Guard. 'Our Guard,' he called it, and, 'Your Guard.' There were other ways of countering air attack than massacring innocent people. And if they attempted invasion from the air, or even from the sea, 'and we must not minimize such possibilities', then indeed they would realize the impregnability of our defences. That mild but studied warning had the effect of throwing the eastern counties metaphorically at the feet of the Flesh. 'Our Guard!' he exclaimed proudly. He said nothing about the carnage in the Hunslet Road nor was that reported in the news-sheets.

II

While renewed hope and loyalty were stiffening the quaking spirits of a scared populace we, the visible objects of these emotions, were spreading our battalions eastward in ever-increasing numbers, jeering at our smart road gear, laughing at our military leadership until it became too irritating for laughter. The idols of the girls, the envy of the men, we behaved ourselves outwardly and scoffed and cursed amongst ourselves. We had no more stomach for adulation than we had for flags and politicians. We were workmen taking our legions to the kill, a job to be done, and it would have been more to our taste to do it naturally and dirtily and without show.

We were a denomination, a new and different loyalty threading the old, our allegiance given to Dax-Beldite's and the spirit of the Congo Compound. Led by young gentlemen in khaki who had to consult us on every detail, inspected by brass-hats who knew not what to praise or blame, we represented something wider and more brutally honest than they. The Guard our sole *raison d'être*, we were the essence of carnage, the careless harbingers of internation suicide.

When General Tankerley was dragged from his retirement (the Hour had found its Man, we were told), we made a choice song about it and sang it on the march. Not until we heard Godman's version did we withdraw our ribaldry in respect for a workman as honest and ruthless as ourselves.

'Damn and blast your Guard! Why d'you ask *me* to command it? You've always had your eye on me, Vessant. Because I'm a soldier and not just a showpiece you think I can face wholesale, universal slaughter as part of the day's work. You politicians are the most bloodthirsty crowd on earth. You're so damned urbane.'

'We're only microphones,' laughed Vessant; 'we say what we are told to say.'

'Bah! *That* for a blazing tale! Who tells you? Beldite's. And who's behind Beldite's? Politician Vessant. Your *damned* circle. Why don't you give Godman here the supreme command? He knows more about it than I do. The country wouldn't stand for it? Another blazing tale!'

'I suppose even a general has to earn his living,' he surrendered; 'and if my job's killing, I'm too old to change it.'

'Damn and blast this Guard!' he said, after his first review. 'Why the hell didn't they give it some buttons to inspect!'

III

We slept that first night on the bare floor of the Market Weighton Town Hall, and in the early dawn were out feeding our contingents. They had been brought to rest overnight on an open grassy space at the entrance to the town on which what was humorously termed a 'filling station' had been established.

Halting the Guard was a matter of exact timing and knowing the nature of the brutes. Once over the brief torpor which followed every meal, and set upon the road, they would march through anything short of steel plating, and would continue to do so until hunger reasserted itself when their awakening faculties made them more tractable. They had a strong sense of association, and the custom was to run up the feeding drums from the rear and space them at intervals along the sides of the column. The sight and sound of these and, possibly, the odour or other emanation suggested food and, whilst they tugged and blundered to a stop, struggling to break column so as to reach the drums, long tanks would be thrust between the ranks and a general halt ensured. The linked quadrifanes were sufficiently long to allow of their bending to the food, and would sometimes entangle themselves in the creatures' feet, so that the guzzling diners stumbled and fell in the most ludicrous manner. How they slobbered and gobbled at those nauseating pans of ketchup!

We had to treat the ground with chemicals afterwards to prevent the seedy stuff taking root.

Altogether an OK business, halting, if taken to schedule, but woe betide the roadmen who delayed and allowed the hunger anger to mount!

Immediately after feeding they were extremely docile and amenable to hefty whacks on the sensitized parts of their legs, and it was only a matter of patience to push them into resting formation, which consisted in linking the front rank of a section of fifty to the rear rank of the same section, so making a circle which could bump and fall about as it pleased but could neither separate nor progress. This was 'corralling'. Sufficient of a contingent was always kept back to form an outer circle of similar pattern round all the clumps of fifty.

Throughout the night sentries stood guard over this molecule of disordinate atoms. All trying to go different ways they struggled and blundered through the dark hours, gasping like grampuses, but sometimes the outer ring would begin to march and go round and round like Kiss-in-the-ring until the very sentries grew dizzy and were all but hypnotized into taking part in that tireless roundabout.

Resting formation was designed solely for the benefit of the human element accompanying the Guard. The only rest, apart from some five minutes' stupor, that the units knew was the digestive process and that was accomplished on the march. Hence they were always certain of sufficient exercise during the night to ensure a healthy appetite in the morning.

Everyone in the little market town was out that dawn, I imagine, standing in crowds at a safe distance to inspect those unbelievable breakfasters. Feeding, they looked comparatively harmless lumps of useless life engaged in the immemorial process of stupefying themselves with food. They rose glutted, their retinae insensitive, their limbs lazy; dully and instinctively they clutched their quadrifanes and sagged into torpor, and we left them there for our own breakfasts at the Town Hall. The rustics gaped at us as though we were merely a more refined class of pug.

After our meal, its duration strictly limited by the digestive powers of our charges, we returned in shimmering early sunlight to unlink the fifties and thrust and drag them into the first semblance of marching order, by which time they were capable of moving on their own.

'Them's snails!' I heard an old man in cloth leggings and a thirty-year-old tweed hat remark. 'They we'ant do no scrappin'.'

Our officers tended to share this opinion and were hard put to it not to believe that the War Office was making fools of them.

'What's the Service coming to!' exclaimed one. 'Can't we fight our own war without dragging this dirty stuff into it! Is it any good? How can it fight? It's clogged. It's like leading somnambulists into battle!'

'I feel a bit like a chorus girl in charge of a menagerie,' said our pleasant young captain cheerfully. 'We were ordered to march with the Union Jack flying,' he confided to me, 'but it's just damnable to fly the old flag over *them*. And they promised us a band. Thank god I haven't seen a crochet of it. Glory be, a band!'

That first day we had done close on forty miles, we mere humans taking rests on the cars in relays, and the second day was to carry us beyond Bridlington, a prosperous little pleasure-town on the East Coast. During the night we had been disturbed by the rumble of bombs and answering gunfire inland, and half an hour afterwards new gunfire broke out coastwards. That must have been the second raid on Leeds.

It was not unexpected that even our highly skilled defence failed to locate the invaders on their outward journey until a very few minutes or even seconds before the attack; but the machines and strategy developed on the Continent during the long silence of disarmament were introducing elements altogether new to aerial warfare and setting the defenders problems they had never foreseen.

Silent as birds they came over at an altitude of many miles and, guided by radio beams, almost as accurate as though they had been trailing sensitive fingers along the ground, did not descend until close upon their objective, when they dropped earthwards like their own bombs. Two-hundred-ton 'Mother-Machines' they were, and along their fuselage clung anything from a dozen to two dozen 'bomb-pluggers', according to the carrying capacity of the 'mother', small, high-powered, practically wingless monoplanes – they had the appearance of grey sharks with fins on their sides – which took to the air a mile or more up and would have crashed with the weight of their own explosives had they not begun to release these almost immediately. Travelling at five hundred miles an hour and more, they provided no appreciable target surface and so great was their impetus that, when unloaded, they could mount to the upper atmosphere again with the aid of their powerful engines at almost similar speed. In extremity, and providing they did not slow down, they were capable of reaching their base though it were some hundreds of miles distant, but the custom was to reland on one of the mother-machines for recharging with explosive or return conveyance. Projectiles, they were, more than airplanes. They had superseded the much-dreaded 'sowing-machines'.

The first sign of a coming raid as often as not was the release of the bomb-pluggers which were the very antithesis of their soundless mothers, roaring and clattering as though they were themselves in a state of continuous explosion.

IV

Evening was drawing in as we neared our destination.

The main road to Flamborough passed through what was still traditionally called the 'Old Town', though in fact it had become a very pretty suburb of ultra-modern villas. The Priory and an ancient gateway linked their twentieth-century surroundings with the far past, and excited great interest in some of the Congos who had never seen a good-sized church near at hand, and were amazed that there should once have been sufficient religious minds to fill it. 'Muggers who built that believed in hell, didn't they?' asked Haggard, and when I said I supposed they did, 'That's queer, ain't it? We don't an' we make units an' quads. Hell must ha' made 'um think pretty.'

'This Guard almost makes one disbelieve in anything, doesn't it?' said the young captain to me. 'It's hard to fit it in with churches and all that. They haven't *blessed* it yet like they bless big guns,' with an insight into patriotic limitations. 'Not that I know of.' That captain had more imagination than the average officer. Glancing back at the dusky pile of the Priory, twin monoliths against the fading sky, 'The first shell will knock that to smithereens,' he said. 'We're like worms – eating up the bodies of our ancestors! Though perhaps it does not matter that high ideals seem to get nowhere: they meant something while they lasted.'

Half-way to Flamborough we turned off the road down a steep slope into great concrete undergrounds, 'filling station' attached. The excavators were still standing in the fields nearby and the concrete was new and damp. 'Talking of worms!' exclaimed the captain.

But there was no room for us down there. We camped in the open in a lush, breeze-blown meadow, with the sough of the scattered woods and the heavy undertones of the North Sea to lull us to well-earned sleep. The contingents had the raid shelters. It would have been perfect, a scrap of idyll in waste, but that a couple of hundred units were also crowded out, and even the most imaginative could not pretend for long that their all-night circus was only the homely cattle restless with the heat. Their discordant rumpus was added to by horses in a neighbouring field which thundered and snorted in alarm night long.

Early in the morning sightseers began to assemble along the road and the cliff path, and soon there was a huge crowd agog with interest. Revolutionary feeling was a mere sputter beneath the surface in this district and the Guard propaganda was taking good root. So the spectators (it was largely a holiday crowd) were orderly and good-tempered and comforted by our presence, and the only current of criticism was over the raid shelters. There had been a popular impression that these hurried works were for civilian use.

There was nothing in the least exciting about the Guard in resting condition, but no doubt from a little distance they were impressive enough to strangers with their complicated accoutrement and hugely muscular appearance. Sentries were posted to keep adventurous sightseers at a safe distance and, by late afternoon, the roads and cliffs were choked and police were there moving on the cars. As dusk came the crowds thinned, but throughout the night one could hear approaching vehicles drawing to a halt. No doubt the curious occupants descended and peered into the darkness towards our lights and listened to the grotesque animal noises in the adjoining meadow.

That night, as on the two previous ones, the raiders passed inland. We knew nothing of it until guns from hidden emplacements across the fields woke us startlingly from our sleep and then we saw the sky alive with searchlights ready for their return. The great beams from the air beacon on Flamborough Head, swinging at the top of a huge steel tower and erected for peace purposes originally, seemed to inflame half the sky. At a spot so easily located as ours we probably owed our safety to its vigilance and the encompassing brilliance of its rays. Bombs fell in its vicinity and a hotel near the North Landing suffered damage, but they came from a great height and were merely chance slots.

There followed two days of peace. It was our truthful boast that, apart from shooting at raiders, we had made no effort at reprisal. This, I fear, impressed the Continent as being more cunning than an honesty of peaceful intentions, but it solidified much wavering opinion at home. The first passionate wave of insurrection had broken, the muggers in the factories had responded only half-heartedly, and the more violent elements among the strikers were baulked for the nonce. Vessant's smart manoeuvring had complicated their argument: that this was a 'different war' was becoming evident to all but the most well-versed in political involution. The dancehalls of the country spun to the catchy tunes composed for the occasion. 'It isn't the war we thought it would be, They're *forcing* us to fight.' 'The Peaceful Mother in her Shell-swept Home,' etc. One could buy in almost every store pictures, busts and road-car mascots of Vessant and the Prime Minister, of my grandfather and, a flagrant fake, of Goble.

Lectures, placards, broadcasts . . . The sterios were boosting Vessant's Saviours almost hourly, and there was a full-length film out – it must have lain in stock for some years – which dealt with an imaginary invasion in which brave officers led hordes of shouting Death Guard into action against howitzers and tanks. Parts had been shot in the Congo and cooked up to fit in with the heroic love interest later in the studios, and it was all entirely ludicrous. The Guard could not shout and the officer who would have dared to lead them into action would have been impossible to find.

It served its purpose.

The toy market was flooded with a fine variety of 'Cuddly Brothers', humorously passable imitations of the real thing; advertisement writers found – or were given – a fund of good material in the Guard, and those lively, impolite Unknowns who originate the more verbal, *sotto voce* type of jokes discovered a new variant for old themes. There was no side of modern life, I imagine, into which the Flesh did not penetrate. Its frightful purpose was obscured under roars and sniggers of laughter and patriotic fervour.

The song which was heard more than any other ran to a very ancient tune once popular on the old music-hall stage. It was considered highly suited to singing by some pretty girl dressed in fancifully scanty military uniform and firing souvenirs into the audience from a golden blunderbus.

> Hello, hello, hello,
> It's a diff'rent war again!
> Different guns, different noise,

But the same nice girls
. . . For the same brave boys.
(*Drawled with a fat wink.*)

Baroom, baroom, baroom! (*stage imitation of bombs bursting*)
Who fears the raiding 'plane!
We've got all the enemy guessing – it's
A different war again!'

And on to the stage would come a crowd of chorus girls wearing tights with balloon-like muscles and carrying pasteboard quadrifanes, and would dance round the pretty, patriotic singer.

THE HUMAN WAR

The invasion of England, to us, is an historical fact, and it is a little difficult to reach back to a period when a majority of minds were comfortably oblivious of any such possibility.

That the centuries-old boast of Britain's inviolable shores was a pleasant myth likely to be exploded any moment had to be broken to them gently, for the days were long gone when a navy or even an air force could keep any shores inviolate, and it was not public policy to pretend otherwise. The existence of such a land force as the Guard must have awoken many. Vessant's studied warning of land attacks to come completed the awakening.

Its place in enemy strategy was too obvious to be overlooked.

The power of a modern nation rested not in the armies it had placed in the field nor even in its reserves, but in the munition factories, which were capable of replacement at an unprecedented rate. These had to be destroyed – and occupied – before victory could be assured, and, as our chief source of power was in the Flesh factories, it was easy to predict that invasion would take place along a direct route to those centres via the coasts of Yorkshire and Lincoln.

That it would be the enemy's first assay was not, perhaps, so generally recognized, witness the comparative calm in the East

Riding. But to any well-informed mind not only was the battle beginning to shape itself days beforehand, but the date of its opening was predictable within a week. The Continental powers were aware that each day's delay meant a further forty or fifty thousand of the Guard in marching condition, and only the needs of preparing their own forces and reaching agreement amongst themselves held them back from immediate attack. There was no announcement of their general confederation nor final ultimata, but the Leeds and subsequent raids were a sufficient indication that the advocates of open warfare were now in the ascendant and the storm about to break.

Not one power but had employed those weeks of warning in high-speed rearmament; the studs and the buttons had been pressed and the super factories of the age set to turning out the munitions of war in unexampled quantities. Close upon five hundred millions of people must have gone about their daily business scarcely aware of the racing machines smelting and cutting and lathing within a few miles or even yards of them. The lighted windows would be visible to them by night, there would be much extra work for many, but there was little of that age-old calling to the colours, little open preparation to show for the devil's work in hand; only the incessant propaganda that Great Britain was the enemy of the world, that Europe, even mightier Europe, was massing in honour bound against her. It must have strained the ingenuity of the propagandists to the utmost to convince their nationals that their governments were not planning a war of sheer, brutal aggression based on fairy tales, but were forestalling a world calamity.

Never since the ancient days when armies sallied forth en masse to meet in open and final conflict the total strength of their foes had nations arrayed themselves in such battle order. Like a machine which when made springs incontinently into motion, the European fleets, naval, transport and air, left their bases concurrently; like a machine the defence waited on the appointed battlefield. The maximum available force of each side was concentrated, face to face. There would be no preliminary forays, no outpost skirmishing, nor would either side waste itself in murderous but ill-advised efforts to terrorize civilians from the air. Civilians had grown accustomed to leaving their governments undisturbed in peace and, patient or panic-stricken, dying in their own homes or fleeing in millions across the countryside from the enemy gas, they would not be allowed to disturb the governments' war. Battle was to the machines, and the only morále which counted that of the men behind the machines.

Such was war in its latter days, the completion of a cycle.

II

The first we knew of its imminence was that unprecedented orders had been issued for the immediate withdrawal of the entire civilian population of those parts of the coast which presented suitable landing-places. Any day, across those lowland stretches, the Death Guard battalions might be released to their work of massacring the invader and, arduous as the alternative was, it was patently impossible at such an early stage in an unpopular war to allow them to slaughter the civilians they were supposed to be saving.

Like a playing-field the prospective battleground was to be cleared for action.

The populations of Scarborough, Filey, Bridlington and other towns in the vicinity extending southwards to Spurn Head were given twenty-four hours' notice to leave. In Hull and along the Humber the orders were to provision raid-shelters for at least a week, to fix gas-nullifying sprays at every corner, to put the anti-panic organization into operation forthwith ... a long series of directions ending with explicit instructions as to how to behave if any roving units of the Guard approached. For the evacuees state conveyance was provided, and all the trains of the north must have been torn away from their timetables and rescheduled into an endless circular service running on double tracks from New Malton and bearing their living freight inland via Leeds, a slow progression from sure death to mere danger.

Road traffic, apart from a minimum for invalids who could not travel by rail, was prohibited; all roads leading east were reserved for the tank corps and Guard contingents. Gliders were allowed to depart for specified dromes.

Followed the first proofs that the Government was standing no nonsense from the civilians, that they were, for the nonce, nothing but so many impediments, and would be treated as such. Whole regiments spent the last few hours before the first battle of their lives herding them from their houses, helping them to pack necessities, transferring valuables to special safe-deposits in the raid-shelters, lining the streets and ruthlessly crushing any sign of panic. Panic there was, but it was in the minds of the people, given no slightest chance of outward expression. A group of men in the Bridlington Quay Road who began to run were shot down in the legs. In Scarborough sleep-gas was used in some quantities, the compulsorily pacified panickers being bundled into the trains with the rest. A screaming woman was gagged and bound.

Psychology had ruled the plans, and they were not without their humorous side. In some quarters every child under fourteen was given a bag of sweets and a comic paper before it left its home! The sight of soldiers with gas-masks, sleep-bombs, and fixed bayonets handing out the goodies and chuckles must have been one for the gods! Pets were allowed to be taken: an hysterical woman torn from her Pekinese might easily start a panic.

Along the streets loudspeakers played the brightest of jazz; waiting for the trains there were radio services and popular concerts (side by side), and the actual loading was done to the most encouraging voice in England (chosen after considerable research), bidding all be of good cheer, promising a speedy return, restoration of all homes, victory, victory, victory, until the once frightened evacuees were cheering at the tops of their voices and were well on the way to being convinced that by doing what rifles and sleep-gas were compelling them to do they were helping to win the war. Cameramen were present. Many must have got quite a kick out of the thought of the millions of steriogoers inland actually watching them help to win the war. So good-humoured and courageous! Abandoning their homes, and gardens, and businesses, for the sake of their beloved country!

With songs, prayers and lies, this unparalleled exodus went through with a minimum of casualties. It was, perhaps, not very much more difficult than the handling of one of the immense Cup Final crowds of peacetimes. At the end of the journey tents and frame-huts and hot meals awaited the travellers, and there were more concerts and services. Organization was triumphant and shouting its own praises from every radio.

Before the twenty-four hours were past low thunder was heard beyond the sea horizon. The guns died down again and there was no news. The last trains moved southwards out of sight.

Then, in the early evening, a host of tiny specks became faintly visible in the sky, dropping earthwards like vultures, enlarging to a size we had never imagined could rise from the ground. At a set altitude, as it fell, each had the appearance of suddenly breaking into pieces. These pieces, after the first silent off-take, broke into an angry mechanical roar, and the mother-machine was seen to be exactly the same size as before she appeared to burst and, in some instances, was still casting loose her screaming devil-children to the destruction below. They swung down in beautiful curves, grey sharks of the air, and as they sped they, too, seemed to give birth to children, black streaks which fell, disappeared, and then gashed into flame and thunder.

That was how war came. Sudden specks in the high sky then death within seconds.

Far to the east, as if it were a part of the rising night, a deep rumbling began and continued without cessation hour after hour. The bulk of the great air armadas of the Continent and the water squadrons of the more northern countries were engaging our North Sea Fleet.

To us it was an enigma of distant thunder. None could prophesy how the reputedly unsinkable, gas- and bomb-proof battleships would fare in actual fighting, whether the seaplanes catapulted aloft from the aircraft carriers would repel the attack or whether that unparalleled swoop from the skies would end the fifty-year-old controversy of sea versus air for ever. Not until the victorious 'planes came swarming southwards did we know how that unequal contest had ended.

III

That vast annihilation, thorough to the point of wanton massacre, occupied the main Continental air forces until well into the following day. Warning of their approach, I understand, came in the late afternoon and, almost before our seaplanes had risen to join their distant scouts above, they were overhead.

Fighting opened above the clouds far out of sight of the waiting ships and, as they watched, the sky darkened unexplicably. There followed the bomb-pluggers to explain that darkness, hurtling from the battle above to the battle below. They must have looked like mere, tiny darts descending, grey flashes which fell, levelled, and were gone again above the clouds. As they passed they spread their bombs, bombs which exploded with no very terrifying sound and belched out thick black smoke. As it expanded the smoke lost none of its density but clung blindingly round every ship it touched, so that the gunnery officers were unable to see beyond their hands, and sighting instruments became useless.

Ship after ship was shrouded in gloom from which no speed could carry it. They had been widely outspread with the intention of closing in on the enemy when he took to sea and of intercepting the transports if they followed, but with the coming of the bomb-pluggers that plan died and they turned to saving themselves.

They slowed to a bare five knots an hour, blinded monsters crawling in their shrouds, their sea-guns afraid to fire for fear of hitting each other, their air-armament blazing its thousands of shells a minute aimlessly through the enveloping fog. Invisible to each other, they drifted like derelicts at the mercy of the enemy, each billowing cloud having a ship at its centre.

To these clouds the pluggers returned, dropping their depth-bombs on a helpless foe. The Continental ships circled nearer, adding their gunfire.

No plating could withstand that ceaseless bombardment of highly penetrative explosives indefinitely. The whale-like, stream-lined vessels which had outplaced the old battleships with their complex superstructure and vulnerable decks were as near being unsinkable as any floating thing could be, but the destructive powers in nature will always be stronger than the constructive abilities of man. The expansive force of humanite, for practical purposes, was as powerful as those 'atomic energy bombs' which were once so confidently adumbrated, and British engineers had not foreseen that Continental chemists would add to this power by solving the problems of directing the force of explosions. Depth-

and surface-bombs, 'deferred detonators', and 'triple-exploders', were novelties for which our ships were entirely unprepared.

The North Sea fleet was not sunk, it was blown to pieces, unit by unit, their sides and decks shattered in, their inner chambers destroyed, steadily and patiently, until the one vital spot, the magazine, could be penetrated. In a sea boiling with submarine explosion, ship after ship blew skywards throughout the night and the following day. Those which had exhausted their ammunition survived longest and were seen many days later, husks of disillusioned might, floating southwards, their tattered metal flying like flags frozen in defeat.

The only struggle in the North Sea battle was above where our seaplanes, quickly deprived of their floating bases, were shortly joined by many of the land squadrons. They put up a brave defence. But, before long, many of these too were struggling in the black clouds like netted birds, their target surface quadrupled for the gas-shells which followed.

IV

No one who survived knew the nature of that gas, for those who encountered it fell forthwith to join the dying navy beneath. Only later when it came to be used in the land attacks and in the process of disorganizing the country did it acquire the name of 'electric gas' from its quality of being attracted to moving objects, its intense adhesive power, its undoubted electrical effect upon all it touched.

In truth, it was more a dust or powder than a gas, though gases of a wide variety were usually blended with it. It would flow as though with conscious intent to whatever attracted it, billowing and contracting, spreading and humping itself up like some ghostly land jellyfish. It is said that in some way it collected and polarized the natural electricity in earth and air, creating powerful currents which perished the strongest gas-suit, allowing itself and its companion gases to enter and suck in through lungs and skin. Those who did not perish forthwith went mad with irritation. Men have been found electrocuted by the natural electricity within them; buildings rotted and corroded under its persistent influence, and machines were rendered useless instantaneously.

The black smoke owed both its adhesive quality and its blinding opacity to the presence of a proportion of electric gas in its composition, which held and concentrated it densely around the object it first encountered and, though this proportion was not deadly, the clouds could be supercharged, as in the case of our aeros, if bombs or shells containing electric gas were exploded within their area. Used separately the gas was practically invisible except for a feathery flickering, like hot air, noticeable in shadowy places.

In the air there was no means of countering the two in conjunction, except by avoiding them entirely; any aero in the vicinity of an exploding smoke-bomb was quickly enveloped and its airmen gassed, roasted or electrocuted by the supercharging process. By morning our squadrons were withdrawing to the assistance of the land defence, leaving the slow massacre of the navy to reach its predestined end.

In comparison with the onslaught on the battle fleet the first attack along the East Coast was a mere preparatory action directed mainly at our shelters and at the gun-pits at the back of the town, then spreading inland over the wolds in a somewhat hopeless search for the greater contingents deploying eastwards from York.

Our undergrounds had been rapidly enlarged since our arrival and, though not complete, sufficed to give shelter to us and that residue of the Guard which had been corralled overground. We had to break resting formation under a hail of bombs, but at that hour the units were in good marching condition and went rapidly and easily to the shelters. Three dozen or more were shattered into fragments and a number of our soldiers were killed. A couple of Oxy-Exys were badly wounded. Rifle-fire was useless against the pluggers, nor could they usually be seen quickly enough for an accurate aim to be taken but, on the uprise, a shell from the anti-aircrafts accounted for one.

The gunfire, however, was directed chiefly on the mothers, a mile or so up and one spun down into the bay flaming. As it touched the water its magazines detonated and the whole bay became a scurry of outspreading breakers. The sea was empty of shipping except for one small fishing-smack which was torn to fragments. A jagged section of the bows was flung on to the cliff-top.

I have no very distinct impression of that first experience of concentrated bomb-fire. One moment we were spectators, nay, listeners, for we were too busy on our work to stare; the next, we seemed enclosed in a deafening mechanical roar as though the very universe were thundering at us, and the entire ground in sight was being hurled upwards and over us. Surface bombs were in use, bombs which dug no useless holes nor wasted their power upwards, but expended a maximum of explosive energy on a level plane with themselves.

All sense was dulled in those wild minutes. The earth leapt and flared about us, the air bellowed and buffeted us hither and thither. Then we were safe – who should, from the sound and sight of things, have all been dead – and the whole affair was over like something on which a thick door shuts. Everyone was breathless and staring madly. I had not been afraid. I suppose no one had been afraid: there had not been time.

No further attack followed. Perhaps because of the darkness and the dust of the bombs the pluggers had not at that time an accurate location of our shelters.

Night deepened, a soft night of summer haze lit by a continuous flicker of reflections in the east. We saw nothing of the rest of the air fighting until close upon midnight, stifling like rats in our earth chambers and hearing only a dwarfish replica of the battle which raged intermittently over us, swinging seawards at times, dying into silence inland, then reviving like a patter of rain directly over us.

We were not entirely blind. Though deep underground and sealed in, little observation instruments connected by wires to concealed visors on the surface kept our military in touch with outside events, but those events were too swift and chaotic for any coherent account to be given. Radio instructions received from unknown headquarters were to keep the Guard constantly within one hour of fighting condition and await further orders.

Soon after twelve the enemy decided to put the Flamborough beacon out of action. At first they had probably wished to preserve it for their own use after landing, but they suffered too heavily through that design.

Haggard and I saw the attack upon it and the beginnings of the land invasion.

We had sweltered long enough below ground and, against orders, dodged through the gas-excluders and up the new entrance runway, and concealed ourselves from the sentries there behind a pile of sandbags. The change to the breezy open was delightful, though it brought us within clear hearing of the gunfire. Every now and again the searchlights would pick up one of the enemy craft and then, as if by a miracle, it would be encircled by bursting stars. The enemy was still trying to locate us and, while we crouched there, more than one depth-bomb crashed in our vicinity to be followed by a rain of earth and stone and unseen objects, which thudded unnervingly around us. We did not fear gas. Chemical gas-detectors were thickly scattered to a half-mile radius around us, and their characteristic flames would give ample warning unless the first bomb fell very close to us; nor was a force contemplating invasion likely to spread death-traps in its own path.

There came a long pause, one of those pauses for the reloading of bombs which took place beyond all earthly ken in the higher strata. Stratosphere flyers, themselves having been loaded miles up, brought the replenishments over, but I do not know how the transference to the mother-machines was accomplished. It was automatic, rapid, and apparently not dangerous. Perhaps they also landed on the great mothers like the little pluggers did.

In that pause we heard the Priory clock chiming the half-hour, the clearest, loneliest voice I have ever heard. The four great beams of the beacon were pointing zenithwards, waiting.

A quick succession of flashes spat out on the horizon, then the dull thud of heavy guns reverberated in our ears. There was an unimpressive crackling sound of bursting towards the headland, and the lights were suddenly blotched and broken by swelling black clouds. A second volley followed and others in quick order. Ships were firing, preparing the victim for destruction.

They employed the same means to destroy the beacon as were being used in the North Sea battle. In five minutes it was a writhing pillar of blackness through which chance rays found an outlet ever and again, vivid streaks against the ebony cloud. And with that the bomb-pluggers roared into hearing, driving unseen towards the point from which the struggling rays came. Like insects laying their eggs in flight they passed over the pinnacle of the cloud, and were half a mile away before the bombs they had left burst lividly in the surrounding black fog. When at length the cloud dissipated, our keen eyes could still distinguish the towering lattice of twisted girders, but the light and the brave men who manned it were gone.

Forthwith the guns of the European fleet were turned on the town and, under their covering fire and the pattern bombing of the pluggers, the first landing took place. Though we stayed on we saw little of that except glimpses of huge, shallow-draught motor transports like immense surf-boats churning landwards in the uncertain moonlight. One went up in a gush of flame and the sentries cheered madly, waving their rifles in the air. We heard the telephonist passing on the news to our captain below.

Haggard glanced at his watch. 'Gone one. We'd better get down. Orders may be coming any time now to get the old pugs going. Josh!

'Gorey,' he hissed, gripping my arm. 'D'yu get it? I've thought of this for fifteen years. All the boys have. Guess yu think we're a bloodthirsty crowd, but a pack o' praying curates who'd done our job would be the same. When yu've made a thing yu can't help having an itch to see it work. This ain't just a test in the Compound, pugs agen' pugs. It's the Red Try-out in reality, the real thing. Think of those foreign muggers swanking up across the sands, almighty struck to stick their dirty feet on England. Proud as pink pugs with their surfboats an' devil-bombers. They've swiped us so far an' they think they're going on swiping us. And in a few hours . . .'

I did not listen to the rest. I never liked Haggard to talk that way. It was sheer workman's pride in an efficient instrument produced, I know: bloodshed and suffering were by-products he did not consider overmuch until they were thrust before him, and then there was a soul in the man, sympathy, help. But he gloried in the thought of the Guard in action, and I hated to hear these enthusiastic periods of his. It always seemed to me that he was gloating over a power greater than humanity's, smacking back savagely and gleefully at a world which did not understand him and which he despised.

*

V

Along the coast north and south as far as could be heard heavy firing continued incessantly. Splinters of news, like debris flung from an explosion, reached us, a cumulative story of defeat.

In Bridlington street-fighting was in progress, an old-fashioned, hand-to-hand struggle; bayonets were in use and hand-grenades. The landing had been covered by the feed-guns of the surfboats, anchored on the edge of the beach, by aircraft above, and the battleships now drawing nearer over the horizon. It was a victory of sheer weight of explosives. Evaporating gas was used along the front, sprayed from the transports, and the first invading parties were rubber-garbed from head to foot and carried decontamination gear. Speed was on the water as well as in the air and wave after wave of infantry followed, rushed across the North Sea under the very nose of our helpless navy.

The battle starred outwards from the front, advancing from corner to corner. Officers must have charged at the head of their men as of old ... Gas played no further part, the fighting was too close. The barrage of the enemy shells fell in a devastating semicircle round the whole town.

Within that semicircle the regiments which a few hours before had been assisting the civilians to escape were trapped, struggling in the little streets against every demoniac device which could be used against them, their backs not to a wall but to a flaming explosion, thousands of them with no protection against the pluggers racing above their heads.

Beyond the semicircle, twenty or more columns of the Guard were advancing nearer, too far away to be of use. The attack had come a little earlier than expected and more swiftly than our defence could have imagined.

Our shelters were beneath the barrage. A squad was detailed to search for cracks in the walls and strengthen these if they appeared. A constant tremor vibrated through floor and walls and into our already jangling nerves. Bad temper was rife. Men cursed at each other over nothing or mooched around broodingly silent.

About 2 a.m. a good cold meal with beer was supplied and then the captain, still dandified but rather pale, came to give us the latest news.

'It's on you and yours, boys,' he quipped jerking a thumb towards the eternal grumbling of the Guard. 'Our chaps are entrenched half a mile outside the town but they're being pressed back. Everything is against them. They say the whole of the Baltic and German fleets are out there putting across this barrage – Heaven knows what's happened to *our* navy! – and they've made a second landing southward near Auburn and another at Hornsea. They've tanks with them and things that are both submarine and land-machines. Come crawling up from nowhere. They've thought of everything, these foreigners. They're pouring troops in like it's never been done before. Our air-force hasn't a damn chance against theirs and, in any case, most of it's not here; they say it's helping our navy, whatever that means. Navy shouldn't need help,' he grumbled.

'We expected this attack – here! – now! – and damn all, we're not ready for it! It's the old game of muddling through again but it won't act in this kind of war. Machines, god alive! and ammunition that would have lasted a month in '39!'

His voice suddenly became faintly querulous, suspicious.

'You're sure this circus of yours is what it's said to be? It seems it's all we've to depend on. I never could believe in – in zombies,' retrieving an apt word from his younger days. 'I can't believe it *now*, doing damn all down here and waiting for a lot of imitation swine to digest their suppers so that they can defend *us!* You're sure –'

Haggard bolted the half of a sandwich he was chewing.

'Captun,' he said. 'Yu'v no faith in yur superior officers. Yu may think yu'v got yu'self billeted in a fairy tale, but I grew up in it. I've had my bottom kicked for throwing stones at the pugs. I've grown up with 'em an' I've seen 'em rip the guts out of each other an' not shed a bloody tear. Them foreignors, yu, us – beside them we're all –' He ceased with a choking sound and began to clear his throat of an errant crumb.

'Spawn,' I supplied, laughing though feeling far from it.

'Spawn?' inquired the captain.

'Just little, pink, wriggly spawn,' said Haggard, having conquered his crumb.

By three the defensive gunfire had almost ceased. Our troops, or what was left of them, were said to be retreating inland on a swinging line with one end holding on grimly round our shelters, half a mile to the south of us. They were being massacred by the barrage. Tanks which should have come to the rescue were not there. It was rumoured they had met with some unexampled disaster.

'Test,' came the order and we commenced to inspect selected members of our contingents to learn how their reflexes were working. They were fidgeting and breathing more heavily than usual, becoming a danger to us unless they were released or fed very shortly.

'Give them a hundred yards and they'll do,' was our overseer's decision. 'Marching order. Clear runways. All REs to the slopes for uncoupling.'

I got to my less skilled job of herding the units straight and Haggard made for the main runway, and it was he, I believe, who struck apart the first two ranks and let them loose into the world. One deft stroke on the quadrifane couplings and they went ahead of their fellows jerking their weapons as if in pleased surprise. For twenty yards they moved at little more than their customary marching pace. A shell burst to the right and another close in front. They paid no attention to that: it had no meaning for them yet. They were hungry, but the anger in them was only beginning to translate itself into movement. As a third shell burst the front couples quickened their step and trotted on to the main road.

'All clear,' I heard a voice calling from behind. 'Message says: Left flank now retiring through the woods. All safe for Guard advance.'

Over the fields where the shells were bursting we had a brief glimpse of little khaki figures springing up from their concealed trenches and running for the shelter of the trees. In that fashion, hurrying in open order, casting curious glances back through the woods, the infantry arm of the British army began to answer the last Retire into the darkness of history, surrendering its proud place to the 'artificial fighting contrivance' which had superseded it, which brooked no allies in the field and knew neither fear nor courage nor pride. In thunderous darkness, splashed at second intervals with the glare of bursting shells, those historic little figures raced stumblingly along, leaving the field clear.

RED TRY-OUT

In five minutes when a thousand units had been uncoupled to drive down the main road the order, 'Extend Formation', came. Restless, and dragging at their couplings, a thousand were marched across the fields towards the cliffs and a second thousand inland. In blocks of ten they were then faced towards the town and let go.

I was with the seaward force. Until they had been moving a short while the last of the dope in them would not wear off and they would continue in the direction in which they were headed without endangering our lives; nevertheless, I had to take a firm grip on my nerves to prevent bolting for cover as soon as my work was done. We stood for a few moments watching them separating searchingly into the dark and crashing through the scattered spinneys. They showed up dim and pallid like ghosts in the watery moonlight and then only their receding thunder could be heard, a thousand units of death released to kill and to continue killing until they too were killed. Like Tchaka's impis we sent them out never to return.

As we raced back across the fields keeping in the shadow of the hedges, for shells were falling at intervals and there was a peevish, whining sound which I was told came from enemy bullets, we heard the clash of forces in the suburb of Sewerby a mile down the road.

That meeting was nothing but a distant, featureless pandemonium to us. It commenced with a sudden rattle of rifle fire, followed by the spitting roar of some quick-firing machines. Here and there we could see the flashes. Then a rising crescendo of panic shouts shot with the shrill screaming of horses and a sullen rumble of wheels dwindling into the distance. Rifle-fire again, spasmodic as if men in flight paused to fire backwards at random before racing on again. Then silence.

We stood looking at each other in the darkness, questioningly.

A hurrying roar in the sky broke our party into wild flight to the underground entrance. I saw the bomb-plugger a good mile away, a black, enlarging blotch against the low sky, twisting and turning with the bends of the road and raining bombs like splashes of whitish gold. The road into Bridlington must have been a sorry mess after its passage, but it came too late for its purpose of catching our first block in close formation between the hedges: they had separated minutes before.

As I disappeared below a soft inland blowing breeze sprang up and, as if it had found a message on the way and were carrying it to us, a second muted pandemonium rose from the cliff-top fields, mass fire, queer, inhuman crying, scattered shots, silence. It recommenced, dwindling townwards.

We foregathered in the runway listening intently. Behind us the reserve of the Guard tugged and rattled, anxious for release. I found myself near the captain who was standing with a glass of rum in his hand and a cold cigarette in his mouth.

'I don't like it,' he kept repeating. 'Don't like it. This isn't war. It isn't anything. Just – letting beasts out.

'What's happening down there?' he snapped, turning on me. 'It's quiet. That firing's miles away out on the wolds where our men are defending. I saw the barrage they're putting up, Kilham way. Down here – nothing's happening. Even their pluggers have stopped.'

'Afraid of bombing their own men,' I suggested. 'Listen. That's in the town. Machine-guns. Shouting, too. That hum.'

'Like a football crowd from a long way off,' said someone.

'I don't like it,' repeated the captain; 'I don't understand.'

We were silent again, straining our ears. Four of the Experts settled down to a game of cards on the slimy floor, lit by an electric torch well concealed behind some boxes. The Reserve was being fed with a modest ration to keep them docile.

'Oh, damn those slobbering swine!' muttered the captain.

Haggard moved away and returned after an interval from the depths eating a sandwich.

'Poor dope this,' he said. 'First time I've ever wished I was a pug. They're having the luck.'

Across the fields a voice was heard shouting, a wild, lonely voice emitting guttural cries. It passed up the cliffs. A high drone of aircraft came and went. The breeze had veered and we could hear nothing of what was happening in the town.

*

II

The prisoners came in a little batch from a clump of trees over to the right of our main runway.

They revealed themselves first as shouts, muffled and indistinguishable, then quite clearly in English hardened by a foreign accent I could not place. 'Surr-enderr. Us – we – surr-enderr. Cappy-tlate. No gunz. Prizners. Can we come, advanz? Not shoot?' The captain went forward to the open, shouting back, and they came across the moonlit sward hurrying, five of them. One limped extravagantly and was half dragged along by two others. A short man a pace or two in front waved a handkerchief in his hand.

As they came down the runway, hemmed in by bayonets, they caught sight of the Guard reserve in the dimness ahead and came to a sudden halt. One of them emitted a goat-like bleat and stepped back almost impaling himself on the point of a bayonet. I saw his eyes. They had turned up until only the whites were visible. His mouth drooped open inanely. The others cringed together, holding on to each other.

Two of our Tommies gripped hold of the fainting man and the whole bunch was hustled down a side passage. Behind their escort we Oxy-Exys formed an inquisitive tail to the little procession. The Overseer pushed his way forward to make himself evident.

'Have y'any coffee?' he asked a lieutenant.

'Coffee? Yes. There's gallons back there.'

'I mean fu' them. They needs it, the poor stuck devils.'

The lieutenant stared at him in amazement. It transgressed his military etiquette that prisoners – and those the very first he had ever seen – should be regaled with hot coffee on arrival.

'An' sannijes,' ordered the Overseer. 'Plenty rum in the coffee. Get 'em,' to one of us AREs. 'See here, Lettenunt. Them forren spivvies needs hot coffee an' sannijes like hell. All we do is be stuck here an' swig an' scoff an' send Brothers on the joy-run. They've *met* 'em.'

The lieutenant nodded, not entirely comprehending this unexpected humanity in an Expert, and so the prisoners clumped together in a side chamber and ate and drank in amazed suspicion with a varied audience gloating, mostly sympathetically, upon them. The man who had seemed about to have a fit nibbled at a piece of bread absent-mindedly with constant glances over his shoulder. Then the Overseer pushed himself forward again and engaged the one who could speak English in conversation.

They were part of some internationally composed force, it tran-spired, early volunteers for service against Britain, this one, their linguistic leader, being a German. He told his story in good English with excited lapses into his native tongue. The captain came in to listen, a little impatient at having to postpone their interrogation on military matters. 'There ain't no military matters left this side o' three miles but them,' said the Overseer. 'You listen, soldier.'

Our five prisoners had been stationed on the fringe of the outer-most houses of Marton. Apparently the extended line to which they belonged was merely holding its positions not aware that the British troops in front were retiring westwards, for a skeleton defence had been left to keep up a pretence of fire. When this had ceased some five minutes they received an order to advance cau-tiously. Men were valuable until a greater number could be landed and were being used sparingly. Anticipating a surprise, a message was sent back for reinforcements, and these reinforcements being in readiness a few hundred yards to the rear they were soon close behind deploying along the suburban avenues with a large force marching up the main road. We gathered that the whereabouts of our underground was known approximately and that the plan was not to rush it but to enfilade it from inland once the British infantry were pressed back sufficiently. After a few unguarded words our informant avoided this aspect. But he would have given nothing away: it was all past history now.

Their first sight of the Guard was similar to our impression as they went into battle, scattered ghosts in the trees and shrubberies. The moon came out more clearly and they saw helmets glinting dully. They took them for helmets though they were too high up to be worn by men.

From the main road to the right there suddenly arose an inde-scribable noise. 'Like cattle. Somet'ing.' That was too far off to concern them.

At a signal they sighted their guns and opened fire on the

enigmatical attackers ahead. Did they think these were the Death Guard? we asked. Yes, they had thought they must be the Guard but, though they had read and heard about little else for weeks they had few details whereby to recognize it. They had been warned that a few of the creatures might be with the British defending forces and had been given certain curious instructions upon how to combat them, instructions obviously based on little more than imagination.

'Fire at their eyes,' they had been told.

'Dummer!' said our German prisoner. 'Dey had no eyes. Not till dey vas close. An' den dey vas not *eyes*! But dey zeemed to know ve vere dere. Zum – eenstingt.'

Much trust had been placed in advancing nests of motor machine-guns. These five had comprised such a nest, each with his own gun. They had been placed together because, though of different nationalities, they all understood French.

They could hear their reserves coming up the roads behind and were much heartened by the sound, and at any moment they were expecting bomb-pluggers to come to their assistance. They fired for some sixty seconds at the ghosts in the trees but without visible effect. Our German admitted that, for a while, he thought they *were* ghosts. Then the crashing of undergrowth and the heavy palpitation of their breathing became audible in between the rattling gasps of the guns and they all ceased fire to listen.

'Dey had nod told us dey vas zo beeg. Ve thought – like men, perhaps. Fat, jah, fat; dey had zed zo. But Gott in Himmel! Der zize!'

Then they saw that some of the others nests had crept forward reserving their fire until a more effective moment. These, some four or five, perhaps twenty guns in all, opened out as the Guard began to emerge from the trees. Momentarily black they were, in deep shadow, then moonlit and ghastly white in the open. Their hoofs shook the ground – though that might have been the guns.

Three appeared, shoulder to shoulder, hunched, mighty forms, with the lowered vans of their quadrifanes glinting a couple of feet or more in front of them. Our German could see that the quintuple barrels of the nearest nest were blazing straight at them, hundreds of bullets a minute. Probably their aim was none too good. The units went straight through that hail as though it were sand, and in two seconds they were on the machine-gunners.

'I heard five screams. Five!' He held up outspread fingers. 'Von gun vent on firing, itzelf. De beazts vos pulling out dere spears, bayonets, vot dey be! Von turned to de gun and – vot iz de vord? – vrust, speared at it and it vos silence. Ve could ze it een de moonlicht.' They passed twenty yards to the side, breathing like heavy engines, and our prisoners saw that the meadow beyond was alive with the advancing hordes. Right and left the concentrated fire ceased in screaming and cursing. Gun after gun spat its last.

Our five and an auxiliary crouched watching without trying to fire, hidden in deep grass and bushes. One of the Guard came shuffling at great speed towards them and either they were spellbound with fear or instinct told them not to move. They crouched back, almost flat, all but the auxiliary who shouted and began firing his automatic. He remained standing, pumping lead into the brute until it drove down on him, 'zblitting him een two', and passed on. Probably his suicidal action saved the others' lives by attracting its attention. In passing it trod on one of our prisoners' legs, laming him.

They lay for many minutes until the meadow seemed clear, and then went forward hoping they would not meet a second wave. Not knowing where they were going they blundered close to the main road. They could hear terrible sounds back towards Marton, but the stream of the Guard drove on without pause. They had seen three of the beasts dead in the meadow, but were afraid to approach too closely being uncertain what constituted death to creatures which seemed bullet-proof.

At this point our German held a conversation in French with one of his companions, a Swede, I imagine, then repeated the latter's description of one of the dead units. Like a sieve, he described it, a mass of bullet holes. The top of the mask was blown away, at least he thought it was, for never having seen it in full life he could not be sure that the pulpy mass he saw was not natural. Its hands – he called them hands – were still moving.

And so, by chance, they came in sight of our underground, recognizing it by the excavators in the field and the humped earth.

*

III

While we were gathered down in the store-chamber listening to our captives' account of that first outpost meeting between man and Guard the battle without had become a far-off struggle, a receding settlement in which now we had no part. As if we had lit a fuse ... And distant, featureless explosions all we should ever know of its results.

Dawn found us tired and cheerful but without news. It was a misty dawn with the promise in it of a brilliant day and it seemed to bring peace to the world. Desultory fire from over the wolds mingled with the soft crying of sea-birds. A far, intermittent thudding and the mellow hum of unseen aircraft seemed a part of that dawn. Thick mist veiled the ocean from our view and trailed and dissipated and came again across the near landscape. We went up into the open where the distorted images of cattle across the meadows gave me a momentary start. Rooks were busy, cawing and circling beyond the trees.

Gas tests were made; quite an intimate interest was taken in the shell-holes. 'Dopey' tanks, for use against errant members of the Guard which might have turned on their tracks, came clanking up the runway to their stations. Everyone was yawning and laughing. Two unexpected corpses, one decapitated, dulled our pleasure for a while.

The attack on the underground came with that unexpected suddenness to which we were now becoming accustomed. One minute we were lounging like lords in the filtering rays of the early sun and discussing whether it would be a good idea to bring our breakfasts into the open and have a damp but welcome picnic amongst the sand-bags. The next there was a shattering concussion, so close and loud that I do not think one of us knew where the bomb had landed, and we were bolting like big, muddy-looking rabbits for our burrow.

So rapid were the bombs that they kept time with my falling feet. I ran six paces before I was under cover, and in that time six violent explosions had rent the air, and God knows what the things were which were flying about. One of the excavators leapt feet from its seating then a vast gush of earth and lacerating stones engulfed me from behind, flinging me on hands and knees down the runway. I saw Haggard in a miniature sandstorm, his mouth wide open, and one of the Tommies was standing quite still with his eyes shut, swaying. He collapsed and, before the emergency valve closed behind us, the ragged body of a man was hurtled in and passed me and smacked against the runway wall. Then the only sound for some seconds was the closing of the gas-proof valves. We were sealed in, theoretically safe from all bombardment, and without possibility of egress until the valves were opened again.

I lay still for a good minute, my mind hovering between my own ubiquitous bruises and the splashed man across the runway. I suppose I was only half conscious. I recollect musing unprogressively on the arrant foolishness of Edom Beldite's only male descendant having run himself into such a situation. This train of thought ended at the realization that it was probably the justice of fate, whereat my bruises swamped all other thoughts and I realized that Haggard was hauling me up roughly. I swore at him and he grinned cheerfully as though enjoying himself. So I shook him off irritably and made my own uncertain way to the deeper chambers where I found everything in turmoil with the news which was coming in from our surface visors.

The fleet was shelling us: the flashes could be seen in the mist and they had their bead on our entrance. Overhead, miles overhead, but dropping like hawks to the kill, was what must have been a part of the main Continental air-fleet fresh from its victory over our navy. Their enfilading plan having failed and, for all we knew, their whole land attack with it, the enemy was concentrating on us, perhaps under the impression that we sheltered the main reserve of the Guard. Our own planes were in the sky as well but they were outnumbered and, unit to unit, no match for the aggressors. A unit in the British fleet was one, though maybe a very powerful one. In the European fleet it was a triumvirate, stratoplane, mother-machine, and bomb-pluggers with anything up to a dozen of the latter acting in unison. Not a sigh of that aerial struggle penetrated to us.

Then, as though a giant with a hammer were attacking our

underground fortress, depth-bombs began to fall on us, triple-exploding depth-bombs. Thud, and an audible shudder in the air which rocked our walls, followed by the sullen rumble of a confined explosion as the bomb, having gouged a hole in the ground, detonated for the second time, driving deeper still to a third and imminent roar close over our heads.

We stared at each other aghast.

'Bomb-proof, by gad!' exclaimed the captain, staring up at a thin fracture in the concrete roof.

'Guess they tested it with the wrong sort o' bomb,' laughed Haggard. 'Looks though we came down here just to go up again.'

Many of the surface visors were already destroyed. From the remaining ones came the message that pluggers were swooping down directly over us and had our position to a nicety. The voice of the man at the seeing-post was as calm as a radio announcer's.

'Still driving over, dropping bombs.' Useless information, for we could hear them. 'Coming much closer now. Few yards above surface. Gor! One's laid an egg. Just popped his bomb down one of them holes. All the blamed pluggers are laying eggs.'

Some of the faces around me were laughing, strained and hysterical, but laughing.

'There goes some more of 'em.' And at that there was a grinding, tearing sound like the roof being ripped bodily away. Over where the Guard was shackled the concrete split and fell crashing. A couple of men were thrown off their feet. The lights disappeared incontinently and immediately new lights from portable lamps flooded the darkness away.

'Open valves. Clear runways. Uncouple units.'

The orders for the evacuation were carried out in disciplined, exact fashion with sections of the roof cracking over our heads. There was a pretence of boisterous spirits. Death was close and some men must laugh to face death bravely. 'These ain't the shelters we thought they'd be,' sang someone, parodying the song. 'Bury us first and kill us afterwards. Some bloody shelters!' To the right one wall was bulging inwards where bombs deposited in a hole in our earthen surround were exploding. Within short minutes we were facing the naval barrage at the runway entrance.

The Guard having been headed towards Bridlington, we Experts were ordered to make our way inland. We passed into a world of flying fragments and fire, with bomb-pluggers roaring close above our heads. There were some who would not move into the open, standing white and shivering, preferring death to come to them than go to meet it.

The last I saw of the interior of the underground was a sudden blaze of fire which came rushing up towards me, engulfing those staring figures. In that explosion many of the soldiers and units were caught, and killed or imprisoned under tons of earth and concrete.

CHAPTER SEVEN

From Flamborough Beacon

INVASION

THE GUNS OF the fleet, which had paused during the final destruction of the underground, opened out again, but now their aim was directed a quarter of a mile farther inland as if to cut off our chance of escape in that direction. Haggard, some steps in front of me, glanced back, signalling me to follow him towards the cliffs, and perhaps a dozen of us went with him, dodging in and out of the patches of ground mist, hiding at times flat on our stomachs from the searching pluggers which, ever and again, raked the fields with automatic guns. We came to temporary safety at length in the lush grass of a deep gully leading steeply down to a precipitous drop to the beach below, and there we crouched, our faces turned skywards, our lungs panting.

I glanced round to see who was with us and found that Haggard and I were alone. He raised one hand, indicative of the cliff-top, and shrugged his shoulders.

'We were lucky,' he whispered. 'Better get on while the mist's about.'

'Where?'

'There ought to be some kind of shelters under the beacon. That's where I thought of making. We'll be safe there as anywhere, safer than out here in the open.'

'Gas,' I suggested. 'Those clouds?'

'Chance to test our fancy bonnets,' he grinned. 'They may shell it, of course, but I guess they think they've cleared this patch of England.'

Half an hour or so later we had traversed the intervening mile and were in the lee of the old lighthouse with the vast, twisted framework of the beacon straddling high above us and not a sign of gas. At the base of the beacon, as though he were a moth caught in its flame, a foreign airman lay, his partially opened parachute spread round him like big, useless wings. He had been dragged along the ground and mutilated. His blank, boyish eyes watched the sky from which he had fallen.

Scattered about were various loose articles, an air-chart of which we could make nothing when we examined it later, a short, heavy-barrelled gun of a type unknown to us, a pair of field-glasses and a slab of chocolate. We took these and Haggard would have gone through the dead boy's pockets, but I stopped him, and then we hid ourselves in the generating house which was in a state of wreckage where one of the giant reflectors had crashed on it. The living quarters, though also in ruins, would have provided better shelter, but something had been splashed and spread about inside the entrance and, after peering at it, we chose the generating house.

But worn out and in danger as we were, we could not settle. We went back to the door again and stared at the remains of a row of anti-air guns and transports which blocked our view. Then I conceived the possibility of ascending the beacon.

It was a foolhardy idea which instantly appealed to Haggard. Curiosity altogether swamped our common sense and he led the way. The elevator being blown to pieces, we had to ascend by what was left of the emergency stairway at imminent risk of being seen, and so, after a stiff climb, came in view of the battlefield. In an angle between two girders and one of the great, sloping uprights we found a suitable perch well sheltered from the wind and the enemy's notice and with sufficient space under our feet to give a nice sense of security even at that giddy height. Unless we were actually seen there was small chance of our eyrie being shelled, for in comparison with aeros it had no value as a look-out or signalling post and, otherwise, was merely one of a growing number of ruins of no interest to the invaders.

East Yorkshire was like a map before us.

II

Our view extended as far as Whitby Castle on the north and the dim line of the Humber on the south. A great pillar of smoke shot with red showed where Hull was burning, but inland the mists were still heavy on the wolds and of what was transpiring there we could see nothing until later.

We took little more than a glance at that vast, surrounding scape before turning our attention to the little spa at our feet (as, indeed, it seemed) and its immediate environs. These, with the aid of the dead pilot's field-glasses, we could examine as under a microscope.

At right angles to the south cliff the invading army was actively engaged in entrenching itself with an appearance of extreme haste. Besides the travelling excavators normal to trench-making, hand spades were in use and, on both sides, the morning mists had been replaced by low-lying smokescreens which must have hidden these activities completely from anyone on the ground. The works extended inland in a curve round the outskirts of the town and caterpillar guns were being settled into position a mile west of the Driffield road. The guns were being placed back to back and, seeing this, we turned our attention to the town.

It could not have been more than four hours since we had first uncoupled the Guard but, so far as we could see, not a living human being was left in the streets of Bridlington. It was a town of slowly moving automata which paid not the remotest attention to the scouting aeroplanes circling above in the sky and studying their movements with, no doubt, the liveliest surprise. They ambled about aimlessly, having nothing to re-arouse their combative instincts except when at times some airman carrying out prescribed tests, we assumed, dropped a bomb within their sight. Then they became galvanized with sudden rage and plunged headlong at the centre of explosion, at falling walls, and at the threshing carcases of their injured fellows. A moment gone and the stimulus having passed, those which had survived these insane onslaughts would go blundering on angrily to fall again gradually into that slow, searching prowl.

Every street was littered with dead, human and Flesh together, and over these the units sometimes paused and bent down with some dim realization of a thing once living and moving. So far as we could see they made no effort to eat them, and, indeed, ravenous though they were, such was entirely against their nature; without the characteristic odour of 'ketchup', food held no attraction for them. Nor could they have made any manner of use of such solid fare had they taken it in their mouths, for they did not swallow and digest as do natural animals. At the back of the mouth gap was a mass of absorbent tissue through which a speedily liquefying substance such as ketchup could be assimilated as quickly as they could gulp it down, but which had no power of deriving nutriment from solids. Through that same tissue they breathed with all the strain and noise which I have described, and would also suck in gas though with very different effects from those sustained by a human being.

At many street corners wreckage of feed-guns, flame-throwers, and other weapons was visible. A convoy of lorries stood abandoned and, farther along the same road, a tangled heap of what appeared to be motor cycles surmounted by a tractor which had crashed into them. What we would see of the Marton road was a lane of trampled bodies.

It was a scene of uncanny desolation half encircled by that busy fringe of workers; its deathly aspect was emphasized more than denied by the prowling units. They were a part of the prevailing death.

As we watched, a group of units emerged into the open from behind an outlying avenue of little villas, close beyond which trenches were under construction. A whistle sounded, shrill and distant, and in a second every man within a hundred yards was hidden either below ground or flat on the surface. That second, however, had been sufficient, for apparently the smokescreen had thinned at that point. The quick stir of life had awakened the instincts of those seemingly insensate, aimlessly drifting pugs. They hunched their shoulders and shuffled forward at some speed.

An air scout appeared above them swooping down. Its aim was not quite accurate, the bomb exploding slightly too far in front of the group. Two of them went down but the remainder quickened their pace and, in a moment, had driven over the top of a slight rise which brought them within sight of the motionless soldiers.

It was against human nature to lie still with those monstrous forms approaching however strict the orders. A drab-clad figure scrambled to its feet, panic-stricken, and began running.

In this new warfare it was the crime of crimes, and it revealed to us that the invaders were already learning something of the tactics necessary to combat the Guard, for from all sides came a sudden rain of fire directed, not at the Flesh, but at the fleeing man. His nerve already broken, he screamed wildly, and then stumbled forward, rolled over with his legs waving ludicrously in the air, and was still. But further concealment was useless. From right and left machine-guns opened on the Guard, a whistle shrilled twice and the sputtering whirr of automatic rifles joined in the fight. The remaining brutes must have been riddled, but they went through that concentrated fire to close quarters. Outnumbered by fifty to one they were literally cut to pieces before they fell, one by one. Their victors gathered round in a thick crowd, gesticulating and pointing and even prodding the still-writhing flesh and paying no heed to their own considerable dead, until the whistle sounded again to send them variously back to their digging and to ambulance work.

All was silent again apart from the remote sounds of that distant, pigmy activity beyond Bridlington, the occasional faint zoom of aircraft, and the singing of larks. Haggard and I fell to discussing strategy and speculating on the further outcome of this strangest of all battles.

The appearance was that the enemy had gained a firm footing on the southern, low-lying margin of the bay and were, no doubt, pressing steadily towards the Humber if, indeed, they had not already constituted that natural boundary as their left flank. Northwards we could discern no sign of them (we knew nothing then of the electric gas bank over Scarborough), but, apart from our great height, the low, graceful hulks of their fleets, strung out in an endless line, were visible and, from beyond these, the surfboats, as I have termed them, came scudding to land, bearing five hundred or more reinforcements each load. They were landing at the rate of many thousands per hour, and not only men but mobile artillery, tanks, ammunition and stores.

The invasion of England was an accomplished fact. From a twenty- or thirty-mile base, a base which could be widened in a northerly direction as soon as they had troops to spare and found it advantageous to clear the gas bank, it would be possible for them to drive a wedge across the industrial districts inland. The signal success of our contingent in clearing the town seemed a little affair, a freakish setback in comparison with the immense preparations afoot. The remains of it had degenerated into something little better than a broken herd of abnormally dangerous wild animals, fighting, when they came upon an opportunity to fight, in tiny bands or even singly against numbers which, individually negligible against them, were in the mass insuperable and, as Haggard put it, spent the time in between trying their best to commit suicide in the bursting bombs. As a background to all this was an ocean now free and open to the enemy's transports and the air over which they held almost undisputed sway.

That was the manner in which a stranger would have read the meaning of our bird's-eye view, but to Haggard and me it held a very different content. Those suicidal wanderers in their deserted town were nothing but scrap-stuff which, had our underground base not been discovered, would have been destroyed by us as mercilessly as by the invaders or, according to convenience, retrieved and corralled again or sent raging forward into further battle with the infusion of new battalions. They were a residue, an overplus, to be killed or used again according to circumstances. Somewhere out on the wolds, hidden from sight, the greater contingents were drawing nearer.

'It seemed a big thing to us last night,' I said. 'I almost forgot that we were just one little packet out of – how many are there now, a million?'

'We were just telling the fleas to bite,' said Haggard. 'I've a feeling – maybe I'm wrong – we were put there just as a blind. Make the foreign spivvies think that's all there was. P'raps our top-knobs sort of wanted 'em to land just so they could get the full blast of what's comin' to 'em.

'Look,' he exclaimed sharply, pointing across the undulating country; 'the mist's rising!'

THE MISTS RISE

As the soft, early fog vaporized and passed we found ourselves overlooking a battlefield of close upon a thousand square miles. Its nearer aspects were revealed to us as suddenly as a grand finale when the curtain is raised.

Some four miles inland the outlying entanglements of the invaders became visible and, already, overnight, rough fortifications had sprung into existence behind these, a scarred line disappearing into misty obscurity and extending to the north-west of us into the tiny village of Bempton so that, apart from a narrow strip between this near flank and the sheer drop of the cliffs, we were entirely cut off from the interior. Whatever plans existed for following up the first offensive, it was abundantly clear that the enemy was intent for the while to consolidate his position.

Some miles away British artillery could be discerned, a brave, midget array like toys spread for mimic action, for in that bare country concealment was wellnigh impossible; and between these opposing lines lay the homely no-man's-land of the wolds, devoid of any suggestion of human life, as though there lurked in it some invisible danger which neither side dare face.

The reason for this reluctance to come to closer quarters became evident with the dissipation of the further mists.

As far as the eye could reach, their columns stretching back into the hazy distance, the Death Guard contingents were heading coastwards. Beyond the British lines every road stood out as on a map, dark and dusty with their passage, and in between those widely spaced ways further columns were trampling their own paths across the open country. On the one side the British forces had withdrawn to safety, for at any moment the legions might be released to the kill; on the other, the invaders were concentrating on the strongest defensible line hoping, no doubt, to break and disperse the attack before ever it reached them over that unprotected, intervening space. The battlefield was set, and the beast battalions were marching in their hundreds of thousands to defend the factories from which they had emerged.

We were not the only observers of that great land armada.

High to the zenith tiny gnats hovered, fluctuating in and out of sight. To these, infra-red photography must have revealed the plan of that advance with the first faint dawn of light hours before but, perhaps because they were exhausted of ammunition and had been awaiting new supplies or because, for all its added danger, daylight fighting was an advantage in their cataclysmal method of warfare, no effort had been made during the early hours to stem it.

Even now, with the day bright, they withheld their attack until the heads of the columns were far out into no-man's-land, and the British artillery had commenced a steady shelling of their wire. Then, in answer, the land batteries opened to be joined after a brief interval by the guns of the fleet.

'Pharaoh's hosts – up to bloody date!' ejaculated Haggard. 'I'd like to see the Red Sea that'll wash *them* up! That's out of a book I read,' he confided. 'Things sort of crop up out o' those books. As if they belonged.'

'Bible,' I reminded.

'No. Something about a test. Savage stuff.'

The air attack opened immediately to the west of us and spread swiftly southwards. There had been fighting in the air beyond our sight. It lulled. An airplane came spinning through the higher mist, trailing flame. The mother-machines did not descend to within range of the anti-air guns below, but flung their pluggers earthwards from a point beyond our vision yet less than a two-minutes' journey to those speeding flyers. Exactly spaced, one following another, they streaked down like a black chain through the smoke-smudged sky, raking the nearest column with surface explosive which, bursting just before it touched ground, spread destruction over an immense radius. Down and up and, as they rose, a following chain of bomb-pluggers started their thunderous descent. Before they were in action the second Guard column was under attack, then the third and fourth until, as far as we could see, the sky was festooned with their passage. Hundreds there were, black bugs of the air.

It was as though the parts of a monster machine had been let loose and, still keeping to their mathematical exactness, were warring on a helpless defence. There was rhythm in the ghastly scene.

That rhythm lasted five, perhaps six minutes. It seemed impossible that any force, human or inhuman, could withstand that hail of hyper-explosives for long. Five or six minutes, then from guns placed far beyond the immediate field of action, a shrapnel barrage spread like a froth over the heads of the marchers and, as the pluggers dived into this and were caught in the deadly spray, the perfect arcs of their descent became uncontrolled spins, each ending in a rush of fire skywards and the crash of the whole cargo of bombs as the machine struck ground. Over human troops it would have been an impossible tactic, but the rain of metal on the steel helmets and shoulder-plates of the units affected them but little. Though their surface flesh must have been cut to ribbons, fighting creatures which could go through feed-gun fire to the kill were proof against half-spent shrapnel.

In seconds the pluggers were changing their method of attack and, side-slipping steeply, were plunging in between the barrage and their prey. A quick bank and they were flashing on only a few yards above the contingents; ten seconds and, half a mile or more on, another bank and they were shooting up like arrows. But for this manoeuvre their speed had to be lessened, and immediately the cloudy barrage began to writhe like a snake to intercept their daring dives. Low ground guns came into play. As a plugger levelled out to place its deadly eggs on the column it found itself flying along the face of an arranged target, the narrow space between the marchers below and the barrage above, range and position known to a nicety by the distant gunners. Plugger after plugger displayed in that corridor as effectively as a moving target on a range was hurled to its own explosion a hundred yards clear of the Guard.

The heads of the columns were already breaking and the component units spreading out into loose order. Apparently uncoupling had taken place while they were still in marching condition only, but the dope was now passing and the bombardment was greatly assisting the awakening of their instincts. They fanned outwards, increasing their pace.

Along the line of the enemy trenches and wire and into the bay beyond, the shells of the British land guns fell increasingly. Some of those guns were thirty miles away, immense barrels sunk muzzle-deep in the ground, loaded from undergrounds a hundred feet beneath. The calm waters began to churn and rise into great billows rushing hither and thither but, unsinkable except by a direct hit, the transports, tossing like cockleshells, continued landwards. Little effort was made to silence that fire; the Continentals concentrated everything on the advancing units. A triple barrage was placed in their path, infernos of flying flame and fragments into which they plunged unhesitatingly, attracted by the violent commotion as though it were a haven from the storm.

We were witnessing the end of a military epoch. Never again would armies entrench themselves month- and year-long, pricking and pecking at each other over a few scarified yards between; never again would human armies dare to march or camp in the open, nor war be confined to known limits. The whole of the sky and land were the field; a battle which began over some stronghold might be a hundred miles away within the hour, the fort a gas-enveloped ruin untenable by life. These were only the opening passages of the new warfare which we were seeing. Behind were the factories, ever-increasing, the training-schools turning out pilots to fly the fool-proof machines of the time as quickly as they could recruit them. This was but the curtain-raiser.

Through that unbelievable hell of explosion, of gas and liquid flame and electrified barbed wire, the Death Guard went forward, the only living creatures which could have penetrated it alive, burnt and blown to fragments in their thousands, uncaring until beyond the smokescreens which were the enemy's last defence, the ripped, mutilated vanguard came in sight of the trenches. Seconds and they were on their foe, cutting through his ranks like butchers' knives through meat. Those which had encountered the electric gas carried it forward with them to the destruction of its senders. Barbed wire trailed from their legs and bodies, catching in the clothing of those they killed and dragging the corpses behind them, bouncing grotesquely. Over ground prepared for their advance the greater contingents followed.

Haggard was growling in his throat in an effort, I think, to cheer. Teeth and hands were clenched. 'Pharaoh's hosts!' he repeated obscurely. 'No spawn on 'um! No spawn on 'um! If only thu was French an' German Brothers 'stead o' squeally little men ... Josh, what a fight! What a fight it'd be!' So enthralled were we that anyone could have shot us down without our knowing but, even if we were seen, we two specks on our windy height had no importance; had there been dozens of us we could have watched unharmed.

Near Bempton the fighting was distinct. There was an effort to hold the railway embankment, a hurried rushing and mounting of machine-guns, whirring fire into the fields below. Before ever the heads of the Guard appeared up the far slope, men were abandoning their weapons and racing down the track. Many of those who stayed fought with their bayonets. Through our glasses we could see the units cutting them down, smashing the still-spitting guns. They turned to follow the runaways. A batch of units had mounted the lines nearer the station and the soldiers were caught between them. Some jumped from the bridge on to the road below and lay writhing. Along the road came others of the Guard trampling them underfoot.

Farther south beyond the Old Town were deep trenches. Into these the first units fell to form a bridge for others to cross.

It was I who first saw the catapult gliders west of the Driffield road. They came swiftly from beyond the smoke and fury of the barrage, two huge, wide-spreading, low-flying airplanes, skimming towards the coast at great speed and too low for the anti-air guns to concentrate on them. Except for their extremely broad fuselage they looked oddly flimsy things. Gyroscopically balanced they sped nearer, growing larger and larger, and not till they began to tilt earthwards and travel more slowly (probably with the action of air brakes opened automatically by the inclining of the prow), did I realize the strange cargo they carried. Each of those wide bodies was crowded with the unmistakable heads and shoulders of the Guard, a hundred or more in each, their quads upright between them.

The first landed heavily but safely on its giant springs, the sides and planes collapsed downwards as some simple mechanism was actuated, and the living contents tumbled out well behind the enemy line and within a few yards of a battery of field repeating guns. The second was less fortunate. It lit on a hummock, and rolling over spilled its load like so many sacks from a wagon. The speed having been slowed to a mere fraction during the last few yards, however, only one of the brutes failed to rise. It could be seen floundering helplessly, crushed against a gun wheel.

The unique invasion from the skies had taken the enemy completely by surprise. Gunners turned from their guns, some glancing round for hand weapons, other fleeing. A string of quick-firers came to a halt and was unlimbered into position in seconds. They never fired. Before the entrenched infantry were even aware of what lay behind, the artillery men and machine-gunners in the vicinity were dead, the guns thrust over, and the units were advancing on the parados.

As more and more of those swift, low-flying planes skimmed over my first surprise changed to wonder that I had not foreseen this most simple of expedients. Had I not often used catapult gliders myself? But Brighton, calm and luxurious beside its peaceful ocean, seemed less real now than the speeding death-carriers I was watching. Pretty dreams! Brighton, my grandfather; Gregory Beldite 'getting a grip', 'going to school'! Probably as not blown to blazes by night. Much it seemed to matter.

Flimsy things of canvas and fine steel, the gliders soared, levelled, and returned to ground. The pluggers swarmed around them like flies, hurling them over in flames, bursting them as a July bug is burst. For each one which went through to the enemy lines a new panic started, a new sector of the defence was thrown into rout. Cheap things, their cargo, cheaper even than real soldiers and much more durable.

II

I have no aptitude for describing sheer slaughter nor is there interest or excitement, after the first wild, hot-blooded moments, in seeing one's fellow-human beings, temporary enemies though they may be, butchered hour after hour. For a while I sat with my head in my hands sickened by the nauseous repetition of gutting and blood-spilling. Haggard, too, fell to silence, muttering at times to himself. Loathsome it must have become to him also, that ruthless carnaging, despite the fascination of seeing his beloved units in action.

It was all so far away that the plan of it, if there were a plan, was impossible to follow. Smoke and dust clouded everything. Once the extended line to the west of Bempton was swept clear, and the Guard had passed through the Old Town to join their fellows in Bridlington, the fighting became almost indistinguishable. With the battle at close quarters the Continental aircraft turned their attention to the distant British lines and there, wherever a settled encampment could be seen, tank parks, convoys, road-stations, the clinging smoke was dropped and humanite, the basis of all depth-bombs, was flung into the swirling clouds and the whole engulfed in immense pits.

Some, however, stayed with the coastal defence, circling low overhead, to execute a new tactic which was practised wherever possible. Hasty retreats would be executed and the units, left to themselves, would be assailed and blown to atoms by the bomb-pluggers. That tactic lasted only a while. Within an hour or two the whole army of the invaders was in helpless disorganization, degenerating at points into rout which, as the day wore on, became general. Whole battalions were marched into the houses to hide, to be discovered and slaughtered, sooner or later, as surely as though they had remained in the open to fight. We saw men piling dead bodies over themselves. Over the littered streets the Guard ploughed on to the very edge of the sea, and waded out after the overloaded transports so that many were washed away.

We witnessed a hundred outstanding incidents that day. Field-guns firing point-blank into the charging Guard and being lifted and flung from their carriages as the flood overtook them. Tanks plunging their way through beasts which fought against them as living things, until finally they stranded in the welter of bodies they had crushed. And one incredible little hero in a grey-blue uniform who fought one of the Brothers single-handed with his bayonet, dancing round and round it, thrusting and ripping at it, screaming and cursing, a tiny David who finally embedded his blade to the rifle's foresight in the animal's stomach and clung there, half-fainting, until he was shaken off and ended with one stroke. His conqueror stayed with him a long while, making sure, and then went off and killed five other men in as many seconds.

As twilight fell we descended from our post and searched round the dark buildings below for food of which we were badly in need. The splashed and bespattered doorway no longer appalled us, and we went into the living quarters. There was a considerable store when at length we found it, the beacon minders having left in a great hurry (if they had left), and we sat out in the open in the gathering dusk eating silently and watching the little houses of Flamborough, dead and unlighted, disappearing in the dark. Refreshed, we dragged the dead pilot out of sight into the silent company of some artillery men we had not noticed before, pondered a while over the problem of covering them up, and left them. After our day in the high open we felt as though we had descended into a pit. Only the dull thudding of distant guns broke the silence but, over the unseen battlefield, at intervals, great lights flared. Beyond our horizon the pale reflection of fires danced mile after mile, brightening as the night came.

No one approached over the windswept headland and, feeling little need of caution, we felt our way into one of the bedrooms and feel asleep.

GASFARE AND THE HUNGRY GUARD

Perhaps two hours later we were woken by intense anti-aerial fire from the batteries west. There was no accompanying sound of bombs and, puzzled by this, I went to the window to stare up at a sky which seawards was dead black, and inland presented the most amazing pyrotechnic display I have ever seen. Haggard lay on the bed mostly sleeping through it, but cursing vigorously each time he woke. Though we knew nothing of it then it was the opening phase of the new air strategy which the necessities of defeat were forcing on the enemy.

Out over the wolds the bomb-pluggers were laying the first of the 'gas fields', a novelty of aggression which was later reproduced in the most divers forms throughout Britain and the Continent.

I listened to the one-sided bombardment for a long while and, unable to make anything of it, went back to bed.

II

It was in the nature of latter-day warfare that its major battles, involving the use of forces hitherto undreamed of, should quickly assume uncontrollable proportions and should leave behind them not merely devastated areas, but whole districts inhabitable neither by one side nor the other; the mustard gas patches of previous wars were magnified to an immensely greater scale and were much less easily decontaminated, and specially left 'gas pockets' and unexploded landmines, not to mention drifting units of the Guard, were endemic.

Had the Continentals repelled the British counter-attack their further advance would have been incommoded beyond measure by their own defensive actions; paradoxical as it sounds, the price of their victory would have been comparative defeat. The price of the British success was a danger area of some hundreds of square miles aggravated by our own blunderings and, subsequently, rendered nigh untenable by the enemy's new gas policy; for once they realized that the East Riding would be of no more value to them, they concentrated on making it as lethal as possible to its rightful owners. It became an integral part of their general disorganization policy.

During the later bombing, in preparation for this, the pluggers had focused their attacks mainly on our gas-layers and on the requisites of field clearance, with a discrimination which suggested a very accurate knowledge of positions; destructor and dopey-parks were blown to fragments, and with them the stores of gulleting-gas and ketchup which had been brought into the field. We lost heavily in mobile decontamination gear. And, whilst we two slept beneath the beacon, they returned and, despite the intensive bombardment which woke me, smothered the wolds in sticky gas. Along every road they laid it while other machines flew across at right angles making a chequer of gaseous death. Not an explosive bomb was dropped. It is said that the pluggers flew low, a mile under the barrage which was shattering the sky above in search of them.

Where the gas fell it stayed after spreading a little; and when the surviving gas-layers and destructors started out in the early dawn on their work of field clearance, machine after machine ceased movement as the electric vapour entered its works and could not be started again. Engineers who endeavoured to locate the trouble fell forward dead into the machinery as the gas ate through their rubber gloves.

Of the destructors which escaped the electric gas belts, all turned back when air scouts informed them of the numbers of units ahead. They knew their duty, but it was not suicide. Many were caught in the gas on their return and others, endeavouring to avoid it, were met by the Guard and trampled out of existence.

For the gas deposits were not the only difficulty. Fear and optimism, in equal measure, had created a second and more lively problem within the first.

*

III

That second problem of whole contingents alive and unapproach-able in the gas-field, was due not so much to individual blundering and bad technique in handling the Guard as to the fact that war itself is the supreme blunder and demands more than the most astute generalship can give. Can one expect a vigorous military command, facing the unknown imperatives of a brand-new war, to visualize and avoid all the unpleasant after-effects of the victory for which it is striving?

No one could have foreseen the intensity of the enemy bombard-ment nor the rapidity of their landing and, faced with that un-precedented onslaught, it is not surprising that our defence found itself unable to trust the methodical, strictly controlled method of counter-attack prescribed for the Guard, and had struck almost simultaneously along a twenty-mile front.*

The havoc wrought by the bomb-pluggers swooping over the marching columns must have shaken all faith in that method, and have indicated in terms of the visible dead that unless an uninter-rupted advance were kept going no units would ever reach the distant enemy lines. Contingents which should have been held in reserve were hurried out to the shambles, new and unnecessary columns were formed and launched on their deadly march and, at a late hour, when even the most pessimistic commander could not have doubted the issue, still further contingents were thrown in ap-parently to complete the good work more speedily. Is there a gen-eral on earth who would not revel in the opportunity of sacrificing

---

* The correct method of deploying the Guard along such a front as the sea-bordered coast, where there was no follow-through into enemy land and danger of backdrift by the units was correspondingly great, was to break the line at one place only and, using that as a feeding-point, to drive along the frontage as though one were rolling up a carpet, other parts of the supporting army retiring meanwhile, if necessary, until such time as the enemy was out-flanked and general advance by infantry and tanks became safe. Under this scheme 'field clearance' of the units would always take place in a limited area, viz. to the rear of the advancing Guard, 'cleared' troops being utilized again from the point of greatest vantage instead of being destroyed, and the numbers unshackled being strictly controlled according to need. – G.B.

troops ad lib without either fear of depleting his reserves or need of human compunction? One can imagine a period of intense jubilation, a reaction from the first semi-panic and doubt of their newfangled troops, before realization of what they were doing – perhaps in the form of some undisciplined Expert pushing his way into a Staff Room uninvited – came home.

And then the hurried call for dopey-tanks and destructors to be rushed out into no-man's-land, curt reminders from the REs in charge of these that though they were prepared to deal with normal backdrift they were not going to sacrifice their valuable men in endeavouring to destroy the surplus thousands of massed and battle-conditioned units which misguided enthusiasm had let loose upon an enemy already routed. Infantry which were on the march to reoccupy the coastal sectors after field clearances had taken place were recalled; airplanes which had been driven to earth by the bomb-pluggers during the battle took the lower air again and attacked the rearguards of contingents which were still in column. Followed a general retirement of an army all too victorious, placing mile upon mile between themselves and the troops which had won them the victory.

At one point half a contingent turned back on its track to be met by a charge of battle tanks. For one almost unbelievable ten minutes British and Continental aircraft were assisting each other unknowingly in the destruction of their mutual foe. The issue became plainer and they turned on each other leaving the Brothers below to their indiscriminate ravaging.

IV

Haggard and I climbed into sight of the aftermath of that mad night with the first rays of the sun.

The scene was one of desolation, an enlarged replica of Bridlington on the previous morning but devastated by bomb and shell-fire to an unbelievable extent. Not a living sign of the enemy occupation remained, only their abandoned guns and stores, and their dead like overthrown sheaves of corn. Seawards the fleet was still visible and towards it a few belated surf-transports were making their distant way.

Firing had ceased and the air was free of their machines; but British scouts were abroad apparently inspecting the battlefield and, miles away, the smoke of many fires rose into the still air where the army of defence was preparing its breakfast undisturbedly.

Scattered about the wolds were little groups of figures gathered around their motionless destructors and dopeys and near these clusters was a busy traffic in stretchers and first-aid. Gas cases. It was all too far away to be seen in any detail.

Over the whole nearer landscape there was a strange, lethargic quiet. What, in theory, should have been a scene of intense liveliness, destruction of surplus units, shackling teams, scurrying dopeys, and all the other energetic accessories of the Guard, was void of any sign of human activity. It was as though another world had been superimposed on the familiar little watering-place and its environs. Farther out there was an irregular, misty film over the countryside which we decided must be gas, visible only by reason of its distance, and so provided ourselves with the beginnings of an explanation of what was transpiring down there.

It was all too evident that we were cut off from the interior, confined to our headland as effectively as during the fighting.

Our first thought on realizing this was to return to the ground and rig up a vast white flag out of the bed sheets as a signal to the scouting 'planes, but we delayed a while watching the Guard units and, Haggard having muttered a while and thrown out an inexact quotation or two, he decided to stay aloft.

'The spawny-witted muggers!' he ejaculated, surveying that field of dubious victory with an expert eye, 'I could have done it with a quarter the number. If Hell yawned it wouldn't clear up *that* bevy in months! That's what comes of letting soldiers run a war 'stead of handing it to fellers who understand it!'

'O' course the enemy's made it worse,' as I indicated the gas deposits. 'What's the bleeding enemy for!'

I descended after an hour or so and commenced work on the ambitious flag we had in mind. I planned on the grand scale and successfully but laboriously hitched six sheets firmly together with strips torn from a seventh before hunger began to assert itself, when I went into the kitchen and dug out a meal for the two of us.

The splash in the entrance was quite dry by then. After this I signalled to Haggard, still perched on high, but his answer was a call to me to rejoin him so, fortified with four fat sandwiches of some stringy but tasty meat preserve, I climbed up the beacon ladder again, resting at intervals to take a bite out of my dinner.

'Gorey, the chaps who started this war ought to be gulleted,' was his greeting.

I stared across the miles of carnage, the streets and gardens and fields strewn thickly with distorted, trampled bodies over which the Brothers shuffled and squelched like swine in manure, the whole filthy waste of death as far as the eye could see ... and, 'They ought tuv had another war furst just to learn how,' he continued, beginning to wolf down a sandwich. 'That technique of ours was just bloody theory, paper stuff like that Shakespeare an' all the others. I guess it was as spawny as the generals.'

He launched into a discourse on the one subject which enthralled him, the art of using the Guard, revealing to me in fuller detail the course of the previous nights' events which I have already outlined and which he could read as in a book from the signs before him. Slovenly as the unshackling had been the technique of field clearance was, it seemed, OK; but its organization had been smashed, ruthlessly smashed. He began to sketch future possibilities, the probable behaviour of units left too long without food, the effects of gas on them, what ought to be done to remove this blot on the Experts' record. That was how he treated it. He was especially concerned with the Guard dead, much more so than with the human ones.

'Can't leave muck like that lying about in this heat,' he muttered more than once.

It seemed to me an obvious enough comment at the time.

The somnolent Brothers in their dead town had an air of mute suffering altogether delusive. Hunger with them implied ferocity and they mooched about meaninglessly only because there was so little on which to vent their feeling. It smouldered. The swaying of branches and leaves above their heads was an attraction and they lingered around such centres of movement. At times bigger interest came their way. While we watched we saw a dozen or more cows slaughtered – they had broken their way out of a ruined mistle –

and, at one time, a hullabaloo broke out in the far streets and was over in a few minutes. What happened there we could not tell. Possibly hidden human beings had been discovered.

Ever and again the Brothers would batter through the doors and windows of houses following their instinct that living things were at hand. There was no means of knowing whether it misled them or not, but after a long while they would issue into the open once more ... Once, for certain, it was only a cat. There was a great chase when it fled and I think it escaped. Farther south towards Hornsea there was mist in the fields. Wreckage of boats was scattered along the beach amongst the bodies of hundreds who had died on the edge of escape. Many units were there, hunched, prowling figures like old men searching for flotsam.

We watched through that weary afternoon and late into the evening. For all we knew many stragglers from the invading army were still in hiding, watching in terror from upper windows, wondering, perhaps, in semi-madness, whether they had been killed in the battle and this that they saw was the aftermath of death. Ever and anon some scramble would arise and die down. No sign of renewed activity came from the military encampments and the scouting 'planes did not come our way. The little groups out on the wolds had long ago withdrawn, leaving their useless vehicles behind, and all effort at field clearance had for the while been abandoned.

Great flocks of gulls and other sea-birds had gathered over the battlefield circling and screaming. At times they would swoop on the corpses. A few moments and some group of units would come charging along, unconscious, self-appointed guardians of the dead, and the gulls would rise like whirling snow to the sky.

Haggard said that very shortly the units would begin to move inland again. The herd instinct which kept them passively together when doped for the march was reasserting itself now that the fighting passion was no longer at its height and they were massing in increasing numbers. Whereas at dawn they had been scattered along the whole low-lying coast hundreds were now gathered in the open spaces where the brighter light had drawn them.

'Somebody'll start a trek one way or the other an' then they'll be off,' said Haggard. 'They're hungry, Gorey; their glands must be dry as sand an' gritting like it. They may come this way or they may go that way, but before long they'll get down to some solid marching. It's thur nature.'

The first sign we saw of any definite movement was just before dusk when some three dozen appeared in Flamborough village less than two miles from us. They did not seem to be moving in our direction.

By the following morning the impis which had been sent out to die were returning inland, for there was no enemy left for them to kill.

V

But before my rather fanciful parallel of impis takes too strong a hold on the reader's imagination I must correct a widespread, romantic delusion that the return of the units was in any sense a revolt of starving, battle-weary troops marching to add their armed power to the reviving revolution inland.

Nothing could be more fantastic; even the sentimentalist view that in some dim way they realized the foul debasement of their lives and turned upon their oppressors knowingly 'to carry out their destiny of death' is quite impermissible. The Guard was entirely incapable of any such ideas: its only instincts were to feed, march and kill.

From a killing standpoint it was the perfect military tool and, as such, had need of neither brains nor emotions. Dangerous as it could be on occasion, if managed properly there was no more risk in its use than there was with certain gases or with high explosive, the problem of discipline being overcome by drugging before the battle and slaughtering afterwards. I have heard that for some while Goble experimented with a variety which would die spontaneously after a given spell of fighting (like the drone dies after mating) but the creatures lacked the whole-hearted vigour of the less-obliging specimens and the scheme was abandoned.

The impis returned like the brute things they were, not in organized contingents but in aimless herds which went gas-mad out on the wolds and became an inherent factor in that festering sore of battlefield which it was in the nature of latter-day warfare to leave.

In between making our flags, Haggard and I spent our time

watching them through our binoculars or staring at the enemy fleet which continued to occupy the horizon. After nightfall an aerial bombardment began far inland lasting into the early hours; the tiniest affray it sounded, like pin-pricks exploding. Only the seaward wind made it audible to us.

The stratoplanes must have passed over the East Riding quite unheard.

That was the beginning of the systematic destruction of all regular communication in the north. Each night the enemy came over to deliver their methodical attack on railways, roads and bridges, and on key towns. Sometime during that period the first electric-gas raids were made on Darnley and Leeds and other centres of Flesh manufacture.

We saw nothing of it all except the second night when an air battle swept high over us, a swarm of giant, sputtering bees spitting flame at each other. At one time it was like a roof over our heads. We hid until it passed seawards.

VI

We were rescued on the fourth night when what was left of our food had gone bad with the heat or had been stolen by unexpected rats which still lingered in that country district. We had made up our minds to set out across country that very night as soon as it was fully dark, risking both gas and Guard which we knew from our daily observations to be scattered over the whole countryside between the headland and New Malton. Thirty miles of death-strewn country had not invited us while our food lasted, but we had no success with our flag – it blew away the first time we hoisted it and another one had to be made – and in any case the airplanes never came within three miles of us. If they saw our signal they probably thought it was a parachute entangled in the girders.

Then, suddenly, a scout came skimming down to us from the evening sky and a smart young pilot jumped out to discover us in deep conclave over a piece of mouldy bread trying to decide whether it was worth taking with us.

'Saw your old handkerchief,' he greeted us, cheerily, 'and guessed it was someone doing a desert island stunt. What's that you're staring at?'

'It *was* food,' I answered. 'We're a couple of Experts from the 27th Contingent. Went into action the first night.'

'Been acrobating up the sticks for the last four days, watching the army taking its summer nap,' added Haggard.

'Got any *real* grub?' I asked.

'Tons. At least, tins,' laughed the lieutenant. 'It's the job I'm on. Hunting out survivors in the derelict area and, if I can't take them off, dropping food to them. Regular service of us starting. There don't seem to be any up this way, only stiff ones, but farther south they're out on view, sitting on the house-tops. Mad, some of them. There was one old lady thought I was an angel from the look of her and started to pray to me.'

He was a cheerful boy who had seen death only from above, foreshortened and undetailed, and he was still excited at flying a real 'plane in a real war. He brought in some cans of a pemmican-like stuff, very sustaining, he said, and gave us all the news un-asked.

'It's jolly thrilling,' he announced. 'We've got our backs to the wall against the whole bally Continent.'

'Where's the wall?' chewed Haggard through a mouthful of the pemmican-like stuff.

'That's where it's so exciting. There isn't a wall. We're not only practically surrounded but there's this ghastly mess of a battle about here and gas spilt all over Yorkshire and Lancashire; and there's a big strike on and shooting and rioting. Our navy's less than an also-ran now.'

It was the first we had heard of that and for our benefit he told what little he knew of that day- and night-long tragedy of the sea.

'I've always said that the navy was only an accessory to the air arm, but it's too late to argue about that now. Our seaplanes hadn't a chance. Like flies fighting vultures and not too many flies either! Some of their aeros were nearly as big as battleships!

'And those bomb-pluggers! More bombs than machine; they couldn't possibly *rise* with such a weight. They just *drop*, unload like things being sick, and go up empty to be fed again. Like having a belt-feed, one of those endless chain affairs up in the air.'

He pondered on this unsporting arrangement for a while. 'They say we're going to have a new sort of 'plane soon. Perhaps we'll have a chance then.'

'Of course, it's pretty damned awful when you look at it fair and square,' he said, cheerfully. 'In York everyone's in a fearful stew. No one expected it to be half so bad as it is; just don't know which thing to attend to first. Your Expert fellows say the first thing to do is destroy all these – units, d'you call them? – which are strolling about, and the army says it hasn't the shells to spare and I know as a fact that *we* haven't either the bombs or 'planes. Frightful shortage of ammunition. and they're biting each other's heads off over who's to blame for it all.

'You chaps seem bally hungry,' he broke off, taking a forkful of the pemmican stuff for himself. 'I should eat as much as you can now. Back in civilization we're rationing. Like hell. We've got what some jokers call the "order of the tight belt". Oh, the country's full of food, it's the one precaution which *was* taken, but they can't get it to us. The Conties are smashing up all the roads and rails and most of the transport that's left is too busy bringing eats for your bally Guard to attend to us poor immortal souls. I can never remember the blasted names, but dump after dump of the swill stuff they eat went sky high in that hell-fire bombardment. Ketchup, that's it. Funny sort of name. Reminds me of mushrooms. Well, as I was saying, *Our* Guard mustn't starve –'

'Hell, it mustn't!' said Haggard.

'– but the Officers' messes can eat their boots if they're peckish. I don't mind gas and bombs but I *do* like my meals at the right time. It's these peacemonger crowds in the towns.'

'Oh, them!' from Haggard, no doubt with memories of Manders.

'It's all right saying, "Them!" I don't know what they're getting at but it seems to me they don't want either war or peace but just a hell of a mess. The road- and rail-men started it, stopping the trains and lorries out in the country, smashing open the drums, and letting the – ketchup run out. They refuse to bring it to the front, say they'll *starve* the Guard. They're smashing up the factory storehouses and pouring the beastly stuff down the drains. At Hunslet they've burned the factories to the ground and at others they've surrounded them and barricaded the gates to keep the

Guard inside and the ketchup with them. They wear the masks which have been issued to civilians so tear gas and sleep gas aren't any use against them. The police seem helpless, can't cope with thousands.'

'The army?'

'The army's busy guarding the roads and bringing the stuff from other stores which aren't destroyed. It seems that's what it's for now: to wait on your beastly Guard. Filthy swines! I'm sorry; I suppose you're proud of them, but they *are* swines. And we've to go short while they choke the roads with tinned swill!

'There's been fighting in the towns, of course,' he revived; 'quite a lot, but nothing much will be done while Pollen's in charge. He's too weak; hasn't the guts of a louse.'

'You fellows will be sent to bomb them,' I suggested.

He did not answer, only stared into the empty can of pemmican. We fell to silence, pondering these internal complications.

In my mind I looked back into the troubled hives of the industrial districts, miserable enough in their normal existence, driven to fighting frenzy by the prospect of even deeper misery. I could imagine the scores of secret meetings, the clash of views, wise and ignorant, rancorous, pacific ... the theoretical disagreements of many powerless years evaporating before the one united demand that the Guard must be abolished; all those little dabbling democracies, idealists, crude workers, scheming local politicians, polyglot but now unified, voting for chaos, voting to burn their fellow-workers if they were fools enough to stay inside when the factories were fired and – their master-stroke of unreality – agreeing to starve to death all those thousand and more contingents which had already taken the road. Perhaps some opposed this, explaining that if the Guard were not fed it would become a dire menace to the country; and others, impressed but doubtful, welcoming assurances that this was only another of the clever lies circulated around the great Beldite conspiracy and, after heated debate, voting for mass starvation. To this disastrous extent had they accepted the one-time incredible Guard, applying to it the common facts of animal existence with no conception that these had been modified out of all practical meaning. The units had not been created to die quickly.

Was that the way out? Greater chaos?

'Pouring it down the drains!' Haggard expressed himself violently. 'Ketchup's seeds an' grows fit to bust itself. Yu'll have all sorts o' funny forests in yur old country before long. Hell in flames!' he ejaculated; 'those ketchup plants'll feed all these bloody little neoblasts which'll be coming . . .'

'Neoblasts?' I queried. 'What d'you mean?' for until that moment I had understood neoblast to be nothing more than fleshy deterioration, excrescences, scabs. 'Any unit showing neoblastic tendencies should be immediately destroyed,' ran the factory regulations. I began quoting them to Haggard, and he wiped me aside. 'What's cellular deterioration from our point o' view is just thur spawny way of trying to reproduce thu'selves. Cut out all the injections an' leave the flesh to go its own way an' d'yu suppose it'll stop at knobs an' rottenness? I know I ain't told yu before. Who the hell're yu to know everything! D'you suppose we're proud of it an' spill it to ev'ry Oxy an' mugger we meet! Besides it wasn't in the firm's interests; might ha' stopped sales.'

'You don't mean – you don't mean – the Guard's going to have babies!' exclaimed the lieutenant, understanding gradually. 'God! crèches on the march! It isn't decent!'

'Thur ain't no bloody decency about anything the units do,' said Haggard; 'an' thur ain't no crèches. Yu see all those carcases down thur, thousands of 'um, acres of 'um? Well, it's those'll give us the 'blasters not the living units. As you'll probably be eaten up by 'um yu may as well know. Those carcases are no more dead than a tree is if yu lop off its branches; thu'r just not pugs any more, that's the only way thu'r dead. Thu'r lumps o' living oviplasm an' the only thing that's killed is the centralizing force which kept 'um working prop'ly an' stopped 'um from germinating. An' the injections, neutralizers. When thu were alive all thu could grow was lumps an' things, but now . . . Thu'r just a mass o' seeds let loose. That's all a "dead" unit is, a mass of seeds, an' thu'll grow thur kind like all seeds, like ketchup does.

'Say,' he broke off, 'hadn't we better get? Those French stratos'll be piping round soon.'

The little scout leapt into the air and in three seconds we were level with the top of the shattered beacon. The open sea became half our view, Flamborough Head fell below to a dusky outline and the dim wolds came hurrying beneath like shadowy waves. A lost land, a ghost world which a short week ago had been homely and bright with busy human life; still and lifeless, and breeding ground of none knew what foul births, pestilence and worse. I glanced at Haggard and he, too, was staring down, his face more serious than I had ever known it.

Little towns, battered and lightless, came into view over the horizon and passed. In a quarter of an hour we were dropping steeply over York to the landing fields.

VII

But here, before passing on to the actual coming of neoblast upon the deserted scape of the battlefield and the air war which preceded and accompanied it, I feel I owe some slight physiological explanation to my more serious-minded readers.

I have mentioned in an earlier chapter how Goble contended against the inordinate growth energy of his specimens, how they sprouted new limbs and sometimes whole though immature imitations of themselves, and how this proclivity was not limited to any particular portion of their anatomy, but was common to their entire structure; I have explained how he found it impossible to eradicate by a centralizing of the reproductive and other organs which by providing vital spots would have negatived his conception of the perfect fighting animal. He strove for and achieved a creature altogether animal in its power and mobility, but structurally more akin to plant life. His phrase, 'cells in a living machine', expresses not only his vision of the units in relation to the Guard as a whole, but the literal truth of the millions of cells comprising each individual unit.

Each cell was an organism to itself, subdued to playing its specific part and acting in concert with all the other cells in the unit, so that while the brutes were intact the bodies as a whole would respond to certain influences and all the parts act in unison. Periodic injection counteracted both the ordinary growth capacity of the cells and also their inherent reproductive powers; but once the bodies were chopped up sufficiently, their main sensory nerves and ganglia destroyed or separated from the rest, then agamogenesis, non-sexual reproduction, immediately started in the then uncontrolled cells. Many cells went to waste, neutralized by chemical suppressors and other abnormal stresses, but the remainder was as prolific though not so reliable oviplasm as that from which they had originally grown, and retained, more or less, the capacity to reproduce further highly organized creatures similar, in varying degree, to the Pug Brothers in the factories.

'For every unit that's left out in the sun, disintegrating, germinating, hell knows how many there's going to be,' said Haggard to me that night. 'The heat'll bring them on hand over fist. Not that they'll be such prime beauties as the Brothers: there'll be no special feeding for them an' no injections, but there's nothing on earth can kill 'em unless *we* do. They've got an Eden all to themselves out there beyond the gas, unless we can get through in time an' they'll people it with devils of every shape and size.'

Neoblast has been made the subject of the strangest and most grisly of fancies. It has been compared to disease which is one of the normal consequences of dead things left unburied. It has been likened to the dead returning from the battlefield, their suffering, fear-warped minds manifested in uncouthly formed flesh, their wounds and mutilations still with them, for its products, as I have indicated, were most erratic in their growth, blind, half headless, and limbless, or otherwise deformed specimens being quite common. Though it is understandable that some unscientific minds should view these deficiencies as inherited injuries, I hope I have made it clear that such was not the case and that their variability, suggestive and sickening as it was, was entirely due to imperfect heredity, to faults in the oviplasm genes.

Neoblast was the most natural of phenomena, as natural as decay, and as inevitable.

BOOK III

CHAPTER EIGHT

The Battlefield Gives Birth

BACKGROUND TO WAR

THE BRITAIN OF that blazing August may be visualized as a patchwork of intersecting pictures framed in the flash and fury of air bombardment. The whole is shortly in flux. Scenes run together to become one; they flow westwards away from the scarred battlefield, away from the air front of the industrial districts leaving blank, death-infested spaces behind, gas-fields and areas where the mutilated remnants of bombed contingents are still at large. No air-force can prevent the steady, scientific destruction of communications, nor guard more than a few chosen spots against the massed superiority of a continent. The mother-machines are in control of the upper strata, and though they cannot occupy the land as they have the air, this is at the mercy of the bomb-pluggers which can destroy almost as they will. Humanite and sticky gas are cheap so that it is often more convenient to devastate a whole town than to search out separate military objectives.

At strategic points around the coast Guard contingents are stationed to repel any further land invasion, but neither these nor the home air-force can prevent blockade nor bring new supplies to the island.

Within a very few weeks there is an appearance of final disintegration, of that crash of a civilization long prophesied. But it is not yet that: it is an immense readjustment, compelled both from within and without, in which thousands are dying and millions are rebellious, but in which encampments if not homes are provided, food of a kind is distributed, and a vital minimum of law and order drastically enforced. Civilization has grown cunning and knows how to keep its essential core in safety, and there is no intention of allowing a maddened populace to defeat its own racial interests. For civilian morale matters little; the only morale of importance is in luxury and safe-keeping, together with the new Flesh manufactories which are growing in the depths below London. It was always known that the country as a whole could not be protected from the air, and though the resultant chaos passes expectations national policy cannot be altered. For the while the country must be abandoned, its detailed history a grim recital of whole districts blown to ruins, of town-wide conflagrations, roads and rails rendered impassable, disasters which personally I never saw and of which I could only tell by hearsay. When the few chosen centres which can and must be protected have fulfilled their purpose, the chaos around will be ruthlessly stamped back into order. That purpose is to break out of the frame of blockade and bombardment which is closing in on them and to spread a worse confusion abroad.

Meanwhile, as soon as the first stampedes and horror are over, the emergency Labour Bodies will recruit all possible persons to establish a new order of life and to counteract the spread of revolution. This, however, may need more drastic action and should provide suitable employment for the human military forces, particularly those surviving from the navy for, since ships became little better than practice targets for the ubiquitous powers of the air, these have become more restless even than the army.

II

London is the hub of the new scheme. From the moment war broke over the marching Guard in Leeds its millions were gripped in an organization long and diligently designed to avert panic; they were flattered and bullied, harried and advised in a manner so vigorously efficient that they were confused into the belief that they were being adequately protected. The famous balloon barrage speckled the sky, aeros zoomed over the outskirts without intermission; no one took his children to zoos any more, they took them to see the Death Guard, specially doped, cleaned, non-perspiring specimens, pleasantly varnished and in highly polished harness and shining helmets, on free show in every park of importance. There was no threatening night sky above, only searchlights and invisibly protective blimps. The earth felt more solid for its being honeycombed with raid-shelters.

One can think of London as a stupendous organ with ten million keys and stops; expert fingers were constantly playing on it lest the organ should suddenly change into a land hydra, each key and stop a panic-stricken head.

The organist played, 'Business as Usual', and all the pipes cheered. At a word the tune changed and the pipes were silent, stupefied. The balloon barrage, a doubtful asset to the new form of centralized defence, disappeared to Brighton, London's annexe and war playground, and the centre of the city evacuated overnight. Though much normal work was still continued, workers entering by special permit only, the great ebb and flow of the traffic tides was over. Followed a spate of new regulations, new work, new price controls, rationing, orders, orders, orders, compelling study, keeping the people busy, convincing them they were still under protection. 'For your own safety, *keep in the outer belts*', ran the proclamation. The wisdom of this advice came home with the first raids on London. Each night and many days air battles raged over the militarized centre and the home counties shuddered beneath the passage of the bomb-pluggers. In the morning roads and rails would be found impassable, many citizens were dead. But they were dead inadvertently; it was the transport ways the enemy wanted to destroy, not the citizens. There was no gas, no fiendish massacre.

More slowly did they realize that this concentration of defence involved their relative abandonment, that safety and food supplies were also being concentrated on the principle that if only a minority could be saved the privileged and their minions engaged in defending the country must be that minority. Some said there was a month's food in the country, some three, some six, but it was mostly in great, guarded storehouses and the problem of its disposal to the people at large was increasing daily. To have spread it evenly to all and sundry would have been as reasonable as dividing the cartridges and shells so many per head.

This was the logic of modern war for a tiny land set in the sea, it was the logical destiny of a majority now powerless and meaningless, useless even as cannon fodder. They were the People, incapable both of fighting and of making peace, onlookers, encumbrances, doomed to die patiently or rebelliously – did it matter? – whilst others starved them that they might be saved! In their name thousands of aircraft were under construction, secret factories were turning out submarines, the legions of the Guard were being bred, equipped and housed, housed in the very underground shelters which had been prepared for the People. In their name some vast counterstroke would in time be delivered; perhaps they would hear of it, would cheer victories which swept over them like avalanches, leaving them dead in their train.

In procession they marched to the city limits, here a mere cordon of soldiers and machine-guns, there a flimsy barricade, in the East End sand-bag walls and barbed wire, and, as their tempers ran, presented petitions or stood staring, wondering whether they could break through and to what end; or flinging themselves at the barriers in crudely armed masses. There was much parleying with the soldiers, but these were well fed and housed and saw no good prospect in the hungry crowds either for themselves or their country.

On the Whitechapel and Commercial Roads and south of London Bridge, a hundred yards behind the walls which cut off all access, contingents of the Death Guard stood, day and night, fed in their chains, grumbling and thudding and jostling, injected every half-hour to prevent their wakening to fighting condition until needed. They were there in the name of the People, a warning to those threatening to overthrow the leaders who held the safety of that People in their hands.

Contingents were in depot at Croydon beneath the old airport, at Guildford and Gatwick. From Croydon also the balloon barrage restarted, forming a high pseudo-protective barrier as far as Brighton. London had chosen Brighton for its scanty relaxation and it liked its Brighton safe and bright. Outside the militarized centres its shelters were unequalled; the heavily mined channel guarded it from invasion. Though it could have been destroyed from the air in a day, so could any other town if ever the enemy turned to sheer massacre. It was handy. It had all the facilities for wartime amusement.

The first semi-panic had been ended by the unleashing of every publicity device the Metropolis could command.

'The Safest Overground Town in England.' 'No Danger from Refugees.' 'Spend the War in Brighton', cried the adverts, and while armed patrols headed away undesirables, the wealthy went south to pay their Safety Taxes with comparative content. Officers and others whom duty kept in London flew over for afternoons or evenings; the hotels were thronged, the great dance-halls flourished, the Flying Stage became a centre of more hectic gaiety than it had ever been. It's a different war again! (in Brighton). Behind black windows Brighton merrymade into the early hours, loose-hearted and undisciplined. The air-front of London needed its Brighton like the trenches of old needed their Paris.

Within hearing of this orgy my grandfather lay on his sick-bed, studying papers, listening to the radio and, as these grew dumb under censorship, meditating and worrying and dictating long letters to people of influence whom he thought he might sway. He wrote more than once to Goble and to Dax, for it had not been thought wise to tell him that they were dead a month gone.

III

While Goble and his helpers were still engaged in arranging the conveyance of their more valuable specimens to a safe spot, alien bombers attacked the Compound. Before help could reach it the pluggers barraged in circles, one mile, half a mile out, spraying gas into the centre meanwhile. Those who escaped were shot down by machine-guns. No doubt they would have preferred to take Goble alive, but that was not possible.

There was one survivor, a negro attached to the laboratories, who had rather a miraculous escape. He left Goble and Professor Dax busily destroying everything of value. One wonders what Goble's thoughts were, but that we shall never know; he went about his last work of firing the laboratories with hunched shoulders and a dark scowl, but now and then he laughed at remarks made by Dax who seems to have been optimistic about escaping. He had always been buoyant and irrepressible. Goble told the negro to run for it and hoped he would get through. 'Let out some of the doped units and keep with them; they'll help to suck the gas away from you.' Perhaps they planned to follow the same tactic later. The negro thought they were blown up. All that was left alive an hour later was a considerable number of units in various stages of growth.*

To have told my grandfather would have been equivalent to killing him, for he never tired of talking about Goble and their early days together. 'Those little pugs blundering about in the Congo sun, silly fat things! They made us all roar with laughter. And then as they grew up! Terrible creatures!' His old eyes would glow and a glint of tears dim them, tears of childish disappointment. 'I never saw them march,' he said. 'No. I never saw them march. They got me out of the way before then. I never shall now – marching out in their thousands . . .' Behind the film of tears they could see the excitement in his eyes.

IV

In this complex picture of misery and luxury, of devastation and protected privilege, the Northern Armies are to be seen as an inset struggling with the aftermath of their victory. This battlefield on which they made such proud triumph is not merely a desolated area to be reclaimed at leisure; it is a sanctuary of death which each day makes more difficult to penetrate.

Though few know it, it is the potential breeding ground of living plague; in their zeal to defend themselves they have let loose a laboratory and now the laboratory is about to experiment with them.

Even as all the scenes in that palimpsest summer are flowing, so too is this. A few weeks and the Northern Armies are retiring; they have become the steadily receding shore of a great bay in which a relentless tide of life is advancing, a tide of life which multiplies as it is destroyed.

---

*There is a rumour that some of these units are still alive in the African jungle, but this may be merely a fable originating when the Compound was still in existence. – G.B.

THE GAS-FIELD

Within less than an hour of landing in York, Haggard and I were back in the thick of it. 'Just the men we want,' we were told at the Road Depot where we reported. 'Get your field-clearance kit and stand by.'

'Don't we have some sleep?'

'What the hell's sleep?' We were drafted to different sections, I was instructed in the use of gas-gulleters, told a dozen and one things and expected to remember them, and then given a job helping to mend a dopey-tank due off at dawn. 'Where do I look for letters here?' I asked.

'What the hell're letters?' I had a nap in the dopey on its way to the gas-field, some hard rations, and – well, looking back it seems to me I woke up again at the end of three weeks and realized who I was. If death keeps close to you long enough you forget it's there, but you also forget what has gone and what is to come and time itself. With the rest of the Experts, Oxys and soldiers, and every-one else who could be roped in, I became a salvager in a lost land, a glorified scavenger. Scavenger . . . We were scouts, fighters, disin-fectors and scavengers all in one. Our work was to destroy or reshackle such units as bombers and artillery left alive, to locate and thoroughly dispose of all Guard dead, to treat chemically the ground on which they had lain, to aid the gas layers, and otherwise to make the East Riding clean and wholesome again. Our ultimate object was to reach through to the shambles in the coastal area. Twice in the first week I applied for leave and heard no more of it. No word came from my grandfather. I did a job and was glad to be alive at the end of each day.

II

Field-clearance in the gas-field.

We travelled in dopeys, swift little tanks which could chase around like sheep-dogs after sheep and which derived their name from the gas apparatus they carried; or in acid destructors on tractors. A battle-tank or so, equipped with point-blank guns, always accompanied us. Throughout each day irregular gunfire was to be heard where the howitzers, eking out their ration of ammunition, were destroying the drifting Guard; each day at dawn air squadrons rose and the heavier note of their bombing would be heard at intervals until sundown.

Respirators and gas-suits were our normal dress and we had to test our ground every yard for uncharted gas-banks. Our one blessing was that gas and Guard were rarely found together. Not that it killed them. Unless it were very highly concentrated their breathing gullets would not absorb it and coughed it back; but it injured the tissues, eating them away internally, and that, in conjunction with the action of vesicants on the outer skin and electric gas on the whole organism, had the effect of driving them mad if the term is permissible. They would fling themselves indiscriminately at walls and trees and at each other and, ceasing their uninspired prowling, would be in constant, violent movement. They never stayed long in the gas deposits.

The life was hellish but fascinating. After the first day I thought of nothing else. The hope of getting through to Bridlington and seeing what had actually happened there held me.

Death licked men from us daily, silently, and without warning. A shimmering as of heat above the dry grass, a sudden respirator-dulled cry of: "'Lectric!' and some incautious man would suddenly stiffen in his walk and shrivel before our eyes, or come gasping and swaying back for help we could not give. Or gas-mad units would come upon us unexpectedly.

Six of them came hurrying across an open field. The scene was as peaceful as it well could be, early morning, birds singing, the slightest of caressing breezes, nothing in heaven or earth to stir them to anger excepting their own raging selves. Not until we appeared crashing over the hedgerows like huge hooded toads, and then they had thought for nothing except the dopey immediately ahead, and that was the one in which I crouched staring along the barrel of my gas-projector.

Straight for us, hell-for-leather, heads down. At twenty feet we had to open fire, and in the intervening seconds correct the aim of our gas directly into the units' open mouth-gaps. Nothing, but the highly concentrated stream full on the gullets at the back would stop them. I thought of a heavy engined battle-tank Haggard and I had seen in Bridlington stalled in the welter of flesh it had ground under it. Poor little dopey! Then of Bloody Omega and that rhino he had killed in open combat. I thumbed my projector button wondering where Gregory Beldite was due for next.

Our commander bungled the order. His tongue froze or would not work, and all he emitted was a queer stuttering sound. One man glanced back. He tried again, and by then the beasts were not more than fifteen feet distant.

The man who had looked away had no chance with his aim. The other shot had his unit out in three seconds, a lovely shot – and my projector jammed. The five remaining pugs came on us like living battering-rams.

They caught us standing and we lifted bodily up and backwards, swayed on our rear tractors, and over we went, those tearing brutes thrusting at us through the projector embrasures. In the fall the door was strained and sprang open, and the blood-rusty vans of a quadrifane drove in and began jabbing right and left. A second came over the first, their steel ringing together like a dull bell, jarring and echoing in our ears. Others were battering at the gas-projectors, smashing them from their pivots. Our commander was spitted. If a snail has feelings I know what they are like!

We crouched together, silent as the smashed machinery and the dead man with which we were mixed; then, as quickly as they had been on us, the Brothers were gone, abandoning our uninteresting silence for the other dopeys, and when we clambered into the sunlight the last of the five was just going down. They were our first catch and, instead of chucking them into the destructor to be dissolved in the acid vat, we fed them ketchup when they came round, crowned them with daisy chains, and sent them back to York. Scraggy and blistered though they were we did them prouder than most prisoners get. Then we were off again, happy as sparrows, until an hour later one dopey tippled into a concealed gas deposit and had half its crew asphyxiated.

That was the way of our life in the gas-field. Though we gasgulleted plenty we sent no more units back to depot; mostly they were useless specimens, all bulges and growths in between the scars of their brief fighting career, and they found their only suit-able resting-place in the destructors where they were soon reduced to a slime like that from which they came. Some days were spent purifying a meadow where the bombers had caught hundreds and scattered them to shreds, and there we engaged in daylight bonfires with what we could find of the bodies and for the rest were spraying the surrounding ground with acid. It was such a foul business that we had to laugh about it to keep control of ourselves. Never did flesh and corpses yield such a crop of grisly jokes.

At night we parked our flotilla in circular fashion and tented it over with a frame and rubber arrangement so that we could have light, and heat for cooking. The weather was blazing and we spent the evenings half naked, playing cards and singing our bloodthirsty ditties from the Congo. Gas and units and common accident thinned our numbers steadily; bomb-pluggers spotted us more than once, and accounted for many good men. I was in charge of a dopey after a week, and Flotilla Commander in less than three for promotion was quick. Haggard had gone to the Head Field Control. Some of us were still alive at the three weeks' end when the imminence of neoblast put an end to our useless sacrifices.

Struggle as the gas-layers did the gas-field was growing. Their nearest bases only an hour's flight distant, it was impossible to keep four thousand cubic miles of air free of enemy craft. There was fighting over the wolds day and night. Along the line of the Derwent great preparations began, the first intimation that hope of success was being abandoned and an advance by the surviving units feared. Broad barriers of close-netted trip-wire were erected which, when electrified, were designed to operate automatic acid sprays. Haggard had told me sufficient for me to know that not only units were expected. The country that way became alive with soldiers cheerful at having work to do.

It was about that time that I came sane (or started to go mad), and reached my decision to finish with this madman's life before it finished me. I realized again that I had come into this bloody business of war, and worse than war, with some kid's idea of stopping it and, though that might be lunacy, it was time this wild, forgetful play of being hard and courageous ceased. I had a look at my disgusting self in a bit of broken mirror, tanned, whiskered face, torn, mud- and bloodstained jerkin, and swore by the hell which had made me so, that if I were going to die I'd die fighting death and not perpetuating it.

Just a bloody scavenger of Flesh in the gas-field! Me!

ON THE AIR-FRONT

I was in York at the time. We had come down from Malton district for repairs we could not execute in the field, and had found the withdrawal of the Northern Armies already in progress. What remained of the civilian population was loafing about the streets laden with their few treasured goods and the scanty food they had scraped together, watching night-long and day-long as the guns rolled and the soldiers marched, the drab, khaki-clad end to a once glowing pageant, delaying, doubting until the last ranks were gone and the dust subsiding. They could not believe they were to be abandoned; they knew but could not believe. If an enemy had been advancing on the city ... But this was the aftermath of victory. Throughout the district it was known that the living plague from the east was coming, but they could not visualize its meaning. Was there something an army could not fight? Were armies, then, use-less?

York had been our base, sending us reinforcements in exchange for our dead. As the centre of the Northern Armies it had enjoyed a brief spell of prosperity prolonged after the invasion by the westward migration, bewildered country people mostly who shortly before had obediently followed locally appointed cheer-leaders in speeding the contingents on their way to the coast and had now been warned to leave their homes because the queer, frightening beasts they had been told to welcome were likely to return across country to kill them. Sometimes organized into trudging caravans for safety and companionship, more often in separate, miserable twos and threes, these unaccustomed nomads thronged the city and continued westwards when it was found there was little food in York and no air safety, the shelters being altogether monopolized by the Guard reserve. The wretched exodus passed on leaving only its younger men, most of whom were enlisted for gas-laying or field-clearance, or to fulfil an enigmatical demand for 'national helpers' which took them into the new Flesh Factories or the great new industry of road repairing.

What there was of news had come to us via York. The one regular news-sheet and the radio spouted national boost more than news and postal censorship rapidly became prohibition, but truth leaked through by mouth and a blotchily printed paper issued by the West Riding strikers and smuggled about the country which even its fiercest opponents were glad to read for its items of genuine war reports. In one or other of these ways we learnt of the blacking out of the Tyneside dockyards and their following destruction by humanite, of how Darnley and Burnley and other Flesh centres were rendered untenable by electric gas; of roads pulverized beyond hope of repair, dams burst, intensive culture lands poisoned; of riots and the shooting of riot leaders, and how a pitched battle raged in south Leeds with tanks and artillery engaged. Swiftly, a deeper night fell and into the smoke clouds incendiary bombs rained and ended the futile struggle. Strikers and soldiers ran blazing through the streets together to plunge into the river.

Our whispering gallery told us how Flesh manufacture was still in vigorous progress and of a strange new London growing below ground to accommodate it.

But until those strangest, most startling reports which ever emerged from a stricken battlefield began to percolate from high quarters into the streets and homes of the people, York, though bombed almost nightly, felt itself safe from the worst stresses of war. Then tales brought in by the airmen began to spread, reports of hosts of the Guard lying dead and how, when they passed over a few days later, the dead were shrivelled and unnoticeable and in their place was a movement as of busy, new life, reports of Experts in conclave with local military as ill-prepared for their careful technical explanations as they would have been for expositions on Black Magic; stories brought in by muggers of incredible things seen in broad daylight and how all this was week-old news carefully kept secret and that now the whole east coast and for miles inland was alive with this new germination, with vigorous, insatiable life.

From an incredulous whisper it grew to be the main fact in

existence. Like all the hags and monsters of war the Flesh conceived not only in life but in death also. Like pestilence incarnate this scourge was coming westwards out of the battlefield.

II

The coming of neoblast must have been simultaneous over a very wide area. Wherever the Guard lay dead there that most revolting of all natural phenomena began to reveal itself. It has been calculated that nearly a hundred thousand units were 'killed' in the fighting in the East Riding, a hundred thousand centres of neoblastic activity like as many heaps of dung breeding flies. To these our bombers and artillery had added further centres in their efforts to destroy the roving units and, as the new gas-fields were created by enemy aircraft, still others came into being, in south Leeds and Darnley and westwards into Lancashire, wherever manufacturing had taken place, in and around the old coal-mines of Barnsley and elsewhere on the sites of the Guard depots. Our field-clearance was infinitesimal compared with the needs of our problem.

It is said that the soft west wind which was blowing intermittently throughout that summer carried minute seeds coastwards from where the strikers had emptied the ketchup loads, thus establishing new oviplasm growth areas close enough to the now barren birthplace of the first neoblasts to attract the ravenous hordes inland.

We Experts, who alone realized the full portent of this new calamity, were the only ones to be pleased about it. We cheered the rumour that, certain defensive preparations having been completed, most of us were to follow the troops south. We were pestered with questions by citizens visibly blaming and hating us.

A once popular general addressed a crowd from an extemporized platform, vociferating optimism, saying that Britain would triumph, that great counterstrokes were in preparation. They listened sullenly – it filled in the aching time – but they knew they were no longer Britain, that victory would mean nothing to them. They were fleeing from one victory. When he finished they hissed him.

I came across another crowd being harangued in a hoarse voice by a fat but semi-starving man in a quaint old-fashioned hat and check coat, obviously a race-course tipster, who was selling scraps of news, 'guaranteed uncensored', scribbled on slips of dirty paper just as a few weeks before he had been selling tips. I was his only customer. He asked for food but accepted money as it might have value somewhere else. I forget what the news was but there was a Biblical text attached.

'I never held wi' the Last Day or anything,' he told me, 'but there's a lot o' tork about it. Signs, they say.'

'Signs be darned!' said an old man. 'I never see nothing queerer in this Guard than in aeros long sin'. These things come. It's science. If there's other things coming, then they're coming. Nothing good never did come out of a battlefield not even out o' your Biblical battlefields.'

I left them arguing and went on to a dressing station for a poisoned finger and there, as an Expert, I took precedence over a hawk-eyed old Colonel who stamped about angrily nursing a bandaged arm while I had attention. 'It's a pity they didn't let you damned Experts run this war,' he fumed. 'Experts! Neoblast! They'll be telling us next that the tanks are cohabiting. The army's an anachronism, a show, a parade, a recruiting dodge. Nothing to do but wire and dig trenches and blow up the ugly brutes they've put in place of us! Not even that unless the Experts tell us! General Tankerley is in command! Hah! Of a lunatic asylum! Christ alive! Is any of us in command of anything!

'At the beck and call of every roadman in the country!' he grumbled, pacing round.

'I'll submit your complaint to Vessant when I see him next,' I jeered, but he took me seriously. My extreme filthiness probably persuaded him that I must be a Head Expert. I told him I was Beldite and he was extraordinarily impressed. 'Tell him the military are extremely dissatisfied. Impress it on him that if this war were run in the proper manner, the orthodox manner, that we could win – without all this upset.' Upset he called it and suddenly grew suspicious that I might be lying. 'You wouldn't be here if you were who you say. Why, Beldite and his grandson have a power equal to Vessant's!' That was not true, but it impressed me. Perhaps if I saw Vessant, and Human, and Rufus, and the Prime Minister I should find them fawning round Godman like this old Colonel was doing with me. Well, if rumour were true, I should be in London shortly ... By that evening only casual, lurking thieves and hangers-back prowling for leavings were left in York apart from a skeleton detachment of troops and us depot hands. These, and a few hundreds of unpretentious but strangely steadfast people who might be seen during the day carrying on their precarious life undismayed and uncomplaining. At night they came together to declare their faith and to give thanksgiving for the death which was coming upon them.

III

In wartime superstition finds perfect soil, well manured with fear and helplessness. Talismans are sought eagerly by those whose lives are in the hands of the gods; news of the future is demanded by those who can no longer control their destinies; religion cowers back into its dark origins, reviving the black dooms and prophecies it had hoped to forget.

Each night a preacher mounted the city wall and reverent crowds gathered round him. If aircraft passed and sirens and explosions sent others shivering to shelter they knelt in prayer unafraid.

'Man has poured the evils of his soul into a beast,' cried the preacher, 'a beast that ravages and slays, that is the Beast of the Pit come to earth. When the Beast is dead still its evil goeth on. It riseth from the dead in mockery, it is an hundred beasts, it is the sins incarnate that Man hath harboured in his bosom all the days of his fall.

'God hath not judged for God is all-merciful and would save the very damned. But Man has chosen to perish in his pride, to die blaspheming in his White Man's Glory. And there shall be no more repentance for those who have chosen death, for the day of repentance is gone and now is the hour of last damnation for all but the few who are with me in God. They shall rise from life to life knowing no death, but Man who dies shall not rise from his dead. Nay, the Beast shall rise, yea, the Beast shall rise and the earth shall be peopled with the children of the flesh.'

'Cometh the Day! Cometh the bright day!' chanted the crowd of the truly repentant.

*

IV

Rumour was not true. Troops to the west of Hull were in danger of being cut off. Gas hemmed them in and plague and Guard were likely to wipe them out unless help came. We were routed out of our sleep in the darkness of an air attack, a dozen flotillas and gas squads, and within the half-hour were moving once more to the gas-field to which we had hoped to say 'goodbye' for ever. We made a bee-line of it, tanking across everything, heading straight for neoblast country where our new job lay. Curiosity damped disappointment in some, but not in me.

I was found hesitating a yard away from my dopey by Haggard who summed me up in a glance.

'Yuv got bugs, I know, but this ain't the place to air 'um. In yu go. Yu'll enjoy the little 'blasters until they enjoy yew.'

I was commander of that flotilla and Haggard of the entire fleet and he and immediate duty clouded my judgement. By noon I had my first glimpse of neoblast.

CHILDREN OF THE FLESH

We had been out since early morning in as scorching a sun as I had ever known, footing it largely because the dopeys were like ovens. More than one fainted with the heat and the suffocation of his respirator. We had discarded our gas-suits by eleven o'clock: danger or no danger they had become unbearable. We must have looked the queerest scum of Hades in shorts and open shirts, some of us naked to the belt, and topped by oxidized muzzles, metal tubing and goggles. An absurd compromise, for most of the gas could have reached our vitals as easily through the skin as through our mouths. We put our trust in the little gas detectors shot ahead and off came the smothering head-gear as well. And no one who has not worn one of those hell-masks for hours on end on a glorious day can know what breathing really means.

At noon we rested, finding shade under a clump of trees. So jaded were some of us that we slept before eating and then decided to sleep again. The sun was coming round in our direction and for this second nap I and a Congo went deeper into the trees. They were dark in comparison with the outside.

We had gone some ten paces into the shade when I saw something moving in the underbrush. My immediate, casual thought was of rabbits. The next moment I had gripped my companion's arm tightly and had drawn him to a sudden halt.

'That!' I exclaimed stupidly. 'What's that?' He, too, was staring. We stood quite still. From the undergrowth a heavy-bodied, club-headed little monstrosity some six inches long bobbed out at us and withdrew. It was eyeless and noseless or nearly so, but it had arms and legs and my swift impression was that it was standing in semi-upright position.

It was gone.

From a clump of fern a scurry of the little imps appeared, shuffled across an open space . . . They also were gone.

My companion growled something which I missed because I was not listening. I was wondering whether I had really seen these creatures or whether the checker of bright light and shadow under the trees had tricked my eyesight. I stood, dummy-like, asking myself whether this unnatural life was beginning to tell on me, giving rise to hallucinations, and knowing all the while what the true answer was. When I came to myself the Congo was gone and the recall whistle was sounding prematurely.

All the crews were gathered in an interested cluster as I left the trees. In five seconds I was renewing acquaintance with the vision I had tried to disbelieve. Someone had caught a neoblast.

It was – no, not struggling – palpitating in the hands of one of the men and another, who had captured it, was glowing with pride over his shoulder. It was slightly bigger than the ones I had seen and was all lopsided as though one side had grown more quickly than the other. The mouth-gap was twisted grotesquely and it had one recognizable eye surface and one smeary-looking blotch. It gulped and seemed to be nibbling at the air for food. It looked like a botched kind of monkey freshly skinned.

We all stared at it silently, knowing it for the precursor of the most evil experience in our lives.

'Bah!' said the man who held it and, dropping the distortion to the ground, stamped on its head.

'Damn you!' its captor shouted. 'I wanted to keep it. I was going to dope it and send it to my girl just to show her what we're up against.'

'If she lives within fifty miles of here its brothers'll reach her quicker than the post,' I laughed.

The little body with it squashed head was still squirming.

'Boys, thur's a change coming,' Haggard told us commanders. 'Tell all to keep near the tanks till I say. These critters about here mean the whole lot's moving inland an' when they decide to come thu'll come with a rush. Thur big as hell, thu say, along the coastline. Thu'll bring what's left of the Guard with 'um.'

II

By nightfall, after communication with York, we were under new orders not to move from our position until further instructions came through. We were too far north. Early to bed, and by eleven we were all awake again. It was a windless night but beyond the rubber walls of our bivvy was a constant movement as of rustling grass.

'Hell, I can't stand this!' said our second-in-command and crossed to the radio to get through to York again.

'Stay put!' he exclaimed. 'We're in no danger. I wish to the devil we *were* in danger. Cronking here! Those *lice*! Like ghosts!' He cursed himself back to bed and, 'Don't bother about 'um, boys,' said Haggard from his corner. 'It's only the little 'uns we hear. Thu can't hurt us an' we can't do anything about 'um because thur too many.'

I lay in that moving, whispering darkness, listening, unable to sleep. Quiet fell. There was a remote concussion of distant bombs but that was normal and lulled me. At two by my luminous watch I woke to Haggard's voice at the wireless. Lights came on and everyone rose. Orders were that we were to break camp and move south-south-west for five miles; apparently we were to be steered through this neoblast country by radio. The news was that the coastline breeding grounds were emptying and the migration was heading due west.

Lights out and the clumsy, blasphemous folding and packing of our gas-proof contraptions in pitch blackness. The neoblast had passed for the while but now and then we trod on a straggler. An hour and we were strung out on the trek, a metallic pandemonium waking the night wolds, our engines grumbling sullenly beneath the clangour of our passage. There were constant halts. Messages came at intervals steering us on a zigzag course which towards dawn was taking us on a direct line to Market Weighton. With the light we tested for gas and left our tanks for the open air. Somewhere *en route* we had passed over neoblast. We had felt nothing, but the tractors were coated with slimy substance and here and there oddments of limbs and flesh told their own tale. We might have been ploughing through a field of babies. We had escaped the main flow.

Market Weighton was empty except for a frontier depot at which we learnt that what we had passed through was one of the breeding grounds created by our bombers within the previous week and not a part of the main movement. This accounted for the smallness of the neoblasts. But, as if by some uncanny interchange of thought, these too were on the move, the true reason no doubt being a meteorological one.

An air scout described what he had seen east; millions, he insisted, and ranging from a foot to three feet high. Going headlong and eating on the way. Like locusts but worse.

'I wish you'd left your biology in the books instead of bringing it out here for me to deal with,' he said. 'Nasty nuisance!' He was under immediate orders to return to his scouting and, I heard later, did not return. Presumably his engine failed and he had to make a forced landing in his nasty nuisance.

III

The flotillas were now in position to cover the retirement of the troops along the Humber. It was to be field-clearance on the grand scale. We were to wipe out all later growth areas in the district, well advanced by now, and acidize every inch of the countryside so that if the main migration came that way it would find no food but plenty else. Beverley must have been particularly succulent and held them interested, otherwise we should not have had a chance.

For some days we circled out from Bishop Burton and became as familiar with the smaller brand of Haggard's 'little 'blasters' as we were with their parents. There was quickly a shortage of acid and we took to burning them. Our fires had to be out by dusk but more than once secured too strong a hold on the dry vegetation so that the night came lit by flames and pluggers swooped out of the unseen to bomb the neighbourhood around this suggestive phenomenon.

I fell in with a laconic little Cockney, full of news which reminded me that there was still a war on. He had come from London to complete training in the field as one of the new Experts. The *In*experts, we dubbed them. 'We'll awl be back there soon,' he assured me; 'cahn't stop this rot an' awl fleshers wanted there. Notser poster tell,' he said, and told.

'Wot they cawl Overseas Stytions started. Awl over plice. Fact'ries down below turnin' out Guard. Dohn' know 'ow far. Right down. Enemy'd 'avter sink shahfts ter reach 'em. Then there's –' He stopped, his snippet tongue balked for the nonce by more complicated details. 'Wotyercawlem. Miking gloiders an' rocket thingmebobs, send 'em orf. Catterpult guns, sort of. Ye'. Goin' ter shoot the Guard acrost.' His thumb jerked south-eastwards in a circular swing. 'On'y wye out. Cahn' do nothing 'ere. Scrappin' arselves. My be ett up by these 'ere rodents if we ain't eatin' each other. England sittin' on 'er backside witing ter be kay oed! No bleedin' fear! Not 'arf!' That was a long speech.

'Ever 'erd o' Vessant sittin' still on 'is bottom. 'Asn't one. Leastwyes doesn' need one. Uses 'is legs an' brines. Shoves the others. Like 'apenies!'

'Catapult-guns?' we inquired. 'You can't shoot gliders sixty, eighty, a hundred miles.'

'Cawl 'em catterpults. Not rubber things. Prest air, 'xplosives, 'ow should *I* know! Used up 'ere onner smawl skile, th' tell mi. Why not? Blighter not long since goin' ter shoot 'imself ter th' moon. Thinks 'e can do that, we can do this. Wot's it matter if they bring 'em down. Plenty mor. Dohn' cost as much as a shell them gloiders an' Guard two a bob. Ye'.' Pressed for fuller details he had exhausted his knowledge but had a background to give to it. 'Fed like 'ogs 'ere. Up London wye jest scraps. Dolin' out. Synthetetic food an' stuff. Wooden known London, you. Awl one bleedin' basement now. 'Tain't no use bombin' their plices. They've got us beat at that. Bung th' Guard acrost, onertwo milyons. Bring 'em ter their senses. Ye'.'

On that, lying awake at night, I made my decision. My grandfather must have had a load of conceit ever to imagine he could control the business of life-making he helped to start (or to dabble in it at all), and I suppose the same fool confidence came uppermost in me. Have you ever looked at yourself in a mirror and whispered, 'Jones!' or 'Robinson!' or 'Fothergill!' and, because you'd had some little success, it sounded big? I stared at myself in the dark and murmured, 'Beldite', and, God knows, it was about the only thing I had from which to draw strength of purpose, a name which had smashed a world – and if it tried could remake it. I made it sound bigger than all the other names in the political galaxy and it put a meaning to the callous, hard-bitten hell-hound I had become. I never let the grip of it fail until it nearly drove me mad in defeat. It was a psychological trick, but without it I'd have got like Haggard. You know what he was like.

'We're not letting them do this thing,' I said to him in the morning. 'We're not letting them spread this hell over to Europe.'

'Might as well,' he disagreed without heat. 'Guess yu always had a bit of an itch against killing though. What yu thinking?'

'Bolting. We'll never get south otherwise. It's deserting in the field. You could have me shot for suggesting it.'

'Sha'n't know anything about it. Yur tired of the "thur's not to reason why" balls, eh, an' want to do a spot of reasoning for yu'self. That's more yur job than this, Gorey; anyone can burn spawn. I'll stick round an' report yu dead. Maybe I won't be exactly lying except by a few days. Pipe the word when yuv packed.'

IV

All day in the field, sweltering, cursing, the sky clouding up for a storm like a roof coming over the world, the heat growing more oppressive as though it were being forced down upon our bodies. The first real rain for weeks was coming. Rain! We had almost forgotten the feel of it.

About three we ran across neoblast in a spinney, two-foot high beggars eating ravenously. Unlike the artificially treated units they had a natural appetite and, sucking what juice there was out of anything which came to hand, they spluttered the solid residue out. They had more the appearance of being continuously sick than of eating.

There was no acid so we fetched out our tinder and ringed them in with fire.

'Makes me gip,' confessed Haggard. 'I'll stick a knife in where it's needed or a bullet, but burning – even these slimy vermin.' He was taken that way sometimes, what he called his 'sick-livered streak'.

It had to be done. I was more used to it than he. But I turned away so as not to see the blindly attracted little animals plunging into the gasolene flames. They spluttered like grease. Some came through and we all had to share in that. Handwork it was, for they were slow enough at that size to catch, but they were clammy and oily as pugs going through the wash-ups and we used specially roughened gloves so that they should not slip away. Then, whush, a dose of gas into their gaping gullets and, whizz, back into the flames. If viewed rationally I suppose it was nothing like so foul as any ordinary battle in which you spread the flames on human beings instead of throwing them into the flames, but it seemed worse. Like slaughtering children. The difference was, perhaps, that we knew exactly what we were doing and could see them die.

The fire did its work well, but we had failed to isolate it properly; we should have spread the extinguisher liquid more thickly. It was a whale of a fire too and seemed to lap up the extinguisher like a cat milk.

A radio message from above told us that units had been sighted a mile north, but we could not leave our job. A blaze once well started might spread any distance in that dry weather and endanger the lives of other flotillas. The units might not come near us, but, if the fire continued, we knew the bomb-pluggers would and we had to mask up as a precaution. Jamming the respirators over our sweating heads we went at it with greater vigour; we sent back for reinforcements and more extinguisher. Over us that canopy of slatey sky spread like black cataract over the eye of the sun. Then the rain came, slowly, in huge drops, followed by sudden deluge, and the smoke from the flames thickened and became an opaque, swirling cloud like a part of the thunder sky above descended. Lightning flashed before my eyes, half blinding me; the rush of the downpour was lost suddenly in a concussion which seemed to come from everywhere at once. As a second grinding explosion followed hard on the first I looked round for Haggard to suggest we should stop work and leave the rain to do the job for us.

Into the lightning and flame-lit struggle came the Guard, driving pell-mell. One moment we were like devils dancing around the flames and the next real devils were with us.

An inarticulate screaming drew my attention. I stared through the blinding smoke in its direction and then ran a dozen paces, stumbling over the rough, invisible ground. The smoke lifted and a man came flying towards me. Other dim figures were beyond him, towering immense in the exaggerating cloud. From his run I knew it to be the snippety Londoner. He fell and squirmed and I knew what was following him.

I continued to run forward, Heaven knows why, for he had not a chance, and, too late, terror seized me. Through that terror ran a streak of sanity telling me that, though I could not save him, I might warn the others.

I swung round and went sprawling on the slippery grass into some sort of hollow and the herd went over me. I had my eyes wide open, glued open, my head twisted sideways exactly as I had fallen. Their huge, glistering limbs flashed over me, pounding mud and grass into my face, the thunder of their hooves and raucous breathing beating into my brain. I remember that I was screaming in my brain, delirious with fear, but I doubt that a sound of it passed my lips.

Something crushed my side, there came a sharp rap on my head . . .

V

I came back to consciousness sometime in the early evening but it was no real waking. Dream, reality and delirium were all confused in me; my thoughts drifted from gulfs of stagnant pain to airy states in which this pain was not wholly mine but a quality of some extraneous being which I shared, as though I lay on pain and the air were pain about me but my thoughts were free to wander brightly, flimsily happy and nonsensical.

There were lucid intervals. I recollect gazing up at a singularly black sky in which a bright star shone, sometimes here and sometimes there; I suppose it was different stars, my eyes being able to concentrate on one only at a time. The star seemed to drone with the sound of a distant aero.

Then, again, it was broad daylight. I struggled out of a delusion that I was pinned under a furnace to realization of my true position.

There was the hot sun I had known for so many days and I was lying in steaming slush, soaked, miserable and with an immense dullness pervading my whole body. All my enfeebled energy must have gone into this effort to understand, for I made no attempt to rise. Then my attention was attracted by movements over to my right.

I am not altogether sure that what I remember was not returning delirium, but it fits in exactly with what I know to be the truth of the thing I saw. The carcase of a unit was lying there perhaps ten feet from me. I should say part of a carcase, for its head was gone and it was studded with lumps of metal from some heavy shrapnel. It was a horrible thing to look at and I could not drag myself from the thought that so men lay out after battle, ort, garbage, with everyone too busy adding to the human refuse heap to heed them. I might soon be so myself. Though, even then, I should have a head. The thought consoled me ridiculously. But what was going on around this unit's body very quickly absorbed my interest and I forgot the beastliness of the thing in a new horror.

Parts of the creature were as if they had melted and run, forming glutinous, pool-like extensions and, whereas the body was still and dead, each of these spreading protrusions had the appearance of life or of something in which life throbs and thrusts. They pulsated irregularly, or was it that beneath the caul-like membrane living organisms moved? As I watched one of them commenced to strain and expand visibly.

It burst with a minute, crepitant sound and forthwith there

came a tumbling flow of tiny, pallid shapes moving of their own volition into the blazing heat. I have seen seed-pods break in similar fashion, but never with such an urge to endure, such eager sentiency. The sporocyst flattened and crinkled, an abandoned parent vesical the purpose of which was fulfilled, and all the little spores became still. I counted – or perhaps I imagined I counted – some fifty or more and, as I was straining my aching brain over this feat, another sporocyst crackled and another and a further hundred or more embryonic neoblast were let loose into the stimulative heat of the sun.

A sick dizziness took me back to unconsciousness ... then I was watching again. Though it must have been hours later the two views seem parts of one. The sun was still high and now there was dry ground beneath me and a raging dryness in my throat. The spawn which before had been like little bundles of tissue were perceptibly larger and had thrust out five stumpy, cactus-like projections, elongated swellings which I dimly realized would soon become arms and legs and heads. As if to find confirmation of my hazy understanding my eyes drifted farther afield for the first time and there was what had once been a second carcase but was now just a dried thing, a residue of unproductive gristle and skin. All the life which had once been in it had passed out into a multitude of separated organisms which now crawled over and around it sluggishly. An inch or more long they were and blotchy yellow, blind things in their thousands.

In nausea objects swim before the failing sight, grow larger and vaguer. So these urgent embryos began to grow in a sick imagination which had captured all my senses, visibly they grew until they were many feet high and their numbers covered the fields to the horizon and beyond. They were moving, hurrying inland in their lust for food and I too was moving, leaving my body behind already consumed by them. Together we crossed the wolds, mouthing and sucking the vegetation in our path, leaving the villages like dry skeletons, until the empty shell of York was before us and we were flooding into it, breathless in our foul haste.

All things were ours, the bright streets, the little, once-cherished homes, the ruined Minster. How we breathed and pawed over the altar finding it the poorest of food and, trapped within the barren walls, turned on each other to satisfy our appetites until chance found us the sunlight again. Even the burial grounds were not sacred to us. We left York behind, left the ravaged inset which had become my life, and hastened into the wider world where the myriads of people awaited our coming in horror, where there was war and the new dead were fresh and our numbers would multiply in decay. We were disease and we were the dead returned from the battlefield, we were the risen Beast and all the evils of Man ... we were the life and the breath which Man had made, the foul life and the fetid breath of war.

Haggard's face was peering into mine. It seemed too huge, too vague for a human face, and there was that pain in my side ... Other faces were in that pain, swollen, silly faces.

No faces – pain – the carcase and its busy spawn cut out very distinctly in the evening light. Haggard's face again, persisting, refusing to be disbelieved.

I was back inside the dopey tent and there was watery sunlight outside and a scent of disinfectant and brandy. I discovered myself to be sipping brandy, Haggard leaning over me. My side was burning in a hellish way and a constant buzzing in my head seemed to be keeping time to the aching throb of my skull.

'Yur a lucky mike,' Haggard was saying. 'That mob must have known who yu were. Just trod on yu they did instead o' slitting yu up. Real consid'ret Brothers, them.' I lay back shivering and he covered me with heated blankets, tucking me in with roughly gentle hands. His smile did not impress me in the least; even to my enfeebled mind he was forcing his jest.

'Trod on me?' I whispered and, 'Kicked yu on the head an' took a fat lump out o' yur side,' he said. 'Yu'll soon be in marching order again.'

I lay still thinking my way through the burning torture under my ribs to something which I dimly knew to be fretting at my mind, something which was before this pain, before the neoblast spores. I reached it, lost it again, and then found it as clear as though I had never forgotten it: how I had intended to desert and get free, the great work I was going to do ... It returned wildly exaggerated as though imminent success had been snatched from me. Dying in the field! Yes, I was dying: Haggard's effort to smile had told me that. I began to jerk and it made the pain worse.

'Get Haggard. I want Haggard.' He was with me again in a minute, chewing his supper and grinning cheerfully.

'That get-away,' I whispered. 'I'll never go now. I'm done for.' I could see that his eyes did not deny me though he shook his head, still smiling. 'I want you to go south. Try to do what I would have done.'

'Queer,' he said. 'That's where I'm going. Orders came through, all Congos to get to London quick. Did yu dream it?'

'I didn't know. That's good. I wanted you to go anyhow. Get straight off. A town called Brighton. The Carfax. Go there first whatever the orders are.' He had to bend to hear me. His eyes brightened.

'Yu mean that gurl? Yu'd like me to take a message to hur?'

'Girl?' I whispered, and remembered Paddy Hassall as something infinitely remote. I had not heard from her since the battle; no doubt she had written but there had been few posts in our frantic world. And probably she had not written. What did I mean to her? Or she to me? There must have been other men since, clean, amusing, secure. Young officers; Brighton full of young officers ... Not filthy with neoblast slime, as good as dead. What did she mean to me – to Beldite! My wavering senses were still clinging to that conception of myself as a great name. A girl in a porch at dusk! A parting kiss which could have meant nothing. Sympathy. She must have felt that I should die like this, babbling, sweating.

'I want you to see my grandfather,' I said. 'Tell him – tell him –' What was there to tell him?

'He's probably dead; he was old flesh. About that gurl?'

'Hell, Haggard,' I snarled 'I –' I thought I had it all clear and understandable and he was perversely dull. The pain racked me suddenly and I shuddered and became quiet.

'I didn't want to leave yu,' he said, a hint of sulking in his voice. 'I was going to dodge that order an' stay with yu.' His horny palm touched my brow and gave place to the soft backs of his fingers. He was puzzling something deeply.

'Goble, Edom Beldite – didn't intend this,' I muttered to him. 'They'll do something if you make them understand.' My eyes bored into his, trying to convey what I wanted, what I could not even have expressed to myself. 'I'll be there to help, later. You hear? You think I'm all spawned up, dying, but I'm not, I'm not.' I rambled.

'Course yur not. Dope yu up an' yu'll –'

'I'll escape. Tell him – I'll be at – yes, View. At View. I'll rest there and get strong.' It had always meant rest to me. I know my words wandered on, reiterating aimlessly, telling him impossibilities, telling him I was dying but would not die ... 'It shouldn't matter that one man dies,' I remember raving. 'But it matters, Haggard. He mustn't die. He's Beldite. I'm Beldite. I – won't – die.' My mind was failing.

I seem to remember his mentioning Paddy again. 'I'll be getting now,' he said. 'Young Gorey ...' His hand lingered on mine.

So I gave Haggard my message not knowing what I meant myself. He left our feverish little land of intense, concentrated struggle for a changing world of which neither of us had any comprehension. The furies of a social system in collapse, the terrified ruthlessness of a whole continent, were black and featureless in my mind. Somewhere in London or other underground fastness hard driven, anxious minds were planning to break the death clouds over their very heads, having no greater pride than to die fighting though the world died with them. I felt that Haggard would prevent them, would save them against their wills, not knowing that to him they and all others were only so much human flesh and his one idea was to help me.

VI

Fever held me semi-conscious and mostly delirious for – but I have no record of the passage of time. I do not know when Haggard left nor when it was that I was sent back to the road ambulance train. I came to my senses in an ambulance tank which was taking me and some dozen others across country, making what little use it could of undamaged secondary roads. I was told we were well west of Goole and that this route had been chosen because the troops retiring towards Doncaster were under constant bombardment. We kept to a south-west course. There was talk of a hospital ahead, I do not know where. There was a man with bandaged eyes who kept telling us that there was more bleeding neoblast this way than that. There was a man sympathetic to the revolutionaries who wished to God he could get to Leeds and died somewhere south of Pontefract. There was mention of the Mercy Gangs. I was not interested but listened. In the absence of any adequate ambulance service for civilians in the desolated areas these voluntary bands had organized themselves to scour the West Riding for wounded and gassed people, assisting them if they could though they had little backing in the towns and the poorest of equipment. They originated in Leeds, but Leeds could not take those they saved, needing all its food and hospital room for its own casualties. Two men argued interminably as to whether it was right for these gangs to put away painlessly those for whom they could do nothing or to leave them to die in anguish. One said it was not mercy but murder; the other, in between fits of coughing, disagreed. I listened.

There was a string of ambulances and some anti-raid tanks with us and the whole train was destroyed one night out in the open Penistone way. There had been gunfire and, later, the ripping tremolo of machine-guns not far above us. Then bomb-pluggers took us endwise. I was awake and much better. From the noise we might suddenly have been led into a gun barrel doing rapid fire. They took us from end to end, returning twice, and when they were gone I was lying on soft, tumbled earth in the deadest silence I have ever known. I lay there till it was light, having no reason to move. Then I stumbled and crawled away from the bloody havoc. There seemed to be no one else alive. I dragged myself a long way into the fields and, blundering upon a haystack, tucked myself into that and fell asleep. It was the best thing which could have happened to me, for the hay made a warm bed and I was exhausted as only a very sick man can be.

CHAPTER NINE

Little People in the Audience

DEATH OF EDOM BELDITE

IT MUST HAVE been while I was still in the gas-field in the Beverley sector that my grandfather died. Since the north-eastern invasion he had changed. He rarely referred now to the past though, from odd remarks, it was evident that his mind was still intent upon it. He seemed to be withdrawing himself from the world and its troubles, often falling into long silences which would last for hours. No longer visibly distressed, it was as if he sought something hidden deep in himself like a man grown cool after irrational fear searches for the true cause of it. Sometimes he was quite childishly happy.

He had no sense of personal danger nor of danger to me, though at times he wondered why I did not write. At night when bombs falling on London were distinctly audible he was not troubled. 'Listen,' he would say, and lie very quietly. 'It's worse in the north where Gregory is,' he said once.

Edom Beldite died to the boisterous sound of music from the Carfax dance orchestra below. He had been moderately well and trying to understand what was taking place in the country.

'There must be millions homeless,' he decided; 'whole towns wiped out.'

He collapsed without warning while Paddy Hassall was reading an evening sheet to him. He preferred her to his nurse. Doctors were sent for hurriedly. One of them, a locum tenens, was very distressed.

'I don't understand,' he said. 'He is in a very serious state. One would think his friends would be here, ministers, the Prime Minister himself. Not even the Press!' He had a strong sense of his patient's immense standing. He considered that there should have been more doctors present and extra nurses.

'Mr Beldite was a great opponent of the war,' Paddy explained. 'I'm afraid his friends have all deserted him and the Press only uses him when he is useful,' she said bitterly.

The locum was frankly incredulous. He had always understood that Edom Beldite had believed in the war, not opposed it. Was he not Britain's greatest patriot!

In any case he had never heard of a myriadaire being unpopular!

Only one nurse!

And no specialists!

The regular doctor knew that Edom Beldite detested fuss, and nurses, and specialists and would die more peaceably without them.

In the dance-hall below the dance was well under way and the overheated, flowery rhythm beat upstairs to the sick-room, mingling with shouts of laughter and an undercurrent of a hundred blended sounds of gaiety. Paddy rang for an attendant.

'Is it possible to stop the dance or make the noise less?' she asked. 'Mr Beldite is seriously ill, perhaps dying.'

'They're celebrating the victory,' the attendant explained uncertainly. 'There's a special exhibition dance coming on.' He looked about him as if wondering how to approach this problem against the immense, pillared magnificence of the Carfax. 'So many people are dying,' he said vaguely and, with insight. 'They've come here to dance and forget.' The orchestra broke into the sobbing strains of 'Don't You Get those Air-Raid Blues'. Loud clapping greeted this popular number.

'But this is Mr Beldite. Edom Beldite.'

'Edom Beldite,' he repeated. 'Yes, of course. They wouldn't have had a victory to celebrate but for him would they? I'll see what I can do. It wouldn't do to tell them. *All* the best people are there,' he muttered in distress, hurrying away. The composer of 'Our Guard' ('Which held our Shores Inviolate') was present in person and was going to sing his famous march song. London had overflowed into Brighton that night.

Paddy returned to the sick-room and found my grandfather whispering weakly to himself.

'They're marching,' he whispered, 'marching. On, on. I can see them. I thought I'd never see them but I can now. Thousands and thousands. They're going over the hill. Right across the world. Goble said they'd do that. "Let them march, right across the world, right into the hearts of men."' He became silent, his eyes closed.

'Ought we not to telephone the Prime Minister?' asked the new doctor. He had never seen a myriadaire die before.

'No,' said Aunt Fertile and, 'He doesn't need the Prime Minister,' rapped the regular doctor. 'Specialists are coming but they will not be able to do anything.'

'Who am I to stop them!' my grandfather's voice resumed very faintly. 'No one listened to me . . . Across the world.' He mumbled a while. 'Marching,' he whispered.

The attendant returned to begin a long, apologetic explanation. The manager would be up in a moment. Thick curtains, felting –.

'Tell the manager it does not matter,' said Paddy. 'We don't think he can hear it. It isn't troubling him.'

My grandfather suddenly broke into uncontrollable tears. Turning half on his side he sobbed himself to sleep.

Sudden shrieks of young laughter sounded on the stairway. Feet went padding by on the thick pile of the corridor. Voices shouting. A girl called, 'You can't catch me-ee!'

'Make way for the Flesh Guard!' shouted a boy's voice in reply and there were renewed shrieks of mock terror.

Then another voice requesting them to return downstairs.

'Very ill. Very ill, indeed.'

'Doctor,' whispered my Aunt Fertile. 'He – he's not holding my hand – like he was. It's – limp. I think . . . Doctor; come.'

Edom Beldite's eyes were open, staring fixedly at the wall, staring beyond all things in their final fascination.

II

At three o'clock, two and a half hours after my grandfather died, an announcement was made from the bandstand and the Victory dance brought to a hushed close. From the ballroom many famous people ascended to file through the death chamber. Now he was gone he was the great myriadaire again, 'the man who made victory possible.' Vans were out in the streets calling the news.

Among the mourners at the bedside was Sir Godfrey Human, silently dignified in a frock-coat so well cut that it matched his bulging head to perfection. The financier, Rufus, a trifle crumpled for one so powerful but still gleaming and alive, accompanied him. The Rt Hon. Rupert Vessant attended the funeral.

He was a trifle more heavily built than either my aunt or Paddy had expected, sturdy more than fat, and was faultlessly clad in traditional parliamentary style, with a tiny spray of pale exotic flowers in his buttonhole which, unable to name, they placed as one of Goble's charming cultivations. It seemed a strange finish to mourning-dress until it was seen that a great wreath of similar blossoms had been sent in his name. My grandfather had loved Goble's flower gardens.

He was the greatest man Paddy had ever met and she studied him carefully. His jaw was projecting and rounded without that softening concavity beneath the lower lip which is normal. An intractable jaw. During the service his lower lip projected slightly and his head sank forward on his chest, increasing the bull-like thickness of his neck. It was a mannerism of his. Some said it was in conscious imitation of Napoleon and others that it had been insensibly acquired through many hours of watching and admiring the Death Guard. His eyes were large, slightly protuberant and of a palish blue and, Paddy felt, oddly childish; keen and vitally interested but more staring than understanding. It seemed strange that he should be genuinely grieved over the peaceful passing of one old man and unconscious of the violent deaths of thousands.

They had a short conversation. Vessant was surprised that I was not at the funeral and more surprised to hear that I had been in the battle as a mere ranker. He was not surprised that they had heard only once from me since the invasion. But vital negotiations for the transfer of Flesh manufacture from Dax-Beldite to the Government were taking place and my presence was urgently needed. I must be found.

'I hope you will find him,' said my Aunt Fertile. 'I hope you will find him a very different man to deal with from what my father was.'

Sir Godfrey Human, who was present, smiled charmingly at Paddy and leant on his gold-headed cane, silent and statuesque. For a moment Vessant looked more like a Flesh unit than ever.

It was a little over a week later that I was reported missing and, probably, dead.

III

I was traced, it seems, with some difficulty and located as being in the ambulance train not more than a few hours before news of the attack on it reached the mobile field depot to which I had been attached. The warrant officers actually accompanied the salvage corps which examined the wreckage. The destruction was so complete, most of the dead being quite unidentifiable or entirely blown to pieces, that it was assumed I was one of these as no other trace remained. As, however, there was a chance that I had lived and had wandered away delirious into the Darnley gas area (there had been similar cases before), all military components were notified to watch for me though this must have been a purely formal precaution as no special search was instituted. My Aunt Fertile was fully notified immediately.

Paddy Hassall received and opened the telegram. She was still holding it limply in her hand when my aunt found her, staring unseeingly out of the window at the sunlit promenade. 'Is it – Gregory?' she said. 'Gregory?'

'I wrote to him only yesterday,' said Paddy. 'I can't believe I shouldn't have known – if he were dead. *Writing* to him – when he was dead!'

IV

Though I never received that letter I knew its contents. It was quite short. It told me of my grandfather's death and of Vessant's wish to find me; it pressed me to return immediately, suspecting that something unknown, something wrong, was being done without my consent. It ended in a way altogether typical of Paddy by saying that unless I answered or came within a week she would come to find me.

There was a postscript, longer than the letter.

DECISION AT THE CARFAX

It has never been my intention to try to lighten this story, loveless and harsh though it is, by dwelling on my most private affairs and so introducing what novelists would call a human love interest. I have no desire nor faculty for such intimate revelations being, I know, rather old-fashioned in such matters and of the opinion that they are no one else's business.

But where they bear directly upon history I have no option and, though it makes me cringe a little to do so, I have to make it clear that when Paddy said she was coming to find me she meant it.

And why she meant it.

'I told him I loved him,' she confessed, clinging to Aunt Fertile. 'I told him over and over again. I felt it would bring him back if nothing else would. I *knew* it would bring him back. I couldn't have felt *that* about a dead man, could I?'

She stared at my aunt with wide eyes, refusing to cry, refusing to believe the obvious, and with a certainty which makes one wonder whether the human mind is merely a supreme trickster or whether it knows and sees without the senses' aid.

'Why shouldn't I say that? He *isn't* dead. He couldn't be dead. I told him he was a big fool not to know I loved him, and that he was blind and it was more important than fighting or peace or anything, and that I was going to find him somehow even if I died or we both died. I'm going; I'm going now,' she said. 'You're not going to keep me back.'

'And this is true – what you say?' said Aunt Fertile doubtfully. 'I – I was never quite sure.'

Paddy nodded. 'It's true about me,' she answered. 'That's all that matters.'

'I'm going to write to the War Office to tell them they must find him,' Aunt Fertile said. 'If he is alive . . .' She bustled about for pen and paper and commenced to write in her large, stiff-necked hand and phraseology. Before many lines were penned I think they both broke down.

Into that room of quite unwarranted grief Haggard walked behind the deferential tap of an hotel servant. 'A messenger from

Mr Beldite,' the office 'phone had announced and fluttered them both to sudden excitement and facial restorations. He must have looked the toughest specimen who ever entered the precincts of a famous hotel, weather-beaten and rugged to the colour and texture of his stained, shabby road outfit, dirty and unshaven as he had left the field and with a new, half-healed gash on his jaw. He still carried his uncoupler swinging from his belt together with hand-gulleter, gas-helmet, thermos, knife and all the other small service kit, and his jerkin had a foot-long slit on one side and a pocket torn out. Paddy described him as a steel trap of a man with a smile in his eyes and murders in the background. He drew up at sight of the, to him, very distinguished ladies.

Filthy as he was, in a moment Paddy was hanging on to his arm asking about me, making a fool of herself, she says, and nearly kissing his grubby jowl. Haggard, at unimaginable heights – or depths, for I have no means of knowing how Paddy's onslaught affected him – began blurting out some modified version of the truth as far as he knew it. There seems to have been a difficulty in understanding his accent or idiom, but it was only a minute or two before they realized that the telegram gave later news than any-thing he had to tell. He read it, with some difficulty, being no reader. 'D'lirious? Does that mean bats? He *was* a bit spawny witted when I left. He'd bugs before that even but ... Don't seem right he could be blown to bits,' he said irrationally, or perhaps to comfort them; 'an' if he wasn't, an' his side's held out, an' he's looped the gas, an' hasn't bin chewed by 'blasters he must be alive all right. Somewhere.

'Yu don't know Young Gorey,' said Haggard to the aunt who had nursed me though childhood; 'he ain't sick-livered or broody like once. Found his guts in the gas-field. He was all set for something big. Still is – if the units haven't got him or the 'lectric.'

'My father mentioned you often,' said Aunt Fertile trying to make him feel at home. 'You were the boy who cut open Mr Goble's best specimen to see the works, weren't you?' She insisted that he should take a bath in their private bathroom and have his chin attended to properly, and at the meal which followed she encouraged him to talk about me and our life together. During this time she was thinking very deeply, studying Haggard and keeping in line with Paddy's thoughts which she could follow quite easily from the expressions on her face.

II

My Aunt Fertile established herself firmly at the beginning of this history. Without her well-cooked meals, her broad-minded understanding, her tact, it is probable that the whole course of the world would have been changed, that there would have been no homo wigglies, no Congo Compound, but only a disillusioned genius pottering pennilessly with his dreams.

And now I have to admit that had it not been for this faded elderly lady, quietly rising from the tea-table to resume her knitting where she had left it at Haggard's entry, I should in all probability be long dead and, because chance had it that my name and the peculiar influence it carried could not be reproduced, the siege of Britain would have risen to its climax, the Death Guard landed in Europe and, who knows, its processes of manufacture spread broadcast to the world's destruction. Paddy would have gone north alone . . . But it was always Aunt Fertile's forte to take charge of the inevitable and turn it to fruitful purposes.

'Miss Hassall has practically made up her mind to find out the truth for herself if that is possible, and I thought of going with her. What do you think of the idea, Mr Haggard?' she said.

'I think yur a couple of – well, I mean yu just couldn't.' He glared at Paddy and, 'I'm going,' she confirmed softly. 'Yu *can't* go,' Haggard snapped. 'Yu don't understand. Women up thur! Tell yu what. I'll go; I'll forget those orders. London won't miss *me*. Guess I shouldn't have left him at all, spawned up like that.'

'Then you can accompany Miss Hassall and I will stay here. I can trust you, I know. Eh? You say there's no *spawn* on *you*? Well, I'm not sure what that means but it sounds trustworthy. I hope you will not get into trouble disobeying orders.'

'I'll take care o' that. An' I'm going alone, see?'

'Which was why you came, of course? To have tea with us and to tell us he was badly wounded and then go back by yourself? Piffle, Mr Haggard, piffle! You came for Paddy because you thought it might be their last chance of seeing each other alive. Don't be ashamed of sentiment. You're not the first blood-and-thunder man I've met and I can see through you. But now you've seen Paddy you think she's too soft and ladylike to go. So do I but –'

'Course she is.' He sought arguments, arguments to hit this fool of a 'gurl' as hard as possible. 'He didn't ask for hur. It was just an idea of mine. Yu can't think of gurls up thur. Find a gurl an' like hur – an' she's in bits the next day. No – stability 'bout anything. An' Gorey . . .' He hurled his clinching argument. 'It's rotten to say it to a gurl, but he ain't that fond o' yu. Fact is he'd practic'ly forgotten all about yu.'

'He merely remembered her address,' said Aunt Fertile, with a speculative eye on Paddy, and Paddy suddenly flung away from the table. 'I don't care; why should I care! I can't live – thinking of him – lying somewhere . . . I'm *going*.' She ran out of the room.

'You see, Mr Haggard,' said Aunt Fertile, 'I used to have to decide matters for both Mr Beldite and Mr Goble and I am deciding this for you. Women have to do. Gregory *needs* Paddy though he probably does not know it, and Paddy needs Gregory. There are some times when just because a woman *is* a woman she must face all the dangers men face. I shall be all right. She cannot go alone so you must go with her.'

She was as straight-backed and decisive as on that distant day when she decided to make View her home, as when she decided that Goble and his oddities must leave Darnley for ever; she was as alive as though she had been saving energy for this moment for the whole of her seventy years.

'I am talking of him as though he were alive,' she murmured, and, 'I will let you have my car. I hear the roads are very bad but it will take you at least part of the way.'

DOGS AT THE CITY GATES

They left little more than an hour later to make what use they could of the daylight. Avoiding the main London speedway which was liable to bombing, they went west with the idea of making through Horsham and Guildford and possibly avoiding the city entirely. Paddy drove and Haggard kept his eyes on the road ahead for danger. Both were silent. Haggard seemed irritated or nervous of her. He took over the wheel as it grew dusk. In Guildford, which was unlighted and busy, Experts were visible, their characteristic garb standing out noticeably. Haggard sunk low into his seat. 'From the Hog's Back,' he said. 'Big undergrounds there. Heard about 'um.' Beyond the town they were stopped by a dimly lit white barrier. Sentries stood guard over it. A huge, phosphorescent notice informed them that beyond the road had been destroyed and that no vehicular traffic could proceed farther.

'They've done it to every main entry into London,' they were told. 'Them bomb-pluggers. They just swoop down and follow the road dropping bombs every fifty yards or so. Special road shattering bombs they're using. Isolating London, that's the new wheeze.' Their informants, soldiers, did not veil their curiosity at the sight of a ragged Expert in the company of a beautiful girl in fashionable driving costume.

Before taking the alternative road they made a fruitless search for food to add to the stock they had brought with them, but though shops were open there was little on sale but raiment, masks, fire extinguisher and a sweetly acid concoction, flat capsules in tubes, which were advertised as fine for allaying hunger. They bought some of these. Five miles out they decided it was too dangerous to proceed in the dark and put up at some village between Aldershot and Pirbright where at an exorbitant price, they secured accommodation. The landlord gave them some tea blended with a herbal mixture and promised eggs in the morning if the hens laid. He was suspiciously amazed at their taking separate bedrooms, but later this turned into half-veiled ridicule. 'Pretending, silly fools. Comes from Brighton where the morals still is,' they overheard him say to a concealed wife. 'As if we'd care, these times.'

Tired as she was Paddy lay for some while staring at the night sky between the scraggy curtains. There were a few faint stars across which swung the searchlights of the depots and camps surrounding them. At intervals a dull, almost inaudible pulsing throbbed in the air. She had no idea what it was. Then a distant clattering arose Aldershot way and seemed to travel backwards and forwards, backwards and forwards interminably. Some machine, perhaps, night working on one of the main arteries to repair destruction. She was very lonely and cried herself to sleep.

II

Dawn saw them on their way again. Very shortly, having passed the ruins of Woking, they were held up once more when they came upon the main speedway running to Wimbledon.

It was easily recognizable as a road, as a first-class motoring road, but its appearance was as if some stupendous giant had been walking along it, a club-footed giant whose footprints were ten and sometimes fifteen feet deep. At times, it seemed, he had been unable to keep to so narrow a path as the sixty-foot highway and his feet had smashed down on the hedgerows tossing mounds of soil and roots and unexpected litter in all directions. Each of these giant footprints was a bomb hole. They stretched into the distance each way, unrepairable except through weeks of work, an impassable barrier to all traffic, useless almost to pedestrians.

There were houses along this upturned road, blank-eyed, empty skulls with shattered windows and some tottering walls. A few women were visible, one hanging out some washing, and there was a bent old man rooting in a garden. A couple of young fellows came out through a broken doorway, plodded heavily over their tumbled garden, and began to make a precarious way citywards along the speedway. They carried empty sacks over their shoulders and one swung a heavy walking stick.

Haggard backed a short way down the side road to turn off into a bumpy lane where the going was awkward enough but there was a sense of sweetness and health. There had been a queer grave-like smell about the road. Half a mile on an old-fashioned terrace of stucco houses presented itself ahead and Paddy insisted on stopping again. There was a little crowd round the last house in the row which had been thrust in as if by a kick and had the appearance of imminent collapse.

'They're all dead in there,' they were told; 'leastways they've left the children. They're dead. On the floor in the front parlour with the ceiling fallen on them.'

While they were talking an old man was passing from house to house, apparently collecting rents. He joined the crowd and shook his old head drearily. 'Times are bad every way,' he told Haggard. 'Only two paid this week. *Two*! If the men were here they wouldn't pay at all but they're mostly in the new Labour Bodies. There's free rations there and some say drink if you can pay. They're still spending their money on drink,' he hissed, 'instead of leaving it at home to pay the rent.' He refused to go into the house which was dangerous but said he would notify someone, after which he hurried away.

Paddy and Haggard went up the garden path to look at the children lying huddled on the floor beneath a fallen joist, some bricks, and a scatter of heavy plaster. It was quite obvious they were dead. Paddy would have gone in but Haggard stopped her. They wasted a little time over one of the women but she was nit-witted with worry. 'Aye, it's bad; everything's bad hereabouts. They buried five last Monday and a bomb dug them up Tuesday,' she kept telling them. The best they could get out of her was that the Labour Bodies would be coming round shortly and would see to everything; it was not wise to touch the children as there might be disease; or the parents might be mad and in hiding. Such things happened.

'They leave them there, babies! and still go on paying their rent . . .' said Paddy. 'It isn't possible!'

'Yu'd better go back. It ain't fit for yu.'

'I'm not going back.'

They spoke to one or two people. All police had been withdrawn, they learnt, and the Labour Bodies were still in a very rudimentary state. Disasters came so suddenly they were difficult to deal with.

After that they talked with each other more freely.

'Guess it's difficult for yu, tied up as yuv been,' Haggard sympathized. 'Must be spawnish having ties, an' relatives, an' home stuff hanging round yu. I've never been that way. Missed something I guess but all that dope, fam'ly life an' Sunday afternoon's over now so what hell does it matter if I missed it! I could have done with a bit of cush though,' he ruminated. 'Looked forward to it.

'Doesn't seem I'm having any,' he decided some minutes later, still pondering this aspect of his isolated life. 'Guess it's all done for most. 'Tain't fair on *yew*.'

He made Paddy laugh with his quaint wording. 'That aunt of Young Gorey's has glory in hur. Most women I've known seemed fat in thu minds, all men an' eating, but yew two's a few breeds up. Yur out of books,' he illuminated.

He talked continuously, apparently to take Paddy's mind off the children. 'Great place, that hotel. "Mighty pleasure dome,"' he tried. 'Doesn't quite fit, eh? Are thur any poems about hotels?'

They came upon the outskirts of the new Metropolis about noon on the Wimbledon High Road.

III

What they saw of the south-western suburbs that day was typical of the whole of the outer belts. The reorganization of that vast agglutination which was the London of those days, dissolved almost overnight by necessity and disrupted a dozen times since, was scarcely begun. Its clues to life gone, the authority above it, once near and homely, now removed and threatening, it seemed incapable of adjustment. Great crowds blocked the streets day-long, aimless struggles arose ... Labour officers would harangue the fighters, silencing them, and, as often as not, the brawlers would form up after a time and march cheering to the labour recruiting centres.

Paddy and Haggard, having parked their car in a ruined garden, found themselves near a ration station where soldiers with automatic guns, tear-gas projectors, and smoke-spreaders stood on guard. The method of distribution was efficient but offensive to suburban minds and caused constant trouble. Each applicant had to have his wrist stamped first with a small die, differently shaped dies being used each day. A wrist would conveniently hold six marks after which the first impression would have faded sufficiently for the space to be used again. Only injurious acid would dissipate it more speedily. The applicant having been branded, he would immediately receive his ration which, that day, was a tin of synthetic nourishment.

It was a dreary-eyed crowd inclined to dawdle and dispute. Sometimes a spark of humour revealed itself as when an old seaman without arms presented himself to have his wrist stamped.

Paddy had thought to draw rations, but it would have taken too long so they went back to the car.

Nearer the city limit the crowds grew denser, respectably dressed people mainly. An agitator on a box received scant attention from them; possibly they disapproved of his rebellious spirit. Nothing could be done that way, by force; at least, they were not the people to do it. They had been trained to submission and self-effacement, they did not know how to start trouble. In the East-End it was different.

There was much talk about the East-End and some were wishing them luck and others expressing fear that they might break through and disorganize what small organization there was. That might mean even scantier rations. They still clung to faith in their superiors like dogs will hang round a master who starves them. But in the East-End they fought daily.

Spreading revolution, deepening war, blended in the conversation, these suburbanites appearing to see little difference between them. The general opinion was that the war had scarcely started but that organization would improve steadily.

'Let's trek out,' said Haggard; 'there's no way through here.' They backed precariously through the throng into a side road and the action drew attention to the car. The uniform of the Expert was recognized and immediately, unexpectedly, boos and hisses rose from all sides. There were elements seeking a chance for trouble in the otherwise resigned crowd.

'Shows the new wind. Ought tuv had a big coat. Oughtn't tuv brought yu this way.' Haggard sunk himself deeper in his seat. 'It's a damn not knowing the country an' yu not much better.'

A stone whizzed by Paddy's head, one of the car panels resounded and cracked to a heavy blow. The example had been set: a fusillade of stones and empty synthetic cans began to fall around them. A shouting mob congregated at the entrance to the side road like angry sparks thrown up from some deeply smouldering fire. Here was an enemy they could hurt and whom they did not fear or depend on, who was alone and helpless. Many who a moment past would probably have lauded the Experts as the country's only hope were caught in the new mood and thrust forward to join the mob. 'Mind the girl,' someone called.

'To hell with the girl! Expert's mistress!' Foul epithets were flung at Paddy and a shower of heavy oddments lashed over the car. Paddy was cut on the cheek by some sharp fragment.

'I think they're only letting steam but keep 'um back with this while I turn the car,' Haggard snapped, thrusting a short gun into her hand and she half stood up in the car not pointing it but merely showing it to the crowd. A renewed scream rose but those at the front pressed back. The car swung round and bumping over a causeway shot off between narrow, dingy houses.

'Work west – to the left,' instructed Paddy, dabbing her bleeding cheek. 'We'll get out Windsor way.' She was breathless and Haggard was laughing silently in a peculiar, grim fashion.

'Someday they'll bust thur city braces an' do a killing. Might have been now,' he said. 'Yuv guts. Give me the gun back.'

CHAPTER TEN

Silence Over the North

WRECKAGE AT VIEW

HAD THE SEARCH for me which Vessant instituted been started only a few hours earlier it is possible that I should have been discovered still asleep in my haystack close by the wreck of the ambulance train. I imagine that even as the mangled bodies of my late companions were being examined in the hope of finding some trace of me I was only a mile or two away staggering more than walking across the fields like a mesmerized man with one idea implanted in his mind.

I woke, I think, not because I had finished my sleep but because something was nibbling at my hands and persisted through muddled dreams and half-conscious irritation until it had me wide awake. Then I saw it to be a little neoblast not more than six inches high and it was struggling with all the strength of its tiny, loose-textured jaws to derive sustenance from the knuckle of my little finger.

I shook it off and discovered that it was only one of an indeterminate number which were sprawling about in the hay like exaggerated pupae. They were nothing in themselves, but where little ones were big ones might also be about, and at that realization I came to my feet and though I was tottering my mind was refreshed and it was not long before I began to recognize the West Riding scenery about me. I calculated that I could not be more than seven or eight miles from Darnley. In prospect it seemed more like eighty, but the thought of seeing View once more and perhaps finding someone alive there gripped me irresistibly. Making an adjustment to my bandages which were chafing abominably and continued to do so, I set off, securing a very useful stick to help me along, a hedge prop of some sort. The sun was up but it was cool.

303

Knowing the general lie of the country I made no major blunder in direction and came within sight of View on its hill by early evening after another sleep and many rests and the avoidance of anything which remotely suggested the proximity of neoblast.

That first view of my home affected me as the most unreal happening of all the many strange experiences I had encountered since I left it. It must have been visible before but I had not realized this and then, suddenly, as my eyes wandered along the horizon, there it was, flat-faced, a little stodgy, provincially commanding and, to my weary homing sense, crushingly bleak. The trees did not look the same, threadbare, or missing; there was an irregularity at one side and, close by, something lay on the side lawn, a long, black, lumpish object.

I had to go downhill and to pass the old sewerage works in the valley before I could reach a clearer view and I lengthened that journey considerably for fear of what might be in the neighbourhood of the growing-pans; I skirted round the lower hills and did not even look that way fearing the effect of what I might see on my tiring nerves. It seems strange to me now that I was so conscious of neoblast, accounting for the absence of other human beings by its presence, and never for a moment thought of the gas deposits into which I must frequently have been in danger of blundering. My mind was beginning to play queer tricks and that was one of them. I clung to the sight of View knowing that it, at least, was no mirage.

Nearer inspection showed it to have been struck by a bomb and the lumpish thing was a bomb-plugger, or what I took to be one, for I had never seen these machines at rest but only flying at blurring speed. That held me up for a while but a rational perspective soon asserted itself. Foreigners, after all, were human and more inviting than a night out in the silently crawling open. Coming closer I convinced myself that there would be no foreigners, that the plugger had been abandoned.

A further half-hour and I was pushing through a hedge towards the big lawn, now quite certain that the plugger had crashed and that no living person was with it. Late evening was thinning out the sky into pale threads of mauve and silver; there was a hush over everything which was like the stillness after snowfall, that hush which is more akin to sleep than death but seems no less eternal.

The open door gave me a start until I saw it had been forced. I swung it wider nervously, on mental tiptoe, and then after a pause during which my courage nearly broke I went round the old house room by room like a ghost might wander through its one-time habitation knowing itself real and the life it had left, a shadow. Room by room – one wall of the study had been burst in – until I came back to the broken door and stood under the porch looking at the fields below me settling into the dusk, slipping away as if in doubt of the world they had graced. I was frightened of the house behind me as a soul might be frightened of its dead body. The massive furnishings, the great gilt frames with their dim interiors which had always held romance and friendship for me, telling me stories and responding magically to my childish fancies, held nothing now, gave nothing. They were husks from which I had withdrawn myself for ever. And all the unobtrusive little knick-knacks and curios – I felt Aunt Fertile must be dead and these of her alone were left.

Fear is a sickness I have always fought against. I struggled with myself and at last emitted a meaningless shout, meaningless both because it was nervous and rasping and because I knew it could receive no answer. I had to convince myself that I was alone. That shout was so lost, so echo-less that it emboldened me and in a few seconds I was shouting my way round the outside of the house giving vent to all my pent emotion in loud yells. 'Hullo!' I bawled; 'hullo!' The horror which underlay my certainty that there would be no response was brought to the surface of my mind by that shouting and became a thing I could face and on which I could reason. Even death can be faced if only one will face it.

Three-quarters round as I came by the corner near the stables my last shout dwindled in my throat and became a startled gasp. I had come upon the bomb-plugger which I had forgotten, like a huge grey moth crouched on the lawn and, standing at its side, leaning forward as if he bent over the control pit, was a figure in same grey uniform. I stood, in the exact position in which I had been walking, petrified. Then, I think, for a moment I went crazy. I shouted at it. As if the shout I had curtailed blended with the one which would have followed it, I screamed at the figure. It gave no sign, the most motionless figure I have ever seen. A dead man does not look so motionless: he is frozen, inanimate, movement is foreign to him as to a stone. This man looked living yet devoid of all that minute motion which constitutes vitality.

I hesitated nearer until I could peer into his down-turned face and found it withered and empurpled in death. Beyond, crumpled in the control pit, distorted amongst its levers, was a second dead man. Between them on the floor was a gas-gulleter such as we Experts carried for emergency use against units. They had found it somewhere and, thinking it some type of syringe no doubt, had experimented with it. I had never seen men gas-gulleted before; the visible instantaneousness of their death was awesome.

I touched the outer man and, as he did not fall, I examined him more closely. Beneath his leather and wool uniform he was encased – there is no other word – in a jointed, metallic suit from neck to toe, gas-proof, bullet-proof, cold- and wind-proof. I discovered later that it could be heated to a required temperature. There was a helmet in the pit, a many-piped contraption, with a transparent proboscis and an auditory arrangement with a protected sound-box over each ear. It suggested to me that these aeronauts could speak to and hear each other even through the terrific noise of a plugger in flight or in the rarefied atmosphere of the higher strata.

I left them and went back to the house shouting no more, my brief excitement wasted away into trembling reaction. That man in his metallic shell which kept him standing even when dead! Some day his bones would fall apart, rattling on the metal, and he would still be standing! Like the great furniture I faced again.

I peered into the study once more in the deepening darkness and felt afraid of its ruinous state; something might come for me through that jagged hole. I did not like the faint whispering of the trees beyond. So I decided to spend the night in the drawing-room and fetched blankets from above to wrap over me in a chair. Overtired, I should still have lain awake but I was suffering from an exhaustion which was filling my mind with weak terror and, frightened to lie there with this as companion, I drove all thoughts out of myself.

II

In the morning the sun was shining invigoratingly, the living birds were twittering, and there was a brisk, healthy hunger in me, a hunger not only for food but for life. All the nightmare was gone out of me and I was myself again and though, as I shall tell, worse was to befall me, that fatal sickness of the mind never returned. I decided, at the obvious expense of not eating, to rest for a couple of days, sleeping as much as I could, and then to make my way back to humanity. I began to plan even further than that, to sort out the hundred and one ideas which had come to me in the gas-field . . .

On the second day I tore open my wound endeavouring to move the dead airmen; in their metallic under-uniforms they were twice as heavy as normal men and, thereafter, I was a cripple, limping about in intense pain and growing weaker daily. All thought of departure had to be abandoned. Only gradually did I begin to think of the bomb-plugger as a possible means of escape. My farthest journey was when I hobbled down through the gates to the cottages, keeping myself to it by trying to recollect the names and appearances of the last tenants; they were all empty and the place was swarming with incipient neoblast. The hardest task I undertook was horrible but necessary. Unable to bury my putrefy-ing companions I dragged them gradually away from their machine and burnt them with oil discovered in the stables.

Luckily for me, whoever had ransacked the house had done it hurriedly and badly. Though there was no food worthy of the name and no water in the taps, there were some scraps and an un-opened tin of biscuits and much wine in the cellar. I drank the wine sparingly, aware that in my broken state intoxication might lead me to the point of madness and possibly suicide. Never for a moment did I allow myself to think that I should not live to get away and to this end I began to develop plans for the future, preparing to take what seemed to me my rightful place in the running of the war. The plugger and its practical problems kept my mind keen so that I did not dwell on myself nor my destiny nor the dangers around me except after darkness fell.

There was no reason to suppose that the plugger was not in perfect condition for, from the pilots' attitudes, it was clear that they had been on the point of rising again. It was some twenty feet long, not including the heavy rudder, with a tapering fuselage some five feet broad at the extreme front. Its colour was a peculiar slate grey, varying in tone, and capable of chameleon-like changes when subjected to electrical influence. For propulsion it had a complicated tractor propeller which could be withdrawn under cover when diving and extended again for ascent, and also a series of blowers on each side, and its planes, which at their extreme projection were little more than balancing fins, could also be slotted back into the body. Every available inch was devoted to bomb space which extended along both sides of the pit and engine to the very front, or to mechanism controlling the releases. Its streamlining was as perfect as that of a bullet.

These facts were either known to me by hearsay or easily discernible. Control of its highly intricate and sensitive mechanism was a very different proposition.

I sat for long hours in the control pit studying and fingering the many levers and wheels and other gadgets, trying to puzzle out their uses. Familiar as I was with 'plane controls, my knowledge was of doubtful assistance. I worked it out that the plugger was not so much steered as set at intervals to automatic courses, its speed on occasion making continuous human control wellnigh impossible. These courses I judged from an electric pin-point contrivance would be visible in diagrammatic form for some miles ahead, the pilot's position on the course at any given moment also being shown. They were almost infinitely variable and mathematically exact. In those perfect flight curves was the explanation of why pluggers did not dash themselves to extinction when they descended to low altitudes; it explained how they could follow and bomb the most winding of roads, the route being set beforehand from a photographic map.

A system of adjustable dials was obviously the setting gear and a board bearing over fifty dials and electric pushes was clearly for timing and releasing the bombs. But though I satisfied my reason on these points I made no experiments in projecting myself into the air. The plugger held my only chance, it seemed, and starving and sickening as I was I was determined that chance should not merely lead me to a swifter kind of death. I would master my machine first.

On the fourth day I began to suffer from giddiness and once I fainted in the cockpit, cutting my face badly in two places. It began to seem that by the time I had solved the plugger's mechanism I should be too weak to fly it. A new dread was beginning to gnaw at me. Who knew but that neoblast spores had penetrated my wound and were germinating in its rich though unaccustomed soil!

The rest of that day I spent at the upper windows of the house playing again with the idea of trying to walk across country. Already I had noticed solitary, distant figures in the valleys but I was more than doubtful of the reception a badly injured, starving man, an Expert at that, might receive among the struggling population still lingering around Darnley. No one but the infirm, I felt, would have remained through the weeks of constant gasfare and if any had returned it could scarcely be for pleasant purposes. Darnley, I knew, was a death pit where thousands lay rotting, a spot so bad that no ambulance work nor field-clearance was possible there, and I discarded a chance that the harsh law established by the revolutionaries in Leeds might be spreading round the hills to which the gas had not risen. I discarded it as much from preference as from reason, for any such sally would probably be headed by those Mercy Gangs of which I had heard and God alone knew what manner of mercy that desperate hope of a city might sanction.

Nevertheless, I derived some comfort from watching those distant people; they kept my eyes and thoughts away from the valley where the dead lay in heaps and where, at twilight, a faint shimmering could be seen to warn me that electric gas still lingered there.

Gas and neoblast in the valleys around and humans conceivably as dangerous to me: in my weakened state I might have to crawl and stagger for days through a death-infested country before I reached safety. I returned to my bomb-plugger. It was not only my own life I had to save: on my life depended the lives of untold others.

I clung to that thought, making the utmost of it. I found no amusement in this fantasy of myself as a great leader, a great leader a hundred and more miles from those he would lead, as alone as any man on sea or desert could be, a cripple, perhaps dying; I regarded him solemnly, at first without belief, then compelling myself to believe. What were these leaders? Men who could shout the right words at the right time, who dared to perform the inspiring acts, who could, above all, conceive themselves without doubt as leaders. Strutting, posing, cruel or cunningly merciful as need demanded. Masters of self-deception. There was that painting, 'The Conquerors', famous military leaders of all times from Attila to Napoleon, proud, evil, limited men. But they were different: their modern counterparts were only tools in the hands of such men as Rufus and my grandfather, quiet, unassuming men, friendly and kindly when not driven by the dyspepsia of power-seeking. Such men controlled the modern Attilas. Any fool, inheriting a vast fortune, could be one providing he could also control himself. I had only to pull myself together, to reach London ... then I, too, could be the tiny lever which commanded the mechanism of war. A human key, that was all I was.

I drank heavily of the wine to keep myself to it and on the sixth, or was it the seventh day, I felt satisfied that I had mastered the last of the plugger's secrets. By then my regard for it was almost animistic. It was like some hellish creature asleep and I think I loved it as much for itself as for the promise it held. In between my studies of it I had taken to polishing it, never tiring of the touch of its glossy metal sides for, unlike most aeros, lightweight cellular rubber played little part in its construction; that 'imitation muscle' would not have carried the weight of bombs. I succeeded in making parts of it shine a little in the sun.

Perhaps with starvation and increasing illness the human dynamic which impels men to action and risk had become dormant and the primeval instinct to lie low, watching my opportunity with infinite, catlike patience was beginning to dominate me; indeed, to any observer, I must have looked very like some wounded beast, limping grotesquely and with features distorted by pain, bright, feverish-eyed, furtively harbouring its residue of courage. The fact is that now I felt confident of escape I did not grasp my chance forthwith; I stood back, as it were, to take pride in my knowledge.

I laboured upstairs again to the top storey and began to examine the countryside for possible changes which need no longer affect me. I began to think of the past and how the future might be linked to it and that took me into Paddy Hassall's old bedroom where the few personal possessions she had left had the oddest effect on me. Some obscure mental process had convinced me that both she and my aunt were dead, for that is the way of wars. One kills people in the mind in preparation, one thinks of them as dead long before the news comes.

There was a group photo of a crowd of young people with Paddy near the middle, half her face, only partially recognizable, and one shoulder. I tried to recollect her; for a few minutes it was my greatest wish to remember her in exact detail, smiling cheekily as she had always done at me. I could have loved that girl ... I could have stayed with her, living the life of a human being. Even if, at last, we had been killed together.

Wine and weakness took hold of me and I smashed the frame across the room.

Later, I thought to return and rescue that insufficient photo, but I never did so. When next I was in that room love and the past were the farthest things from my mind.

It was after I had descended and, still half thinking of Paddy, was staring proudly at my plugger that someone began to shoot at me from the fields.

III

I make these notes of myself not because of any egoistic sense of my importance in this narrative but because they both symbolize and epitomize the world at that time. Suspicious self-sufficiency, dogged hope, and a deliberately delusive faith in my destiny kept a dying body alive. And wine, much wine. To keep alive I would have murdered as the world was murdering, as indeed from that first shot I planned to do. That will always be the last hope: whatever man may do to himself in fear or in luxury, there will always be some who will refuse to die, who will see themselves and themselves only as saviours and, foully and ignobly perhaps, will save the race.

Sometimes, I know, this very thought was in me and I would stand gazing at myself in one or other of the many mirrors of View, amazed more than worried, conscious that the emaciated figure before me typified what was coming to a whole civilization, individually and collectively. Already the process in short weeks was advanced, the country was spotted with blotches such as this in which my own waning life lingered, gassed, blasted, overrun with noxious rivals to man. These blotches would shortly be running together, spreading and thickening. Perhaps Europe was already being systematically infected to the same death.

I no longer doubted the purpose of the pain-racked creature in the mirror nor feared that death might defeat him before he could achieve it. A key, that was all I was, and why should a key doubt itself?

There is little to tell about that shooting. The bullet rapped into the woodwork of the porch as I leant there gaining breath, then another starred the stonework a foot away. I drew back into the shadow. After some ten minutes I tried again, going out through the hole in the library. As I came near to the plugger the ground in front of me splashed up twice. A third shot whistled by my head. He had the plugger covered.

Whoever he was I knew him to be a bad shot, a fool, and an arrant coward. He could see I was crippled and harmless; he could have walked up to the house and shot me down point-blank. Instead he potted at me whenever I showed myself, from about a quarter of a mile away I judged. I scarcely tried to consider why? It confirmed my suspicion of human beings in that area and that seemed enough to me. Perhaps he knew of my wine store and wanted it.

I slept upstairs that night, waking every few minutes to listen though already I felt he was too big a coward to come to close quarters. No, he would stay out there and pot and keep me away from my plugger. I debated alternative schemes: to fly the plugger by night, to sleep in the pit one night and go up at dawn. In the morning he had changed his position for the shots came from another direction. They seemed to come from two directions but it was far-fetched to suppose that two men with guns would not have rushed me. One nearly scored. I got clipped on the shoulder and the muscle stiffened damnably so that I could not properly use that arm.

They were hounds and bloody swine to do this to me. I could have made a dash for the plugger and got away for they were the rottenest shots out of hell. I would not. Before I went I was going to get him. If there were two I would get them both. With my hands.

PADDY GOES ON ALONE

Haggard and Paddy went northward through a country which was only the shadow of England. At Windsor the castle was a black ruin; from Henley onwards there had been fires and much wreckage of aeros and guns strewed the river and banks. Above the distant Chilterns stationary gyros guarded something below; ever and again great freight 'planes shot up from some hidden work-place and sped towards London. From Oxford the tendency was for the larger towns to cut themselves off from the outer world, to become as medieval cities, self-sufficient and barred. Civilians guarded the ingoing roads. A new word was in vogue: 'town-crasher'.

In the Midlands that was changed and towns were open, having nothing to lose. The fields were bare of produce, nor was any livestock in evidence. There was much talk of the new organization but little of it to be seen; they passed through rumours of armed bandits and lynchings.

The main, north-running roads became impassable and they tried throughout an entire day to make headway without success, finding road after road demolished. Once more freight 'planes swept over them labouring south. They reached west as far as Wolverhampton, avoiding Birmingham, and then they worked eastwards again, making endless false starts. There was excitement in the streets of Wolverhampton, meetings, and shoutings, and a big placard on a building declaiming, 'They've took the food to London. Join the March.' But in Derbyshire, after a troubled journey through Stafford, where they were nearly mobbed more than once, much was normal. Part of the synthetic nourishment industry centred there, intensively cultivated allotments were occupying the people, there was air traffic, decent roads, soldiers. One of the chosen!

Beyond, everything was in patches, keeping going more or less under the gloom cast by the Sheffield gas area; here a kind of warped trade would be in evidence, strong local control, stress laid on an onerous routine. Five miles farther they found four men dangling from a tree from one twisted rope, their heads touching. They were not the first dead bodies they had seen.

It took them four days in all before they came into neoblast country in the region of Barnsley where huge quantities of oviplasm had been stored in the mines, to be raided and scattered later by the ex-miners to their own undoing. Each night they slept in the open, Paddy in the car and Haggard nearby in a field; she felt sure he was awake most of the time watching over her. They ate little. Very rarely they succeeded in buying food and twice Paddy had her wrist stamped for free rations, Haggard not daring to accompany her for there was no plausible excuse why an Expert should go hungry. In between they scrounged, wasting much time over it.

For half a day they were held up with exhausted engine batteries but, after a long search in some town, procured new ones in exchange for their spare wheel. They were lucky in having a new-model car not dependent on spirit, for all petrol had disappeared a week or two before.

Haggard accepted Paddy's presence the second day; her motoring tunic, leggings, and breeches had eased his mind considerably it seemed and the discovery that she could face a mob without quailing completed his change. 'That frock!' he scorned. 'It was a lovely frock,' Paddy expostulated. 'Never seen anything like it. Not used to 'um,' clinched Haggard. Thenceforward he became brusque and frequently rude, but she perceived, as I had done previously, that this was the sign of his friendship. He guarded her like a child, allowed her to drive only when he was sure the roads were safe, and ordered her about without ceremony, calling her, 'gurl', when he called her anything. Most of their talk was on his argument that she should not be there. 'Yu Gorey's gurl. D'yu suppose he wants yu all rough an' sick, yu damn fool?' Paddy's determination was stronger than his. 'And I'm not his girl. He doesn't care what I look like.' They always pretended I was alive.

Their first sight of the oviplasm growths was a patch of whitish fungus on the drab green of an overgrown slag-heap.

Haggard pointed it out then drove on quickly. He had seen a movement as of big maggots in the shadow of the flaccid plants. Paddy had seen them too but did not tell him. The whole journey she had been afraid that he might find some plausible excuse for leaving her behind.

II

It was a deserted country, a place of evil, broken villages, straggling and decayed, half deserted these many years and now abandoned. Humped mounds narrowed them in, refuse from a distant, dingy industrial prosperity, some still bleak and aching in their ugly nudity, others soothed to draggled green by a scanty overgrowth of grass and weed. Like skeleton monsters bending over something hidden the winding gear of the deserted pits straddled amongst them, ghostly in the early morning. Here and again hastily made runways projected their brick entrances between the rotting sur-face buildings, cavernous vaults leading down to the herd stables where the reserve Guard had been packed in the sweltering depths of the mines. They were empty now. At each of those dark arches fleshy oviplasm growths were in abundance, three and four feet high in parts and seeding and spreading rapidly. There was no wind, but their watery heads were in constant uneasy movement; waves seemed to rise spontaneously in the flabby profusion, hurry, and stop as instantly as they had begun. Haggard glanced at Paddy and saw her watching this phenomena curiously.

'Isn't there another way through?' he growled.

'This is the most direct route providing the roads are passable,' Paddy answered. 'What's wrong? You're frightened; I mean there's something troubling you!'

A pack of gaunt mongrels shot out from between dilapidated cottages to tear yelping down the rough street, became a snarling, fighting mob fifty yards on. As the car jolted past many scurried in fear, others remaining in a ferocious clump around some silent object.

'I didn't see what they had. Was it a cat?'

Beyond the village the road became more than usually treacher-ous and the car floundered sickeningly.

315

'That's two questions I've asked and you have not answered. What's *wrong*?'

'It's wrong that yur here. It's like saying something rotten to a gurl to bring yu through here,' he said surprisingly.

'It's interesting.'

'It's dangerous. I don't know how dangerous it is. There's been gas all over here but it's got laid somehow, so why aren't the folks back? A few anyway. There's not even a garbage scrounger. It means – well it don't need guessing to me but yuv never been prop'ly told what's happening. An' yu don't ask. Can't make yu out.'

'If I knew too much it might frighten me. It's this neoblast you're talking about? We've got to get through and it's no good me getting scared until I see something to scare me.'

'Guess yur right,' he mumbled, driving with close attention to the rough way. 'Hoped to dodge this. Fault of being sort of foreign, not knowing places. Sun's getting up,' she heard him mutter. He glanced right and left as if for a side road which was not there. In miles there was only a rough pit track.

'I never thought thur were gurls like yu,' he suddenly said. 'Gurls I've known, some of 'em had pluck an' some looks but they never gottem together. All hard things or glittery. Yur soft but yuv grit in yu, sort of belong somewhere else. Gorey showed me a photo once an' I've not forgotten it, not till I see yu then the photo seemed punk. Don't mind me talking to Gorey's gurl like this way, do yu? I'm just saying what's been in me a while. Seeing yu's sort of put something –' He paused, seeking suitable expression. 'Well, shackled, something up which was running all loose. Guess most of ours think women're a joke an' the women like it that way long as they get all doped up an' plenty else. Cow-running! Guess I can't see straight or they can't. Women never got me that way, they sort of give me a better itch.'

'You're the straightest man I ever met,' Paddy answered. 'You've been – I suppose it's silly to say you're wonderful, it's so ordinary. I'm nothing special; it's only because I'm different, better dressed, and have been trained to attend to myself.

'I like hearing you talk,' she added; 'I'd like you to talk about yourself. You say so little.'

They were running towards small woody country, saplings mostly like delicate wands lifting out of the thick undergrowth of the oviplasm.

'Talk about *me*!' Haggard jerked out a laugh. 'Pugs and flesh and muggering round, try-outs an' stuff I couldn't tell yu! The only thing worth telling about me is what I've thought now an' then an' I've only thought in scabby bits. Gurls.' He had not looked at her since they left the village, staring straight ahead, but now he seemed easier in his mind. 'If I wasn't so raw I might have found a gurl like you. I don't mean *same* as yu; just to me like yur to Gorey. A gurl who'd – give me a jump when I saw hur but would take me up like yuv done him an' give me what I don't seem tuv ever got. Delicut an' fashionable like yu an' with guts like yu. I couldn't like a gurl without guts.

'Guess I'm talking queer,' he cut off, shortly. 'We're a crowd, yu know. Think almighty of ourselves. Cuss at Mike, we would. Never felt I wasn't anybody before but guess we're throw-outs when yu come in. Experts of the Guard! Dirt in charge o' muck!'

He was scowling. Suddenly, on the very edge of the sapling wood, he brought the car to a jarring halt.

'We're going back,' he said, and shot into reverse.

Something had moved in the high plasmic undergrowth confronting them, something which seemed to rise up like a bald head and be drawn in again. Then the whole surface of fungoids trembled and broke into motion and the sunlight and shade went rippling left and right like smooth water suddenly disturbed by a deep undercurrent. Haggard was cursing in an extraordinary manner. 'Hell take me!' he rasped.

From the damp shadow below animals came loping, animals with pallid, mottled skins, bending forward from their heavy waists and seeming to drag their thick, doubled legs along with them in their headlong rush. They held their stubby arms awkwardly, one thrust forward in front of their bodies, the other pressed back close to the side as though they carried invisible weapons in a charge. Their featureless bull heads were sunk low on massive, convulsively breathing chests, the gaps of their mouths hung wide in their effort to breathe. The sound of it was like a shudder in the air.

The car started backwards and they were on it, clambering over the wheels and body, surrounding it, soundless except for the pulse of their breath and the scrabble of soft, padding feet.

With a snapped, 'Take the wheel. Get 'ur clear,' Haggard had swung out of the car at a vault. In his hand he had a tyre lever. He smashed down at the blob-like head nearest the seat and it disappeared from Paddy's sight, not cracked but doubled in as soft, rubbery substance would double. The lever made a lifeless, flat sound. Then the creatures were swarming over him, clinging to his legs, dragging on his arms so that he could not swing his weapon. Their greasy skins glistened in the warm sunlight, their breathing grew shrill with strain. Flinging them off he began battering with the lever, and as they fell beneath his blows they still squirmed, crippled but active, around his feet, struggling to renew the fight. The limbs of one he had stamped almost in two were still clutching at the air. There was a thing whose head and body seemed one, all encrusted with scaly protrusions, sucking avidly at his leg.

'Get the car back,' he shouted. 'I'll foller. Quick, yu fool . . . only way.'

Paddy hesitated, fear and common sense impelling her to get clear, other, deeper qualities telling her to go to his help, girl though she was. The little beasts were clambering on to the car again. The lumpy fingerless pads and stumpy thumbs of two hands grasped the door top to draw up into her view the slobbering, gasping mouth of a neoblast. Its pulsating sight ganglia seemed fixed on her avidly.

'Get back!' screamed Haggard.

'Hurrh,' it breathed; 'hurrh.' Its body humped up jerkily, a piglike leg was dragged over the door. In that position it poised itself, thrusting its arms out towards her, the left one almost straight, the right with the elbow nearly touching its body. For a second Paddy had a grotesque sense that the creature was pleading with her, its attitude was one of dumb supplication, pleading for its foul, meaningless existence to be ended as some being in a fable, damned to dwell in horror of its own repulsive form, might plead. Then she saw the close crook of the hands and understood. Jerking its hands back like a man withdrawing a bayonet it thrust again, obeying the mechanical instinct in it to fight with the quadrifane though no weapon was in its grasp. Its expressionless face was motionless; it thrust again and drew a second leg into view, a leg pulped and hanging from some blow but still in use.

The car was already backing at a good speed. Leaving hold of the wheel Paddy thrust at the thing as it balanced precariously. Her hands seemed to stick to it, to hold and press into its gummy skin. Its mouth was gasping at her, its pads were clutching at her hair. Then it toppled back and was gone. The car, swerving to the road edge, jolted violently and heeled over to one side. It held for a moment, caught against some obstacle, the wheels whirring uselessly, then dragged free and drove on backwards. She caught the wheel in time to prevent its running off the road down a slope.

Haggard's struggle with the neoblasts had receded a hundred yards or more. He was on one knee and a beast bigger than the rest had its mouth gap fixed on his arm and its hands gripped round him. He came free and was running limpingly down the road towards her as she turned the car. His face was streaming blood and one arm he held close to his chest with his other hand. His jerkin was in shreds and trailing behind, his face set with pain as he blundered into the seat gasping some unintelligible word to her.

In his hurried escape the neoblasts had lost sight of him. There were hundreds of them now, peering and groping about blindly. Then the movement of the car caught their sight and they came busily in fruitless pursuit.

One of the rear wheels was clattering and flat. Paddy could feel it oscillating and breaking beneath her.

III

A mile back they came to the narrow pit track and this they took in preference to returning to the last village where there was now, in the sunlight, as much danger of neoblast as ahead. They had been travelling along it but a few minutes when the erratic motion of the car increased and the steering became almost unmanageable.

Paddy drew to a stop only a fraction soon enough. As the car stopped it dropped over at the back and the broken wheel spun away to the side.

Haggard half rose then fell back, his eyes partly open and staring blankly, his mouth sagging. Until she bent over him Paddy thought he was dead.

It must have been ten minutes before he revived with Paddy's fairly competent aid and then for a further time he sat staring unseeingly. She stood on the car seat looking round hopelessly for some help in that silent country. Panic was beginning to seize her. Suddenly:

'I frightened yu,' she heard his voice, and he was looking up at her, smilingly dimly. 'Did I – slump? Spawny fool! Lost a lot of blood. Arm broken. Chewed through. Gosh! the devils suck like leeches; get their gaps on yu an' squash the veins. Sooner – meet a real Brother: they're clean, spit-yu-through fighters. They don't manhandle yu and suck yur blood. They seemed to think I was a mushroom, a lump o' walking ketchup.' He tried to smile again, but the effort caused him intense pain.

'Car's busted now,' he continued after a moment. 'Look here, Paddy gurl, yuv gotter get on. One of my legs is torn an' I couldn't walk any case. Fix me up a bit decent an' then – yu'll have to risk it alone. We've been damned days on this running.' Wincing, he tried to look for their map but could scarcely move. 'Can't be far to some sort o' town. Yu get going.'

'I'll make you comfortable and then I'll find some help,' Paddy disagreed. 'No, you needn't argue. Do you suppose I'd leave you here? Those horrible things!'

'They'll stay where they are a while, near the food. I'll holler an' someone'll hear. Must be someone in this empty place if he's only got bogged up by mistake like us. Anyhow – yu get on. Don't come back for me. I wouldn't send yu if yu were safe here, but yur as safe going nearer somewhere else as staying stuck.'

'There you are. You say you'll be quite safe but that I shouldn't.'

He grinned weakly.

'Guess I can't argue. I just know yuv gotter go. It's Gorey yu came to find an' don't forget it. Yur as likely find help for me that way as nearabout. Send 'um to get me, yu go on. I'll follow. No damn use sticking round here with me. That's straight as gulleting, ain't it?'

She set to work to bind up his broken arm so that it would not jar and tried to apply salve to his crushed leg, but the flesh and cloth seemed pulped in together and blood was oozing from it in a dozen places. She wrapped it round tightly with strips of the car rug, hoping to stanch the bleeding, nearly fainting as she did so. He made a gritting sound with his teeth when the pain grew too intense. Afterwards he lay for a considerable time without movement, only partly conscious. His face was clotted from two deep abrasions, but he would not let her waste time on these.

'Thought it over? Thur's me here an' thur's Gorey somewhere else, both like half-made pugs. We're spawned up, no saying not. Thur's yu, bit of a gurl, with four good legs as they say. It's yur's to go or nix. D'yu suppose I hell like it, yu going! It's yur only chance *an*' Gorey's. I'm through unless yu get help. Yuv guts. Yu neck's stiff even if yur delicut. Keep away from the plasm an' yu'll be all right. Yu may hit on Gorey, think o' that. No, he ain't dead, yu spawny gurl. D'yu suppose we've come this hike to find him dead! Josh, how yu make me talk!' He continued his argument while Paddy debated to herself, his voice growing weaker.

'If yu don't I'll shoot myself,' he said. 'Got me gun stuck in me ribs now an' yu can't get it away. Get going.'

She stood looking down at him and suddenly tears started to creep down her cheeks. He did not tell her not to cry, to cheer up; he held out his good arm and she crept close to him and sobbed out all the strain and fear of those past days. His hand smoothed her tangled hair gently.

'I'm better now,' she said after a long time, rising and smiling at him bravely. 'Guess I'm the spawny fool.'

He looked strangely happy. He was laughing quietly, afraid to strain himself.

'Thought yu'd be better. Yu can face leaving me now. When yu see Gorey tell him to remember *he*'s the joss now an' all the others just black flesh. That's just till I get back then I'll tell 'um hell myself.' She bent over him and for a moment the tears were coming again. He looked so white and weak.

'What, some more!' he chuckled. 'Here, take the gun. It's a good thing to show.'

'No, I won't take the gun,' she said. '*You* might – need it.' She knew now why the country was deserted, knew that there was little chance of her finding anyone who would dare to return to him.

'Yu take it,' he insisted. 'If the little 'blasters come before all the juice has drained out of me I've got me gulleter. I'll find an okay way out. Hi, don't do that.'

Her lips touched his swiftly, their hands gripped, and she was hurrying down the slaggy path, the map and gun clutched in one hand. 'Keep yu guts *tight*, Paddy gurl,' she heard his voice. Ahead of her the scarred land was bleary before her eyes. The ragged ruins of a village, drab mounds and baked, empty stretches; distant pit-heads, sentinels who had died at their posts. The path wound down to an old rubbish heap. Over to the left the leprous whiteness of oviplasm shone in the sunlight. When she glanced back he was propped up watching her with the open container of his gas-gulleter in his hand. He waved it to her, feebly but cheerily.

IV

She had no hope of ever seeing Haggard again, of finding help in time to save him. 'I've left him to die,' her mind repeated over and over. She began running; sometimes she shouted. She talked aloud, telling herself she ought to go back, that *I* was dead and she was a coward pretending she was trying to find me. Their plans, made on the journey, to visit the spot where the ambulance train had been destroyed, if they could find it, to question everyone they met, to search out the hospitals ... all seemed fatuous, impossible. She should have stayed with Haggard and died with him when the time came.

There seemed to be no one in the whole country. Once, in broad sunlight, she crouched with her hands over her eyes, imagining that neoblast was bearing down on her from a wood nearby. After that her courage returned and she was able to face a district where the dead were thick on the roads, some visibly trampled to death, others, she thought, shot; it was the first sign she had seen of the stampede from the West Riding during the final raids. There were a number of mangled airmen fallen from the skies. Beyond these somewhere she decided to turn back.

For about two miles she was successful in following the way, guiding herself mainly by the kind of dead she had passed. A uniformed policeman with a battered head fulfilled his last duty to her at one point and, at another, there were two stout women lying across each other. When, beyond these, she came upon a living man she screamed. By then she had lost her way entirely and had sprained her ankle badly so that she could scarcely walk.

The man was a rough brute of a fellow, a farmer, with a snarling tyke at his side and when she tried to explain to him about Haggard, shouting from a distance, he only bawled to her to clear off. Then a woman came out from a house, calling to him, and he went back to her and talked. Paddy stood watching until finally the man shouted to her and, without apology, told her to go into the house.

'Ain't much grub,' he said; 'not enough for uz but yer can be an 'elp. Ah'd forgot but the missis thinks o' nowt else.' And two nights later, knowing less it seems than the rough man but a godsend to the woman, Paddy assisted at the birth of their child. When it was over she and the man sat by the bedroom fire to dawn with the mother asleep and the baby puling behind them. The man told her how all the neighbours had fled from the threat of gas and how his wife had refused to go, preferring death in their familiar neighbour-hood to the starving, congested terrors of the westward-running roads. The neighbours had taken everything they could find from the fields and houses leaving them a scant sufficiency for a few days and he had added to this by bashing some thieving boy over the head and taking what the boy had already stolen from others. He went to look for the boy next day to see if he had killed him, but he was gone. Paddy decided that the boy was not the only one, for he was a big, brutal man and there was more food than this version explained. It was hidden somewhere well away from the house.

'We've become beasts,' said the man; 'all on us.

'You're no beast,' he said, turning a newly bright eye on Paddy and then, that half-born mood dying, he began to wonder aloud whether he ought to kill the baby while his wife slept and pretend it had died. It hadn't a chance, he argued; bombardment or gas or 'those filthy lice' would kill it soon and in any case it could not be fed. 'Tear the life out o' her it will.' He was a blend of duty and affection to his wife and abjectness and increasing desire for Paddy with small concern, it seems, for himself.

Paddy nursed her leg and the mother, keeping her revolver always handy, and the man did not kill the baby. Perhaps he did later. When, the fourth morning, she awoke feverish and ill the farmer turned her out, threatening her with a gun she had not seen before. She had served at least part of his purpose. Having blundered a mile or two away she was picked up many hours later by a gang of armed people who, unlike the farmer, were interested to hear her explanations about Haggard and me. They said it was their job to find people like her and us and help if possible, and they knew the district and its changing aspects like a map for many miles round. Haggard, they said, was bound to be dead, but they would make sure when they sent for the car; this Gregory, however (Paddy withheld my second name being uncertain how they would take it), well, that was rather remarkable. At least it might be. There was a big man in the outfit of an Expert behaving very mysteriously at a house near Darnley, the house where old Beldite used to live; he was doing something to a bomb-plugger and though only the one man had been seen the circumstances suggested that others might be there in hiding, that he was only a blind to cover some foreign plot, preparing for a parachute landing perhaps. Some of the comrades had the house surrounded . . . It was interesting but – Better let them get on with it and find out afterwards, was the general opinion. At that a frail-looking young woman in man's clothes who had been very kind to Paddy, after taking her revolver and everything else from her pockets, intervened imperiously. She had found a photo of me and said she recognized it. 'Did I meet him!' she exclaimed. 'He was a fine guy, that Comrade Gregory.' She winked at Paddy and smiled, a sidelong smile designed to hide a gap in her teeth. 'Call the comrades off toot sweet. He's one of us. A bit bourgeois but . . .

'Wish you'd gotter cig,' she said to Paddy; 'but as you 'aven't I'll keep 'is photo instead. You'll have 'is real dial.'

UNDER THE WAKENING SKY

That last afternoon, seated close inside the porch debating how I could best reach that hound with the gun, I must have looked the sorriest of all earth's creatures. I was starving, and drinking more and more wine, gaunt and feverish with a weary, twitching drag to all my limbs. Flatulence racked me and distended my wound agonizingly. I had shaved twice, in wine with a dull razor, but that day the stubble was thick on my bony jaws.

Throughout the morning and afternoon, at intervals, there had been a murmur in the air which I had recognized as the sound of very high aircraft in great numbers. Nothing was to be seen. Gun thunder sounded later and sometimes I could hear the concussion of individual bombs without being able to locate their whereabouts. The lull in the northern fighting was over it seemed.

It was a long time since I had heard the sounds of battle, and the familiar drum of explosion excited and pleased me and gave me new courage. I limped out into the porch to see if the sniper would have another go at me.

On the opposite hill some miles away there was a change in my landscape, a humping and bobbing of erratic movement above the line of a hedgerow, extending out of sight in each direction, into the dip of the earth west and eastwards amongst the outlying, broken villas of the town. My sight was unreliable and I had to concentrate to confirm my first impression that this could only be due to the passage of many people crossing the field path I knew to be there, people laden with bundles or pushing little carts, one of those purposeful, weary migrations with which the East Riding in exodus had familiarized me. I strained my eyes and imagined I could separate one head from another, humanity from baggage. Here and there were flags, yes, certainly flags, and then for perhaps a minute as the wind veered the yawning, nasal notes of an accordion. Or many accordions.

In those days people marched to many strange ends, for safety, for marauding, as demonstrations, and in rebellion against the maddening inertia of their home lives. These, I reasoned, were from the direction of Leeds and might be heading Londonwards, possibly revolutionaries abandoning a city grown untenable or anti-revolutionaries thrust out as traitors. The flags portended some purpose other than a mere march to safety.

I made my way with what haste I could to one of the upper rooms to gain a better view. I must join these people. The field path, as I remembered it, would lead them through the valley half a mile away. Many hundreds, even thousands there must be and one more, ready enough to starve if only he might go with them, would not be resented. In a very few minutes I would be in the plugger and be damned to my sniping enemy. Let him live and shoot someone else. I would set the dials to a straight course to the zenith and then, from an altitude, safe for experiment, change them to a gradual spiral. I would land well away from the marchers who would probably attack me until they saw who I was. Then — but I was a welter of possibilities as I climbed the stairs, drawing myself up by the banisters. In the excitement of those moments it escaped me that if I could work the plugger at all I might as well fly to London or Brighton as risk death on this tiny hop I projected.

I was on the landing when the sound of tiny, distant voices shouting came to me through a broken window and turned me towards the front of the house instead of the back to see what this new invasion of my silence might mean. I went into Paddy's room and to the window.

II

They came in sight together, hand in hand, the man dragging the woman, running from behind the quaint little lodge which guarded the gates of View. Perhaps it was they who had been shooting at me, having been in hiding all the time since I came. Perhaps it was they who had ransacked the big house, intending to return. I must have looked a fearsome, cut-throat character. No wonder they tried to kill me.

They hurried forward, glancing back. The woman screamed. Then, from amongst the trees and bushes which long ago I had peopled with dwarfs and wizards, came one and then another of the Death Guard, their shoulders hunched to the charge, their mouths wide gaping. There followed a string of units as if they had been passing through a narrow aperture. I remembered that there was a little gate on which I used to swing. Maybe they were of the last contingent in the Darnley mills, released by some explosion. Who but God can ever know!

The woman tripped, her hand jerked away from the man's, and

she fell. In a second she was up. The man was some feet in front of her, apparently unaware in his terror that she had fallen. He was moving in long, painful leaps as though injured. She screamed after him or tried to scream for I heard no sound. Perhaps he heard. He turned, raised clenched hands in a wild gesticulation of dismay, and went back, and the next moment . . .

Such was my state of mind that I watched until it was over. Not long, and I will not describe it. I recollect listening intently to the dull thudding of the units' hoofs on the lawn below me. Like sodden drums, I thought, and knew they were probably the last drums I should ever hear. Only the nearly dead could have taken it so calmly after the desire and hope of life had re-risen so shortly before. They spread round the house and from the west lawn there came a noise as of many road-cars smashing one into another, smashing and smashing. I knew what that was. They were breaking up my bomb-plugger. Only that morning I had felt proud of the manner in which the sun glinted on the parts I had polished so carefully. To the units that flashing was movement, a thing to be destroyed.

All the exciting little dials, the plunge, the first clear cut into the air. Often I had imagined how I should have risen and visualized some unseen observer watching. My clattering passage, an eddy of sudden wind. Then gone, the drum of my engine resonating in the air like one note stuck in silence.

That was over.

There came a heavy creaking from below, the broken front door swinging on its hinges, and then a great blundering in the hall, the crash of furniture overturned, glass breaking.

III

Until early evening I did not leave the bedroom. Tearing a slit in one of the curtains I used this as a peep-hole to what was transpiring in the garden and, after an hour or so, became convinced that I was in no immediate danger; but the beast which had blundered into the house below was still there and that precluded any thought of escape through the lower floor. I could hear it moving from room to room. For long intervals it was silent then, suddenly, some heavy movement of the furniture, the clatter of pans in the kitchen, would mark its continued presence. Once the stairs creaked.

I debated the feasibility of descending from one of the windows. Providing I were not altogether surrounded this might have been possible but had I the strength for such a venture? Perhaps the units would leave. A murmur in the air betokened fighting somewhere and I hoped that sooner or later bomb, airman, or 'plane, it did not matter which, would fall to earth near enough to attract them away. The marchers would have gone by then . . . The murmur grew louder. For a second, bomb-pluggers roared somewhere close by, bombs were exploding. A mile away perhaps. Or less. I wondered what could be attracting them. Was my fate to be death from a plugger instead of safety by one?

I could observe the beasts in the garden with loathsome distinctness. One and all were caked in thick mud with weeds or grass clinging to their legs and sometimes trailing like veils along the ground, and they were thinner and less alert than newly matured specimens. Their immediate purpose of death achieved they lingered, bereft even of the instinct to go forward. They would stand, their vacant ganglia staring at nothing, their muscles lax; then the breeze maybe or a passing bird would stir their impulses to movement. They would amble forward a few paces, heads sinking, then become still again. Never before, despite my close contact with them, had I fully comprehended their entire meaninglessness apart from their vocation of killing: they had no life of their own, no volition, no intercommunication. Perhaps I am wrong on that last point. At times they drifted far apart and then that invisible bond between them would reassert itself, drawing them close again. Who can be sure that some dim interchange of instinct did not play its part in that. They showed a tendency to cluster round the porch drawn by their companion inside, but there were always a few absent on the other lawns.

Many were injured as if they had healed into ugly scars after being caught in an explosion. One was minus an arm and another gashed fearfully across the mask. Their excrescences suggested to me that a perverted neoblastic tendency was working in most of them. Probably portions were already 'dead'. I observed all these details with minute intentness and so the time passed. Most present in my mind apart from plans to escape was the queer thought that these abysmal monsters had come out of the little books in which Goble used to write. I had kept one of the clocks going, bringing it upstairs the previous night for company, and shortly after it had chimed six I ventured out on the landing to peer and listen over the banister. Thirst was maddening me.

It was a mistake I should have been compelled to make in time unless I had resigned myself to death, but I had no conception of the risk so slight a move involved, knowing little of the Guard's faculty of discerning the proximity of concealed living creatures. I had not been at the stair top for fifty seconds before sounds of quick, determined movement came from below. So cautious had I been that I did not associate it with my presence on the landing.

The heavy tread came across one of the rooms and I had a glimpse of vast, blackened shoulders issuing into the hall before I stepped back. As I closed the bedroom door with infinite care, again the stairs creaked. They continued to creak. I had given myself away.

The slovenly, shuffling tread mounted to the landing, seemed to hesitate, and then continued along the corridor in my direction. It knew something was there.

I could hear its stertorous breathing approaching. From that sound and the cessation of its dragging steps I knew when it halted outside my door. There came the ring of metal on wood then nothing but that leathery respiration like the softened pulsing of some slow-moving machines. I had a thought to barricade the door, to pile bed and chairs against it, but afraid to make the slightest new sound hesitated on the hope that it would come no farther. I backed towards the window to glance through my peep-hole. Did I imagine it or were the beasts showing signs of excitement? They were mostly out of sight in and around the porch but the sound of their quickened breathing rose to me.

There came a distinct movement from the passage then the floor vibrated and with a harsh, rending crash the heavy oaken door split down the centre and burst inwards with the great, rusted vans of a quadrifane driving through. It flashed back and drove again and the panels cracked open and were flung aside to make way for the vast, filthy body of the creature behind. It came thrusting through with the torn woodwork ripping strips of flesh out of it. The head was down, the chest muscle huge with exertion. I remember noticing that one of the arms was a mass of lumps and ridges as though pieces of metal or stone were embedded there and the flesh had grown over them. Its mouth-gap streamed foam and the white froth mottled the muddy shoulders below. With it came a stench as of putrefaction.

It was the incarnation of death but not my death.

The thing was blind. The top of the head was one huge sore, the head smashed in at the side. It stood aimlessly, its instinct for the moment at a loss to locate me, perhaps inhibited by the strain of action. It shuffled forward two short steps, its crushed head moving as if seeking me, and then I had dragged myself past it and was stumbling down the corridor. The sharp movement cause an agony of pain in my side but I went on, down the back staircase and into the kitchens which I had chosen as the safest means of egress because of the partly enclosed yard beyond.

It was empty as were the smaller yards. I hurried across the first flagged space, through the narrow gateway into the next. No units were in sight. Passing the old stables I noticed oviplasm growing out of the doorway. Goble's big window was a black, broken space. A tiny face peered out at me from the gloom and there was a quick scuffle of soft pads. I had not thought them so close. At the next gate the fields and buildings began to oscillate about me in the fading evening, lights danced before my eyes. I supported myself waiting for this giddiness to pass. My figure must have stood out boldly, almost silhouetted.

The first shot got me in the arm, the second in my right side. A stone cracked at my feet and a fourth had me bleeding all over my face. It came to me that the man the units had killed had not been shooting at me at all, that perhaps he had been shot at as well, and that the skunks with the guns had been in hiding all the time watching their chance in case the Brothers did not get me too. They were skunks but they must be brave to stay anywhere near the Guard just to get a chance at me. A wave of dull heat spread through me suffusing my whole being. I remember struggling on some paces and that there were other shots but I was partly under cover then and none of them touched me. Then the shots stopped;

possibly they thought they had killed me or were afraid to follow because of the units.

I was never wholly conscious after that. I recollect soft air on my face and a sense of going on and on in a broken manner and with no feeling of self-volition. I thought myself dying, a dying thing continuing to move. There was a descending field, palpitating with strange red and ochre light, concussions above and around which may have been guns or the sound of my blood beating, some voluminous noise quite close which must have been a bomb. After the way I had stuck it out – to die!

There is an intermittency in my impressions which suggests that more than once I fell unconscious. Or perhaps my mind lost understanding while my body blundered on. I was flesh and ganglia like the units, following a blind instinct.

IV

I came upon the holocaust by bright moonlight down in the valley below View.

There was a man lying face down on the grass whimpering without consciousness. It seemed to me he was armless.

Then, beyond a hedge, I fell headlong down a bank, lying where I fell. The dead were all around me, bodies and portions of bodies, piled up, all very distinct in the brilliant light. It seemed natural to me, not loathsome. There should be dead. But I hated the sound of their groaning and one agonized voice which damned God even as it screamed.

I lay there through the night. The fall had injured my leg and I could not move. Lights began to come and go in the sky as the moon went down, wee flashes and tiny bursts like stars opening and closing. The muffled rumble of unseen fighting was like a far-off gusty wind rising and falling; I have known a forest make the same unearthly, almost soothing sound. I lay until the sun was visible, content with my dead who was to die so soon himself.

I knew who they were without the effort of reasoning. They were the people I had seen marching. Here they had reached when the pluggers swooped and those who had lived had fled on for there was no hope of helping the dying. One of their flags had fallen erect and was fluttering in the dawn. 'Brotherhood Out of Arms', it said, extended, and folded and rippled itself around these brave words, and spread them to the dying once more. Manders and his army of peace. I remembered. They had been marching for the great assembly. Maybe the plugger pilots had mistaken them for military. Maybe not.

A bloody face raised itself to stare at me. We two dying men watched each other silently for a long while. It lay back slowly.

The sun was high when I first saw the gas-garbed figures moving through the field. They must have been at work an hour or more before I noticed them for they were quite close to me. They carefully examined every body worth calling one. They were a mercy gang, risking their own lives to bring help, or peace, to others. I watched them dispassionately. The hooded forms were spread widely examining everyone, turning them over, looking through pockets; where one lived there would be concentration over it, an exhaustive testing, one kneeling and speaking to those gathered round him. Twice they carried people away, both women. Some of the others cried out, screamed at their saviours.

Silly, bloody fools, I thought. There was no cure for them, no bed, no restoratives. Would they sooner lie out here for days? Were there not sufficient living to be cared for without cumbering the starving cities with useless cripples to fester and spread disease and undermine the morale of others? This was the day of the Death Guard, of ruthless survival. When they reached me I was ready for them. I would not complain. One side eaten away, neo-blast spreading in me, three bullet wounds or more. Perhaps the leg was broken. I was in the last stages of exhaustion. I would tell them who I was first but – then I would take the little capsule and be done with myself, be done with Gregory Beldite and his foolishness. I lay in the hedge bottom, to me a kind of wobbling balloon. Up and down, up and down I went with mottled shapes going and coming.

Large round rimmed eyes looked down at me and I knew that they were kindly eyes though I could not see them properly.

'You're conscious,' said a muffled voice. 'Feel all right? Think you can walk?'

'Sure,' I said, 'I'm in great trim. I need a bit of care but I'm worth it. I'm Gregory Beldite. I could have stopped this war if they'd let me live.' I said more than that but none of it sounded on my lips. Rubber fingers were feeling all over me and my clothing. The goggles came nearer. 'This looks like him,' said someone. 'This is the man we shot,' said another. Some had guns. I could see they thought I was no good though they did not say so. One of them put a little flask to my lips. That was to dull my last pain. Silly, I did not seem to have any pain. A syringe came near. How I wished they would stop their interminable argument. 'Stop chattering,' I said silently. 'Get it over.

'Get it over, get it over, get it over,' my mind repeated. Ever since I fell beneath the onrush of the Guard I had been dying and fighting against my death; now when at length I was resigned these bearers of final mercy was still keeping me lingering, arguing whether I was worth saving or not. Ah, the flask again, little drops of hot sweetness pouring down my parched throat. 'Have it your own way,' said a voice. Why the hell did they shout at me when I was dying! I was having it my own way.

Death became movement and a sound of sobbing. Were there really angels and did they sob when a man died? Then there was dimness and calm. The movement continued, a rushing in which all things accompanied me.

CHAPTER ELEVEN

The War Metropolis

RESTFUL INTERVAL

IN THAT WAY I came to safety and, by devious ways, to the country house of the Rt Hon. Rupert Vessant who, on hearing I was alive, commanded that I should have the best possible attention. The revolutionaries did not wish to be burdened with me, even though they thought I was a comrade, and on Paddy's assurance that I had friends in the south and would prove useful there if I survived, they passed me over their 'frontier' to partly sympathetic Government troops, after which Paddy felt free to reveal my identity. There was a suggestion in Leeds that the unsuccessful shooting of me should be completed while I was unconscious, just in case I were a spy, but this passed over.

I knew nothing of that at the time nor recognized any of the ghostly visages which peered down at me during the journey, impinging meaninglessly on my semi-conscious brain. Vessant's face must have been one of them but I did not meet him knowingly until three weeks later. And for many days I could not understand what had brought me to that gracious, most soothing of all sick chambers where I lay. I was only intermittently conscious of any of these things. But I must have recognized Paddy, or dreamed of her, for I knew it was her hand holding mine – even, I suspect when it was not – and that gave me a great contentment. When, later, she explained my rescue I accepted my fate as a pseudo-prisoner with invalid calm and a keen appreciation of its amenities though I was not blind to the ulterior side of Vessant's hospitality. Maybe I had reason to regard him as an arch-enemy but, even in his absence in London, he was the most considerate of hosts and I was too sick a man to criticize the hand which was supplying me with such rare comforts.

While I lay half consciously in my bed the second great invasion swept on to England's shores and was repulsed. I heard nothing of it except, perhaps, of the air fighting, the sounds of which were so familiar that they meant nothing to me. All one night and the following day Paddy sat at my bedside though she was ill herself, alone in the upper structure of the mansion, with the nurse and servants hiding in the gas-chambers below. I was not to be moved for fear of haemorrhage, and as I had to risk death, knowing nothing of it, she risked it too, wearing an oiled suit and mask most of the time and having at hand one of those most evil of contraptions, the invalid's gas-protector, designed for sick people who could not be trusted to keep breathing in the ordinary headpiece.

The mechanical robot-killers, which provided the basis of faith for this second land attack, came ashore at Pegwell Bay, near Ramsgate, one midnight, and clanked and murdered their way as far or farther than Canterbury before the Guard hosts, swiftly dispatched from the underground depots of London, met them. I have no adequate description of that strangest of all battles when Flesh and metal met on the plain of Kent and automatically hunted and destroyed each other for the better part of a week; it was not a battle which any man could witness and remain alive. It was seen, however, from the air, and news was flashed to London telling of its general progress, of how within a few hours the wireless control-led robots were scattered and the Death Guard driving through to the human troops following behind their mechanical vanguard with pathetic confidence; how the slaughter of the East Coast was repeated but the units kept strictly under control so that similar disaster should not ensue. There had been no ordered removal of the civilian population, the time for such considerations was passed, and these must have been massacred by both sides. There is a story that the Flesh broke through the barriers of the Chisle-hurst caves which had been gas-protected to hold thirty thousand, with beds, rations, hospitals and artificial light; there the foulest carnage of the war took place, a hell's festival of death ninety feet below ground.

The accompanying air onslaught of which I had heard the open-ing, stretched from Dover to the Humber, preceding the invasion by two days. Its object was to prevent our air arm giving full assistance to the Guard by destroying it beforehand, and in this it was largely successful. Few bombs were dropped; the fighting was between fleet and fleet.

An end to that second gasp of fury, so far as we were concerned, came after some five days, by which time I was beginning to take in something of my novel comfort. A hundred outstanding incidents must have happened while I lay there and later sat at the bright window recovering strength. Echoes of the East-End riots came through to us. It is said that the rioters burst through into the City, leaderless and uncontrolled, seeking the food they knew to be hidden in the undergrounds, and that aeros, flying low, gassed them in the narrow streets by the thousand until from St Paul's to Aldgate was a silent waste of bodies. Whether they were killed or merely rendered unconscious is lost, perhaps intentionally, in the exaggerated rumours of the occasion. There followed the assassination of Erasmus Pollen who, shaking with fear they say, mounted a barricade in Whitechapel behind which the Guard was shackled, and pleaded with the people beyond to suffer in silence a little longer. He spoke of the increased demand for workers in the Labour Bodies and of the great work these corps were doing in restoring order; he had lists and statistics to prove that normal industry was still functioning. Since the encircling raids had abated it had become possible to restore many roads; the new currency and barter systems were working excellently; recently completed submarines were gradually breaking the blockade and food would again be entering the country shortly. He spoke of our impregnable coastline, of speedy victory, of how the enemy had learnt that the underground fortress of London was unassailable.

It was his own idea, his own futile, humanitarian effort.

They listened to him for a good hour and then shot him down.

We heard much of reprisals on Continental cities and a considerable proportion was true. The blowing-up of the Essen humanite works for which our airmen were given credit was, however, quite fortuitous: that most dangerous and destructive of all explosives was never to be trusted. Of the coming counter-invasion not a word was breathed beyond the confines of that deep, thronging world in which it was being so exhaustively prepared; it was perhaps as great a reason as any for the exclusion of the majority from the central ring and was too precious a secret to be used even to placate the angry populace outside. News of home disasters did not penetrate to our comfortable country sanctuary.

The landing of foreign airmen by parachute in the Welsh hills with a view to the establishment of a depot behind the mobs of refugees occurred during that time. The mobs suffered the growth of the depot for some days but perceiving the inability of our aircraft to destroy it, so cleverly hidden it was, and hating the Guard as much as the foreigner, they took war into their own hands and heedless of losing the lives which were nothing but a misery to them swarmed up the hills to wreak vengeance.

Yorkshire was mostly abandoned, town after town being finally evacuated before the famishing pest of neoblast. They ate up the country and passed on like a nightmare of leprous beggars come true, a drift of meaningless, voracious life. Leeds and Manchester became walled cities during that period but as the country cleared their revolutionary councils began to exercise increasing power over their districts. Radio returned to the air. Day and night if one tuned in one could hear them calling upon the refugees to return to the help of the 'New Civilization' which they were establishing, to join in fortifying against the return of neoblast eastwards or its ravenous spread to new areas. Northumbria had the same message. A snatch, a dozen or two words, then the stronger Government stations would blot them out with words of cheer and fortitude and rival calls to the defence of the Midlands' 'neoblast limit' which was being established. A twist of the knob and Leeds or Newcastle would be rediscovered on a different wavelength. Again the official transmitters. It was an endless chase from wave to wave.

Of more immediately relative events I learnt much which I was probably not intended to learn from my only visitor of importance, Rufus, the aged banker, my co-director in Dax-Beldite.

II

Nothing but a name and a news-sheet photograph to me up to then, he became almost a close familiar during the week prior to Vessant's return. He flew over from London daily and I believe his object, or Vessant's, was to eradicate foolish tendencies in me and prepare me for helpful participation in their schemes. It quickly became evident that I was to be fully accepted in my new capacity with unquestioning tact, or cunning, which left me at first at a loss to solve the complexity of doubts rising in me. That I was suspected of planning to oppose my co-directors, that my views were certainly 'anti-war', that I might even have sympathy with the revolution, these were points not to be mentioned openly in the new relationship. So I reasoned; and these persuasions, together with a somewhat amusing though, for one with such a finance-besotted mind as he, probably natural respect for me as head-director, engendered in me a much-needed confidence.

Rufus commenced my education in the manifold details of Dax-Beldite and its related concerns and undertook to arrange a meeting with my solicitors in regard to my vast inheritance as soon as I became well enough. It seemed that law, its controls and safeguards, were still in being for such as us. I began to see that I was now accepted as one of that select aristocracy destined to keep civilization going. If conquered we should be treated as gentlemen worsted in fair fight: we should be expected to retain our supremacy and privileges at the expense of the human herds then far beneath our ken in destitution and misery. As victors we should recognize a similar oligarchy, preserving its dignity before its inferiors whilst humbling it to our will. Though civilization perished for the majority our fratricidal strife must not be allowed to result in our overthrow by the dispossessed.

Rufus was a poor watch-dog if indeed that were his role. He was old and lonely and deadly afraid for his life and wealth, which latter he could not credit as being already more a tradition in others' minds than a fact, and had been shocked into rediscovery of his soul by the immeasurable disasters of which he was a minor and indirect cause. He made me his confidant in these matters. I grew to like what was left of a character which may once have been impressive and charming. Nevertheless, his was a mingy, grubbing mind, albeit it grubbed in millions and spheres of worldwide influence.

He respected Paddy, with his eyes as well as his words, and I liked him for that. It may have been sheer age.

Three meetings were sufficient for his creaking manoeuvrings to make it abundantly clear that whatever course I eventually decided to take my wisest policy at first was to be non-committal. He told me of the directors' decision to sell out the Flesh secrets and then regarded me expectantly, positive that the offer of safety embodied in the terms would win my agreement. 'We are not soldiers,' he said; 'our business is selling. Providing the national interests are not adversely affected, what is wrong with selling?' I pretended a convalescent dullness of perception, laughing that I felt just a *little* like a soldier at the moment, if a reluctant one, and led him into a solemn admission that he also was a pacifist. 'But how else can we have peace except by assisting our country to win?' He grew shrewd. Now was the best time to sell; for the while Vessant had a sufficient supply of oviplasm for his purposes and was inclined to be generous. If he became hard pressed, if his ambitious plans were hindered, he might adopt less pleasant methods to gain the knowledge he required. Humanite had destroyed most of our factories (Sir Godfrey Human, apparently, being in no way responsible for this). The new factories were Government ones. Confidences ensued, the old man's gnarled face coming close to mine.

Vessant was not really cruel or callous, he was merely logical. He could be sympathetic when there was no good reason why he should not be sympathetic. But his sympathy was 'like the little flower in his buttonhole'. It was not really his; he had acquired it from someone else. 'It tickles his fancy, I'm afraid; that's all.' Nevertheless, he was no Hitler nor Shanks. He was a true Englishman.

'Yes,' I said and, 'Yes,' and committed myself to nothing.

He told me of a wonderful spot in South America to which modern war could not conceivably penetrate; there an old man could spend his declining days in happiness and a young one speedily recover from the poison which was invaliding him. Whenever I mentioned my experiences in the north he would turn the subject to South America. It amused me to see his shuddering rebound.

Once Sir Godfrey Human accompanied him and disposed his dignified silence over our conversation. He was very interested to hear first-hand accounts of the effects of humanite and nodded understandingly a number of times.

*

III

A hundred incidents of world importance, as many promises of wealth, and power, and security to come ... Of them all, such is the shape of the human mind, one persists as being of most importance to me. Persists. And because, through this book, I have perhaps encouraged others to be interested, I do not propose to keep it hidden where it really belongs, in me and nowhere else. The laugh is on me but it is a happy laugh.

It seems I was a bad patient during the first days, furious at times in my delirium so that I had to be fastened down. They say I wanted to kill someone; and then again it was as if I had already killed him. I cursed and fought and bled copiously because of it. I came back to consciousness very pleasantly to find the sun shining on me and Paddy standing at the window looking out.

I was not surprised to see her for she had been present in some dim fashion for what seemed a very long time. And now she was there in strong reality I watched her with an interest which excluded all else. She wasn't dead. Where had I lost her photo? Why had I not kept that other photo? I must have made some sound for she turned quickly to come to the bedside.

Was it really Paddy? She seemed altered. The brightness had gone from her eyes and there was a scar on her cheek. 'Greg'ry. You're awake. Are you really awake?' she whispered. Yes, it was Paddy, Paddy's voice. She was crying.

I tried to smile to reassure her but my jaw was too stiff; it was swathed in bandages. So I tried to raise my hand but that too would not move. Then she bent down, kissing me softly, and I felt she was holding me very tightly though her hands were barely touching me. I was such a mass of wounds I was scarcely touchable. I lay there with her lips on mine watching the sunlight searching out the ruddy glints in her dusky hair. It seemed quite the best way in which to spend my first moments of consciousness.

I fell asleep that way. When I woke Paddy was still there, sitting at the bedside. I waited for her to kiss me again but this time she

was very business-like, a nurse. Perhaps she thought I did not
remember. I let her feed me with broth and listened to her talking.
She talked because she was nervous. 'I went all the way north to
find you,' she said. 'Silly wasn't it? I met such wonderful people
there and they found you for me. *I* just went sick. All spaw –' She
drew herself up; she did not tell me Haggard was dead until some
days later. 'When you're better,' she said, 'I'm going back to help
those people. They need help so badly. I'll be a nurse or anything
they want me to be.'

That was all wrong, immensely wrong. It was *I* who needed
help, needed *her*. I must make it clear I remembered that kiss and
understood; that I would have kissed her first but was fastened up
like a mummy. Always had been it seemed until now!

'You went to find me?' I murmured indistinctly, for my jaw did
not move very well. Wonderful thought, that! 'I went to find *you*, I
think.' She looked at me sharply. 'I mean that,' I said; 'I'm not
raving.' Words were unaccustomed tools and the ideas seemed to
slip about. 'I remember it all. Was that you crying after the Mercy
Gang killed me, I mean after they *didn't* kill me? How did you find
me? How did you get there?'

'Sh-sh, you're asking too many questions. You're talking too
much.'

'I'm going to ask more. When you go north again will you take
me?' It was great to joke. As if I'd let her go! 'And we'll find *us*?
And will you kiss me *every* time I wake?' Her eyes stopped me,
solemn eyes rebuking me.

'Greg'ry, don't jeer. I know it's nothing to you but – but it hurts.
That kiss – didn't mean anything really. I'm still just a silly little girl.'

Jeer! Didn't mean anything! All my ideas went into a jumble. 'I
suppose it *is* pretty dumb for a scarecrow to imagine you could be
fond of him or dare to be fond of you! Tied hand and foot! Why did
you kiss me at all if I'm so horrible? Why didn't you leave me to
die up there?' I was furious. 'Damn these wrappings!'

'Greg'ry!'

'*Damn* these wrappings!' I found part of myself which would
move and before she could prevent me I was half out of the bed.
'Nurse!' she screamed; 'nurse!' 'I don't want the nurse; I want you,'
I fumed. 'I'm going back north where I belong.'

A scared woman entered the door and, 'It's all right, nurse,' said Paddy. 'I thought he was going mad but – but he's just a little excited over something. I'll get him back. Please – please go.'

The door closed. Paddy's soft face was next to mine; I could feel it through the bandages.

'You *have* me,' she said. 'Don't you understand? You always had. No, I'm not just saying it to get you back to bed. I thought you didn't bother about me at all. Yes, I *do*. I always *did*. I always *shall*. But, Greg'ry, dear, you're ill; this isn't the time to talk about it.'

It wasn't. I went over like a log and did not come round again until evening. But I am sure that those were the happiest hours of unconsciousness I ever had.

IV

In between the visits of Rufus, long letters from Aunt Fertile, and Paddy's insurrectionary enthusiasm (not to mention our more personal revolution), I would sit at my window, oddly placid and unworrying, and stare at the landscape. Beyond the house stretched the most beautiful of all flower gardens to distant, lichened walls. Ruin, death and desolation might lie beyond. I could not see them. I need not see them ever again, nor need Paddy, if I ordered my life according to the tenets of financier Rufus. There could always be a flower garden, always a high and kindly wall . . .

Oddly placid and contented, for I had no intention of staying in a garden. In a while I would be seeking the guns again, sweating, struggling. A key. That was a good thought. There did not seem to be any lock though, only flowers and love.

Well, that would come. In the meanwhile there could be no safer nor pleasanter place, nor one so delightfully ironic, as that which served as an occasional rest home for the warlord. There was supreme comfort, and a luxurious plenty to eat and drink, and night and day our sanctuary was guarded by hidden soldiers and aeros. I did not know where it was; that was of no importance to me. If I went to sleep – Paddy would wake me up; and not with kisses.

There was an anxious but cheerful flurry in the house when news came that the great man was to take a brief holiday at home.

The house thrilled with expectation of this man whom holocaust could not disturb and who cherished his garden more than the dying country around.

'One has to forget the people so as to concentrate the power. Never dissipate comfort. Concentrate it for the benefit of those who count. They will count for all the more.'

He said that to me over breakfast the following morning.

BREAKFAST WITH THE RT HON. RUPERT VESSANT

On the morning of the day on which the first of the overseas contingents was due to be shot across to Europe, the Rt Hon. Rupert Garner Vessant, having decreed a brief rest for himself, rose punctually at 7 a.m. as was his invariable custom, and bathed and dressed with that punctilious interest which graced him in all his affairs.

Like the leisurely breakfast, the quiet reading of letters and cuttings, and the stroll through his flower gardens which always followed, this unhurried, early toilet was an essential part of his preparation for the long day ahead. During these dawdlings and amiable chattings, for he was fond of visitors, he sorted out the hundred and one prospects of the next sixteen hours.

Perhaps the best dressed, most soothing man of action of all time, he planned a way through life as immaculate as himself, spotless of irritation, void of surprise. Careful premeditation prepared each hour to function smoothly and effectively. The smoothing began in his refreshed brain as he placed his plump feet in his slippers and watched his valet letting in the sweet air of morning. Thenceforward the most exacting of days became merely the fulfilment of his leisurely decisions, a continuation of the routine which had opened so placidly in his peaceful, spacious bedroom.

This particular morning was charming, a foretaste of a benign autumn to follow, in which the all but imperceptible mist seemed to have filtered away the grosser and more glaring elements in life, leaving a mellow message of peace and understanding. Like unexpected forgiveness.

It was suggestive of anything but war, yet war and its grim

appurtenances could have been the only thoughts in his mind. To be exact, those thoughts were moving gently across the dirty and slightly inhuman vista of the new Flesh factories down in the bowels of London. Having expressed his pleasure at finding me so well he told me as much.

There was trouble in the depths. That was not unusual but this trouble was more subtle and dangerous than hitherto. Its origin lay deep in the hearts of the negroes and there was a suggestion of complicity in certain Experts. He showed me a portion of a report signed by my old friend, Coe Gardy, a crude but illuminating epistle. One could almost smell the underground yards with their reek of oil and ketchup and fleshly admixture as one read it.

At the table also were Rufus and Field-Marshal (late General) Tankerley. They too read the report and we discussed it together. I was one of them, listened to with respect.

One of them. The thought amused me. Beside their healthy delicacy I felt something of a monster. My face was no prettier for being cadaverous and scarred and my hands looked quite capable of tearing neoblasts to pieces which they had done more than once. Tankerley and Rufus, I think, regarded me as a bit of a brute and felt a little neoblastic themselves in my presence, but the refined unit at the end of the table had not reached a decision. Nor had I.

'These black fellows have never been told of the deaths of your grandfather and Goble but they seem to know or imagine they know. You had the same trouble in Darnley, I remember, even before it was true. That time you killed the girl. I hear, by the way, that she is still used in the insurrectionary districts. A modern martyr. As if the whole world is not a martyr!'

'You'll stamp on these grumblers?' Field-Marshal Tankerley rumbled. 'Who's responsible for them? I'm not.' He glared upwards under shaggy eyebrows, including me in his scrutiny.

Rufus, who crouched a little over his food, bent lower and grunted. Vessant pondered thoughtfully on his gently moving dessertspoon and appeared to sanction a slight furrow of worry to crease his brow.

He had that faculty – once mentioned by Goble as characteristic of immature souls – of pulling flies to pieces to an extreme of dispassion so that he could view the imminent dismemberment of civilization with equanimity, seeing it as an anatomist would and never for a moment divorcing the cringing little, blasted and seared components from the whole. He could view it as a film editor views his celluloid, his to cut and prune and rearrange until from world catastrophe and that philosophically accepted suffering which was an inherent part of the process, there would emerge – perhaps the Rt Hon. Rupert Garner Vessant, planning the new earth over his grapefruit.

But this matter of a few thousand disillusioned and restive negroes was a matter nearer to the military heart. It might conceivably affect the dispatch of the overseas contingents.

'Stamp on them,' he repeated, unfavourably. 'Crude. Crude.' He rarely crushed his opponents, he dissected them. 'This, my dear Tankerley, is an age of technicians. Technicians hold the effective power. One does not shoot nor even imprison them; one does not despise them because they have black faces. Most of these nigs possess a high degree of skill which we Europeans cannot yet equal. They wash their pugs with – delicacy and understanding. And there are other tasks of the young ones which no white man would undertake, not even though he were offered the income of our friend Rufus.'

Rufus grunted into his plate. I nodded agreement.

'One becomes a greater technician, a technician of their minds,' explained our host. 'One leaves them largely responsible for themselves without too visible a control. They are extremely democratic, these skilled workers: democracy gives free play to their jealousies and rivalries. The Experts call me "Rupert", and I say, "Put it here, Bughouse", and "Cheerio, Coe". If they found me visibly dictating they would probably shoot me or gas-gullet me. The nigs, of course, have their Glory Service.'

In those days there were a number of rare and expensive fruits, a recent triumph of the scientific orchardist. A selection of these was on the table, newly imported no doubt at some risk to the airline handling them. Trade in luxuries still flourished for such as us. There were gorgeous blooms from the garden and other flowers, freshly cut, from California. Vessant sorted amongst these with his pale blue eyes as if seeking words of an equal rarity.

'I fear they are worshipping differently. They are in fear, fear of the vaults in which they work, fear of the aeros above. In fear the simple mind turns to superstition and that, I think, is the way of it.' He selected one of the fruits. 'They are worshipping a supernatural Goble, a supernatural Beldite, now their demi-gods are dead. A dangerous development easily productive of blind fanaticism.'

It was Tankerley's turn to grunt.

'Fear and fanaticism have a way of spreading and, under stress, simple minds, white or black, tend to run together. Like electrons when a contact is made. There are many thousands of electrons down there, Experts, negroes, other workers, muggers as they are termed.'

'You expect serious trouble?' Rufus, having listened with scant interest, was suddenly alarmed.

'The contingents are due to be shot across tonight. A very few grains of sand in a complex machine can made it unworkable. I was thinking that if a living Beldite could be produced, an earthly divinity, as it were, to give earthly guidance . . .'

'What's this! What's this!' growled Tankerley. 'Why, damn and blast, you're not thinking of turning our young friend here into the Big Joss?'

I was not prepared with any answer nor did Vessant expect one of me.

'Try one of these,' he said, proffering me a silver dish of purple fruits. 'Milk plums.'

He rose to greet Paddy who entered at that moment, inclining his plump body with old-world courtesy. Lady Vessant and her daughter were, it transpired, breakfasting in bed. (The men in the house that morning did not interest them.) Vessant smiled at Paddy and kept the conversation lightly upon serious, confidential topics.

II

'You must not allow over-vivid experiences to destroy your sense of perspective,' he said to me as, breakfast over, we strolled on to the terrace and descending to a little path of crazy-paving and quaintly cut shrubs made our way to the flower gardens. Paddy was with us but the elder men had stayed behind with their cigars. 'Nor you,' he smiled at her. 'I know how you both feel. Britain is defeated, civilization doomed. More than that. You feel defeated, not by your own suffering but by that of others. The old order passes and you are looking for the new, perhaps among the northern revolutionaries or the books of Mundaine and other pacifists. But the old order is always passing, in peace and war – and *never* passes. The past projects its withered branches into the present, the present is gravid with the roots of the future.

'Excuse my eloquence,' he smiled to Paddy. 'In these days of activity and snappy orders my holidays are my only opportunity of practising a little rhetoric. Britain is far from defeated,' he resumed, and proceeded to sketch the revival which was taking place: how civilians in their thousands were being organized to combat neoblast, how shortly an army of tanks would advance on Leeds and 'decontaminate that human gas-field'. I saw Paddy wince. How that very night the contingents would be shot over to the Continent, turning dreary defence into triumphal attack.

'I have never been accused of being romantic,' he smiled, 'but there is a stir in me which has perhaps some slight kinship with romance. London has become a gun, a city-wide feed-gun with a score of muzzles from which living shells will be shot, five hundred at a time. Five muzzles, five soundless, high-power catapults will fire at once and each rocket-plane they dispatch will carry a hundred units. Until ten minutes before they fire no aero will be able to locate them for they are hidden beneath buildings and many feet of earth. In those ten minutes these concealing obstructions will be blasted away by humanite and the way made clear. Allowing for inevitable losses it is calculated that we can transfer the Guard from London to the Continent at a minimum rate of twenty thousand an hour.'

'These things are not secrets any longer?' I questioned.

'Not to you.' From plain, confident statement he changed gently to a persuasively modified platform manner until an inspiring battle and the breeze quality had developed in his discourse. We had gone down like a brave flag dipped. Now the flag would fly full mast again and the amorphous graves over which it had grieved a moment were already splendidly heroic in retrospect. It reminded me of one of those ennobling pages specially written to inspire youth.

There was an atmosphere in the garden and in the calm grandeur of the mansion behind which matched his words, an atmosphere of inviolable well-being as satisfying and invigorating as mountain air, an invitation to security which made it seem ungracious, vulgar, not to share that inspiration. Paddy's hand touched mine and I gripped her fingers soothingly to bring her more into tune with the garden. There is sometimes a lack of subtlety in Paddy.

'I wish we were not here,' she murmured; 'I wish you were back in your ragged old jerkin.'

'I had hoped for a long conversation with you,' Vessant was saying. 'There are so many things to talk about. You can help us in many ways, I feel sure. But I fear this is our last day here and afterwards I shall be too busy. From tonight this charming spot will scarcely be safe; nowhere above ground will be safe, not even the demilitarized pleasure towns. I have persuaded your aunt, by the way, to tear herself away from her beloved Carfax and move to the London centre. Yesterday.' At my thanks, 'Once the contingents are landing abroad,' he explained, 'the enemy will strike anywhere – savagery, shall we say. They know that even their heaviest depth-bombs cannot penetrate to the new depots and factories; they know central London is self-supporting, that nothing which happens outside can affect our supplies. They have been balked of victory by disruption and attrition as of direct military victory so now they will turn to their last alternative. They will use the lives of helpless civilians as bargaining counters.'

I weighed his words, translating them into the reality which I could visualize more understandingly than he. The Rt Hon. Rupert did not use my unspent millions, my youth and love, to win me as Rufus had done, he painted in broader colours to suit my temperament; he presented an aspect to me blandly, knowing I would weigh the grim alternatives.

'Slaughter?' I said; 'annihilation?'

He frowned, now liking the latter word. 'There is no such thing as annihilation,' he answered crisply. 'Someone, the wisest ones, always live. Slaughter, yes. That, I fear, must be the policy of both sides. They will soon abandon theirs. Our counters, our twenty thousand an hour, are the stronger arguments.'

'The greater slaughter,' I said.

Pausing, he bent his head to smell a proud, snow-white, gold-flecked rose. He nipped it off carefully and, handing it to Paddy, 'This is one of Goble's artistic marvels,' he said. 'Blooming in the autumn, thanks to knowledge of which you two maybe know more than I do. It is strange that a man should produce these roses and also the Brothers. Big Brothers and – little sisters, shall we say?' he added whimsically.

'And which do you really prefer?' asked Paddy, clothing her insinuation in an innocent smile.

'How I am misjudged!' he laughed. 'The answer, my dear child, is just that we cannot fight wars with pretty flowers. So many people are forgetting their past lives and blaming me! But it is not states-men nor soldiers who make wars, it is gardeners, both of the soil and of the mind. They tend their blossoms, their ideals and senti-ments, and when the gale rises to ravage them they accuse the man who has spent his life preparing for the gale. They even demand that he should cry over the flowers!'

'No, not the flowers; the children, the homes,' shot Paddy.

'Quite so; but are they useful tears? Do they merely blind our eyes instead of easing them? In a short while, a few weeks, we are due to celebrate a quaint custom, one of those withered fingers from the past, pointing – perhaps at itself in mockery. Armistice Day. Shall we keep the anniversary this year? Shall we, a year hence, perhaps, institute a new symbol and bury an Unknown Unit?

'You think I am scoffing. Far from it. In my own manner I am crying, not over the flowers nor the children but over the gardeners who grew them, blind gardeners who believed that beauty could be its own salvation.'

'I think,' said Paddy, quite brilliantly and rudely, 'you are only resting your mind in clever words.' She was flushed, angry. Ves-sant's heavy, brooding face, its setting of bloom and blossom re-pelled her; it was his garden and behind its beautiful mask she felt that same expressionless stare.

'It seems stifling in here.'

'The blended perfumes perhaps. Farther on there is a gate and open fields. It will be fresher down there.

'Tonight, Miss Hassall, was decreed many years ago by two such dreamers as you and Mr Beldite. Before them, a thousand million people, a thousand times that maybe, had assisted through the ages in preparing what may well be the most terrible week in history. Socialists have taught us that a man's brains and success are not his own but are the product of the whole human race. So is war. Supposing – who shall we choose? Queen Elizabeth, Gladstone, Mr Baldwin. Supposing that we could bring them back to look at our Flesh Guard, telling them it was as much theirs as ours, that all *we* had done was to materialize a hope common to every age, the hope of an unassailable army. Supposing we showed them our country overrun with neoblast, reminding them that their battlefields also, small as they were, were not merely graveyards but the nurseries of new battles and of every noxious evil to which man is heir. What would they say? They would hide back in their pasts, disclaiming all responsibility for a future so fantastic and horrible. Though time could be recalled and remodelled, not by one iota should we persuade them to alter that future which is our present. They would refuse to believe in it.

'You, Miss Hassall, also refuse to believe though you live in it. You would reverse the car which is already over the cliff. Mr Beldite, of course, says so little that it is difficult to know what he believes.'

We were at the gate. The road lay to the side, a quiet, unsullied road. The brown fields undulated upwards to half-concealed beeches and there was a tiny church spire. Rabbits scuttled in and out of cover.

'I do not believe in either cliff or car,' I said, breaking into the conversation for the first time. 'I would stop the contingents.'

'Still the old sentimental Beldite?' He smiled. 'And their further manufacture?' In all his tentative circlings it was the first time he had directly approached the object of his hospitality and interest in me.

'Still the old sentimental Beldite.' I also smiled.

The exertion of walking had tired me. I leant heavily on my stick, supporting my aching leg on the bottom bar of the gate. And I was tired of his bland arguments too.

'This victory of yours – I don't see it as victory,' I said. 'There could be no end to it. It seems to me like a victory over everything we live for, a surrender to death, not a triumph of life. You have been good to me here – because you need me, I recognize that; but you have been kind. I can only thank you for it. As a joss for your plans, as the joss you are looking for, I am afraid I shall be a failure. Unless we can find a way of working together.'

A dull, bull-like quality had overspread his face as he stared up at me, no longer philosophic but brutal and nonsensical in its desire to drive forward. For a second the eyes seemed to fume as though the bull were about to charge. But Vessant rarely destroyed an opponent: he analysed and remoulded him. He was smiling again. The little flower remained in his buttonhole.

'You are still a very sick man, Mr Beldite. We must have another chat,' he said.

III

As we reapproached the house excited figures appeared at the door, Lady Claricia Vessant and her daughter followed by Tankerley and more slowly, Rufus. Lady Claricia was waving an envelope. 'Rupert,' she called, 'I think it's an advance warning. I'm terrified it's an advance warning.'

'She imagines everything to be a raid warning,' Vessant smiled. 'She heard a bull bellowing one day and thought it was a siren. Didn't you, Clarry?' He took the telegram.

'Is it? It is, I know. Is it?'

'For once, my dear, you are right. Now, don't be excited. Nothing to fear. Intelligence advice, very much in advance. In any case, Clarry, I had decided to take you to London tonight. These constant scares – oh, of course you love your home but they are bad for your nerves, my dear, very bad. Now, now.'

'It's always wiser to do as Rupert says,' interjected Rufus, peering with ill-concealed nervousness at the coded message.

'Exactly what we expected,' said Vessant softly to Field-Marshal Tankerley. 'The ultimatum has arrived. Yes, much sooner than I thought, but trust them to know our plans as well as we know theirs.' He laughed.

'Oh, Brock,' he called as a gardener appeared; 'if any damage is done while we are away don't trouble to repair it for say a couple of weeks. The raids may be continuous for quite a long period.

'At least I am always sorry to leave the little sisters,' he smiled at Paddy, 'and leave them in good care.'

THE LOADING PIT

We left for London by air as night fell. At a thousand feet our two tiny, high-speed aeros were joined from above by three heavy fighting machines and as many scouts which, together with an unseen number of gyros, had guarded Vessant's house during his sojourn there. They formed our escort for the brief journey.

Berkshire and Surrey were shadows beneath us, but as we came in sight of the winding line of the Thames near Richmond we dropped to an altitude only sufficiently high to clear the flying stages which spanned the river at regular intervals. All of these without exception were in a state of ruin; in the half darkness their twisted metalwork had the appearance of some fantastic plant growing in mid-air. Advance sirens with their peculiar, inter-mittent drawl were sounding in the riverside towns as we passed and, once we were low enough to be seen, we too by de-muting our engines gave out our characteristic call so that all should know it was friends who went by. At one point we were so low that we could see the movement on the quays where crowds were making an early way to the under-river shelters. Life, dislocated and impoverished but largely recovered from the first numbness of constant danger, was now running to a new normal established in the outer rings by the Labour Bodies. Little they knew that the raid which was coming and of which, thanks to our intelligence service, they were receiving such encouragingly ample warning, was to be aimed directly at them as civilians, that the moaning sirens were little more than a routine intimation to the condemned that the hour of execution was at hand. Few shelters outside the military centre were deep enough to resist depth-bombs nor were there sufficient to accommodate the immense numbers invading them.

Unaware of any exceptional danger the progress of the crowds had the orderliness of the peacetime drill; viewed from above they might have been queueing for some not over-attractive entertainment. That many would die before morning did not excite them. Many were always dying.

Once on the journey Paddy touched my hand. 'I'm not talking,' she whispered. 'I'm letting you think – deeply.' She smiled uncertainly.

'I remember: Brighton. The night before I left,' I said. I gripped her fingers tightly. 'I'm sorry, Paddy. You'd hoped for something better than this? Just flying off to safety! You heard what he said? "A sick man." That's it; full of holes and limping about on a stick! Tonics and injection! Even the doctor has to come along with me!' (He was in the same aero.) 'That's all I'm thinking, Paddy. And perhaps it's better this way. If I'd strength to lift anything more than my tongue against them I shouldn't be here, going to the only place where anything can be done. *If* anything can be done. I'd be in gaol, out of the way. I know; you're wishing I'd been fit so that we could have run away, scaled a barbed wall at midnight perhaps, and gone north to lead the revolution to victory. Shouting slogans through our armed teeth.' ('Greg'ry!') 'I'm afraid I haven't any heroics left. Even for a cripple there's more to be done in London from an armchair than in trying to fight Vessant's army of tanks.'

She shook her head slowly, knowing I was half teasing.

'You look ever such a little bit like murder,' she whispered, 'and you can't express that mood properly from an armchair. I wish I could put my head on your shoulder.'

'You can't. Not here. No, Paddy; this isn't my battle. You remember my grandfather's big chair? I used to sit in it near the window trying to catch a glimpse of that comrade of yours who was shooting at me and planning how to get him. I'm looking forward to a chair just like that. But my brain's clearer now.'

We rose steeply to make the central city landing and the surface of London opened out below us.

II

Central London was a daylight city only, devoted almost solely to the purposes of war. Its financial life was gone, not collapsed as many had prophesied, but set aside, a luxury of peace; commerce was ended, for everyone in the safe circle was housed, clothed and fed by the State. Many thousands of civilians still lived there, but mostly as curators of a business world now in cold storage, their duty being to retain a skeleton organization and to protect and salvage books and records whenever these were endangered. Of the million-odd inhabitants they were a small proportion, the greater number being workers in the Flesh and munition factories, soldiers, and militarized civil servants. Though danger lurked in the day sky as in the night the streets were busy during the lighter hours, but it was a strange traffic which glided along the great thoroughfares, a traffic bearing little relation to the buildings lining the ways, which rose from the underworld and having travelled its distance returned there, military and Guard transport, ration cars for the outer rings, vehicles conveying the city's treasures to safer keeping. It ran through ways having a peculiarly patched appearance for every street of importance to the new regime was kept in repair, liquid cement being poured into the bomb holes and compressed and smoothed by mechanical stamping machines. The overhead paths, including the traffic spans and suspension routes of the West End shopping centres, were mostly destroyed, the debris having been removed by claw-footed gyros to a vast dump in the Thames estuary where relics of many famous buildings and monuments could also have been seen. It was a city of ragged grandeur and dark purposes.

With night it fell silent, an abandoned mistress, deserted by all who had loved her, a living thing alone on the bleak surface of the earth. Somewhere perhaps in the echoless emptiness of space, such cities people the surface of dead worlds, ghosts of the vanished. As we sped towards the landing I felt I was looking upon such a dead world: I saw the earth in the future, a husk, the empty shell of a life of which man had made nothing. Perhaps the last, crouching remnants of mankind would so stare, wondering dimly what had passed to raise those high, meaningless ruins, to scatter stones amidst the wilderness of posteval forest. Like dead bones the white arms of London stretched to the sky.

I have seen the old city in many guises, the world mart in worried, congested haste, in its weary rest hours, and in anger and violence when thousands swarmed through the traffic-blocked streets in the 'forties demanding bread, or in the absence of bread, bloodshed. I have never seen it so impressive as on that pale autumn night when none but the grotesque forms of masked sentries moved above ground and all life had sunk below the surface. On that night London waited its death knell, its pinnacles staring upwards, its myriad eyes closed but sleeplessly watching. Far in the air silent searchlights fled with the silent machines which carried them, going and coming, ever going and coming, sometimes brooding for an unearthly white moment on some part of the city, then brandished again like swords which left no scar.

We hurried across the dark stage into brilliantly lighted corridors. Paddy was holding tightly to my arm. In front and behind marched armed guards. Then the elevator grids came before us and we were dropping down through the built-up crust of London to the feverish, palpitating heart beneath. We passed through an area where the thunder of machinery drowned our voices. 'One of the new aero works,' I heard Rufus piping in my ear. Floors and galleries, vistas of bright machines labouring, the ever-obedient workers of the modern age supervised by occasional tiny mechanics; then a deafening, earth-shaking roar where the humanite blasting excavators were hollowing our new caverns, a roar doubled by the thunder of earth and rock being drawn downwards into the soil converters to be pulverized and mixed into cement for the roads above. There came a bright, porcelain passage at which we stopped. A faint, familiar tang in the hot atmosphere told me that we were in the neighbourhood of the Flesh yards. A string of men crossed the passage, hurrying, men dressed only in filthy shorts and canvas shoes, their greasy, sweating bodies glistening under the lights. They did not look at us.

Paddy gripped my arm almost painfully.

'It's all one great machine,' she whispered. 'Listen, you can hear the throb of it. Even the workers are just parts of the machine. Men are geared to men: belts, chains, and cogs. Somewhere, I think there must be a man sitting at a switchboard, quite an ordinary man perhaps, and when he moves some little lever parts of the machine stop. Or start. He touches another lever and men go running, begin working, like an electric current.'

'It's a bit like that,' I said.

'It is that. They can't start and they can't finish until the man at the board touches the lever. Perhaps there's another man sitting comfortably in an easy-chair telling the man at the board what to do. Greg'ry . . .'

'The right hand at the switch . . .' I murmured. 'No, it's *not* as simple as that. You're going all imaginative again, Paddy.'

'And they're going to make *you* part of the machine,' she said, staring up at me with suddenly strained eyes. 'I know, Greg'ry. And you won't fit. You'll stand, facing them . . . You haven't seen yourself, Greg'ry. You never *did* know. yourself. You think you're going to sit still and watch and learn; then there'll be a board meeting and you'll try to win some of them to your way of thinking. It won't reach that, Greg'ry. You'll be thinking all the time of the people above and the people abroad –'

'Don't be a fool, Paddy,' I snapped. 'I can't do anything for them. Yet. I'll be thinking of you.'

'Not of *me*. You'll forget me. That's what I'm for. If it's necessary to forget all about me like you did before – please do it. It's what I want you to do when the time comes. I'll turn up again – when I'm needed,' she laughed chokingly.

'I'll be having supper with you soon,' I said. 'Then the invalid will have to have his injection, get a good night's rest. You want to get some sleep yourself, dear.'

'Mr Beldite. Mr Rufus will take you to some very comfortable compartments not far away.' Vessant had joined us. 'You will find everything you want there, including much better ventilation. Mrs Fertile will be there. I would take a rest, Mr Beldite, you're looking tired.'

'I'm going with *you*,' I said. 'Didn't you know?'

It was his policy to humour me. He smiled, a keen little smile. 'Very well. Rufus, will you take Mr Beldite to the control room.'

It was not my policy to humour him; I never had the subtlety to be wisely discreet.

'When I've had a look at this hell's broth you're brewing I'll know better where I stand,' I said.

'It will be nice to know where you stand,' he smiled. 'You know, Mr Beldite, you have become a true Expert. So refreshing and – fundamental. A breath of rude reality stirring the gilded leaves of artifice,' he laughed. 'Shortly, when you begin to call me "Pot-Belly Rupert", I shall know we are really friends.'

I pressed Paddy's hand tightly in parting and we men and our bodyguard mounted a string of electric trucks which bore us along the tunnel into a world of intense, biting vigour, a Hades-like world of shadows and bright lights, toil and weariness.

In a very few moments we were in the control room of one of the overseas loading pits.

III

No. 1 Loading Pit of the Hyde Park Oversea Station, besides having its local control room, was overlooked by the Central Control with which all stations were in direct communication and in which every message of importance from sky, or surface, or underworld was first received. It was the Managing-Director's room and the Commander-in-Chief's tent united into one businesslike but charming whole of hide-upholstered chairs, glass and aluminium desks and tables, and rich oak panelling, with thick pile on the floor, diffused light, and automatic temperature control. Wireless transmitters and receivers were installed and telephone lines, I learnt, specially insulated and concealed so that they could be neither tapped nor cut, ran to every point of importance. On all sides but one it was surrounded by offices where coding and decoding of messages and other subsidiary aspects of the central control were carried on. To have incorporated everything in one room would have been impossible, but Paddy's romantic conception of the master switchboard was not far short of the truth.

Our war front was horizontal, half a mile above our heads, but we could examine many parts of this, the other loading pits, and offices, and even the Flesh yards, in a televisor which could also become a finely detailed map when required. There were diagrams in simply artistic frames and two Venetian vases overflowing with the Rt Hon. Rupert Vessant's favourite flowers. The all-pervading aromas of Flesh and ketchup were neutralized at the doorways by some unseen perfuming device.

One whole side of the room was of glass and through this we could look down into No. 1 Loading Pit.

In this delightfully efficient room, one of a gallery suite, Vessant, Rufus and I settled down to follow the course of death and destruction far above in the cold night and to observe the final preparations for the invasion of Europe which had called it into being. Half of our bodyguard remained with us and there was a diversity of officials, high and higher, engaged in the taking and sending of messages, pressing buttons and ordering buttons to be pressed. Everything passed in whispers except when Vessant spoke or was answered. We were visited at intervals by the Prime Minister, by Field-Marshal Tankerley, by lesser ministers, generals, attachés and others. Godman came in, as unfamiliar in a lounge suit as I must have been in mine. Finding me (he had heard I was in London), he stayed, saying little but with his eye mostly on me curiously.

He was welcome to learn anything he could from his observation, and if ever a man could read another's thoughts he could. It might be good and save a lot of explanation. Or it might not. Though I had said nothing to Paddy I intended, somehow, to get down to the yards, back amongst the Experts to find out what was unsettling them and make my presence felt; I knew their way of thinking and the weight they carried. But here was Godman gone cushy and smart, it seemed, and perhaps they were all that way now. If he had been in his road outfit I should have felt more sure of him; a friend with whom I could talk over things. He wasn't. Probably his mind was in a lounge suit too.

He asked after Haggard. 'Dead,' I answered crudely, and he nodded.

As I sank into my luxurious cushioning, half occupied with the details of the control room and half with the strange scenes visible through the glass wall, there was no thought in my mind that others would be dead and I as close to death as I ever have been before I left that room of supreme safety.

IV

Near the floor of the loading pit, some twenty feet below our window, rested the first of the rocket-gliders. Close behind it was a second, then a third, and the prow of a fourth. Beyond this my view was curtailed by the arch of the tunnel from which they were emerging.

In front of the first glider was another tunnel. Both tunnels sloped steeply, the one rising from the depths, the other ascending, and they were connected by a massive, moving platform to which the gliders were fastened so that as one was drawn upwards to the catapult projectors above another took its place for loading.

This loading was accomplished from a third and higher tunnel from which a raiseable gangway, like the half of a drawbridge, descended to the body of the glider for the units, eight abreast, to march straight down to their appointed places, their backs being towards the front of the machine. When loaded they were shut in immovably, only their helms and quadrifanes showing above the sides of the 'plane. In this position, exactly ninety-six Brothers in each, compressed like sardines and breathing like grampuses, they would be shot anything from a hundred to a hundred and fifty miles and could not be released until the machine sides collapsed on landing.

The rocket-gliders were slightly reminiscent of bomb-pluggers but very much larger. The heavy prow was mostly sheer weight to control the descent from the top of their trajectory, but they were not without internal propulsive power to help them on their way, though how this acted was not explained to me. They were almost entirely constructed of some cheap composition substance and the truly amazing economy of this filled Rufus's mind to the exclusion of more interesting aspects. The gliding 'planes were fitted and connected to the gyro controls far away up the moving platform near the surface and immediately before the rocket went into the grip of the catapult.

Viewed as a whole the loading pit suggested a cubist sterio setting: sloping floor and platform and gangway intersected by narrower sloping gangways; great white semicircles enclosing yellow lit interiors, startling against the blank walls of grey-blue cement; glaring arc lamps shaded beneath an apparently black roof, and bright metallic arms descending from that roof, handling, manipulating and rising again. As a focus to the pattern lay the superbly curving monsters on the platform, black slugs receiving into their maws blocks of other, smaller monsters in rhythmic procession. A futurism of lines and lights, curves and planes, and harsh angles.

Through this strange geometric scheme perspiring, half-naked workers hurried about their tasks, guiding the bright metallic arms, swinging back on to their little gangways to safety, examining and testing. Sometimes negroes were visible on the floor crossing the pit.

And to show that humour still lingered in this home of dark purpose, someone had chalked names on the sides of the gliders.

'Proud Annie' led the field and was destined to head the hurtling fleet across the Channel; then 'Lovable Mary' and 'Gorey Mike'. 'Here We Come' and 'Load of Little Brothers' were also in the queue.

London was a multi-barrelled gun and shortly its living ammunition would be pouring into the enemy's lands.

The platform moved and the 'Proud Annie' was carried upwards on the endless chain out of our sight. 'Lovable Mary' was in place, the metallic arms were adjusting certain movable sections, her load was grumbling behind the grid which kept them in check at the mouth of their tunnel. News came that rhodium detectors had located foreign aircraft over Kent travelling at immense speed and height. Further news followed that our fleet was rising to engage them. Everything in the loading pits was going well; all was ready for the 'surface clearance' which would open the muzzles to the sky.

Vessant called me over to listen as he put through to some part of the outer rings. I could hear the sirens now full-throated and incessant. There was no panic yet, we were told. The people had not heard that this raid was different from others, that if any of the Flesh landed in France or Belgium it was the intention of the enemy to commence slaughtering our civilians deliberately and not to cease while they had aeros and bombs and gas wherewith to continue. 'It will not last more than a couple of days,' was Vessant's opinion. 'When they find that we continue to dispatch our rockets and that they cannot intercept them they will withdraw every man to their own skies to combat our invasions.'

'A couple of days!' I exclaimed and, 'Perhaps I am being pessimistic,' he said; 'two hours would convince me.' I returned to my observation of the loading, sitting with Godman and Rufus and later Sir Godfrey Human.

'Where will the first landing take place?' I asked.

'I believe Flanders has the honour,' answered Sir Godfrey, who sometimes made jests.

In my most comfortable of chairs, surrounded by the easiest and most optimistic of companions, I faced the grimmest complexity of thoughts which ever a man had.

The right hand on the switch! My hand. It would be days, maybe weeks, before I could assert myself in their councils. A cripple on a stick, fresh from his sick bed. Kick the stick away and . . . Perhaps a crippled mind too, its only support a foolish conceit! Gregory Beldite. Edom Beldite again! Lounging with a weak body and a distressed mind while the death machine was prepared for the final horror. *My* death machine! Was physical weakness, was hopelessness any excuse for inaction?

Edom Beldite again. Full of peaceful ideals and occasional flourishes but slave to an unimaginative, easygoing temperament which was always losing itself. Dogged in my way and not without courage but always waiting for the fight to come to me, never able to start it. If I stood up and said what I felt, wiping callous serenity and Vessant's cold logic aside, demanding to go down to the Flesh yards, telling them what *I* would have them do . . . If I did that . . . Godman would call me a spawny fool, and Vessant, 'refreshing'. There were guards with guns . . . I looked at Vessant speculatively and found Godman smiling at me in sympathetic understanding. I *was* saying what I felt – to Godman. Perhaps he had gone through it all before – and had been set back on his cushions!

This was the Flamborough underground again that first night the Guard went into action. A different scene, different men in command, but nevertheless the same night returned. But there would be no depth bombs for us, no suicidal flight.

'We fight our wars in luxury nowadays,' remarked someone as though he too had been reading my thoughts.

'There's not much luxury down there in the yards,' said Godman, his eye still on me. 'There's more trouble than the clever boss behind cares to think of.' He was Head Expert now but that had not given him any more respect for those in authority; he continued to curse them and to do his job. Politics and humanity were not his concern; Flesh and more Flesh and still more . . . that was why he was here. 'Oh, religious trouble,' he told an interjector. 'The yards smell of it. Call the nigs to an extra shift and where are they? Praying. Chanting. Cluthered away in some dark corner. "All others be our enemies." You know the stuff. Looks as if they mean it too. Apart from Coe Gardy and a few of the other old boys they'd as soon set the Flesh on us as not. *And* sing about it. We oughtn't to grumble; we helped to give it to them. Some glory, half a mile underground, kicked and sweated around and the only things they hold sacred jeered at and turned into dirty parodies. The mugger crowds think them a joke; some of them that is.'

'They can't do anything? Can't become dangerous, I mean?'

'They can't do anything,' said Godman, pointedly to me. 'It's my particular job to see they don't and to see that all the thousands of muggers we've got stewing down there, and who *don't* jeer at them, don't start chanting as well. I feel like a bug on a throne but I'm well paid and I'm on the safe spot. I'm paid more than Tankerley,' he grinned, and glanced about to mark the chilly reception of this remark. 'He's only Head Slaughterer.'

'Really, Godman,' expostulated Sir Godfrey. 'You seem to forget that sometimes it is a duty –'

'I know,' Godman interrupted. 'I always drink a glass of pure duty with my caviare.' Turning to me, 'That's the way of it, Gorey. I reckon we two –'

Messages cut short that sentence. There was fighting in the stratosphere. Two of our aeros had fallen in flames on Battersea and another in Piccadilly Circus. We resumed our low-voiced conversation in between these items. In a while we paid no attention to the story of 'planes blazing down to earth; it was an old tale of useless heroism which had long lost its savour.

'I don't know why they send them up against those monster machines with their smoke and electric gas,' said Rufus querulously. 'I call it murder.'

'It's camouflage,' we were informed. 'The Conties think they're destroying our fleet but actually the main body is under cover until the rockets go. When they try to swoop down on them they'll get a shock. We've learned something about air fighting since the East Riding.'

There was liquid flame running through the streets of

Shoreditch. Kensington was said to be largely under gas. More serious from the standpoint of the military command was that some thousands of people in terror were breaking through the barriers into the central area hoping to find refuge in the deep undergrounds. It was the general opinion that this must be stopped. Not that there was any likelihood of their gaining their objective through the steel doors and other defences which protected our entrances, but they were in the way and a bad example to the millions who might follow.

'When the enemy's finished its pig killing upstairs I'd like a talk with you,' said Godman, leaning towards me. 'Alone.'

Refreshments were served to us. Zero hour was approaching when, loading being sufficiently advanced, the expeditionary force could be started on its way with a surety of its uninterrupted continuance. The centre of Hyde Park would go up 'like the top of a volcano blowing off'. Many people from the outer rings had assembled in Hyde Park but nothing could be done about it.

Nothing was done about it.

We were warned to expect a series of terrific concussions and, while we were watching the clock tick to the appointed hour, the Continental ultimatum came through again, this time from the enemy flagship above, informing us that the attack had ceased and would not be renewed if we accepted the condition of keeping our contingents in England. The bombardment had been merely a pre-liminary warning to show that their threats were not bluff.

I saw one of my companions yawn. It was a sickly yawn. Only Rufus showed his feelings openly.

'More pig killing,' said Godman. 'Gorey, I reckon we two have sold ourselves pretty thoroughly.'

As that remark went home I realized that we had only four seconds in which to prepare our nerves for Vessant's answer to the ultimatum.

I came out of my chair with a jerk.

'Vessant!' I said harshly . . .

TEN MINUTES BEFORE ZERO

To those in the sky it must have seemed that London had burst. Five centres of sudden, streaming flame then a wind which hurled the ships one against another and sent more than one crashing through the hurtling debris of high-flung rocks. The explosion was heard on the outskirts of Paris where, for a while, cheering crowds assembled believing that the London undergrounds had been destroyed.

In the Control Room, specially occluded to withstand the shock, we crouched with hands over ears. Walls and floor were vibrant with strain. Rufus had his eyes closed; his lips were shaking. When only the echoes remained he was still whimpering. Those echoes were audible for minutes, beating down to us through the labyrinth of galleries and tunnels.

Before they were gone the loading pit below us was in turmoil.

Loading had ceased while the surface explosions took place.

Then men came hurrying along the gangways staring upwards. There was sudden shouting and figures racing across the floor glancing behind them in fear. In the tunnel entrance where the units should have been, fretting behind their grille, there assembled a crowd of gesticulating negroes who, as we watched, fell on their knees and with arms raised to the protection which had deserted them began the grovelling chant from the White Man's Glory Service.

> 'We are the Black Flesh
> Who work with joy in our hearts . . .'

Beyond the glaring arc lights the pit roof echoed the words mockingly.

'Joy' it called and 'Joy' went whispering along the galleries to meet the last tiny echoes of the explosions from above.

'All others be our enemies,' whispered the black roof.

One of our doors flung open and Experts were crowding into the room, some stripped to the waist but all wearing their flanged gas-helmets and with gulleters and uncouplers clanging at their belts. None but Congo Experts would have been allowed to enter the sanctum, but the guards had orders to let them pass where they willed. For they considered themselves the equals of any and what they considered went. They brought with them the stench of the Flesh yards. Behind came a wave of heat from the pits and galleries where no temperature control prevailed. I recognized 'Sump' Bjorraman, the Scandinavian, then little Coe Gardy came pushing forward, his face still smiling as I had always known it, his round eyes searching. They found me and after a second's uncertain widening lit up with delight. He grabbed one of my hands in greeting even as he began speaking to Vessant.

'They've gone mad,' one was shouting; 'the nigs've gone mad. They thought the explosions was the pluggers coming down. They sez the pluggers is coming down the shafts, the crawling cowards!'

'They're heading some o' the unit loads away from the gangway and're letting 'em loose in the gall'ries,' said Coe Gardy calmly through his eternal smile as though this were a prime joke. 'Folk's running.'

Vessant made a fat little motion with his arms as if drawing himself in.

'Not good work,' he said to Godman, and to me, 'This is where we need your assistance. Your appearance amongst them may go far to remove this annoyance. It is all arranged. But first we have –'

'Get me down to the yards,' I said.

'– our emergency preparations for such contingencies,' he concluded. He spoke to an official who whispered into a transmitter and forthwith a sharp splutter arose from somewhere along one wall of the loading pit and the white semicircle above the kneeling negroes' heads was stippled from one end to the other with black dots. The splutter came again and the stippling was thicker and less evenly diffused. Individual dots revealed themselves visibly as intersecting bullet holes. A spray of white dust was falling. No one was hurt. It was not intended that anyone should be hurt. The negroes had sprung to their feet and, with the exception of one, were racing out of sight. The one stayed kneeling, his arms upstretched.

II

That perfect traverse, so harmless yet so harshly threatening, had the effect on me as though the pits below had spread open before my eyes. Vessant did not use guns where guns were not needed. Slavery, degradation, rebellion and then the inevitable suppression

. . . I swung round. There should be no more of this. It had not
been needed in Dax's time; it should not be needed now. In my
time.

But what was new to me was everyday life to the Experts.

'Yer'll stop those guns,' Coe Gardy's cold voice was saying.
'Yer'll stop yer rocket show till we've quieted 'em down.' His companions were gathered round him in a cluster. Human and Godman
were on their feet in alarm. Only Vessant's expression was attentively phlegmatic unless a slight lifting and lowering of the brows
denoted deep thought. The officials were glancing round from their
work nervously.

'I'm telling yer our job's making Flesh an' sweating it along the
road to the feller who wants it. D'yer suppose we'll take shooting
from you! Yer may boss these spawn but not us. Yer our customer,
that's all, an' what hell's it matter to us _who_ buys! P'raps someone
else'd give us that hell of a good time _you_ promised, not just booze
an' brothels down a bloody coal-mine an' cash we can't sling! I'm
telling yer there ain't more than a hundred of us Congos left an'
most of 'em's ready to set the Flesh on the other muggers just for
the sport of it.' Coe Gardy smiled through his bitter words and his
round eyes seemed rounder in appreciation of what he was saying.
Perhaps the words had always been there inside him and the smile
born of a secret pleasure that no one else knew but that someday
he'd show 'em. 'Them nigs think it's heaven they're after, but it's
raw hell the boys want.' 'Sump' Bjorraman gave a heavy supporting
grunt.

That last sentence came to me distantly as if his voice were
suddenly blowing away from me. There was a thinness in the air
and then a gusty wind in the confined space of the Control Room.
The negro at the top of the gangway had risen and was screaming
to his companions down the tunnel. He turned again, lifting his
face and arms in prayer.

Vessant rarely killed, even by proxy, and when he did it was not
in fear or anger but to exercise a psychological influence on others'
minds . . . There were two black spots on the negro's forehead and
his chest seemed mottled with red. He pitched forward and went
down amongst the staring crowd like a swimmer executing a fancy
dive. Two somersaults he took and – 'That air rush was the first of

the gliders going,' said Vesant. 'Tell someone to close the outer valves, please.'

'And get *me*,' Coe was saying. He had not seen the shooting of the negro. 'Yer needed dirt to run yer war – that's all yer think we are! – an' I'm telling yer wot'll happen if yer shoot any of the old pals – *or* our nigs. Yer'll stop yer rocket show, Rupert, till we've cooled 'em down. These bits o' dirt yer walk on almighty an' pay big as lords . . .'

A faint movement in the air, papers rustling on the tables.

'Lovable Mary' was gone in the wake of 'Proud Annie' and somewhere over the south of England eight other rocket-gliders were speeding on their way. I turned away from the pit. All the grids had been let down. Men were tearing at the bars screaming to be let out of the tunnels where the Brothers were loose.

'Coe. Sump. All you boys,' I said. 'Go back to the yards.'

It had come to me that this vast war machine which ran to the touch of a switch, controlled even as Paddy had said by one man in an easy-chair, was indeed no machine at all but, like all organizations, and cults, and creeds which do not spring from the very heart of man, was merely a cleverly devised pause in the endless struggles of human emotions; that, beyond the window, the cogs were revealing themselves as fear and superstition, murder and retribution, while within the room were the patriots, the mercenaries, and the salesmen who provided the motive power. Its only mechanical part was the loyalty, the faith or pretence that it really was a machine.

An actor ran it, not an engineer, an actor in a frock-coat and striped trousers, with a tiny spray of exotic flowers in his lapel, an actor who in early youth had lost himself in the part which fascinated him, who had charmed an audience of millions into believing in that part, into believing that they were not many but one. Shortly, in this more select and critical theatre of the loading pits, his subtle art would reassert itself, stage and auditorium would become one again as he planned them to be and the drama of the machine would have faith in itself again. Unless there were one man who could deny the machine with a belief in humanity equal to Vessant's scorn of it.

'Tell the nigs,' I said, 'that Beldite still lives in the body of his grandson. Tell them that the Brothers who are loose in the galleries must be brought back before they awake. And that I shall be with them soon to see that no more harm comes to them.'

'Splendid!' said Vessant. 'A glory service to yourself!'

Coe Gardy had had his say. A black man was dead. Vessant had not moved.

In my mind was the thought that if a superstitious nigger could face feed-gun fire to declare his belief in something which did not exist it was a little thing for me to die for the greatest realities in life.

'And tell the boys in the yards, in all the yards in London, not to load one more unit, that I am taking personal charge, cancelling all contracts, withdrawing the Guard from action.'

'Bluff!' exclaimed someone, Vessant spoke to an official, muttered orders passed. Then the voice of the sergeant in charge of the bodyguard . . . 'If any of you move I have orders to shoot.'

'Tell them to prepare for parading the contingents through the city,' I said.

Since the entry of the Experts Godman had not spoken. He had stood scowling at us all probably with a surer knowledge of what we were doing than any of us. 'Stop your bluffing, Gregory,' he said, and 'Leave this to me, Vessant.'

'Don't move,' snapped the sergeant.

I flattered myself that I was too valuable to shoot and perhaps I was. But Godman and Gardy did not know it. I took a limping step forward and they sprang in front of me and it can never be known who drew the fire. Godman took most of it. I felt as though white-hot ratch were tearing across my shoulder, Gardy clutched at a shattered arm, and there was Godman at our feet, as ghastly a mess as I have ever seen.

Someone growled fiendishly behind me, then strong arms were round my waist, and I was being hauled out through the swiftly opened door. I had a half-inverted vision of Rufus's distorted face. The bodyguard was in a heap on the floor and Vessant was still seated at his desk, his features suddenly all black and puffed out so that only by the spray of Goble's flowers in his button-hole could he be recognized.

The door slammed. Fists battered on it. There was a gulping scream, gone in a second.

Coe Gardy and I were in the arms of the Experts who had dragged us out and with us, of all those who had been in the Control Room, there was only Sir Godfrey Human. Next to the closed door was 'Sump' Bjorraman with the eyes of a devil, rehitching his exhausted gas-gulleter to his belt.

'Swine-mug!' he snarled; 'swine-mug! He killed our boss, d'yer hear? *He killed our boss!* Got 'im plug in the mouth I did an' the others too. Plug in the mouth-gap!' At a motion from him we hurried on, clearing the office of its occupants for fear of gas leakage from the inner room.

'Them units must have gullets of brass!' muttered a young Expert with a memory of that swiftly blotched and swollen face.

DESCENT OF THE MOTHER-MACHINES

I stopped them peremptorily at the farther door. There was a tiny piping noise back in the Control Room, unnoticeable except for the silence which had fallen on us. It brought to my momently dulled consciousness a vision of what was still happening in that silent death chamber. The piping was to call immediate attention to news from the surface, the one audible signal in many. In front of a dozen different switchboards lights would be shining telling the operators that messages were coming through, from the loading pits, from the projector and Air Controls, from every point of importance in that underground hive. The Central Control Room was the brain, a dead brain which could neither hear nor answer. In a few minutes anxious couriers would be coming to ascertain what was wrong.

'Keep these clerks in there,' I ordered. 'None of you go out of this room except to take my messages. If anyone enters, keep him. The doors are all gas-proof, but you'd better decontaminate the air – after I've gone. Say nothing about what's happened.'

There was only one course to take. The time I had spent idle and fretting in the Control Room had given me knowledge of the authority Vessant had exercised, through whom and how, and of the characteristic way in which messages were given and taken; very imperfect knowledge picked up through only half-attentive observation, but sufficient for me. I had noticed other points which could be turned to valuable account.

Not often does it come to a man to have to gamble for the lives of nations and millions and to have only a few seconds in which to decide whether to make his throw; yet I can vouch for it that when that chance comes there is no hesitation. It is as if a balance swung. Borrowing a helmet, gloves and other equipment and picking out three Experts to accompany me I returned to the gas-filled room to keep the faith in the machine before I wrecked it. There was no time for my shoulder to be dressed, but I had someone wrap it round with a huge pad to keep out the gas and I borrowed a big leather coat. My side had been wrenched when I was dragged out, but there was no time for that either. I was coldly excited and pain did not matter. The others sprayed the doorway as we dashed through to neutralize any leaking gas.

II

There were two dead men close to the door who had to be pushed aside before we could enter. Others had died crawling towards the door and lay face downwards, some with legs outspread and hands clutching into the thick pile, some doubled up in a last agony. One had clambered to the window; his coat had caught on a hook so that while his legs sprawled on the floor his body was half upright, his dead eyes staring through the glass he had hoped to break. All those who had not received the full outrush of gas were distorted with suffering, but two of the bodyguard looked quite peaceful. Others, and Vessant, were all but unrecognizable and Rufus had died where he sat, his eyes closed in fear before he passed.

We picked our way through the dead and began our work. More than one had died at his instruments, and these were piled in a corner. I posted one of my men at the far door with instructions to close it quickly after anyone who entered, and the other two assisted me at the 'phones.

That door and the queer sound of our voices over the wires were the only things which troubled me.

Our helmets were equipped with auditory and speaking apparatus, and I was afraid that the diaphragmatic reproduction in combination with the 'phone transmitter might muffle our voices and arouse suspicion. Only once, however, did anyone remark on it, and him I told curtly to take down the message and be silent. My verbal messages were already on their way to the yards, and, after I had been in touch with the Air Control and other sections and had learned the latest from the outer world, I confirmed these over the wires as if directly from Vessant.

The attack had been renewed immediately after the first rocket's dispatch and the tale of its ruthlessness continued to reach me throughout the time I stayed in the Control Room. Our defence was now confined almost solely to the pits through which the rockets were being shot, all anti-airguns and 'planes having been concentrated about these centres; nevertheless, more than one plugger essayed a suicidal dive into these holes only to be wrecked on the great steel valves guarding the catapults below. They swung aside only to allow the passage of a rocket-glider.

Over Hampstead Heath and Clapham and Wandsworth Commons machines of unprecedented size had come into view of the panic-stricken crowds. At any time troops were expected to land, not with any thought of permanent occupation but to facilitate the work of destruction from the ground. Intense fighting was proceeding at the central area barriers between our soldiers and the civilians, but there was a tendency for this to slacken as it was realized that there was no more safety within the circle than elsewhere. Bomb-pluggers in diamond-chain formation were wrecking the main city streets unopposed. From St Paul's to Westminster not a building was entire. The whole of London was lit by conflagrations.

Before the war machine could be brought to a standstill it had to be reassured and the pretence that the Central Control was still in command revived. So it was that we sent word round that the trouble in the loading pits was now over but that a sufficiency of the Guard having been dispatched for our present purposes shooting would now cease. There was an instrument on one wall which told us the fate of each individual rocket-glider, when it had flown and, by some wireless device operated by its undercarriage, whether it had landed successfully; in the absence of this latter information it was deemed to be lost. No less than seventy-two had sped and by the time we had been back in the Control Room five minutes their descent on enemy land was being registered. Every half minute or so the little lights flashed on and remained glowing. Out of each flight of five an average of four were landing. News of this triumph helped me considerably as I issued orders for all aeros to return forthwith to their dromes and anti-airguns and other defences to cease action. There were phrases I had picked up: 'Orders of the Central London Defence Council'; 'Official personal message from the Minister of War'. One astounded individual of eminence asked me to express his congratulations to Vessant on 'a masterly stroke'; two other expostulated violently and I had to imitate Vessant's characteristic manner and voice in curt confirmation.

Wonder as they must have done there was no reason why they should doubt the authenticity of my messages: they came from the most carefully guarded spot in London where only the most trusted officials were allowed. Could they imagine that the entire Central Control had been annihilated instantly and silently from within?

Through all our instructions ran the suggestion that our successful counter-invasion had placed us in the position of bargainers with the trump cards. It was a supreme bluff. And there was humour in it, rich, ironic humour which none of us could appreciate at the time though it is true that one of my Experts began to laugh after a while. That, I think, was the strain of the dead, distorted bodies and the thought of the gas-filled room. Laughter and horror can be close companions.

I commanded the withdrawal of all soldiers on duty at the pits and yards to their parade grounds and gave instructions for their immediate evacuation to the surface. This would keep them occupied. A valuable minute was lost soothing a general deeply concerned that the Experts should be left on their own. Then I ordered a strong bodyguard to accompany 'Mr Beldite and Experts' to the Central Landing, for it was there I had decided to make my final bid. 'Inform the Commander of the United European Air Fleets that the London Defence Council is prepared to discuss terms of peace,' was the gist of my message to the enemy. I drew attention to our voluntary abandonment of all defence and to the cessation of our counter-invasion trusting that the orders I had flung at an astounded city were being carried out. The answer was that the Commander was willing to grant an immediate armistice and to meet representatives to arrange the surrender.

My last acts before leaving the Control Room were to send urgent messages to all quarters summoning the Defence Council to meet immediately and one to the Military Headquarters advising them that civilians from the outer rings were to be allowed to pass the barriers into central London but must not be admitted into the underground. I debated a general warning to keep away from the Control Room but did not give it: it would have brought a decontaminating squad immediately. I had to risk the loss of further lives.

We threaded our way again past the uninterested dead and dashed through the door. Vessant had sunk into his chair and now that the gas had partially exuded from him, looked discoloured and withered as though he had exploded. There was wild cheering in the loading pit and tunnels. The version I had given them was that we were going to dictate our own terms of peace.

III

My purpose was as clear-cut and unqualified as – some might say a madman's. At most I had an hour in which to fulfil it and at the end of that hour I intended that the machine over which I had transient control should be set to new ends, the ends of peace, and that whoever essayed to turn it back should find no enemy to fight but only the released millions of London celebrating in wild and uncontrollable orgy the return of life from the living death of war. Beyond that I did not look. I had my few Congo Experts and negroes and, through these, less surely, thousands of disillusioned workers in the depths: I had certain pellucid thoughts in my mind, surpassing thoughts, which I should phrase to the best of my ability. Such was my armoury. Perhaps when my hour was over they would shoot us all.

We should be the last victims.

In my mind was that strange, lonely clarity which comes to one on a glider at a great height, soundless and unsupported and as alone as man can be, yet void of all doubt, supremely without doubt that one is absolute master of one's world, a being beyond the little cells and shackles of crawling human life.

Coe Gardy was seated in the outer office, a new inflexion to his smile as they set his arm crudely.

'Coe,' I said; 'you're boss of the yards, you're top boss now Godman's gone. Are you *really* boss?'

'I'm boss that much that if I told 'em to march the Guard to hell they'd march 'em.'

'That's where you're going to march them,' I said. 'I've been giving a lot of orders in there – fake orders which may be counter-manded any moment. I want to give one order which, once you've started to carry it out, *can't* be altered.'

'If yer mean taking the contingents upstairs yer give me that before. Sump's seeing to it. Huh? Course the boys'll do it if they haven't set 'em off loose already. I've sent word they take orders from you an' that was *my* orders. There ain't no more God-aping politicians an' tinkering Toms for us. We're the gen'rals an' the ministers an' the whole bunch without the sick livers of 'em. We're Beldite's, ain't we, an' you're Beldite? Wot else!' His face screwed up, then he was smiling again. 'Wot's the rest but muggers! There's more muggers than fleas down there an' there ain't a tickle in 'em. Spawn!'

'Why do you boys do this for me?' I asked. 'I said a dozen words –'

'An' they killed Godman! An' Sump got 'is wind for wot he's been dreaming years. Think we loved 'em? P'raps we ain't doing it for you an' p'raps we are.' He eyed me roundly and speculatively. 'P'raps it's something your old grandad put into Beldite's in the early days or p'raps it's your grandad himself. You've got his name an' you've got the guts he couldn't find. Hear 'em cheering? I don't know whether it's your name or his they're shouting but if you'll do the thinking an' ordering they'll follow.'

IV

I found and faced what remained of the Central London Defence Council in a large room some hundred feet nearer the surface. It was heavily guarded, but a message stating my identity and that I came from Vessant gained me admittance. I left my own bodyguard outside and took the Experts with me.

Seven of them were gathered round a table but I only knew two, the Premier and the Head Flight Comptroller. They had a paper

power to overrule Vessant but that they had not hurried straight
to the Central Control to dispute his orders was proof enough to
me that unless they were all assembled together they were ineffect-
ive. They rose expostulating, demanding explanations, Vessant in
person, and Tankerley. I sat them down again with a lie the ironic
truth of which I did not appreciate until long after.

'Vessant is on his way to make peace,' I said. The rest I told was
the truth. 'Your power,' I said, 'rests on a tradition and a few
thousand soldiers; mine rests on the Experts and the Death Guard,
and in a little time I shall have all London with me. Vessant had
learnt that already. What you have to do is to sit still at that table
until you're told to come out. Don't call the door guards in and
don't ring any bells for help. I'm leaving two of the men here with
you and if you do anything they don't like or if anyone comes in
without their telling them to they'll kill you. Like this.' I held up a
gulleter before their scared faces and touched the release. 'If this is
pressed it'll let out enough gas to suffocate the lot of you instantly.
Anyone who comes to help you hasn't a chance. Don't ring any
bells for their sake. You're in secret conclave, so secret that for a
few hours no one will know whether you are dead or alive.'

I chose two Experts, big, impressive-looking fellows, looking
seven feet high in their helmets, and left them to it.

No one rang any bells.

V

I made my way to the elevators via the underworld Flesh factories.
Here the ever-glaring lights gleamed on bare rock walls, often
soaking with ooze, the ground was a slime of mud and puddles,
and filth and grit were everywhere. An artificial ventilating wind
swept through the caverns, sometimes like the breath of a furnace,
sometimes deadly cold by comparison. There was no time for cleaning and the living quarters were little better I was told. As soon as
the excavators had finished their work the hollowed-out spaces
were put to use with as little trimming as possible and the excavators continued elsewhere; the distant roar of their blasting apparatus was constant accompaniment to the more immediate sounds of
clanging drums and shouting voices. So unavoidable was the dirt

that at times it polluted the oviplasm and pugs grew to maturity with splinters of stone and metal embedded in them, but they were good enough for oversea and went into the reserve with the rest.

I did not see the reserve, I heard it; a murmur from dark tunnels which led to greater depths, as though at the centre of the earth an ocean rolled. The brutes stood knee-deep in diluted ketchup swill which, however much they ate of it, never doped them more than a couple of hours from fighting condition. The available reserve space, however, was insufficient and throughout the yards units were to be seen corralled in clumps and fastened to the rock by immense chains.

The overpowering stench of ketchup gripped one by the throat a quarter of a mile away. Because of it men rarely ate and then only to vary the monotony of constant toil, but they drank as men never had drunk, raw spirits and special alcoholic preparations to tempt their brutalized tastes. The weaker stomachs vomited daily. But because men cannot be worked and poisoned till they die and still be of use there were 'rest holes' nearer the surface where medical treatment was given and sleep and quiet assured. Otherwise they lived with and not unlike the Brothers, and if they did not eat ketchup they breathed it day and night long.

Work was at a standstill as we went through. Speculation on whether it were peace or not and wild, drunken roistering held them. I told them it was peace, and eternal death to the Guard, and that, instead of exciting them further, sobered them so that I had difficulty in getting away from their questions as to how it was to be done. I enjoined them to spread the news that it was peace to the furthest limits of the outer rings. The negroes stood apart, little crowd groups, still the most humble where all were now Black Flesh. Only one came forward – I saw the ecstasy on his face compelling him – and flung himself at my feet muttering, 'To the glory of the White Man, to the glory of the White Man!'

I gave him a message to his fellows, that they would be safe and back in the air and sunlight before many hours. I could not tell them that it was one of their number who by his death had woken the 'White Man' to his trust.

As I left that hell, I and those I was taking with me went into a large cubicle where we were doused in vapour with an intense but not unpleasant odour. It diminished the worst of the stenches we carried with us.

VI

We hurried on the Central Air Landing through stone corridors and work-halls where men gathered to shout and cheer; then by lift to higher workings, more corridors, and a second lift which bore us beyond the surface. I was in increasing pain and had difficulty in walking. I was glad of my stick. Sometimes they supported me.

The cold night air blowing through the broken windows of the elevator house set us shivering after the humid heat below. I remember how my body dragged as though it were some other person's, a vital but irritating hindrance. The landing was ringed with fluctuating light from the unseen city fires beneath, a black, almost invisible expanse of buildings and tiny figures and the crouching, beetle-like forms of our war machines, with at its centre a dazzling pattern of circles, one overlaying another, a shining rose-window framed in ebony. On to this steady lake of light a shadow was descending.

VII

The flagship of the mother-machines was guided to her landing by the searchlights of her companions. She was the focus of a thousand beams.

There is no parallel to be drawn either with machine or living creature; she was just a winged, luminous shape, beautiful as all lucent things are beautiful, and with a simplicity of line which made her as natural to the skies as the orb of the moon. She seemed to be pressing her own shadow to earth, or to be drawn thither in its black embrace, and there was a living sensuality in her movement as though she posed indulgently for our admiration. As she came nearer and the shadow spread, faint lines appeared on her sides and outspread pinions to tell where the guns and gas-projectors were concealed, and then line after line of little grey beasts clutching her decks, ready for the spring. She was like some lovely, idle prophetess of the illimitable future man, lazily content in her luxury to allow death's busy parasites to prostitute and defame her beauty.

A haze of whirling propellers brought her to rest. Sharp commands rang in the silence, then the tramp of marching men and the clang of arms. I led my little group forward to meet them. We had a momentary difficulty in understanding each other.

'In the cabin?' I said. 'Yes.' It was as good a place as any and warmer than the elevator house. The little posse snapped round smartly and led the way towards the brilliant interior of the flagship. We Experts followed in ragged formation. There was a pause while I was assisted up the companion-way. Lights had come out on the landing-stage and there was a movement of figures towards the distant edges and voices ordering, taking charge of some unexpected happening. From unseen people in the darkness a cheer rose; they could see us though we could not see them. A few of the airmen joined in.

That cheer seemed to pass downwards, to be taken and sent on to the city streets by other adventurous souls clambering up to the cold, windy height to see what they could of the peace-making.

VIII

As if their shadows were in some way necessary to my design, two isolated memories of that night persisted in my mind, blending with and tincturing my thoughts.

One was of Sir Godfrey Human, white faced and intent, pacing by my side through the galleries and corridors of the underworld, trying to persuade me to sell the Death Guard, irritating me – God, how he irritated me! – with an idea which must have been gestating in his hedged, unfertile brain for many years, irritating me with the mere fact that he had escaped alive where others had perished.

'We were wrong ever to engage ourselves with these military affairs. Dax-Beldite was international in its scope.' His voice was husky with emotion. 'What had we to do with these quarrels between nations? Our sole business was selling, is still selling. World commerce; that is the true internationalism. Financial internationalism. Why should one country monopolize what belongs to the whole world?'

I scarcely listened but his constant repetition drummed his meaning into me. He reached his great thought through ideas and phrases culled from all sources, from books, from Rufus, even from the Experts, garnered slowly through his many attentive silences. 'This insularity! This insularity!'

It was our duty to break with the Government, to sell our process, our millions of reserve units, to all comers. The sure way to peace; the highest form of patriotism. It would break the unity of our enemies, they would fight against each other, leaving us to recuperate in peace.

Multilateral armaments, the one guarantee of peace! Humanite was the proof!

'No one dreamed of using it for *war* until the Death Guard aroused their fear and suspicion,' he hissed in my ear. If only we had sold the Guard as he had sold humanite!

Instead – dockyards and dromes and whole towns destroyed by our own produce, by humanite made in his own works at Sheffield!

'It's a pity the chemist who invented it didn't die before *you* stole his brains,' I snarled. 'It's a pity *you* didn't die.' The elevator grid clattered between us. 'Lock him up,' I said. 'Get rid of him.'

'You must offer to sell it to them,' he called as their hands closed on him. 'Offer to sell it.'

With the memory of his frothy plea for eternal armaments and dividends went that of the only person who entered the Control Room while I sat at my 'phones, Field-Marshal Tankerley. He came unaccompanied.

I did not hear the farther door open nor the Expert's sharp closing of it. I heard – what was it? – the ghost of a familiar voice or merely the rasping breath of a gas-stricken man? I swung round and Tankerley was coming slowly across the floor with bulging eyes and hands to his throat, glaring at our grotesque figures and the scattered bodies of his friends and helpers.

He collapsed as I looked, then I was back at my instruments, and when I glanced again he was dead and the Expert in charge of the door was moving away from him back to his post, re-hitching his gulleter to his belt. I did not think of him any more until I was leaving, when I paused a second over his outstretched form glad that there had been a ruthless hand near to bring death quickly to him. There had always been a lovable streak in the bitter, disappointed old man.

These shadows, the millionaire huckster propounding his creed, and a brave soldier 'put away' like a worn-out dog because there was no time to save him, hung on to me as though they marked the edges of my narrow path.

THE LAST MARCH OF THE BEAST BATTALIONS

In a large, low cabin, austerely equipped with a minimum of furniture and a plenitude of maps, diagrams and instruments, we were met by the Commander of the United Air Fleets of Europe accompanied by a retinue of senior officers. He was a slightly built, stiff little man with bright, motionless eyes set like stones in his weather-beaten face. The eyes were the only living thing about him.

'M'sieur!' he rapped harshly, clicked his heels sharply together and saluted me.

I had no military mannerisms. I inclined my head and raised one hand; then, with an apology, I glanced round for a seat. Someone hastened to oblige me. He remained standing stiffly, impenetrable eyes fixed on me.

'M'sieur is sick?' he inquired. He spoke quickly and without perceptible accent but separating each word with hard distinctness.

'Wounded,' I answered. Through most of that interview he stood stiffly before me while I reclined in my chair. His retinue also stood, a little behind him, and my unkempt entourage lounged around me, some standing, some, without invitation, seated.

His eyes had narrowed faintly at our appearance, but he had expressed no surprise. Now, some slight expression to his conception of etiquette having been given, he allowed himself to question his unexpected reception.

'I did not expect – the famous Experts,' he said with the remotest suggestion of a smile. 'I regret that I do not understand. I thought

– your Premier, perhaps, or your Minister for War? And these crowds below? This cheering?'

I sought words wherewith to express to him simply what had taken place or what, for my purposes, I must assume to have taken place.

'We refused to continue the war,' I explained. 'We Experts – there was a disagreement. We have the support of the people. You have seen that both our defence and our counterattack have ceased. Your last message was answered by us, by me.'

'A purely internal matter,' he bowed, betraying no satisfaction at this revelation of extreme disruption. 'So long as I know with whom I am dealing. You and your friends are now the Government, the self-constituted Government of Britain? You hold the –' He sought a phrase. '– the effective power? The crowds are cheering your accession to power?' Perhaps there was irony in his tone, perhaps it was in my imagination.

'Of London would be more exact. Beyond London –' I shrugged and my shrug should have given him new pleasure as hinting at recognized defeat in all but our main stronghold. He betrayed no pleasure.

'Ah. And in respect of London you are willing and have the authority to negotiate the terms of –' He hung on the last word, his harsh eyes, without apparent movement, taking in the expressions confronting him, my own, pacific but unyielding, and those of my comrades, bitter, steel-sprung, fighting, the faces of men who have paused in battle and are about to return to it, some awkwardly antagonistic before the array of foreign dignity, some carelessly at ease, but all firm in an unspoken determination.

'– surrender,' he ended sharply.

He was an iron little man, the man who had been chosen to carry out the holocaust of London, to undertake the foulest slaughter of all time. Yet he was no martinet. He was a soldier of the wide air, rigid in action but not in mind, a man who knew that the sky was greater than the war machines which thronged it. He had faith in a cause which demanded him to be responsible for untold dreadful deaths, who would without hesitation continue until the work of execution was done. But, until I caught the exact quality of him, that he too was an idealist, I hesitated with my words, my surpassing thoughts were doubtful commonplaces, my ideals sentimental weaknesses he had never known.

'There is no question of surrender,' I answered, and his eyes widened and set more hardly. 'Our message was that we were willing to discuss the terms of peace. You must understand that these men, myself, and thousands who are supporting us are not fighters in this war. We are workmen from the factories, the Flesh factories, and Guard tenders from the roads and depots. We had a job to do and we did it. Tonight we began to fight, not against you nor even against our own Government, but against war and everything which makes war, which perpetuates war. That is why the people cheer. The news is spreading that peace will soon be declared.'

His lips tightened but he did not interrupt me.

'We have fulfilled the conditions of your ultimatum. We have ceased to send the Guard overseas, we have ceased to manufacture the Guard. We shall destroy our reserve. In return we ask that you withdraw your fleet, that a conference should be arranged.'

'But you do not surrender; we do not occupy your London? These are useless promises, M'sieur, unless we can be witness to their fulfilment. If indeed you have ended your invasion of Europe with your beast armies then, in our turn, we cease attack on your civilians. That we have told you. Otherwise, a state of war continues. These are not terms of peace you suggest, M'sieur.'

'They are the only terms on which there can be peace,' I said. 'They are not my terms. They are the terms dictated by the very circumstances of war. As a State, a political and social State, Britain is near destruction. People are dying of disease and starvation in thousands, fighting among themselves, a civilization forced into brute savagery. But these things do not constitute military defeat.' I paused for him to answer but he made none. He was grimly attentive.

'If war continues these disasters cannot be confined to Britain. Our only military defence is to spread them abroad. If you have not seen at least you have heard the truth. No army however highly mechanized, no air force, can hold back the Guard, and on the Continent it will not reach a limit, a coastline, as in this island. It will go forward. If it is let loose in Europe in sufficient numbers

Europe will be ravaged as our north is being ravaged, but on an infinitely greater scale. You have heard of the life plague which is there? Yes, it might take years but in the end the Flesh and the creatures it gives birth to would populate Europe. Whole peoples would die.

'These are the circumstances which are dictating the terms of peace. Any other terms of victory and surrendering would be terms of continued war.'

'So!' he snapped. 'We know these things. We too can massacre, M'sieur. Since soldiering died with the coming of your Guard we too have learned to be butchers.' There was fire in his eyes and in those of the officers behind him. 'You speak of peace! You will abolish your Guard! And now you threaten. I am astounded. You threaten! I came to arrange your capitulation and . . . These arguments! These threats!'

'Threats!' I exclaimed. I believe I laughed. 'You are misunderstanding me. You threaten yourselves. If you cannot make peace without humiliating us there are people back there below who will take the power from me and continue fighting though you kill every civilian in Britain, who have no cause to surrender. You cannot have your military victory. Air and underground cannot meet for one to defeat the other; you can reach them only through the columns of the Death Guard. You are destroying surface London but that is nothing now, a relic, a decoration. London is below, where it was destined to be from the first moment an aeroplane rose from the earth. They could live down there fifty years, a generation of rat-men. Children are being born there now, children who if you have your way will never see the daylight, who will live their lives in dungeons with gas instead of air above them. We are offering to surrender our power to peace and we ask you to do likewise. You want to pit carnage against carnage, massacre against massacre; you are prepared to see half Europe die sooner than forget your military pride, your will to victory.'

I lay back in my chair, exhausted with my effort. The Commander's motionless eyes were fixed on me.

'He ain't understandin' you, he ain't believin' you,' said a tall, blue-eyed Expert, lounging forward and staring down at the little Commander with bitter sympathy. 'This is Beldite, Boss, if you knows what that means. I guess you didn't know it was Beldite. He's telling you what'll happen if you don't make peace his way. Vessant's just a dead mess, an' Tankerley, an' a lot more, but there's others what'd cut our throats slit open to let hell out again.'

There was a stir among the statuesque officers as one translated to the others. The Commander bristled, glared. I saw the thought pass in his eyes that we were common murderers, political buccaneers, and then he saved himself from that hypocrisy and was acknowledging our belated introduction.

II

'And so there is no surrender, M'sieur?' said the Commander.

A truce had been declared in the world's most ruthless bombardment so that one, Gregory Beldite, no fool but visibly a sentimentalist, could have his say ... Perhaps the Commander appreciated something of the whimsicality of the situation.

But sentimentalists might be serving other and more evil purposes than their own. He spoke to one of his officers who left the cabin.

A slight dizziness overcame me. My shoulder was still bleeding heavily. Distant cheering sounded, a host of tiny voices in a vast stillness. I was angry, angry that he could not see as I saw, angry that I should be so simple as to believe he could. The sense of aloof dominance which had been mine was slipping from me even as I began to realize that this ruthless little autocrat of the air was as human as I, had his sympathies and understandings; perhaps because of that realization.

I was only at the beginning of that proud blindness which is leadership and he was at the summit, recognizing in me all that futility of ideals which later I must throw aside if I were in truth to lead. Perhaps even now the first of my murders was being committed in my name, my supporters shot down in defence of me, my enemies whom I would have saved from themselves dying before the onrush of the Guard which I was professing to control.

Symbols bandying words while men died!

I leaned forward in my chair and the raw pain in my shoulder went into my voice.

'*What* do we surrender?' I snapped. 'A chaos from which you can demand everything but get nothing! Our pride! And what do you win?'

'Freedom, M'sieur Beldite,' he answered calmly; 'freedom from your Death Guard. That is why we fight, why we have no compunction in slaying your people or allowing our own to be slain.'

'And your effort, your fear, has turned a few thousand units into millions,' I took him up. '*How* do you gain that freedom? In London, in other fortified towns – the Guard. In our colonies – the Guard. A day unfed and not the whole of your Continental armies would dare to approach them. Even if we Experts were to submit and agree to tend them for you your nations would begin quarrelling over how they should be divided. They would be the only spoils of war.'

I became aware of a subtle vibration in the cabin about me. I glanced aside and through the port which a moment before had been black and searchlit I saw the black outline of a distant, high building passing downwards. The ship was rising. He had summed us up as impostors or usurpers of a power we could not hold.

'A mere precaution,' he said. 'Your crowds. They have climbed to the stage. We do not want trouble in that way.'

He turned to the Experts, watching him in uneasy suspicion, then came forward quickly as though he stepped from his high rank to be nearer to us.

'M'sieur Beldite. Gentlemen. You are brave fighters. I do not know how you came by this power you have, I do not care, but it is – it is the power of a moment. You admit as much yourselves. Almost. You forget that it is you English, your firm and its Experts, who have let loose this indescribable horror, who have brought a fear into the world which has driven nations insane. Where war begins reason and ideals die, and you cannot expect even your own people to believe in them, to follow them, until the calm of victory or the humiliations of defeat are theirs. This Death Guard –'

'It isn't a thing apart,' I snapped, 'a fantastic atrocity beside your winged guns and enhaloed bombs. All we have done is to work in flesh where others worked in metal. But for the chance of a man's birth it might have been any nation's. Would they have rejected it? Would they hold up their hands in horror if it were offered to them now, if they discovered its secrets themselves!'

There was a murmur of impatience from the air officers and, 'M'sieur Beldite!' the Commander expostulated. 'These speculations! If there is no more to be said I will see that you are returned to the landing in safety.' His eyes were set and unrelenting once more. His hand came out with a jerky motion. 'I shake hands with a brave enemy.'

I tried to rise and found that my wounds gripped me stiffly and excruciatingly with every slight movement. 'Allow me,' said the Commander and helped me to rise.

'You have never seen the enemy,' I murmured hoarsely and, still leaning on his arm, drew him towards the westward port of the cabin.

III

We looked down on the great crescent of London and Westminster, a sweep of once graceful streets holding within themselves a hundred years of effort and now scattered and flaming. Buildings which had made London famous gaped up at us blankly, grim caverns, dwarfed and ugly beneath the towering flames which ever and again flared upwards as some blazing structure rumbled earthwards. Dark gulleys and gulleys of fire, and smoke pouring southwards in the rising wind as though the foggy soul of the metropolis were escaping from its age-old prison. Above floated the dark, winged shapes of the mother-machines, some circling lazily, some hovering like bees over the dim flower of an open space. The clinging bomb-pluggers on their decks gave them a fantastic battlemented appearance. Dwindling with distance, ever increasing in numbers, they swarmed to the hidden heights of the night sky beyond smoke and sorrow, and from those nearest to us curious searchlights rested on parts of the city so that black building and white building glistened coldly to their glare.

So empty did the city seem that for a moment doubt seized me, doubt that it were possible for one man so to touch the hearts of millions that they would do what I had planned. Then, by the light of the watching machines, in contrast to the city's lifeless majesty, the streets began to fill with tiny figures, scrambling over the fallen ruins, climbing to roofs and shattered walls. As though an etching were coming to life before our eyes. Little voices cheered spasmodically, an elfin tumult which rose to us above the soft purr of our engines. In the rayon of the searchlight a brighter glow was shining, a half-circle beneath jagged black shadows, and towards this the crowds were converging. It was the entrance to one of the underground ways. The people gathered thickly on the sides of the road into which it led. Some were flung forward from the crush, lay sprawling a moment, then rose apparently in fear and thrust their way back into the crowd or, unable to penetrate it, fled down the street.

In the depths of the brighter light shadows appeared hurrying. A scream rose from the people on the street sides, a scream of derision and hatred which changed to fear as they were thrust forward by the sudden pressure of new masses in the off streets. From the lighted entrance came the great, shuffling figures of marching units, emerging four abreast from the channels of the underways into the cold, brilliant roads like dead things from the charnel-house into the light of living man. The people were fighting and tearing at each other, clambering over each other, some to get away from the advancing column, some to get nearer. A shower of bricks from high up on the broken walls smashed down on the front ranks of the units. A figure in the road, struck down, pitched forward, lay writhing, and was gone beneath the tramping hoofs. Men in gas-helmets and full road gear came running by the sides of the column threatening back the crowd.

The Commander turned towards me and I answered his un-spoken question.

'Within ten minutes, before we stopped our gliders, eight thousand of our war units landed on your territory. Those.' I pointed downwards. 'At this moment they are going forward as I have seen them go forward, killing everything they meet, through shells and wire and gas. Compared with those which might follow they are a small force; we Experts would soon dispose of them though we cannot restore the lives of those who are dying even now while I waste time explaining what should be obvious to you. If the flight is resumed there are millions to follow them, those millions which are now beginning to march into the streets of London.

'You imagine you can prevent this? You too, M'sieur Commander, are an idealist, a romanticist. What chance is there to bring down silent, camouflaged gliders at night, hurled at hundreds of miles an hour, which do not fall when their engines are hit, which have no pilots to kill, and no vulnerable spot. As well try to stop shells! If the flight is resumed a breeding ground will develop in France and Belgium besides which Yorkshire will be nothing, and behind this breeding ground a tunnel will emerge, no great engineering feat in these days; a narrow tunnel less than thirty miles long, high enough only for full-grown units to march through. That was one of the late Government's schemes and the depot from which it was to start is a mile deep in the ground. It is provisioned for years.'

The mother-machine had sunk lower so that the faces of the crowd were visible to us, gaunt, maddened faces screaming their wrath at the oblivious column which thundered between them, hoofs and quadrifanes clanking like the chains of a machine, the piled debris flying before them. A woman dashed forward and drove an axe into the chest muscle of one of the stupefied beasts. It recoiled slightly and passed on with the axe embedded in its rubbery flesh. The screams changed to cheers and wild laughter. A moment and the woman's example was taken up by all who could find a weapon. Bricks and timber, flaring balks crashed into the column. A man with a scythe, an ancient tool he had been carrying perhaps for his own protection, stood in the roadway reaping at them. I indicated him. 'Wherever the Flesh falls dead, neoblast will grow,' I said.

'Supposing you made it impossible for us to shoot our rockets or drive our tunnel,' I resumed. 'Supposing I and my comrades were dead and you defeated our successors. I have a fellow-director in Dax-Beldite whose advice would be more palatable and understandable to most than mine is. No sentimentalist; a clever salesman. Supposing he were to offer our wares to another country . . .'

'God forbid!' A murmur rose from the air officers. One of the Experts laughed sharply, mirthlessly.

'Would France reject the chance of owning the Guard? Would Germany, Russia?'

'The people would not sanction it. No statesman, no general, not even a tyrant would dare –'

'The people!' I exclaimed. 'You are wrong. There are plenty of buyers. These salesmen are subtle, they work nation against nation.

There was a man Zaharoff once who sold submarines. Remember? The nations would buy because they feared that others would buy, not mad but fearing the madness of others. In a short while there would be new wars... No. If you think the people can decide listen to them now and take *their* message. They speak for Europe as well as for Britain. The Death Guard is marching to extinction and that is *our* victory as well as yours. If we are proud and defiant and continue to fight or if we are humble and surrender we murder a world. That – is our power.'

I turned to the Experts.

'We have decided not to use that power? Instead, we have given it to the people. They will know how to deal with it better than any conquering government.'

There was a growl of assent. 'Ten million there are, more'n ten million,' snarled one, 'an' if Beldite wants he can make it twenty or a hundred million. He's the only man we'd do it for an' by hell! if you drop one more bomb we'll man the catapults an' –'

'We shan't man the catapults,' I said. 'If the Commander thinks he is at war, if there are fools below ready to kill us and to fight him – they will be destroyed, wiped out, by the people who have seen their real enemy. The Beast Battalions and all they stand for are on their last march. There will be no more Beast Battalions, neither Flesh nor human ...'

We had drifted south. From the outer rings the crowds were still hastening citywards. Soldiers were with them, shooting into the marching units. From a score of exits the contingents were converging towards the great flares along the Embankment where London was blazing. In Whitehall a battery of feed-guns was pouring lead into an advancing column. With sunken heads and blind faces the Brothers trudged on through the hail until the front fell to pieces as we watched and were turned to slush under the hoofs of the following ranks. Three yards separating them the soldiers lifted their guns and flung them down again for the Guard to march over. Cheering and screaming they raced ahead of them. 'Burn them! Burn them!' they shouted. 'Down with the bloody brutes of war!' and the cry passed on until a million throats were shrieking hatred.

'Burn the Brothers! Burn the Brothers!'

*

'Brothers,' said the Commander softly. 'That is an irony worthy of my own country. It is as if – as if the world were theirs,' he murmured.

'It is ours to give to them if we wish,' I said.

We were silent, watching the endless columns winding their way towards the Thames-side fires which the bomb-pluggers had lit. As they came near the flames the road-tenders at their sides drew back but the contingents went forward. Their skin flushed red in the glare, the steam from their sweating bodies rose in dense clouds. Flames from the burning debris in the road lapped round their legs as though they trod through blazing flowers. Then the front ranks became dusky shadows in the blaze, marching heedlessly with heads sinking deeper on their great chest muscles and legs dying beneath them.

Beyond the roar of the flames a deep murmur filled the air, the murmur of ten million marching beasts and the labour of their breathing.

The Commander drew back from the port and glanced round at his officers. Then he faced me, his living, motionless eyes fixed on mine.

'M'sieur!' he rapped. His heels clicked, his hand rose in sharp salute, 'M'sieur Beldite. I will convey your message.'

THE DEATH GUARD

This is the story of the Death Guard, told for the general interest with what skill I have, and as such it ends with the marching of the contingents into the flames of London. Three nights and days they marched until the stench of their burning was perceptible for many miles round and with each day came greater crowds to swell the saturnalia. Only some few hundreds of units were left alive for the last of the Experts' Games deep in the bowels of the earth and these too in their turn went to the acid vats for destruction.

For details of these events, of the three days' chaos of rejoicing in which lawlessness reigned and thousands were killed and crazy disorder spread throughout the country and to the Continent, and of the efforts to restore control and commence the vast work of reorganization, the reader must await my larger history. In that also will be found a record of the peculiar political conditions of the post-war period, of the great southward march of the revolutionaries and how civil strife was avoided only by the genius of Mundaine, released at my order to take control of London, and the scalding oratory of one, Charlotte, now blind in one eye and emaciated almost to repulsiveness, who listened to the arguments of Comrade Gregory with the most flattering understanding; of problems thrown up which are still only in process of gradual solution. In all of these I had my inevitable share. It is no concern of history though perhaps of some present interest that Paddy and I were married long before the news-sheets were sufficiently revived to make any ridiculous fuss about it and dub our unobtrusive little ceremony a 'Flesh Guard wedding,' and though I have a fond hope that one day young Gregory Haggard Beldite will make history he has certainly no part in this one.

Looking back from the chastened sanity of the present it must be difficult for many to understand how nations which in the coldest of deliberation had decided to annihilate another country could, within a few days, be destroying their own arms and sending help to their late enemy. Even as our soldiery were fastening guns and limbers and all the trappings and baggage of death-dealing they could lay their hands on to the blindly dying contingents, so that they also might go on to the flames, bomb-pluggers fully loaded were launched from the decks of mother-machines to dive into the depths of the ocean, foreign munition factories were burned to the ground and many died in misguided efforts to demolish the electric gas stores.

The passion of destruction broke out in sheer hatred and horror of war with the landing of our oversea units and was carried forward in the flame for peace which was lighted in London that same night.

The exodus from Northern France before our invasion, some units from which travelled fifty miles in the first day, fifty miles of violent death, must have done much to place in immediate control those wiser minds which already knew that to destroy one nation was no cure for a disease rampant in every land and so were prepared to accept the message their Air Commander brought;

nevertheless, rage had first to vent itself in a world-wide 'field-clearance' extending far beyond the dreary beasts which first inspired it before that spirit of hope which underlay it could become evident and that gravity of responsibility which is the keynote of our modern world begin to take its place.

That man has at last passed from his childhood, that war and hatred and the self-seeking of hearts in all their forms are but the childish grimaces of our dawn, is a thought which grows all too slowly, but for those who realize that the secret of life-making is indeed ours and that the mysteries of health and beauty and courage are gradually revealing themselves to us there can be no going back.

We shall make other beasts, of the mind if not of the body. Man, if he is to fulfil that which is in him, must travel a fearless path, fearless of the knowledge which comes to him and of the blunders which must result from his experiments. To cringe before the power which is in one's hand, pleading that one is too ignorant and humble to use it, is to be a savage, nay, a renegade from a mighty destiny too despicable for this world of struggle to tolerate long. There is a humility comes from great knowledge, a silence of the mind which gives gladly of its surplus strength and fears no error, which is forever seeking to merge itself in and submit to a power greater than itself.

That fearless humility has marked all the proceedings of the international trust into whose keeping some years ago I gave the secrets of Goble's processes and which now carries a sole responsibility for the production of humanite and gas and many another beneficial discovery and their application to the welfare of the world. Already it has a latent authority larger than any government and a universal responsibility which not even the most foolish may hope to undermine, though many oppose it with arguments which are nothing but a neoblast of the mind, nasty bits of old life pretending to be new. The world was always choked with such meaningless scraps born of the dead things of the past.

Courage and humility and a will to understand were at the inception of the trust, an informal affair when in the drawing-room at View my Aunt Fertile and I met representatives of the late belligerent nations to discuss a possible basis for my conception.

Coe Gardy was there as technical adviser and, perforce, Sir Godfrey Human in the last of his attentive silences. Paddy took notes though Aunt Fertile said that was quite unnecessary as she would remember every word which was said.

In fact, she did not stay very long. Erect and decisive as ever there was a frailty about her which none could misunderstand.

She set the tenor of our talk, and she did so by suddenly raising her voice from a conversation she was holding with certain of our visitors, so that all could hear.

'You are quite wrong to imagine that Mr Goble was either a dangerous egoist or mad. He was a realist and no more fantastically minded than most people. From the very beginning men have made and worshipped horrible images so that they could hide from the light which was struggling in them, and I hope none of you gentlemen will forget it. I hope you will act just as though Mr Goble were at that table guiding you. He was an artist as well as a scientist, and all he did was to reproduce in living flesh what he saw in the minds of men around him.'

I know of no better words with which to end my book.

THE END

About the Author:

_____

Philip George Chadwick was born in 1893, the youngest son of a North Country family. Although he published many short stories in the newspapers and magazines of the 1920s and 1930s, *The Death Guard* was his only published novel. He lived in Brighton for many years where he raised a family and gained a reputation as a fluent and talented political speaker, initially as a Fabian and subsequently as an Independent. He also wrote poetry.

Philip George Chadwick died in 1955.

**Exploring New Realms
in Science Fiction/Fantasy Adventure**

BATMAN™ IS BACK IN ACTION!

Batman™: To Stalk a Specter
by Simon Hawke

Gotham City Blackmailed!

Drug Lord Caught by U.S. Commandos! Desiderio Garcia to Stand Trial in the U.S.! The headlines – and the authorities – are jubilant, but not for long. For Garcia has a deadly would-be rescuer: the superassassin known as Specter. And Specter's reign of havoc and horror has already begun. The people of Gotham City are held hostage and destined to die by the thousands unless Garcia is freed. The people's only hope lies with Batman's bold and dangerous plan. In a war with only one winner and one survivor, he's going to make himself the archkiller's target, matching his enemy weapon for weapon, deception for deception – and with good for evil!

BATMAN™ CREATED BY BOB KANE

Exploring New Realms
in Science Fiction/Fantasy Adventure

Chronicles of Galen Sword
by Judith and Garfield
Reeves-Stevens

The Epic adventures of a fascinating new hero born into a magical realm ... stranded in our own.

Titles already published or in preparation

Book 1: Shifter

Book 2: Nightfeeder

Book 3: Black Hunter

He was Galen Sword by day ... but who was he by night ...? Galen Sword was known as a rich New York City playboy. The public didn't know that his Porsche contained state-of-the-art equipment designed to track down an extraordinary creature, or that Galen was actually on a dangerous quest to find another world ... his world.

A Gift Upon the Shore by M. K. Wren

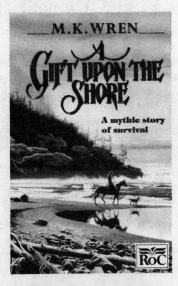

Rachel Morrow and young Mary Hope, isolated at Amarna on the remote Oregon shore, seem to be the sole survivors of the nuclear holocaust, their lives given purpose only by Rachel's mission to preserve whatever books are left.

Until Luke appears – filling Mary with need and desire, both for him and for the Ark, the organized community from which he comes. Yet the encounter threatens everything she and Rachel believe in – for the Arkites are a strict, patriarchal society who think all books but the Bible are evil and who have no place for dissenters. Then Mary becomes involved in a bitter conflict with Miriam, the icy beauty who vows to destroy her precious legacy – even if she has to kill to do so . . .

RoC

**Exploring New Realms
in Science Fiction/Fantasy Adventure**

The Soul Rider Saga
by Jack Chalker

Titles already published or in preparation:

Book One: Spirits of Flux and Anchor

Book Two: Empires of Flux and Anchor

Book Three: Masters of Flux and Anchor

Book Four: The Birth of Flux and Anchor

Book Five: Children of Flux and Anchor

Cassie did not feel the Soul Rider enter her body . . . but suddenly she knew that Anchor was corrupt. Knew that the Flux beyond Anchor was no formless void, from which could issue only mutant changelings and evil wizards . . . Flux was the source of Anchor's existence! The price of her knowledge is exile – the first confrontation with the Seven Who Wait for the redemption of World . . .